Also by
**JOHN A. WILLIAMS**

Jacob's Ladder
The Junior Bachelor Society
Mothersill and the Foxes
!Click Song
Flashbacks
The King God Didn't Save
The Most Native of Sons
Sons of Darkness, Sons of Light
The Man Who Cried I Am
This Is My Country Too
Sissie
Africa, Her History, Lands and People
Night Song
The Angry Ones/One for New York

# CAPTAIN BLACKMAN

01-23-89

To Sandy with many
fond & fine memories
& with warmest best wishes,

John A. Williams

## About the Author

**John A., Williams** is author of eighteen books including *Sissie*, and *!Click Song*. He has been a foreign correspondent for *Newsweek* as well as Professor of English at Rutgers University where he is currently employed. He is the recipient of the American Book Award, The Richard Wright-Jacques Roumain Award, The Centennial Medal for Outstanding Achievement, and the National Institute of Arts and Letters Award, among others. Two of his novels have been adapted for film and television. He was born in 1925 in Jackson, Mississippi, and currently lives in Teaneck, New Jersey.

# CAPTAIN BLACKMAN

## A NOVEL BY

## JOHN A. WILLIAMS

THUNDER'S MOUTH PRESS

Copyright © 1972, 1988 by John A. Williams
All rights reserved
Published in the United States by
Thunder's Mouth Press, 93–99 Greene Street, New York, N.Y. 10012
Cover design by Marcia Salo
Grateful acknowledgment is made to the New York State Council on the Arts and
the National Endowment for the Arts for financial assistance with the publication
of this work.

Library of Congress Cataloging-in-Publication Data

Williams, John Alfred, 1925–
    Captain Blackman : a novel / by John A. Williams
       p.  cm.—(Classic reprint series)
    ISBN 0-938410-68-7 (pbk.) : $10.95
       1.  Vietnamese Conflict, 1961–1975—Fiction.   2.  United States.
Army—Afro-American troops—History—Fiction.   I.  Title.
    II. Series.
    [PS3573.I4495C3 1988]
    813'.54—dc19                                                    88-9748
                                                                    CIP

Manufactured in the United States of America
Distributed by Consortium Book Sales
213 E. 4th Street
St. Paul, Minnesota 55101
612-221-9035

TO
*Gregory, Dennis and Adam*

# CAPTAIN BLACKMAN

# ONE

Tell them that if I am Black I am free born American & a revolutionary soldier & therefore ought not to be thrown intirely out of the scale of notice.

John Chavis, 1832

# 1

The AK-47s were chewing up everything. Not supposed to be any tough stuff out here. Looks like the Major snapped the string on me.

Abraham Blackman tried to force himself down into the wet ground. Buttoned down and they're looking for me, especially that one, he thought, as a patch of grass was chopped up close to his face. Blackman pressed down again, and with that extra movement, thought he saw a cobra slither away. Once any kind of snake might have made him recoil for a few seconds; not now. It was the cobra or that 47; he'd take his chances with the cobra, or two or three of thcm.

There, finally, he thought, hearing a couple of bursts of M-16 fire.

But that hungry 47 was still hunting him; its rounds chewed another trail past him, not four inches away; he heard the rounds thud-thudding into the marsh, a sound like ripping out a wet stitch.

"Captain!"

"Captain-Brother. You in there? You all right?"

Blackman was both relieved and annoyed. They were out

there, Harrison, Griot, Woodcock and the others. He'd have to let them know he was okay, but once he opened his mouth. . . .

"Okay!" he shouted, "But I'm pinned." Once more he tried to disappear into the ground as the 47 opened up again, spattering water into his eyes from its bullets. Blackman began to shake. He heard his men firing at will. They were splashing toward him. Blackman hunched and another 47, a forty-five degree angle away, sent him burrowing into the ground again.

The guys'll come splashing down here, Blackman thought, thinking there's only one or two of em out there, and they'll drop the hammer on them. What to do?

"Captain?"

Why didn't they keep quiet? Why didn't they figure it out?

"Okay," he called. In the momentary stillness he tried to imagine what it felt like being hit with about twenty rounds of 47 ammo. That many rounds, he told himself, you don't feel anything, because you're dead. Five then, or maybe three. He could not imagine it.

Blackman pushed a blade of marsh grass out of his eye. He heard the 16s again, and Griot's M-60, which he liked to hold the way they did in the movies. He heard them closer now, splashing, and he was relieved, because he didn't want to die. But he was angry, too. Only yesterday he'd told them again at the end of his black military history seminar that he didn't want any heroes in his company. Things were close to the end, and even if they weren't, they had nothing to prove. He'd told them time and again, these legs with their mushrooming Afros and off-duty dashikis, that they were not the first black soldiers to do what they were doing. He'd gone back to the American Revolution to Prince Estabrook, Peter Salem, Crispus Attucks and all the unnamed rest; from there to the War of 1812, the Civil War, the Plains Wars, the Spanish-American War—all the wars. He'd conducted the seminar during their off-duty time, without the blessing of the brass, with the obvious, smoldering resentment of the Major, who, for some reason, had let him carry on.

14

"We don't have anything to prove to anybody," he said. "We've done it over and over and over again. No heroes. Just do your jobs."

Blackman's body was tense with momentary indecision. They were walking into what looked like a trap. He recalled in a flash that when the seminar ended, they stood and gave him the salute, the fist, the arm. The same one being used all over the Army these days, wherever there were Brothers. He'd saluted back. He hoped they'd remember the lessons he tried to teach. He hoped they now had that sense of continuity that everyone tried to keep from them, from kindergarten up.

They were closer. He knew the little brown men holding the 47s were waiting. He'd have to do it now; five seconds more would be too late. His mouth was dry, his legs trembling. He thought of Mimosa.

And he sprang up, not wanting them to die for him, thrust his six-four frame skyward, swinging around his 16, screaming, "Get down! Get back!" and felt his weapon kicking against him, felt, rather than saw its bullets attracting the rounds of the 47s, then took the first ones in the thigh, spun around as they clawed for his torso, and he splashed down, sliding in his own blood. He came to rest against a stump which forced his face skyward toward the bright blue Vietnam sky.

As in a dream he saw them, these men in their wigs. They were in an inn in Delaware, a colony halfway between their homes in Massachusetts, Virginia, North and South Carolina. Many had not met except through letters brought by the packet or post, but they were firmly bound together, sharing in the profit and loss of each venture, all tied to the sea and the land, all based on people who were black.

"Well now, then, what is the solution for this intolerable set of conditions?"

They mused until one said, patting his wig, "It used to be a fair

15

go under Burke and Fox, and even now they oppose the taxes George and Lord North insist on laying upon us."

Another spoke: "I suspect that Lord North made too many friends in the service of the East India Company and therefore, not wishing to antagonize them, had decided to levy taxes on us."

The slaves crept around the room pouring water out of thick, clay pitchers. The men in the wigs paid them no attention. A tall thin man uncoiled at the end of the table, moved so slowly that, like an actor stilling an audience, everyone focused on his movements.

"Yes, gentlemen," he said. "There are the taxes. Silly, bothersome taxes: written works must bear a stamp. Fees paid on tea (Lord North's tea from India), lead and glass, and so on. Now, we here have all the glass in our houses we want, I imagine. Our use of lead is now negligible, and I do think that every man here has enough tea among his wares to last at least another two years . . .

"England has not bothered to tax our tobacco or our cotton because it needs and wants those products. It's clear that Lord North didn't want to antagonize his largest resource. He could've taxed incoming slaves."

The thin man with the hair tied behind the nape of his neck, hair that was golden and made his blue eyes bluer still, then said, "We ought to face the meaning of this meeting. We're here to turn the Crown's despicable acts toward the masses into something befitting ourselves. Such as a revolt altogether. Such as forming ourselves into a union free of the Crown, so that we may, since our time here's already proved most lucrative, enjoy not only the profits that derive from the production and distribution of goods, but those higher profits that can be derived by exercising political leadership."

Another man spoke without standing. "The time is ripening. It is true that the commoner bears the brunt of Lord North's ill-advised policies. But, bear in mind that the Crown knows its

16

real enemies, since it's already forbidden several Assemblies to meet. However, once the common man is made to realize that the Crown cares nothing about him—no representation and all that—he will come, reluctantly of course, to know that the only path left to him is to revolt to freedom. In the meantime, we can extend our range from the Atlantic to Balboa's Pacific, increase the slave trade and America will see another, larger Greece."

Knew it all the time, Blackman thought. Chuck ain't shit. Talk about the *Devil!*

It grew light around him and wafting over him came the spring smells of mid-April. Now he saw trees, fields and brush, all filagreed with the first shoots of spring. He walked out of the woods and gained a road, but he was examining the gun in his hand. This is an old one, he thought. Be afraid to fire this one, man. Something thumped softly against his rib cage. He looked down. A powder horn. Now, wait! he thought. He stopped. Where was he? Feeling a weight at his side, he felt with his fingers, found a bag filled with lead balls.

C'mon, man, wake up! You dreamin, baby! Get up off it!

For the first time he thought of the woods, the foliage, and jerked with shock. Maples. Dogwood. Oak. White pine. Red fir, and the rocks underfoot—shale. Yet, when he looked at himself, he was in his fatigues, the camouflaged jacket and trousers, the cap. Bars gone, though, he mused, and the nameplate. *Wake up!* Wake *up!*

Down the road, the road still damp from the spring thaw, he heard voices, then saw, rounding a bend, a mass of men, walking. There were two or three riders, and one cantered down to where Blackman stood and stopped. The rider was a plump, red-faced man. His horse had seen better days, Blackman noticed.

"Whose slave are you?" the rider asked. "Or are you free? Where did you get the musket? Fall in. With the blacks. Strange clothes you're wearing."

Riddled with the questions and confused by the rider's clothing, Blackman fell back to the side of the road, glanced from the rider to the approaching men.

"Are you crazy or somethin?" Blackman asked. "Slave? Man, I'll beat shit outa you, you funny-talkin peckerwood; you an that silly hat—"

"What's that you say? Is your accent from the Islands? Is that where you're from? Anyway, the British're coming and we need every man. Every man, so fall right in the front ranks there with the rest of the boys. Go ahead, now."

The mob was abreast of him now and Blackman, dazed, wandered into the line of blacks who were armed with stakes, spears and clubs. He noticed that the whites behind them were adequately armed with muskets.

"Say, look," Blackman said, pulling his cap down lower over his eyes. "What's goin on?"

Still moving, the blacks eyed him carefully. One said, "My name's Peter Salem. That's Prince; he's Cato, that's Cuff, and he's Pompey—"

"Peter Salem," Blackman said. He looked at the breeches, the worn waistcoats. He glanced at the white ranks. More of the three-cornered hats, but more often they were hatless, their locks flowing freely. "You're Peter Salem and this is 1775 and you're on your way to Lexington because a cat named Paul Revere rode through these parts last night talkin about the British're coming. Is that right?"

They were polite and smiled to one another, as though in the company of one gone mad. It was funny, too, the way the big man spoke. And his clothes: where in the world did they come from?

"Are you slave or free?" the man named Salem asked.

"I'm free, man," Blackman said hotly. "What're you?"

"I'm free, and he's free," he said, pointing at the man called Prince.

"Not Prince Estabrook, is he?"

18

Salem was surprised. "Do you know Estabrook? No. This is just Prince. How is it you know Estabrook?"

"I read about him like I read about you, Mr. Salem, and I sure wish I could wake up and get the hell outa here. Do you know why?"

"Excuse me, but your accent is strange. Wake up? Get out?"

"Yeah, baby, because them Redcoats are gonna lay some shit on you dudes in a couple a days. That's what *all* the books say."

"But what're you saying?"

"I'm saying—the British are going to win at Lexington."

Salem smiled gently. "Are you a voodoo priest?"

"Voodoo, hoodoo, Salem, that's history."

As if they weren't listening to him, Cato said, "They've offered us our freedom, if we fight. So, we're fighting. Is that the way it is with you, too?"

"What should we call you, stranger?" Cuff interrupted.

"Abraham Blackman. That's my name." He turned to Cato. "Freedom? Well, now I hate to tell you guys this, but there're gonna be damned few of you who gonna get all this freedom they're preachin. Another eighty-eight years—"

Blackman broke off because they were laughing at him. "Okay. You guys just go ahead and laugh. Eighty-eight years and another hundred and eight years. You git in this dream with me and see what's really goin down. Dumb-ass niggers. Never learn nothin."

After a while Blackman noticed that the leaders weren't attracting too many of the farmers along the way. The men behind him, also farmers, he gathered, called plaintively as they passed the homes and farms where men and boys strained behind horse and plow, opening the winter-tightened ground to the warming sun. When leaders and farmers both were waved off by the plowmen, they hooted, but when others indicated that they would join the group later, they shouted, "Hooray! Hooray!" And as the group trudged over the miles, slowly now, imperceptibly, it was

19

growing. The riders tried to encourage the mob into formations, but they never held for longer than a few moments.

The black men he marched with were poorly dressed and sometimes barefoot. A part of this mob, Blackman thought, yet prisoners of it, pushed forward by its momentum; they were the expendables, the point of the mob. When the cry went up behind them, "To arms! To arms!" the blacks shouted, too, but absent from their voices, he observed, was the ring of purity he heard in the shouts of the men behind them.

"Where'd you get the musket?" Salem asked, and Blackman knew that this was a question they'd all itched to ask him.

Blackman held it up and looked at it again. "Don't know. I just *had* it. Got to figure out how to work it, man."

Salem smiled indulgently. "The whites don't like it."

Blackman wheeled around and glanced at the ranks behind him. So that's what those looks were about. He turned back and studied the gun. The powder must go here, he thought. The ball in the muzzle, and the ramrod—yeah, this is it. Flintlock? He flicked a metal hook and sparks flew. Okay, now. Powder here, ball, ram and *bam!* Shit! A round every half hour.

They spread out over the Lexington Green. Some lay down, others sat. The riders trotted around placing groups of men. The blacks were in the first group facing the road the British would come on. Campfire positions were set and weapons stacked.

Peter Salem sat under a giant hardwood maple, watching his fellow blacks, particularly Blackman, and thought of Crispus Attucks. Blackman reminded Salem of Attucks, now dead five years in the massacre at Boston. Obviously Blackman was mad. In dress and manner. Look how he was pacing around.

Blackman moved back and forth. He stopped. Closed his eyes. When I open them, he thought, none of this'll be here; the dream'll be over. Now! He snapped open his eyes. Still April in Massachusetts, and Salem was still watching him, the way you watch a nut. Blackman moved another few paces and closed his eyes again. He thought of Mim. When I open my eyes I'll be in bed, she'll be beside me, at her place, and it'll be warm and we'll be sipping a good Meursault and blowing some high-grade grass. That's all Saigon meant, Mimosa. He opened his eyes and found a group of whites staring at him. The farmers. It was still April and he was still in Lexington.

Wearily, he trudged over and sat down beside Salem.

Salem said, "Every white eye here's on you, Abraham. The Brown Bess makes em nervous."

"Salem, you just don't know how old this tale's gonna get, man. White folks're always gonna be uptight about niggers with guns. I can't let that worry me now. I got another problem."

Both turned to watch another company of farmers arrive amid a clatter of muskets. Now, in the afternoon heat, the smell of sweating men mixed with that of trampled earth, grass and things newly green. Additional runners were sent out and instructions were being given in the use of the musket; Blackman was not invited to join. Sometimes singly, sometimes in groups, the farmers straggled in, and by dusk Blackman knew that all who were coming were already there. The campfires were lighted and soon the smell of food began to drift over the Green.

Later, the salt fish and salt pork eaten and the fires reduced to glowing coals of hard maple, the men tried to sleep. Some could not and sat talking quietly. Pickets, flung out from the Green, clumsily patrolled their areas, stepping on the drying detritus of early spring, wind-downed branches, beds of dried leaves, leaning boundary walls of shale. The moon came up a bright, yellow crescent.

A distance away from the black men a group of farmers, also sitting around a fire of heat-giving coals, smoked their pipes and tried to think of the morrow when the British would surely come. But they were being interrupted by the grumbling of one of their number.

"Now, I don't think that man ought to have a firearm. A nigger with a gun is just unthinkable."

The farmers puffed their pipes and thought of seeding. Surely, the nigger, as strange as he talked and looked, had a master in a high place. Who else would arm a black man with a gun? The sight of the big man with the gun had certainly made them pause for a moment, but it had to be all right. Didn't want to antagonize the gentlemen.

"We ought to take it away from him, that's what we ought to do," the grumbling farmer said. One by one the other farmers peeked out beyond the bowls of their pipes at him and said nothing. They thought of the next day. The British had killed Colonials before, in random instances. What about tomorrow? Would it all turn out to be some kind of game? What was going to happen when they met face to face? They thought these thoughts and of their families, their planting and, one by one lay down and closed their eyes, not so much to sleep as to enter privately the deepest recesses of their fears.

But each of them heard the grumbling farmer, some time later, rise from his crouch and step away from the fire into the darkness. They opened their eyes, thinking they could hear better that way.

Abraham Blackman lay on the ground, wrapped in a tattered cape one of the blacks'd lent him; his feet were toward the fire. The snoring of his fellows surrounded him like a heavy, warm blanket, and he felt himself slipping off to sleep. He pressed his fingers tightly to the musket, then opened them and wrapped them around the smooth, cherrywood stock.

He didn't know what time it was when he felt that smooth stock moving slowly out of the grasp of his now relaxed fingers. At first he accepted the movement as a part of his dream or as one controlled by his own body; but as his fingers, slowly and insinuatingly, were left gripping nothing but cool air and cooler earth, he came awake and like a flash his hand moved swiftly in the direction of the gun, recaptured it. He felt it being pulled away again, being sucked into the darkness, and he pulled too, peering intently into the night in which he seemed to see shadowed there, gray and ghostly, the face of his battalion

22

commander, Major Whittman. Blackman felt the gun returning to his control; triumph welled up in him even as a flash of paining, yellow light blossomed silently in his head, then faded slowly to a darkness tinged with red.

The blacks threw more wood on the fire and pressed cold stones to Blackman's head. No word passed between them; they understood. They nodded and smiled at each other when they saw the Brown Bess in the big man's hands. Farmers still awake at other dying campfires wondered why the niggers were getting up already.

## 2

By midmorning the Colonials heard the pipes distantly, carried on a warming wind. They were up and in position, their morning tea already digested.

Blackman'd insisted on taking the center position in the road in the front rank of the blacks, although it'd seemed to Salem, Pompey and the others that he was still suffering from the blow in the face. Perhaps in a good way, Salem observed, for Blackman no longer seemed to be irritated and bewildered. And they could understand him better this morning, maybe because by now they were used to his accent. With the borrowed, tattered cape around him and hatless—Blackman's hat had been lost in the struggle—he now looked more like one of them than a ludicrous apparition. Calmly he'd loaded his musket and now knelt, his gun, butt on the ground, held straight up before him.

The other blacks were also kneeling, one knee down, their stakes and spears straight up. Blackman was staring down the road. Like the others, he heard the pipes, but for the moment the road was enclosed in thin green. The next moment there appeared a regular shape of bright red and white, a centipede. Now he heard drumtaps. Behind him the lines of white farmers rippled with whispers and movements.

"Stead-eee!" one of the officers of the Framingham militia called out. His cry was taken up by other officers.

The British were coming up the road, their pace easy and measured, like a company nonchalant about marching long distances with heavy packs and killing farmers, Peter Salem thought. He glanced at Blackman, then behind him to the ranks of the farmers. Which one had it been? That one? Him? That one over there? That boy? Out of the corner of his eye he studied Blackman again. A slight swelling in the center of the forehead. He'd said nothing about what'd happened in the night.

Blackman could hear the crunch of booted feet, all hitting the ground in unison; the sound chilled him. Black boots, white pants, red coats. Pink faces, some slashed by mustaches. The helmets on their heads made them appear as tall as giants, and their muskets with bayonets fixed seemed five feet long. They came up, their weapons rattling, their gear creaking, and halted on a shouted command. Another cry sent them into a smooth flowing skirmish line. An officer walked to the front to hail the farmers.

"Pitcairn," Pompey whispered to Blackman.

A man, Blackman thought, known for brutality and ruthlessness.

At Pitcairn's order to disperse, the farmers jeered. The officer stepped forward again and repeated his command. Long moments passed, then Blackman heard the farmers moving, drawing back, and his rank backed up, too.

Then a musket was fired, and no one could tell whose it was, a Yankee's or a Redcoat's. Cursing and pushing, the Colonials broke ranks even as the Pitcairn's order to fire was given. The volley cut in among them but the Colonials, black and white, every man for himself, kept running. To hell with the dead and dying.

Blackman found himself with Prince and Pompey racing over the moss-covered ground. They ran at top speed as long as they were unencumbered by brush, and then, panting, glancing over their shoulders, they slowed to a trot but didn't stop until they'd gained the Concord road, where they found Peter Salem, still gasping for breath, waiting. Salem held a Ferguson. From one of the dead farmers, Blackman guessed. They sat wordless, gasping, acknowledging with dull eyes the passing of more farmers, singly or in groups, all on the way to Concord, most out of breath, their faces mirroring shame.

Blackman was the first to regain his feet. "Let's go," he said, and Pompey, Prince and Salem were too tired to argue his assumption of leadership. He led the way, trotting a few paces, walking a few; they matched him. None of the farmers they passed seemed to mind the two guns.

Under the high noon sun at Concord, Blackman saw the group of farmers. Fewer than at Lexington he quickly estimated. At almost the same moment they arrived, another column of Redcoats joined the Royal Marines, already in Concord searching for supplies. The farmers withdrew to North Bridge.

They might have stayed there and returned to their homes afterward, and in the succession of nights converted their rout at Lexington into a victory, the way most soldiers do when they relate their deeds to their children and grandchildren and others who were not there. But from the town columns of smoke, thick and black, rose into the sky.

"They're burning the town!" the farmers cried. "Burning it!"

In a bunch the farmers and blacks began to run toward the smoke, toward the British. Growls and shouts came, as if voicing with shock the realization that, even more than the killing of their fellows back on the Lexington Green, this deliberate destruction of property could not be tolerated.

Blackman, running with Captain Davis, was as surprised as he when, sprinting over the bridge whose loose planks rattled under their weight, Davis took a ball which killed him instantly. Ambush, Blackman thought, skidding to a stop, then shouting, "Ambush!"

26

Once more the farmers broke, but this time for cover. Blackman sought the shelter of a great maple and was joined by Salem.

"How you work this thing, Abraham?" He was fiddling with the gun; his powder horn rattled on the barrel, seeking a place for the powder to go. Blackman had knelt and fired. Now he was back up. The low hillsides around them resounded with firing, the smell of black powder, the hum of lead balls. "Powder, ball, ram, aim, fire!" Blackman shouted. He peeked out from behind the tree while trying to load himself. Ready now, he knelt once again, aimed at a clot of red and pulled the trigger. Nothing happened, and as he lowered the gun, momentarily puzzled, the ball ran out of the muzzle and fell to the ground. He picked it up and retreated to another tree, Salem with him.

What didn't I do right? Blackman asked himself. He started all over again. More Redcoats were spilling out of the green woods. Shouts, explosions. He saw Salem aiming. He fired and tumbled backward from the kick of his gun, but he regained his feet screaming to Blackman,

"I got one! I got one!"

Ready again, Blackman aimed at a phalanx of Redcoats who were making bayonet raids. He got his man, saw him spin backward, jabbing his bayonet into the ground. It seemed that the British were falling back, and around him the farmers were coming out from cover, standing upright to fire. Blackman loaded, cleaned and rammed over and over with a fury; he felt himself sweating. The brush caught at his clothes and made him know he was advancing, not standing still as he believed.

Concord retreated behind them. They advanced over the bodies of British soldiers. Demoralized, the Redcoats were flinging away their packs. The farmers were shouting in triumph. Blackman and Salem fired until their cartridges were gone, but still followed the fight, all the way into Charles Town. Then they followed the farmers back to Concord.

An imposed quiet lay along the line of battle. They'd come

so far to die, Blackman mused, looking at the twisted, shattered bodies. And these, the farmers, almost fifty of them, half the force, were dead.

The blacks drew together. Blackman didn't know them all, but he did know the name of the single black dead man when they told him: Prince Estabrook.

Later, the bodies buried and the weapons collected, the farmers already hurrying homeward, the blacks bid each other good-bye.

"Maybe now," Cuff said, "we can get this freedom."

They all looked at Salem and Blackman, the only men among them who were free. "Where'll you go?" Cuff asked.

Blackman looked at Salem and Salem said, "To Boston."

It was Cuff who said it, slowly, but with the determination of one bound to pursue mysteries. He gestured toward Blackman. "Yesterday you said we'd get beat at Lexington. We did." Now they all, as if in sudden, collective recall, remembered. "How did you know?"

Blackman looked slowly around the circle of black men on their way back to slavery. He shrugged. "I don't know; I don't know how I knew." He sighed. "In fact, I don't even remember saying it."

Cuff, no more than a boy, but with a hard face, nodded. His eyes flicked momentarily up to the swelling on Blackman's forehead. He nodded once again, turned and started off to his master's. The others followed. Blackman and Salem headed at once for Boston, for safety, trailing the Brookline company. They slept in the woods, and in the morning, before breaking camp, they hid their guns.

"We can't walk into any settlement with them, Abraham," Salem said. "They'd tear us limb from limb. We're not even supposed to have clubs, you know."

"And we're free men?" Blackman asked with a smile.

"That's to come, as you said yourself before Lexington." Salem paused in covering the hiding place with branches. "Or don't you remember that, either?"

28

"I don't, Peter."

"And your head?"

"It feels all right."

"Then let's go. Boston it is."

After two months of freedom, of being hounded by British soldiers as well as the citizens; after being checked for weapons almost every day and reading the announcements of the Committee of Safety which said black men, slave or free, were not to be permitted to carry arms in the militias, it was almost a relief to be once again facing British soldiers on the attack. They were down there, disembarking from their vessels in the Charles River.

In two months they'd become fast friends, Salem and Blackman, and had discussed places to go and things to do. Nova Scotia, but that was being flooded with Tories, and besides, black men there complained of their lot. There was talk from the South about the British forming a regiment of blacks, but why should one trust them, either, or accept their many offers to work as free men on their islands? Once they got you on those islands, where there were already slaves aplenty, they could do anything they wished with you. And it was a long way to the South where the Indians would take in a black man and make him a brother in their tribes. The same was not completely true of the northern Indians, so often the mercenaries of the British or the Americans, as they were starting to call themselves.

Blackman and Salem stood together on Breed's Hill; the position was overflowing with men, but Blackman wondered, his eye falling now and again on black men, no longer herded together, why Bunker's Hill hadn't been chosen for its higher ground. Then he chuckled, and that turned into a laugh.

Salem jabbed him with his Ferguson. They'd recovered their weapons when Dr. Warren's recruiters gave in and took in black men to help drive the Redcoats from Boston. "What's funny, Abraham?"

"We've got a hill at our backs."

29

"Yes," Salem said, glancing upward. "You can't run up a hill fast if you're inclined to. They mean for us to stay and fight."

Salem, too, glanced around, saw Cuff Whittemore and Salem Poor, who was with Captain Ames's company, Seasor and Pharaoh, and many other blacks he didn't know.

Their ineffective bombardment finished, the soldiers down on the rocks gathered into formation. The Americans could hear their pipes and drums. The Redcoats started up, their flags whipping in the hot wind, their swords, metal trimmings flashing in the sun. They came up in steady, tight formation, dipping down into the decline behind Maulton's Point, up the incline of Breed's Hill, and the earth began to resound with the tread of so many feet striking it at the same time; it seemed to quiver slightly, as though warning of an earthquake. The Americans, militiamen, clerks, farmers, blacks slave and free, craftsmen, stared as if hypnotized. Captains shouted to their men to break the hypnotic effect. Dr. Warren roamed around the breastworks, instructing, and Captain Prescott was shouting something about the eyes.

"What did he say?" Blackman asked Salem.

"I think he said to shoot them in the eyes." Salem hadn't turned to speak to Blackman; his eyes were fixed upon the approaching red mass. Blackman thought to himself, "They'll have to be very close for that!" and he grew nervous. Now Salem turned to him, and Blackman caught the leading edge of panic in his voice when he said, "I'm not *sure* that's what he said."

Up they came. The men crowded forward to the lip of the breastworks, as though, Blackman thought, they were more afraid of not getting off a shot than being hit by one.

"Look at them," Salem said under his breath. He was admiring the way they were coming up under full pack, drums beating and flutes piping; he could hear them clearly now, together with the tattoo of boots against the hillside.

Blackman strained around those close to him to see Prescott who held his sword in the air; when it fell they were to fire. He turned to the British again. The shapes of their faces seemed to be the same. He could see the designs on their buttons, and now the color of their eyes—

"Fire!" Prescott screamed.

Flashes of red and crooked daggers of black smoked marked the first volley. Blackman peered intently through the curtain of smoke to see its effect. The red line before him had quivered, cracked and tottered and spilled suddenly back downhill, rushing around, over and through officers who pleaded with them, slapped at them with the flat of their swords to stand fast.

Behind the breastworks the Americans were smiling and congratulating each other on beating the Redcoats. Blackman and Salem bent to reload, their eyes on Maulton's Point where the British were reforming. They came back up and were driven down again as word went around that the Colonials were low on ammunition.

An uneasy silence drifted over the fortifications when the British, this time without their packs, came up again. They're brave, Blackman thought. He wondered, if he'd been one of them, if he'd come up a third time. Breed's Hill seemed an awful place to die, he reflected, spattered as it was with dung from Breed's cows. On they came, their ranks considerably thinned, stepping over the bodies of their dead and wounded. The Americans unleashed weak lightning, but the Redcoats, bayonets at the ready, kept charging, on the run now; they swept to the edge of the breastworks and Blackman was swinging at them with the butt of his gun when the call came to retreat.

The steep slope at their backs proved no obstacle; the Americans, those who escaped the bayonets, fled up the hill or down its slopes, Blackman and Salem among them. Later they learned that two blacks, Philip Abbot and Caesar Bason, had not been able to escape the Redcoats' last charge. They paused breathlessly on Bunker's Hill and looked back. The slopes of Breed's Hill were covered with bodies and at the crest of the fortifications were more, these last Americans, who were easily distinguished by their absence of red coats.

Now, walking down the hill, hearing occasional shots behind them and still smelling the gunpowder that lingered in the air, Salem said,

"It looked for a while like we'd whipped them."

Blackman nodded. But he'd never thought so. Men who could keep coming up like that, in formation, under discipline, in the end couldn't be beaten. They just kept cranking up and coming back. Like a machine. You had to strip its gears or jam its mechanisms. Or place a better machine on the field. "Yes," he said finally. "For a little while it did."

They were in a slow flood of men moving turgidly back from the battle; there'd been no pursuit by the British. Men walked with their muskets angled carelessly over their shoulders, their eyes sometimes glazed with weariness or the horror of what they'd seen, or both. It was some time before Blackman realized that he and Salem were walking automatically back toward Brookline to hide their guns once more, like trained animals, and he stopped and Salem stopped too, looking at him questioningly.

"And now what, Abraham?" Salem asked. Blackman looked now, in his worn, castoff clothing, like any other black man of these parts. His strange uniform had since worn away and piece by piece had been replaced with other, more familiar vestments.

"I don't think I'll hide this, Peter. I think I'll go on down to New York. Maybe there things aren't as bad for a black man."

Now it was Salem's turn to nod. He was mildly surprised that he knew this was coming. For himself, he'd met a slave girl he hoped to free somehow and marry. Perhaps by his labors. He knew of no other way. His labor and fighting in exchange for her freedom. He couldn't work or fight in New York; that was too far away from his woman's master who sought first of all to protect what he had in Chelmsford. Too bad, for the big man was interesting, brave and had become a friend. But strange. Salem felt obliged to make at least one plea. "It's a long way," he said, "and dangerous for any man, let alone a single black one. Stay."

Blackman stared past Salem, reflecting. "Well, Peter, I've just got this urge to go. Don't feel right being in one place, so I have to try it."

The two men shook hands and Salem turned north and Blackman turned south, moving with long strides, as if in a great hurry to arrive at or catch up with events still unformed.

Blackman paused and took a firmer grip on the rope knotted around the neck of the statue of King George III. As he did, his eyes met those of a woman sitting on a bench. She turned quickly away and Blackman laughed and took a deep breath before leaning once again into the rope.

Mrs. Frazer had journyed from Pennsylvania to New York City to visit her sister who sat with her on the bench. Neither were a part of the revelry, merely observers of it. The huge Negro had made Mrs. Frazer think of the letter, now in her purse, from her husband at Ticonderoga. "The Yankee regiments," he'd written, "possess the strangest mixture of Negroes, Indians and Whites, with old men and mere children, which, together with a nasty, lousy appearance make a most shocking spectacle."

His description, Mrs. Frazer thought, fitted perfectly those now engaged in pulling down the statue here in Bowling Green. Rabble! And wouldn't you know there'd be niggers here, too? Poor captain, she thought, up there in that isolated place (where in the world *was* Ticonderoga?) with the scum of the earth. That nigger. Looked me right in the eye, the nerve.

The men with the bars strained. "Pull!" they called to those on the ropes. "Heave!" The statue, horse and man, trembled. A shout went up. Slowly, the horse, frozen in its metallic canter, pawed fixedly up off its base into the air. King George, his plump face undisturbed, now stared at the heavens instead of the Hudson River. Over in a slow, heavy arc the statue came until, for a moment suspended by the force of those at the

33

ropes and bars and its own weight, horse and rider gave a little swoop through the air, described a small arc, then crashed to the ground.

Blackman released his rope and walked off.

"We'll want him," one of a group of soldiers said. "When the wagons get stuck, he'll be handy. Get him."

The soldier came at Blackman with the same words he'd been hearing around the city. We can't lose now. We have a General, George Washington, of Virginia.

A slaveholder, Blackman thought, listening.

And we've declared our independence from England.

Blackman knew those words, too, which'd been written by yet another Virginian slaveholder, Thomas Jefferson. He thought of the lines he liked best:

"That whenever any Form of Government becomes destructive of these ends, it is the Right of the People to alter or to abolish it, and to institute new Government, laying its Foundations on such Principles and organizing its Powers in such Form, as to them shall seem most likely to effect their Safety and Happiness."

But the soldier was speaking. "A fine fellow like yourself would want to be a Revolutionary soldier. Who's man are you? We'll talk to your master and tell him we'll take you instead of him—"

Blackman was watching the mob drag off the statue. The woman who'd watched him had left her bench in the company of another woman. Shouts filled the air. To the soldier he said, "I am a free black man, with no master but myself. I'll fight if I'm paid like everyone else."

"But you will!" the soldier said so quickly that Blackman knew he was lying.

Laughing, he said, "You say yes, but the next master-at-arms will say no; the one after that'll say he doesn't know, and after him another master-at-arms'll say he'll find out." But he knew that more frequently now it seemed the rule that black men

34

who fought would be rewarded; slaves would be freed and lands and monies granted. Provided the Americans won, and he agreed to fight, seeing no other way black men could ever be free.

And what if, he thought, they were lying about it all the time?

The war came to New York late that summer, raged back and forth across Long Island and Blackman found himself in the ranks being chased from Kingsbridge to Bedford to Jamaica, from the solid ranks of the British Army with its Hessians in tall brass hats, into the bombardments of the British Navy. The roads of the city were filled with the wagons of people moving to the farms and countryside, with deserting Revolutionary soldiers. Those that remained marched upstate along the Hudson Valley, then crossed the river and began a tattered, cheerless march through New Jersey where they found almost no militias but an abundance of Tories.

Blackman shifted to the wagons, listened to their creaking wheels for telltale sounds of imminent failure, to the thinning oxen for signs of last life so they could be killed and butchered for food. They went a slow and bitter tide over the flat New Jersey fields, desertions increasing, grumbling louder, Washington with them. The nights were growing colder and the dew lingered longer in the morning. Along the route of march, the people drove their livestock off into the woods so the soldiers wouldn't commandeer them and give them a piece of worthless paper in exchange for three hundred pounds of meat on the hoof. At dusk and dawn the sharpshooters were dispersed for the hunting of rabbits, squirrels, deer and birds. And the soldiers sitting before the camp furnaces, the grates empty, listened forlornly to the shots echoing; the more shots, the greater the probability of food.

The blacks set traps as soon as the army halted its march for the day, or, with clubs, set out to trap and pummel to death any

35

edible animal. The rations always became short when it was their turn for them.

But the movement of so large a group chased the game ahead of them or far to their flanks, and meat became increasingly scarce, and as it did, grumbling intensified, and Blackman noticed that there were riders always coming in from Washington's camp to the rear. Something'll be happening soon, he thought. Soon.

And on a morning when fifteen men from the company were found missing, Captain McGruder called an assembly. McGruder was a thin, spare man, better suited to driving horses than men, Blackman thought, for he seemed not to know what to do with the latter. McGruder spoke stumblingly of freedom, the way, Blackman imagined, he might speak of a foal, and of men who hadn't the heart to fight for it. The going was rough now, yes, but the government was doing something about it and was going to show its appreciation. A bonus of twenty dollars and a hundred acres of land and a new suit of clothes awaited the faithful.

A murmur broke out among the men, all except those who were black, and these gazed at each other thoughtfully, each wishing another to speak up to ascertain whether or not these favors applied to them too. Blackman waited and watched, and when it seemed that none would speak, he called.

"Captain McGruder!"

The heads swung around. All eyes swept the group of ragged blacks, then drew up to Blackman. Him, the one who pulled the oxen, lifted wagons out of ruts, pushed the fieldpieces, butchered the oxen.

Captain McGruder had dreaded this moment. Headquarters'd given him no real answer on the question. He believed black men were different from white men, but even so, he thought it fair that every man be paid equally for equal labors. Other matters were not his concern. God made things the way they were, and when He chose to change them, He would. Inwardly

36

recoiling already, McGruder pointed to Blackman. He knew his name for he was obviously the leader of the blacks in his company.

"Captain McGruder," Blackman said again. "Does that mean us, too?"

Blackman felt that the silence had form and motion, but he knew that they knew the blacks'd walked all the miles, killed or wounded their share of the British, marched with fewer rags on their backs than others, gathered firewood and water, and curried and brushed horses while the others sat.

Wearily McGruder summoned Blackman to him with a wave of his arm; he put all the compassion in it of which he was capable. He knew he dare not put it in his voice. Blackman walked through the slowly parting ranks of the whites and followed McGruder to his tent, thinking of the song he wished to shout at them:

> *The rebel clowns, ah what a sight,*
> *Too awkward was their figure,*
> *'Twas yonder stood a pious wight*
> *And here and there a nigger.*

"—and here and there a nigger," he wanted to repeat. "—and here and there a nigger." The Tories at least recognized their presence, though they laughed at it.

"Blackman," McGruder said in his Yankee accent. "I don't know. I've tried to find out. I've insisted on it. They said they'd let me know. I can do no better." Blackman peered down at the thin face, already stabbed with deep lines and wrinkles. "I will keep trying."

"Another thing," McGruder said, taking off his hat and avoiding Blackman's eyes. "No doubt some of you'll now feel that you're free to leave. That's not the case. You'll be shot for desertion if you try to. Like any other soldier," he said, his voice sinking. He waved Blackman out of the tent.

Back through the company Blackman walked aware of the

37

eyes that covertly watched him for signs he could not conceal; the whites were pleased, the blacks confirmed in their bitterness. "It's not the money or the land or the clothes that's so important," Blackman said as up and down the road the army prepared to continue its southward march to a succession of shouted commands, creaking wheels and shuffling feet.

"It's the freedom, real freedom."

The blacks nodded, but all were thinking: This trail of freedom is dotted with caltrops meant to skewer our feet and detour us.

Within days the trees began to flame into color. Chilling rain slanted down the sky, and then the snow came, melting at first, and then sticking. Grippe went through the ranks like the indiscriminate curving of a scythe, and men dropped out of line, their lungs flooding with snot, but were replaced by men thought to have been captured in New York, blacks among them. On Christmas night, the half-frozen army, hoarfrost on the faces of the men, the fieldpieces frozen, came to McConkey's Ferry, on the Delaware, crossed, and with little or no Christmas fare in their bellies, the men broke into two groups for the attack on Trenton, after going back over the river a second time.

Sleet hissed against the already frozen snow. Blackman listened to his footsteps crunching through crusts of ice. Quick-time came the word, quick-time, and they force-marched five miles, each man thinking of slipping away in the storm, but deterred by the fear of dying alone, frozen. Armies, Blackman thought, have discovered an important secret; men did not like to die alone, thus they offered others to die with you, and for the most part you clung to them.

Passing down the freezing, snow-covered ranks they heard the rumor that the gracious government, the new Congress that'd offered the money, land and clothes, had fled to Baltimore from Philadelphia. But the army moved on, from habit and to stay warm.

Suddenly Blackman found himself falling behind. Or was it

that the men ahead were moving faster, fighting harder against the ice and snow? The column was moving faster, the men breathing more rapidly, bending deeper into the wind. Then Blackman knew. Caught between a government, which, according to the recent rumor could not support them, and a Hessian garrison filled with food and warmth, what choice was there but to move quickly and take from those who had it what the ragged, whipped Continental Army needed. Them or us, us or them, and Blackman thought he detected a growl along the line of march, the growl of an animal with its back to the wall, determined to fight for its existence.

Out of the night, then, slipping on rag-wrapped feet, the touchholes of their muskets frozen, the Colonials took out the Hessian pickets and poured into Trenton under the cover of barrages of grapeshot from cannons from which the ice had been dug, killing and capturing with the jerking movements of men whose hot emotions could not match the stiffness of their bodies. And the Hessians, dulled with hot food and drink, Christmas songs still ringing in their sleep-deadened minds, capitulated quickly and watched the ragged horde pour into their barracks.

In the morning McGruder came. He did not order as much as plead with his men to prepare to cross back over the Delaware. Washington's orders. It would be safe there. And, grumbling, the army went, and three days later, faintly feeling like human beings once more, the officers came at them again; Washington wished the army to cross yet once again.

Blackman watched his company, again at the point of dissolution, protest, the men standing toe to toe with their officers, shouting and cursing at them. And why not? He knew some of the men had only three days' service left. They didn't want to get caught up in any action that'd take them past the first of the year.

But, Blackman watched with a wry smile when they agreed, for an additional ten dollars, to remain in the army another six weeks. This time, Captain McGruder sought him out. "I think they're going to give you five, Blackman." Then, heading him off said, "It's better than nothing, now, isn't it?"

"Yes, sir," Blackman said. He was looking out of his makeshift cabin at the snow. Soon, they'd be back in it. "Does that mean we're free in six weeks, too?"

Angrily McGruder spun around and left. Blackman knew there'd be no such luck; the blacks were in for the duration, often filling the places their masters should've been willing to fill. Here and there a nigger, he thought.

He thought it again when, at Valley Forge, the black Rhode Island regiment marched in to give the place the semblance of an army camp.

His aides knew he wasn't well; too many campaigns plus a generally weak constitution. Still, they thought, he shouldn't have said it, not now when it looked like a major victory was in the offing. As a former member of the Continental Congress, he should've known better. But, General Schuyler had stood right there when the Massachusetts regiments came into the camp at Saratoga and said so clearly that everyone could hear him: "Is it consistent with the sons of freedom to trust their all to be defended by slaves?" And the blacks in the rear ranks marched by, eyes veiled but not so much that Schuyler's aides couldn't see the sparks. And the great big one, had he farted then or was his foot scraping the ground? Tactless, General, tactless. The truth need not always be spoken.

Blackman had heard; they'd all heard. Marching past in the warm September afternoon, the cooling Hudson sparkling through the forests, Blackman momentarily locked eyes with one of the General's aides. The aide had been moving slowly up and down, watching the regiments come in, walking up and down as stealthily and carefully as a cat, yet there was something about him that reminded Blackman of a serpent flowing back into itself as it is uncovered beneath a dead log. The man's face seemed to float directly from his body, without a neck; this face, its eyes, locked with Blackman's and Blackman saw that it was whiter than any face he'd ever seen, and the eyes were space-blue, so that he felt as though he were looking into the center of nothingness. The aide's hair helped to give this illusion. It was flaxen, and in the moment Blackman looked at the man, the gold-white hair caught a flash of sun.

Blackman tore his eyes away and farted again. But there was something about the aide, his wordlessness as against the General's, that left Blackman uneasy throughout the campaign.

Major Whittman had been absently listening to the radio. He was sucking on his ragged, wet-ended Roi-Tan, his mind back in Saigon on the talk of promotions. He hoped he'd made the lists this time; time to trade in the gold leaf for a silver one and then, chicken colonel, goddamn. But the crackle of the radio and the operator's monotonous, southern voice irritated him. Out of space-blue eyes he stared at the kid. Faulkner, a redneck from Georgia. The Army was knee deep in rednecks, mountaineers, spics and niggers. Handle em all but the niggers, and the spics were getting out of hand, and shit, some of peacenik white kids—

"What's that about Charlie Company?" he asked the operator. He leaned close to the crackling set over which a flood of monotonous voices, very much like Faulkner's, were crowding in.

"Captain Blackman's been hit, Major. They're tryin t reach him."

Major Whittman straightened up slowly. He ran a hand through his close-cropped flaxen hair. Good, he thought. *Good!* I hope that fucker got it real *good*. "Is he dead?" he asked aloud.

"They doan know, sir. They ain't been able to reach him yet."

Whittman spun around on his heel, biting hard into his cigar.

"Black military history," he muttered. "Teach that black cocksucker. Sonofabitch. I hope they cream his ass good."

"Sir?" the operator called, leaning away from the set.

"Nothing!" Whittman snapped. He stood. "I'm going to my

41

quarters, Faulkner. Let me know as soon as word comes in on Blackman. Got that?"

"Sure, Major."

Years and campaigns later, battles and deaths later, Trenton, Monmouth, Rhode Island, Germantown behind him; the starvation and ineptness, the papers of Paine and Woolman burned into his brain with their truths, the unending parade of sacrificed blacks, slave and free, still like gall stuck in his gullet, Blackman, West Point, Cowpens and Yorktown also now behind him, walked from the discharge place holding firmly to his papers. He walked down the street of this small Virginia town reading them.

By His Excellency
George Washington, Esq.
General and Commander in Chief of the Forces
of the United States of America
These are to CERTIFY that the bearer hereof
ABRAHAM BLACKMAN

in the Ninety-ninth Regiment, having faithfully served the United States from April 15, 1775 to October 19, 1781, and being inlisted for the War is hereby discharged from the American Army.

GIVEN at Head-Quarters the 20th Day of October, 1781
By His Excellency's Command
Registered in the Books of the Regiment,

J. ARMSTRONG,
Adjutant

The above
ABRAHAM BLACKMAN
has been honored with the BADGE OF MERIT for six years
FAITHFUL SERVICE

Head-Quarters, Oct. 20, 1781

THE within CERTIFICATE shall not avail the Bearer as a Discharge until the Ratification of the definitive Treaty of Peace; previous to which Time, and until Proclamation thereof shall be made, He is to be considered as being on FURLOUGH.

GEORGE WASHINGTON

It was a clear, warm day, hinting of Indian summer, the foliage of the Virginia countryside bright with reds, oranges, greens and yellows. Blackman walked easily, scarely feeling the awkward sharpness of the old bayonet he had tucked in his pants.

One block from the discharge place, the whites jumped him, and he knew at once that it'd do no good to tell them he wasn't a slave and had never been one; it wouldn't matter to them. They'd just carry him off, beyond the line of brightly glowing trees to a plantation, and that would be that. He lashed out with fist and bayonet. He was not going to be one of those blacks who moved about plantations in chains because they'd learned to kill white men, but were still good for growing tobacco. He fought them off and fled, and when he was safe at last, under the cover of night, he went on his way, southward under the North Star, over trails of those who were fleeing in the opposite direction.

As he went he hummed a song that came to mind:

> *We had an Army, twenty thousand men,*
> *Five thousand were niggers,*
> *Oh, say that again—*
> *We had an Army, twenty thousand men,*
> *Five thousand were niggers—*
> *Stop! Don't say it again.*

South he went, hearing from blacks along the way stories of Lafayette who told Washington to free the slaves, and Blackman knew as he walked that Washington, like a lot of people wanting to get right with God, would free his own slaves as he was dying, and ask his heirs, of which by blood he had none, to look out for the darkies until they were twenty-five. His body servant, William Lee, would be provided for, with freedom or not, no one would know. Blackman marched South.

# 3

South to sit in the shadows of the Cathedral of St. Louis and the Cabildo, in an inn for blacks, drinking and listening to the French, Spanish, English and Creole being spoken here in the port of New Orleans.

Over his hot rum Blackman reflected that the talk was almost always the same until another ship sailed into the harbor with lowered sails and dropped anchor. The black sailors from those vessels then brought in all the world's gossip, enough of it to last until the arrival of the next ship. New Orleans was a sailors' town and while other inns in other parts of the city were also places of gossip, that gossip was about whites. In La Baleine Noire the black underside of the world was the topic of gossip, discussion and speculation. For here they spoke of the black kingdom of Haiti, of York's journey with Lewis and Clark, of distant African ports and hot tropical islands far to the south.

These days, however, most of the talk in this place of dim sea lanterns and smoky walls, was of the war and where black men, sailors and soldiers, would fit in. The militias had been white for twenty years; not so the Navy.

Blackman was just taking down another hot rum when he was slapped heartily on the back. He knew without looking that

44

it was old Griot, clown, raconteur, black patriot, ancient mariner. Always good for a laugh on these chilly days.

"Mornin sar!" Griot boomed, glancing around to see if his arrival had been properly noticed. "How's de big mon tis day, bien, bon?"

"Criot!" came a shout from across the room. "What's news? What the white folks gonna do with them Englishers sittin out inna harbor?"

"Yeah, Griot, you look like you know sumthin new."

His audience assured, Griot moved away from Blackman to the center of the room, tugging at his striped stocking cap. "Well, mens, we's gonna git us some war, now, don you worry none bout dat. But you know, I made de talk, dina make talk bout Strachan, Ware n Martin, bout dey bein black, n how dey come in here on leave from dey ship, de *Chesapeake?* Come in here feelin low."

Griot walked back and forth, spinning about to make sure every eye was upon him.

"Sar! Come in feelin low n talkin bout how dey no walk de streets enywhere safe cause dey bein black n people spittin on dem n callin em names, wuthless black bastids n alla dat, and dey sailors inna Yewnity States Navy. A crime, sars, a crime!

"Cose dey sails away, sails out onna high seas and goddamn gumbo! Here come de Raidcoats." Griot got into a crouch, his arms out before him, one a little ahead of the other, and he moved his hands up and down and Blackman saw two ships on heaving blue waters.

"De Raidcoats comin in de *Leopard,* puttin on evera patcha sail dey could find, an dey ketch up wid de *Chesapeake,* gonna impress some mo Yewnity States sailors. S now dey snatches off dat boat dem t'ree boys, Strachan, Ware n Martin, n puts dem in de Raidcoat navy! N den, genemuns, we goes t war."

Griot took a deep breath and circled in his space once again.

"De same niggers dat warent safe in eny Merican city now's

45

de cause o dis whole war. Dat's what dey says. Man, dese white folks is a messa *gumbo!*"

Griot led the laughter. His bright red gums flashed in the dim light and Blackman, laughing himself, ordered Griot a hot rum. Griot had told the story before; it was an ironic tale, Blackman knew, and they laughed because it would've been too painful to cry. The laughter was dying now, as it always did when the irony of the war was realized. The drinks were going around now. Blackman basked in the fish-soup-smell of the kitchen, the bland odor of melting wax candles, liquor and sailor sweat. Black, brown, tan and white, the faces of the Negroes glistened in the hot inn; eyes shot here and there trying not to miss any speaker who'd know anything about tomorrow. Their eyes also sought the British ships riding at anchor in the harbor, which could be seen through the small fo'c'sle-like windows of the inn.

Tomorrow, Blackman thought, they will ask us to fight, and he looked around the room again. A lot of strangers, probably farmers who'd come in to find out what was going on. They'd not heard Griot before. This night in La Baleine Noire they were welcomed; war sat hard in the harbor and all black men had the most to lose. Blackman looked up. Griot was at his side again.

"Well, Griot," Blackman said. "They'll ask us to fight, no?"

Griot nodded. "It's down t de skinnin o de shrimp, big man, an dey gonna be askin us to fight; dey gonna say 'now lissen yall black fellers'—dey won't be callin us niggers t'morrow—'dem Raidcoats is in de harbuh, dey comin in here t take over Merica n youse black fellers is Mericans jes like de rest of us, so you got t he'p us fight.' Dey done said it befo n dey goan say it agin, big Abe."

"What you going to do, Griot?"

"Ah'll fight," he said simply.

Black Antoine from upriver joined them. "If they ask, us farmers'll fight too." He clicked his clay pipe against his teeth. "Can't hardly say no, because before this white man'd let us stray

46

loose at his back while he's fightin another man in his front, he'd see us all dead."

Blackman shrugged. The truth.

Griot flapped his arms and laughed. "Fur a fack, now dey might even join togedder t git rid o niggers so dey kin fight in peace."

The inn stayed open all night and the men in it drank, ate and dozed, waiting for daybreak. Faintly, they heard the ships' bells ringing out in the harbor.

Blackman gazed at the man named Andrew Jackson. He might inspire confidence among whites, Blackman thought, but not in blacks. An exterminator. The Creeks would never recover from what this man with the scar on his face had done to them at Horseshoe Bend. Had he done it before? Yes. Would he do it again? Yes, Blackman thought, for a man who'd kill Indians and a few blacks the way he'd done it at Horseshoe surely wouldn't hesitate to kill others. Eyeing the strong, lean face even more closely, Blackman felt that Jackson could take just as murderously as he gave. A tough competitor. One of those backwoodsmen who sometimes saw little difference between life and death; one of those who rose in the morning uncaring about making it back to his bed at night to sleep in peace. A chilling kind of man.

Jackson was speaking:

"Through a mistaken policy, you have heretofore been deprived of a participation in the glorious struggle for national rights in which our country is engaged. This shall no longer exist."

Blackman looked around him. Old Griot stood with the farmers, Pierre, Odum and Jones. Black Antoine on the other side. There were so many, Blackman thought, but why not? New Orleans was as rich with blacks, slave and free, as the soil from the Mississippi whose delta was only one hundred miles away. And with Creoles, the *passé blancs*. They all knew that Jackson

47

with his fine and noble talk was begging, had to be *begging* this cold morning in a frost-girded field, surrounded by blacks. Blackman thought of the streams of fine carriages, filled with ladies and gentlemen and bags and boxes, moving northward out of New Orleans. Poor Jackson, begging blacks to help defend the city because there were too few others.

But they let him continue:

"As sons of freedom, you are now called upon to defend our most inestimable blessings. As Americans, your country looks with confidence to her adopted children for valorous support as a faithful return for the advantages enjoyed under her mild and equitable government."

Griot threw back his head and roared, then slammed himself to the ground still laughing. Jackson swung his eyes to another part of the crowd and continued, a flush spreading across his face.

"As fathers, husbands and brothers," he went on, "you are summoned to rally around the standard of the Eagle, to defend all which is dear in existence. Your country, although calling for your exertions, does not wish you to engage in her cause without amply remunerating you for the services rendered. Your intelligent minds are not to be led away by false representations. Your love of honor would cause you to despise the men who would attempt to deceive you. In the sincerity of a soldier and the language of the truth, I address you."

Blackman could not believe what he was hearing, yet he was hearing it, this bold whitewash of history, this random throwing of compliments, all unmeant, all of which must have fought their way out of Jackson's bitter throat. Listen to him! Blackman thought. He knows what we think and he plays upon it. Honor, intelligence, truth.

"To every noble-hearted, generous freeman of color volunteering—"

A pulsing went through the crowd. So, that was the catch. Only freemen. They'd only have to give them something, not the freedom from slavery whites thought they had now. They'd have to give slaves that freedom, and they wouldn't. They'd see New Orleans burned to the ground first, Blackman thought. Before they loosed the slaves.

"—to serve during the present contest with Great Britain, and no longer, there will be paid the same bounty, in money and lands, now received by the white soldiers of the United States, viz., one hundred and twenty-four dollars in money, and one hundred and sixty acres of land. The noncommissioned officers and privates will also be entitled to the same monthly pay and daily rations, and clothes, furnished to any American soldier."

But the slaves, silently, like shadows, were already slipping away. Some with relief, Blackman imagined, for death in battle instead of freedom might've easily been their reward. Some were sad, for they'd have run the risk, fought and hoped to live, to become free men.

And you, Blackman, he said to himself, why are you here, why don't you go? No slave, but black and there's a choice. Why stay?

He thought then of a quarter section. Land. Land bristling with tall pines, black with weather and heavy with turpentine; thought of magnolias in thick groves and streams and ponds and areas where the earth had been turned over to the warming sun and pulverized by plow and horse, and furrowed. He saw the first green shoots emerge from the black-brown soil and then bushes and then the corn, beans, cabbages and the cotton. There would be cotton, off to a patch by itself, which would bring in the hard money. There would be so much land, 160 acres, that he wouldn't be able to see it all. And it would be his forever.

And his family's, for he thought too of a woman—wife, mother—and of children who would people the land. The woman would be strong, broad-shouldered and under her flawless black skin the bones would be big. She'd walk about with that fine feminine grace large women possess, that grace they were forever conscious of wanting to have—and had because they weren't small—

"Sure could use a quarter section," Black Antoine said, and Blackman came out of his reveries to see him chewing nervously on his pipe. "That's a lotta land, specially when all you've got now is ten acres."

"Griot, what about you?" Blackman said.

"Oh, A'll go," he said. "Git me dat quahtah section n sell it. Dat be wuth mo den de money." Griot looked at them with eyes that in the right light could've been called dead. He'd spent a lifetime dulling the flashes he knew could leap in them. Now, they always appeared lifeless, flat. But old acquaintances, long dead, some washed overboard in rough seas, others murdered in knife fights in ports halfway around the world; these had perceived the cunning that lay behind the flatness of his yellowed eyes.

Looking at Black Antoine, Griot saw a conniving hustler, a land-greedy farmer whose fields one day would burst with the white fluff of cotton bolls. Black Antoine would buy slaves and treat them worse than the white man. Black Antoine had plans and wasn't a good man to fight beside, Griot decided.

He would fight beside the Big Man, Blackman. Didn't know what he would be fighting for except the money and the land, and most of the land he'd put under cultivation for food. Looked like a family man. Hard workin' big nigger. Could hitch a plow to himself and do just as good as a horse. Dreamer. Doer. Believer.

So Griot was prepared when Blackman said, "Sell it?"

And Black Antoine said, "I'll buy it."

To many a man it would have been demeaning to beg for help from the blacks. To some degree Jackson felt this, but more, he was determined to win the battle he saw taking shape for New Orleans and the rest of the South. If you already had pirates,

Choctaws, Creoles and buckskinned Tennesseans, it didn't make any difference about the niggers.

Now sitting in his quarters, Jackson almost smiled. That old fool who was rolling around on the ground this morning. All alone, too. Whatever the others felt about the high-flown speech, they didn't let it show. Land and money in exchange for services. That was fair enough, because if the British succeeded, there'd be nothing at all. You could promise the sky—and pay off, if you won. And he'd see to it that the niggers got exactly what he'd promised, no more and no less. As long as he had the power to do so, and if he won this battle, he thought, a vision of George Washington passing through his mind, he could come into almost unlimited power.

Two nights before Christmas Jackson welcomed the news that the British had landed a squadron of troops and were making for New Orleans by way of the Villiers plantation. The men'd been missing life in the city and were getting restless. You couldn't treat them the way you did regulars; they'd pick up their rifles and start walking back home or wherever they came from.

Which group to send to head them off? The dragoons in their bright uniforms? No, they were best of the few regulars he had. They were needed to set the example in bright daylight, in open field. His native Tennesseans? The Indians? The pirates? The militia? The blacks with some equally unblooded young officers? If they couldn't handle a night attack, God knows they wouldn't stand atop ramparts in broad daylight, and if he lost them and the British squadron did make it into New Orleans, no great harm done, for it would have to be followed and supported by more troops which Jackson was sure he could stand off, if his least prepared fighters were decimated.

Nodding, pleased with his reasoning, he turned to the aides who'd brought him the news and gave the order, then sat down to await its outcome while, for the thousandth time, he studied the American fortification maps before him and the probable British landing sites and routes to the city. As dusk closed with night he heard the cannon from the *Carolina* booming, seeking out the British squadron, and hurrying herself with half the assigned American force into position to trap the Redcoats. The black farmers would know every trail, nook and cranny, Jackson thought again. He'd made a wise choice.

Blackman followed lightly in Black Antoine's footsteps; it was all easy going now that dawn had come and the battle, such as it was, over. Secretly, he was elated that he'd done so well, had not had a single moment of uneasiness. It had been his leadership that resulted in recapturing the six-pounders the British'd taken away from them. Now they were on the way back to their positions on the Rodriguez Canal, not a man missing or wounded, and the British squadron, by now, back on the ships. They could really begin to celebrate Christmas. Feeling expansive, he reached back and helped Griot over some fallen trees. The old man had done well, too, had been by his side all night.

Once settled back in position, the celebration began, sleep forgotten. The sharpshooters roamed the forests and their rifles cracked against the dawn. In camp, the fires were started, the rum and corn jugs appeared magically. Banjos and violins echoed down the line. Here and there squirrels, rabbits and birds were being skinned, plucked and spitted. Griot found a banjo player and danced to his tune, spinning, shaking, sliding, his stocking cap bouncing and whirling on his head. The sun was above the tree line now and the frolicking reached another pitch. The pile of game was growing faster than it could be readied for the fires. More than one man, assigned to watch the cooking meat, fell asleep with exhaustion and a bellyful of liquor, but no matter, there was plenty.

At other positions the celebration was being duplicated. Smoke rose above the lines like signals; whoops and hollers could be heard, and music; dancers among the Indians, pirates, backwoodsmen and even the dragoons could be seen from where the blacks were camped, as well as from the windows of Jackson's quarters.

And he worried. You had to beg people to fight and you had to let them have most of their way or lose them. Every general tries to see that liquor only trickles into his camps, and at the proper times. But out there it was flowing. Jackson didn't worry about the British as much as his own people; they were a volatile mixture, more used to fighting each other than together. He could understand that, somewhat. He had a temper himself, and liked a drop or two.

Outside, the feast continued through noon, then into afternoon and into the evening. Jackson had dispatched officers to keep an eye out, and when the campfires were being put out, one by one, he breathed more easily; Christmas Eve was over.

Blackman felt a sharp kick in his back and heard a muffled exclamation. He came awake in the cold morning, his breath ballooning before him in the air, and saw the whites and Griot, still at his side. The backwoodsmen, and they were steaming with drink. They rambled through the position kicking sleeping blacks or hitting them with their rifles. Now and again a black would leap up to be buried under a clot of whites. In fascination, Blackman watched Griot lift up his rifle and aim, and he too, groped for his gun, found it, and moved its barrel in the direction of the whites. Griot fired high; Blackman fired high. The whites stopped and drew back. The blacks rushed to their feet, their own guns now ready. The whites retreated to the shelter of brush and rocks.

My land, Blackman thought, my land.

And then, from the harbor a British bombardment began and they heard the shells rushing in their direction, and everyone took cover. Before the second shot came, the confrontation had dissolved. Weakly, Blackman sat down beside Griot; neither man spoke.

Jackson, rushing to the area when the barrage ended, saw these two men first. The old one with the stocking cap and the big one; he recognized them both as he went by. In short order his aides assembled all the blacks. He should've been gathering the whites,

53

he knew, but they would've left without their coonskin caps. The thing to do, the traditional thing, was to do as he was now doing, and he shouted out to them:

"To the men of color. Soldiers! I invited you to share in the perils and to divide the glory of your white countrymen. I expected much from you; for I was not uninformed of those qualities which must render you formidable to an invading foe."

Yes, he thought, bring up the action near Villiers plantation; you have to leave them with something. He went on:

"I knew you could endure hunger and thirst and all the hardships of war. I knew that you loved the land of your nativity, and that, like ourselves, you had to defend all that is most dear to man. But you surpass my hopes. I have found in you, united in these qualities, that noble enthusiasm which impels to great deeds."

Blackman exchanged looks with Griot.

"Soldiers! The President of the United States shall be informed of your conduct on the present occasion; and the voice of the representatives of the American nation shall applaud your valor, as your General now praises your ardor. The enemy is near. His sails cover the lakes. But the brave are united; and, if he finds us contending among ourselves, it will be for the prize of valor and fame, its noblest reward."

Now Blackman smiled; he understood. Jackson, looking around the crowd saw the smile, head and shoulders as it was above the other faces. He was pleased; it seemed to have gone down well. Butter em up and slap their wrists ever so slightly, just barely enough so they understand the game too, but then, they always have, these people. He listened as the cheers rang out, and thought as he walked away, "We're all trapped by our history; playing games, doing the easiest and the most obvious, but one day that'll change and it'll be terrible to see."

Blackman lay down, saddened more than angered. He still had a chance at his land. Had he wanted it so much that, had not Griot aimed his rifle, he wouldn't have? Would he have taken anything, everything, without striking back, just for a quarter

54

section. But, 160 acres. . . . Then Jackson came. The whites must've thought to lay them out about firing at their own troops. Smart man, that Jackson. Really talked up that little raid; made it seem like a big thing. "Contending among ourselves." What a way to put it.

The entire holiday week, a restless week, when men thought of their families, homes, friends; their children, favorite inns and mistresses, Jackson's army stood behind their earth, timber and cotton-bale breastworks, waiting. The monotony was broken only by roll calls and patrols. Another week passed and on the morning beginning the third, a heavy fog rolled in from the sea, and with it a strange sound, something akin to silence.

Jackson watched the fog glumly and then, triggered by a thought that had bothered him, almost as unnoticed as a gnat in the dark, he quickly ordered all positions manned. He placed himself between Coffee's and Carroll's detachments and peered intensely into the fog.

"Lissen!" Griot's whisper was like a shout.

Blackman cupped his hand to his ear. The silence out there seemed to have a rhythm, a cadence— The wind shifted and for a moment, through the opening that appeared in the fog, Blackman saw them coming across the cane field, a phalanx of bright color against the gray cloud that'd concealed them.

Jackson, too, had seen them and rapidly called out his orders and with satisfaction saw his firing rows assume their positions and the cannon crews ready to light the touchholes of their guns. He'd been waiting for this moment for weeks, time enough to train some of the troops and to blood others; to get them used to the sounds of war. British naval bombardments had done that, and now the British troops were here. Well, let's see how their regulars stood up against pirates, Indians, niggers and backwoodsmen.

The wind was staying up and blowing the fog away. The British came on, row after row, and now the order to fire came down the line and the first row let go its volley and stepped to the rear as the second moved up and fired. The British marched on, tread unbroken, their lines only slightly bent. As if on some crude conveyor, they marched up to the dry canal and down into it and were slaughtered as they started up the other side. Some wore plaid skirts. Slowly, thickly, the dry canal bed filled with blood. At first it merely soaked into the earth, but as the soil became saturated, the blood began to flow. Not a man reached the breastworks; it was, Blackman thought, like shooting crippled birds, and he was wondering how much they would absorb before quitting when their retreat sounded.

Black Antoine, pushing through the cheering men, grabbed Griot by the arm. "How much you want for it, how much?"

Griot shook him loose and cheered with Blackman. Black Antoine waited patiently.

Even as he cheered, Blackman viewed with awe the great numbers of bodies lying still out there on the field. So many. The fog and smoke were almost completely gone now, and the retreating British at the far side of the field, still marching instead of reforming, and another cheer went up. They're quitting. Suddenly, out there on the littered field, the bodies began to move; packs were slipped from their shoulders, hands were raised in surrender. One, three, eight, and then too many to count. The faces were blackened by gunsmoke and they came toward the Americans steadily.

Griot laughed, "Dey ain no hants; dey plain playin possum."

Blackman laughed uncontrollably. What smart and clever soldiers they were; not cowards. He knew now that he had his land.

For years whenever they met they called each other the name the whites'd given them. Freejacks, and they grew into a tough, isolated, proud clan, asking white men for nothing and giving nothing in return. Griot, whose land was adjacent to Blackman's, did not sell it after all, but leased it to Blackman. Black Antoine bought as much as he could and prospered.

56

Five years after the battle, Griot, hobbling now, his hair fringed with silver, came into La Baleine Noire, unrolled a parchment and asked to have it hung so everyone could see. It read:

February 18, 1820
Office of the Adjutant General
Office of the Inspector General
No Negro or Mulatto will be received as a recruit of the Army.

A group of men sitting around a table'd decided that, Blackman thought when he read it. Groups of white men were always sitting around tables deciding things about black people.

# 4

Johnny Griot rested the M-60 across his knee; he was sure he'd got one of the AK-47s. Make sure. He lifted the heavy gun and aimed for the clump of reeds he'd shot up before. When he finished the clip he signaled Antoine forward while he covered. Antoine signed back; Griot slipped in another clip, ready. If anything happened to Antoine, man. Antoine was his number one nigger. Both outa Norleans; had to look out for each other. And the Captain, too, now. Sure hope that dude ain't hit bad. His ol lady, that fine Miss Rogers at the Embassy sure gonna be tore up if he is . . .

Wonder what the Captain's thinkin—

*Cadences*

*Outside, Cincinnati was gray with rain winding down the sky, but there was enough light and luxury in the Great Hall to dispel the sense of gloom that hung outside the windows, vainly trying to attack the interior of the huge estate and its inhabitants.*

*Lunch was over. The baroque room muffled the sounds of bottles and glasses, of Negro servants picked for their lightness of color, who padded like cougars on carpeted floors whisking away* dishes, bowls, silver, and dressing the tables with crackling white damask covers. It was time for "refreshment" and the talk. Large bowls of pungent, hot spiced rum were brought in. Bottles of Old Robertson's Canadian lent the air of Delmonico's, Riley's and Delatour's to the room. Mint juleps, heavily sprigged and thickly sweet, came last.

Their accents revealed the places the men in the room came from: New York, Boston, Charleston, New Orleans, San Francisco. Random conversations were scheduled for now; later they'd come together at the big table for more formal discussions and dinner. The two sponsors of the meeting sat down in a corner.

"Cockrill, this drift to war is as incredible as it is ridiculous. How can New York and New Orleans go to war? We need each other; we're like the fingers on a hand."

"Then, by God, Cabot, you must stop this opposition to a protective tariff; we won't continue to provide you with cotton; we'll go to Europe."

Cabot sighed heavily. He knew that the Southerners were already firmly into the European markets. "Let's not play games. You're there already. American products don't belong in Europe, not yet, not when you've an obligation still to the American people. You've got to stop pushing for slavery in the West—I know there's lots of land out there; you fellows got us into that war just to expand slavery with your cotton farming. The idea is to withdraw as painlessly as possible from slavery; your entire economy rests upon it—"

"—and yours, dear Cabot."

"But, Cockrill, I'm saying that with immigration wide open now, it's time to change habits. How in the world can these poor Irish and Germans compete with slave labor? It can't be done."

"On the contrary, sir. Were it not for our holding four million or so slaves in bondage in the southeastern United States, there'd be no jobs at all anywhere for the immigrants. It is only because they are so constrained that this European rabble has any chance at all to seek work in your mills. In any case," Cockrill said

59

sourly, "it's too late. The blacks will always be a factor in the labor market, North and South. Indirectly now. But say they were free and joined forces with the immigrants—oh, God, Cabot, what a mess that would be. As it is, we've right now got five million poor whites who hate the blacks because they do the work for nothing that the whites could do for pay. That is good, don't you think?"

Grimly Cabot said, "Sooner or later you've got to give up slavery, you, me, and set our base somewhere else—"

"Yes, and see them come together, the blacks and the whites, and then, my friend, what will we have?"

"You've got to do it, Cockrill. This is serious. In the past, you paid as little attention to our public pronouncements about the evils of slavery as we did to your claims of the blacks' natural backwardness—you've got too many mulattoes and quadroons down there for us to have taken you seriously. Now, it's different.

"Furthermore, we're opposed to the way you've captured political office in Washington with your representation based so much upon the slaves, the very persons you don't even consider to be people until its time for one of you to run for office. God! Open the West and we'd be overwhelmed—"

Cockrill said, "Property is property, Cabot, and according to law, you've got to own property to run for office."

"What we're basically talking about here, Cockrill, and you know it, is sharing the wealth, the sharing the power. We will have our share, goddamnit, or there will be war."

"Now, now, Cabot, you know we couldn't do without you Yankees. You loan us money, let us use your ships, but you ought to know that if there is war, we'll have England and France on our side, because they want the cotton. You could only win if the Almighty stepped in on your side."

"We don't want a war, Cockrill! Think what it'd do to the country."

Soothingly Cockrill said, "We've worked out things before and we can work them out again. The election won't matter, whether

60

*Lincoln or Douglas wins. There're certain hard realities that go
with the office, you know—"*

*"My dear friend Cockrill," Cabot said, and he felt tears coming
to his eyes. "We talk all about the matter, but not to it. We have
got to move the base of economic power in this nation from
slavery, or slavery will move us in one way or another. Now, you
mark my words. Mark them well."*

*Languidly the Southerner said, sniffing of his mint, "Slavery
is only a name. There are others, perhaps less offensive, that can
serve just as well and mean, pretty nearly, the same thing."*

The training was all over now, Blackman thought. All that
marching in the square in those bright uniforms with the women
looking on; that was all over and this, coming up was the real
thing. He nudged Little David Harrison and together they looked
up at the ramparts of Port Hudson. The flat, brown Mississippi
gurgled its way past, cooling the air, and all about them they
heard the jangle of packs and rifles, of drums preparing to dress
them into the line of attack.

Blackman pursed his lips in a silent whistle. This was gonna
be something. "Good luck," he said to Little David.

"Yeah."

On the way to his men Blackman passed Flag Sergeant Ansel-
mas Plancianois. "Ready, Sergeant?" Plancianois asked with a
grin, as he nervously shifted his feet.

"I'm ready. How about you?"

"Ready's I'll ever be, and I'll bring the colors back in honor
or tell the good Lord the reason why."

"Let's hope you won't have to do that, Sergeant," Blackman
said.

Yeah, he thought, continuing on his way. When those balls
start to fly he'll be talking out the other side of his mouth, just
like all the rest of these bad-talking soldiers. Blackman felt his
stomach fluttering and the palms of his hands growing water as

he fell in with his company, row upon row of black faces, men with French names and hard-to-understand accents.

The long roll sounded on the drums. Blackman stared upward at the fortifications again. It was ten in the morning, the day settling firmly in the sky. The insects jabbed and whined at his face. Behind the rows of black troops, he knew that the generals, Banks and Ullman, were there, anxious to see how black troops fought, eager to spread the word of the success or failure of the Emancipation on this one battle.

Now the drums sounded common time and the lines marched forward. Blackman barked at his men, the better to conceal his rising fear, and they, the better to conceal theirs, glared back at him and thought, The big black bastard. His heart pounding, thudding against his rib cage, Blackman moved on as if in a dream.

Quick-time in a series of rolls and flams rocked off the drums and the bugles took up the call. Blackman felt the ground flowing back under him. The clatter of metal hooks sounded in unison as the waves of black men moved on, panting although they'd not really begun to exert themselves. Then: *double-quick time!* Blackman rushed over the ground now; he seemed to be out of breath already, but knew it was from fear, nothing else. For a ludicrous moment there came the twitter of diving swallows. Behind them the barrage lifted, and ahead the Rebels began theirs.

Black powder bursts puffed sharply among them. Blackman cowered at the whine of hot metal seeking flesh. Turning, he saw the lines uneven, bent backwards, strung out, and he shouted into the roar for them to come on. Sharply the bugles sounded the charge and the men, as though stung, leaped forward again, straightening their lines, bending them forward this time, and they burst into a clearing where some of the Rebel cannon had been fixed, firing at the gunners as they tried to escape. They were almost under the walls now and down from them poured Rebel fire, grape and ball, all singing and humming wildly as they slashed through flesh and bone.

Blackman found himself running almost alone; the first line

had been decimated. Captain Cailloux ran up beside Blackman and, turning his back to the fort, shouted at the men, "Steady, steady," in both French and English, his blue-black skin covered with sweat sparkling in the sun. Desperate soldiers rallied to him and he turned to face the fort, lunged forward and took a charge in the arm. Horrified, Blackman slowed to help. The Captain waved him on. "Follow me! Follow me!" He took a shell directly in the torso. Blackman quivered at the sound and wanted to scream when he saw blood, bone and skin unraveling even as Cailloux was moving. He watched helplessly as the half mass of pulverized flesh staggered to the lip of a ditch and collapsed.

Even as he hurtled toward it, Blackman's mind screamed, a ditch! They hadn't said anything about a ditch. You just run up to the walls, batter them in or climb them, or go in through breaches made by our artillery. He was going so fast he couldn't stop; he gathered himself and sprung up and out and came down short of the other side, powering into brown water which gave off a sudden series of silver bubbles as he went under. For a second or two he took shelter in the calm depths. The battle seemed far away, and then in panic, he began to kick and struggle to the surface, nearer the sound of rifle and cannon and shouts. The blacks were bunched up on the lip. Officers among them were urging them back to try again. Struggling up through thick mud, Blackman watched them go, and return, all bent black men, rifles held high. They seemed to be moving slowly as they approached the lip, and then in a wave they took to the air and he heard and saw them fall short, some of them dead, and hit the water behind him. He grabbed a rock with one hand and with the other pulled at as many hands as he could, towing them toward his side of the ditch. Those who could climbed out and cowered under the walls, their rifles useless because of wet powder.

Anxiously, they glanced back across the ditch as the men hurtled up once more and flung their weary black bodies out over the water, some to drown, others to struggle up to where Blackman

63

was, to become victims of the Rebel sharpshooters now shooting directly down from the walls and into the heads of those who'd made it across.

Retreat sounded. Blackman slipped his pack and the others followed suit; they went again into the water, easing past the bodies filling it, and back to the other side.

Later, relieved at having found Little David alive, the two men compared notes.

"We were by ourselves for four hours," Little David said. "And the center and left side sections didn't start their attacks. We took it all."

Blackman sat stolidly. He'd learned that the blacks'd been only one twelfth of the Union forces but had lost one eighth of the total, one tenth of the wounded and three fourths of the missing.

"Pigeons," Little David said. "Or sittin ducks."

Little David Harrison was a small man with a boy's face, but there was something huge and terrible about him, Blackman knew. He was a vicious fighter, a man who killed with equal facility in the heat of battle or the coldness of revenge. "There's no satisfaction like killin white men," he'd said. "Yankee or Rebel, it's all the same to me." And glancing at Blackman in what for him could've been called a gentle manner, he said, "You got too much compassion, or whatever, Abraham. Maybe that goes with bein big. I dunno."

"I kill like you kill, Little David."

The events of the day, like those of other days, would stay with Little David. All that white treachery. And black folks not seeing it just because, back there in January, Lincoln freed the slaves. Freed them because he didn't have a choice, Little David thought. But out here, along this Mississippi and a thousand other places black men were eager to let themselves be slaughtered because they believed in the sudden goodness of those who'd oppressed them for over two centuries.

Perhaps he shouldn't have said what he said to Abraham. Compassion wasn't the right word, or maybe it was in a sense too large

64

for Little David to bother to understand. He has killed like me. Little David shifted his position. "You right, Abe. I didn't mean you're soft."

"Maybe the difference, Little David, is that I kill because I have to—"

Little David smiled, the same kind of smile Blackman observed he smiled when he was ready to sing one of his favorite songs. And Little David could sing. "You mean," Little David said, "I kill because I like to."

Blackman stood up. "We're just runnin off at the mouth, little man. Tired and scared and don't half know what it is we're sayin. Besides, it's time to move on to other places and other killings."

Killings at Milliken's Bend, and in southeast Kansas, brutal, hateful killings that had little to do with war, but everything to do with color, and it was these constant murders of black soldiers that made other black soldiers better fighters, Blackman observed, with each succeeding campaign. For the Rebels there was no such thing as a black prisoner of war. Each battle became a fight not for land or victory, but for survival. Whenever black men and white men locked in fearful, angry embrace, the terror of ugly death struck at both sides; when the balls ran out, they charged with bayonets. Rebel yells and black curses rent the air. Kill close up! Kill with bare hands! Steel! Feel their blood so slick on your hands you couldn't hardly hold your rifle. As if in some wild and ancient euphoria, time after time black and white danced, steel glinting where it wasn't already crimsoned, blood jetting suddenly in the bright sun, all to cries of "No quarter to the niggers!" "No quarter to the crackers!"

Behind their line of march the traded atrocities became legend: prisoners shredded by bayonets; prisoners decapitated; prisoners castrated; prisoners pulled asunder by horses. Still they marched on across the southland, ever fearful that worse could happen, and as they came into sight of Fort Wagner, they exchanged the bitter news of the Draft Riots in New York and of black people hung from lamp posts, beaten in the streets, murdered in alleys, old and young alike, orphans and attached.

So it did not help when they were dressed into line for the attack, the blacks in front, exhausted with travel from Folly and Morris islands, hungry from lack of food. Wagner shimmered before their eyes, a mirage, but a reality, and Blackman saw that even now there were men who were proud to be leading the attack, proud to be white men's cannon fodder, and when the bugles and drums sounded, like spurred horses they charged to the attack as they'd done so many times before, and Blackman moved with them, Little David at his side now, again engaged in survival.

The Colonel, leading the charge, was hit, but he continued, shouting and waving his sword, and Blackman hated him, wished him dead, prayed through gasps of breath for the violent death of this man who'd asked that his troops lead the charge. How much more can we prove, Blackman thought angrily, running hard, all the sounds of his being bubbling up into an angry, frustrated scream which even he couldn't hear for the cadence of war all around him.

Through sand, marsh and water they plunged, sound sucking in air and then exploding it, and up to the walls like crazed dogs, eager to attack and kill the targets for their being there in the first place, and from inside those walls came the old cries: "It's niggers! Kill the black sonsabitches!"

They're afraid, too, Blackman thought, as he blew the head off a whiskered man who'd thrust himself forward on the walls; out of the corner of his eye he saw Little David ram his bayonet into the face of another Rebel, where it stuck, and saw the face disintegrate when Little David pulled the trigger.

Damn the Union. Damn the Confederacy. Kill niggers. Kill crackers.

And, beat down from the walls, Blackman led his men back, reformed them and charged again, this time over the body of the

Colonel, only to be beaten down again and again and again, leaving inside some his troops who'd made it over the walls; Blackman ran back, his chest on fire, hands stiff on the gun he held only by force of habit. He already felt, imagined that he felt, crackers bayoneting him, slowly sawing off his prick, and his flesh crawled. The fate of the missing who'd not been lucky enough to be blown apart by a shell.

The next day, with a solitary drummer, Blackman led out the burial detail under a flag of truce. He always marveled at the quiet that hovered over battlefields after the fighting. Above the vomitus birds twittered and sand flies stung; the stiff sea breeze curled the stink of the dead across the island. Huge flies, glistening bluely, buzzed over shattered skin, sucked drying blood, busied themselves laying eggs that in a few hours would turn into maggots.

The Colonel was already buried. They told Blackman of his naked body, stomped, spat on, and otherwise defiled, and how he'd been put into a pit with his dead nigger soldiers. For a moment, Blackman wanted to uncover the mound, throw aside the black dead just to see what the crackers had really done to the Colonel. Had they cut off his prick, too? His head? Punctured him with their bayonets? He looked to the walls of the fort, gray in this morning light, and saw and smelled a sickness there, defined behind its ugliness; a glob, like the jellyfish on the beach, amorphous, yet containing dimension and sharp pain—a smell of impending decay.

Later, winding through Georgia, a hard, murderous regiment, their cheap, blue uniforms falling in patches from their bodies, they heard of Fort Pillow where General Nathan Bedford Forrest ordered the slaughter of three hundred black troops after they'd surrendered; they said the Mississippi, which flows fast and deep past Memphis, ran red with blood for two days, and that the black civilians fished out heads, arms, legs and torsos, and only six days later, while probing toward Atlanta, they heard of Poison Springs.

There black soldiers were left like hunks of buffalo meat on an Arkansas landscape.

67

The day they heard of Poison Springs was the day they gave up trying to stay human. The change was imperceptible, but it was change nonetheless. Blackman and Little David joined them in the grove that night, away from the white officers. One by one under the moonless sky they spoke the words, each of them, clearly.

"I swear by my ancestors, and by the Mother whose name is Africa, to kill with a swift, sure arm, without hesitation, and in revenge for my brothers at Fort Pillow and Poison Springs and wherever else black soldiers are made to die less than the men they are."

When the oath-taking was finished the chant began like the rustle of leaves in a light wind:

> *No quarter to the Rebels,*
> *No quarter when they call,*
> *No quarter to the Rebels,*
> *Damn them, kill them all!*

Now, Blackman thought, they could drink hot cow's blood and shit, and he dreamed back to Africa's warriors, and forward to 200,000 black Union soldiers who would take the oath and chant the litany; to the white soldiers caught in the path of the black phalanx who would know that their deaths were no longer necessary, but imperative, and understanding that, would tremble when, from outside their walls they heard the chant spring up on the morning wind, the night wind, the noon wind, growing in intensity, in pledge:

> *No quarter to the Rebels,*
> *No quarter when they call,*
> *No quarter to the Rebels,*
> *Damn them, kill them all!*

# 5

Mimosa Rogers quickly unlocked the door of her small apartment and nudged it open with an elbow. "Over there," she said pointing with her chin, and the Vietnamese kid, leaning backward with the weight of the box of books, hurried to a table. Mimosa herself, her arms deadened by their burden—the week's ration of liquor and delicacies from all over the world—sighing, set her load on a chair. "*Merci beaucoup,*" she said, giving the kid a bill. He bowed and went out, closing the door softly after him. Mimosa went to it and locked it; she hoped the kid hadn't heard. She didn't want to offend him. Right off, she placed the Meursault in the refrigerator.

She kicked off her shoes as she went through the flat. She poured herself a stiff gin and tonic from last week's bottle of gin, and then, as she did every day, unlocked the louvered doors and stepped out on the balcony. From here she could see the cemetery and the Embassy, and in the distance, meandering behind the low buildings, the Rachi Thi Nghe, placid and brown.

Her eyes followed the street that would turn into National Highway Number One at Ba Queo, and she wondered where he was. She didn't like to think of the things that could happen when he was in the field. Like now, she tried to think of things to do to be ready when he came tonight or tomorrow; they were supposed to come out then and they'd have lunches and breakfasts and evenings together for three or four days, and then he'd go back again, taking the books.

After the drink, she thought, a nice, relaxing bath. A nap in something real short and scintillating, should he, by chance, come in early and let himself in while she slept. She smiled as she imagined him that way, quietly peeling off his clothes, tenderly pushing up the silk, wrapping his huge hands around her breasts and finally entering her with that gentle largeness that seemed to dwarf and impale her at once. Later, while she was preparing a late dinner, he'd go over the books, express joy with this one, exultation with that, and wonder how she'd managed to get the other, through which obscure black bookseller in which part of the States.

Her smile widened and she stretched. In moments, those garments that held her in, covered her, would be loosened and off. She would be ready whenever he came.

Cautiously, hand-signaling, Blackman moved the men in his patrol out around the plantation. From a distance, the large white house with its Corinthian columns had looked unscarred, but when they came closer they saw that the paint was peeling, the windows broken, the outbuildings and grounds unkempt. Ugly and weathered, the slave huts remained, Blackman imagined, as they always were. By now slave huts were as familiar as anything else in that land of red dirt and dust.

Certain after a while that the place was deserted, Blackman posted guards and led the rest of his men to the house. The interior smelled of mildew and must. The great living room with its french doors, overlooked the slave quarters. From here, Blackman mused, the master must've given his orders, or at night listened as they sang, if they sang. The furniture in the room was smashed, the yards of draperies cut or savagely ripped down. The next room, the dining room with its long line of buffet

70

chests and china closets, tables and velvet-covered chairs was a shambles. A majestic, slow-curving stairway went from the foyer into the upper reaches of the mansion. Blackman detailed some of his men to go up by the stairs that led from the kitchen, a large room with much working space and tables and stoves for an army of house niggers. Others went up the front.

In the bedrooms, wash pitchers and bowls had been broken into shards; pieces littered the chests and mildewing carpets like snow; chamber pots had been shattered with a special vengeance; the coverings and mattresses on the beds, cut to shreds. Axes had been used on the bedsteads. In the master bedroom, which extended across the entire second floor, a portrait lay on the floor, piles of shit on it. Blackman thought of all the blacks who'd trudged up to this empty, foreboding, stinking room just to shit on the face; the ultimate expression of hatred.

Little David broke the silence. "I guess there was some pretty mad niggers around here, Abraham." He unbuttoned his pants and pissed on the portrait.

Blackman looked at him, eyebrows raised.

"Well, Abe, I just ain't got to shit now," Little David said. "I mean, I want to do my share."

"Shoulda burned the place down," another soldier said.

Yeah, maybe, Blackman thought, gazing out the window. Bet they didn't want to call attention to themselves in case there were some crackers around. The slave huts again. Were the crackers so dumb, so damned greedy that they thought they could hold onto things as they were forever and ever? Didn't they feel any heat rising from those shacks?

He saw something move and he felt a flash of terror. Crackers! But silencing his men he peered out and saw three or four black people straining to see the men posted in the yard. Blackman smiled with relief, then his anger came. Could've been Rebels and the guards haven't seen them yet.

Quickly Blackman went down the front stairs. He'd circle behind them, try not to frighten them and get some information.

71

He walked quietly, into the tall grass now, behind the cover of willows, and then thinking he heard something behind him, stopped and dropped to one knee, his rifle at the ready. There, almost like heat waves on a hard road, stood a young black woman, her bright, brown eyes smiling at his fear. Relieved, he lowered his gun.

"Girl, where did you come from?"

She gave him a long, looping look, ducked her head a little and to one side.

"You a Yankee?"

He knew that under her dress she wore nothing. He longed to push up the garment, to touch her flesh. "I'm a Union soldier."

She pointed to his arm. "What them stripes mean?"

"I'm a sergeant."

"Like a boss-man?"

"Yes."

She laughed and her tongue, tiny and pink, played quickly over her lips. "Come here," he said, and she approached silently on bare feet and studied him boldly, her smile forming up and fading, only to form again.

"You kills Se'cesh?"

"If I catch em, I kill em."

"I always thought Yankees was white; they never told us no different."

He put a trembling hand on her shoulder and pleaded with his eyes for her not to run away, for her to be nice to him and to think of all the times when he'd not had the chance to think of it until now.

"What's your name?"

"M'osa." She moved her shoulder so that more of his hand could rest there, warm and kind of shaky. Looking up under lowered lids, her eyes warming and unfocused, she said in a whisper, "What's yours?"

"Abraham," and his voice was also a whisper. He lay down his

72

rifle and pressed his mouth to her neck. She shook suddenly as if from a spasm and he felt her shaking, matching his. Another spasm shook her as he embraced her and eased her to the ground where he pushed up the dress, felt his hands travel unhampered by hidden cloth to all parts of her body, along her legs, thighs and buttocks, and it seemed to him that he'd almost forgotten how to do this, it'd been so long. With one hand he tugged at himself, even as she, brown body exposed to the sun, moved closer to him, wracked now by the spasms, and briefly, the spring wind licked at his penis, already hard as million-year-old stone, already wet; he placed his bigness in the center of her wetness, moved down, then thrust softly up, and she rose with him, a sigh escaping from her at the same time his groan set the grasses about them to trembling.

Afterward, she didn't want to go back with him; she would meet him later. For the rest of the day, while his patrol prepared for the arrival of the first companies, he thought about her, and walked about with a rod of iron in his pants, so hard, so painfully hard that he thought his penis would surely collapse into rubber so soft and limber that it could never be roused again. But it remained determined, and seemed to grow pulsatingly larger when, finally, he slipped away from the plantation to find her. In a small settlement, she'd said, where there were other blacks, some of whom Blackman had seen from the window.

It was late afternoon when he set out to walk the three miles along the way she'd pointed out. Blackman walked quickly, pausing now and again to push down his penis which kept slipping out of its cove in his pants to precede him, wrapped in a bulge of Union blue. An orange glare from the down-turning sun cast huge shadows through the woods, a solid grove of pines. He hastened on, his feet slipping on the needles, until he perceived a clearing ahead. Puzzled, acting on instinct, he slid to the ground; she'd said nothing about a clearing and he'd come only about half the distance. But there it was, at that moment slashed with an aborted scream, one of those ripped

73

ragged from the utmost depths of hate and helplessness. His rifle thrust before him, Blackman snaked over the ground and now heard, as parenthesis to the scream, muffled, breathless sounds, the thud of bodies hitting the earth.

In the clearing, darkening quickly like the rest of the forest, he saw first a diving, rearing little patch of bright gold. This strange bird—for he thought it that for a second—was the hair on the head of a Union soldier who, together with another Yankee, rippled and waved and bent as they held a black girl to the earth, or tried to, and Blackman recognized Mimosa. And he would never forget the blond soldier. When he, Blackman, was through with him, the soldier wouldn't forget him either.

He should have gone silently, but a primal outrage gripped him, and he gathered his great bulk and with rifle reversed in his hands, burst into the clearing with a mad bellow, whose pitch increased when he saw the naked buttocks of the flaxen-haired soldier covering the blackness of his Mimosa. So his murderous charge was single-directed; it was intent on smashing to snot the maggoty whiteness that covered the girl, those buttocks he saw in his rush, now freezing, tightening, humping to get off. His body tensed for the first blow; so anticipatory was it that, for a moment, even after the second soldier'd struck him with all his frightened might, a blow he'd never in life be able to repeat, Blackman plunged on, the world lighting before him in a blinding flash, and as he fell his rifle butt came down with a mighty wind and half-buried itself in the soil, scattering browned pine needles in a miniature tidal wave. Darkness closed about him.

He was alone when he came to, his head wrapped awkwardly in cloth. Peering at it closely in the near darkness, he saw it was a part of Mimosa's dress. The pain penetrated down to his guts and he stopped moving and listened to the whippoorwills, the scrabbling of squirrels along the limbs of trees. Gingerly, he felt for his rifle, felt the cracked buttplate, the hairline break in the stock itself. He stood and swayed and reached up once again to the bandage and took it off. Painfully, he made his way back, wondering at the coolness of the forest and taking great gulps of it, and cursing the water that kept welling up in his eyes. When he reached the plantation, he went quickly to his tent, drew the flap and tried to sleep.

Months later, Blackman's regiment was camped close to Petersburg, the miles and murders, charges and countercharges, nervous drumtaps and shrill bugle calls temporarily halted. But not a day passed when, under the sullen Virginia sun, they did not drill, quick-marching by twos, double-quick marching and the charge at full speed, into and through barriers, heads lowered.

With a cold eye Blackman noticed that while other regiments were rapidly filling up the staging area, his was the only one that was undergoing that particular drill, and he knew that to be a bad omen. But, no worse than anything else, he thought. What could they be assigned that they hadn't already done? Lead another attack? Nothing new. Become a diversion to take all the shells the Rebels could throw while the white boys danced in without getting so much as a speck of dust on their shoes? They'd done that.

Done all of it and raised up a regiment of men who no longer even thought about killing; the days of docile slave and gentle freeman seemed a century away; in reality the precise time was just over a year. In that time, Little David, now sitting silently beside Blackman under the shade of a tree, had got his sergeant's stripes; Blackman was now a sergeant major. They stared toward Petersburg and watched the white Yankees milling about in their stiff-legged marching drills, by turn. The grasses had turned brown from the end-of-July sun, and dust followed the blue-legged units.

Little David watched them intently now. Only that morning had he heard the first rumor; he'd not exchanged it with Blackman. Watching the white troops, he felt it to be true, and he

was both sad and angry, for he knew there were odds that had
to be dealt with, evened out on chance's gambling table.

"You know that crazy drill we been having?"

Without moving Blackman said, "Yeah?"

"They say they've tunneled under the fort. We go in tomorrow
morning and we go first."

Blackman grunted. Well, it had to be something. He'd felt both
a listlessness and an alternating wildness after Mimosa; the wildness an unexpressed desire to live until he had his revenge at
least, and the listlessness because of the haunting sense of futility
that he'd ever have it.

"Don't know about your men," Little David said, "but when
I told mine, they said they'd be damned if they'd lead another
charge."

"What did you tell em for?"

"Why the hell not? You gonna tell yours?"

"No. Whether they want to or not, they'll have to go. Otherwise
these Yankee sonsabitches'll just line em and shoot em and
bring some more niggers in here before tomorrow morning to
do the same thing. Let em get mad when they're on the way.
Stand a better chance of comin out whole."

Little David thought back to their conversation when he'd
accused Blackman of compassion; he smiled wryly. The bigger
the mouth, the sooner it speaks, he thought of himself, without
thinking. Blackman'd been wholly unpredictable after Georgia.

After the evening parade, the Colonel was seen hurriedly leaving his quarters, hurrying to where the generals, Grant included,
were headquartered; his return was calmly awaited by every man
in the unit. They lingered under trees, peeped out from tent flaps
until, an hour later, the Colonel angrily returned and stamped
back into his quarters. Almost momentarily runners were dispatched to the several company headquarters, and they, fastening
their blouses and squaring their hats, trotted across the Green.

The men continued their wait, Blackman bitterly reflecting
that not one, not one black person was involved in all the

decision-making. As night fell, runners to the battalions, the companies, the sections, the platoons, fanned out through the camp. Blackman took the news without expression: the regiment would not lead the attack; a white regiment would. Little David was a broad smile, slapping and smacking at Blackman to get a smile out of him, which he finally did. "They goin, man, not us. *Not us.* Let em earn their goddamn twenty-one dollars a month; we're only gettin seven. Let em go!"

Pleasure simmered pleasantly in Blackman's body as later he watched the white boys dress into line after evening meal. They'd fall out and sleep in position—if they could—and at three-thirty in the morning would hurl themselves forward after the explosion went off. They'd no time to drill, but, Blackman thought, maybe that wasn't a big handicap. The generals back there, perched in their chairs with glasses ready to watch the troops storm Petersburg, had realized, must've realized that their niggers were leading too many charges; there'd be a lot of who-struck-John at this one if the blacks took a bad beating. Thank you, Frederick Douglass, Blackman thought. Thank you, William Lloyd Garrison, Henry C. Wright, Wendell Phillips. . . .

By two in the morning, the entire assault force was ready, Blackman's regiment standing to with the reserves, scheduled to follow the path of the First Division into Petersburg. Blackman was awed by the bigness of the attack. Before night fell, as far as he could see there were tents and blue-coated figures; seventy-seven regiments were there, someone'd said. In the morning now, he heard the massive whisper of cloth on cloth, the surreptitious ring of metal on metal, the muffled hoofbeats of the horses.

At three the blue monster was urged to its feet; it straightened into taut plumb-lined rows; the silence built itself around the measured breaths of thousands upon thousands of men, all coaxed there by the belief that the men standing next to them, not they, would be killed; that they would survive, being immune to death simply because they did not wish to die. If a hundred thousand eyes were capable of blowing up Petersburg, it would've gone up

long before it was supposed to. Instead, three-thirty passed as
tensely and as quietly as had three twenty-nine and three twenty-
eight.

Three thirty-five.

Three forty-five.

Four.

Slowly, the tension drained out of the troops; a foot moved
here; a cough sounded there. A sweating hand slipped on a rifle
butt with a squeak; muffled orders and a smothered movement
of large masses. In whispers came the words, moving through
the ranks like the night wind that now dried their sweating
bodies:

"They've gone down to check the fuses."

"They have to check the fuses in the mine."

"The fuses went out."

Approaching five, the sky lightened and the regiments were
back on line, tense. Trees, ridges, Petersburg in the distance
were black and starkly outlined, and from the fort came distant
calls, languid and as ordinary as ever, but somehow at this time,
with a special clarity.

At ten minutes to five Blackman started as he felt the earth
humping, like the waves of water on a shallow beach, beneath
his feet, and he quickly turned his eyes to the fort just as the
explosion went off. Daggers of orange flame licked and jabbed
viciously at the silvering sky; misshapen objects, men and materiel
rose slowly and with an awful majesty into the sky, as if to display
and complain of the suddenness, without warning, of their shattering. Throughout the Union ranks, shouts, bugle calls and drumtaps sounded again and again, and even as the explosion reached
its crescendo, the blue lines leaped forward, into the Crater of
Petersburg, their own artillery beginning and now sounding pale
and thin beside the monstrous first explosion.

Forward they went, the blue lines, into a gorge thirty feet
deep, Blackman estimated from where he stood, sixty feet wide
and over a hundred and fifty feet long. He watched them pour

78

down the freshly made channel of earth, and their shouts rolled back, brutal and exultant, until a new sound was introduced into the cacaphony of destruction; Blackman started at that, too, since he couldn't believe it possible. The Rebels hadn't been destroyed; their own guns were working, mortar, cannon and rifle, and he could see the blue lines bunching, slowing, like syrup continuing its reluctant flow when the jar's been tipped back.

For over two hours the reserves watched the Union waves blunt themselves in the Crater and Blackman knew they would have to go in, after all; even now the Yankees were streaming back out, shattered, trampling their officers into the blood-soddened earth. *Forward, march!* Blackman swung out to the side and front of his men. *Quick-time!* They moved faster now, closer to the sounds, the screams. *Double-quick time!* Almost like a herd of horses, they cantered ahead faster, seeking a place in the jumble to set the wedge. *Charge!* They flashed ahead and seeing no place to pass, collided with the retreating white troops who fought, clawed and cursed their way past. Their officers stood, whirling, screaming and slapping at them with their sword flats. "Reform! Reform, you bastards!"

Shouldering his way in past them, Blackman heard some of the white soldiers shouting: "We ain't gonna follow no niggers!"

"Out of the way you black bastards! *Move!*"

Momentarily shocked by this meeting with the national truth, the black troops hesitated, fully intending to move aside and continue on alone. They were instantly determined to demonstrate black bravery in place of white cowardice. But the white troops mistook the hesitation for stubbornness and opened fire and charged with bayonets. Wait, *wait!* Blackman wanted to scream. He hurled himself to the ground, hoping he'd be taken for one of the already dead in the front ranks of the blacks, and the whites battered on past. For long moments he felt their frantic feet thudding and skidding on his body.

Those moments past, he thrust himself up from under the

79

pounding feet and battered his way forward with butt, bayonet and fist, his men with him, and as he emerged from the darkness into the bright light, he saw, ringed all around the Crater, Rebels firing at point-blank range. As he started to move, he felt one blow and then another in his thigh and he fell, surprised first that he'd lost his balance, and then feeling the pain and he found himself holding out one hand to his still moving men, one hand in supplication.

*Drumtaps*

The colored division moved out from our works in splendid order. Growlers were put to shame, and most of them fell into line, to go forward. Some few declared they would never follow "niggers" or be caught in their company and started back to our lines but were promptly driven forward again. When the colored assault halted, broke and streamed back, the bravest lost heart and the men who distrusted the Negroes vented their feelings freely. Some colored men came into the Crater, and there they found a fate worse than death. It has been positively asserted that white men bayoneted blacks who fell back into the Crater. This was in order to preserve the whites from Confederate vengeance. Men boasted in my presence that blacks had thus been disposed of, particularly when the Confederates came up.

CAPTAIN KILMER, New York 14th Heavy Artillery

The charge through a broken and demoralized division of white troops, then forming inside the enemy's works, and temporary capture of their interior works, with awful losses in killed, wounded and *murdered*, is a record.

CAPTAIN RICKARD, 19th U. S. Colored Troops

# 6

Only a minute had passed since Blackman got hit, but it felt like he'd been out for much longer. With his face turned awkwardly to the sky, he tried to roll his eyes; no good, hurt too much. He wondered how badly his leg'd been hit; it was starting to pain now, and there was that burning in his chest too. The sensation in his chest, plus some superficial knowledge of what chest wounds were like, made him aware of a peculiarly slick something on his cheek. He tried to blow out his breath, easily, as if to smell it when it emerged, and he felt bubbles inside him. Now he forced his face to one side so he could look at the slickness. Blood. Well, you knew that, didn't you?"

Shit, Mims, it's bad, baby. Maybe not. They'll be gettin here soon. They'll be gettin here.

Sergeant David Harrison finally reached Johnny Griot's position.

"Antoine's over there," Griot said.

"Yeah, okay. Let's frag them fuckin bushes, man. We gotta get him outa there. You think he's dead?"

"I thought I saw him movin a second before you got here. You got a chopper comin?"

"Well, Belmont called for it. They always seem to take their fuckin time whenever we need one."

Both turned to greet the new arrival. Harrison said, "Hey, white boy, me and you're gonna frag them bushes down near the Captain while Griot and Antoine cover for us. Let's go."

Robert Doctorow followed his sergeant, loosening a grenade. Wonder what he'd say if I called him "black boy," Doctorow thought. Hey, black boy. This goddamn racial business, and the Army's scared shitless. Black guys black-power saluting and the white officers saying nothing. Harrison was waving him wide and Doctorow fanned out. He hoped the Captain wasn't hit bad. He could take the other black guys or leave them with their boogaloos, black-power shakes and soul-this and soul-that, but Captain Blackman was okay; didn't take any shit and looked out for his men, all of em. The Captain had let Doctorow "audit" his classes on black military history, over the wild objections of the black EMs, and Doctorow had gone to just enough of them to show he wasn't intimidated by black power. Christ, things he'd never known about black people in the Army, never even thought, suspected or guessed. That was why Major Whittman was down on the Captain along with Colonel Greer. Word'd got out. Naturally he was accused of telling. But nothing'd happened after all; the classes went on as usual.

Doctorow pushed his rifle out ahead of him and stopped as Harrison stopped. He saw Harrison's arm arch briefly through the air, and he selected a clump of grass and threw his grenade with a snapping motion and it flew like a pitch toward his target. Without waiting for them to go off, Harrison and Doctorow, pitched to other possible hiding places and the grenades went off. Doomp! Doomp! Doomp-doomp! Doomp!

Blackman heard the grenades go off and listened for the singing fragments. The rifles started up and the machine gun. He was puzzled by the absence of the VC guns, but glad they were gone. Pulling back, maybe. Now he heard Harrison shouting, heard the swish of grass, and they were there.

"Captain? Captain-Brother?"

They were standing over him; they shaded the Vietnam sky

82

with its blazing sun. Got to see, he thought. See their faces, so I can read them. But they were too smart; there were no expressions.

Harrison was looking him right in the eye, his eyes blank. Doctorow, what was he looking at? And Griot and Antoine—Shrimp and Rice, he called them.

"Woodcock!" Harrison was shouting. "Medic!"

Still matter-of-factly, Blackman thought, and he spoke or tried to and it came out a whisper. "All right, Harrison, what's it look like, bad or good?"

Blackman now saw decision being formed in Harrison's eyes and almost knew what he was going to say.

"Captain, it looks to me like you're somewhere right in the middle, somewhere between them."

Shit, Blackman thought. He wanted to care, but caring kept trying to slip away from him. He thought of Mimosa. Tonight it was supposed to be or tomorrow, and I'd have hitched a plane down there, got me a ride into town and hoofed it on over to my baby's crib. Might've been late. Let myself in, tiptoed to the bed, smelling her perfume. Slipped to the kitchen, got a taste. Back to the bedroom. Undressed; into the bed, slipped up that silk to get at the silk underneath. Digging her little sounds— *oh, shit! Maybe, I'll never get to joog her again, maybe—oh shit!*

Harrison signaled sharply as Woodcock ran up. Harrison didn't like the medic. Newblack, he called him sometimes. For Woodcock was light-skinned and as if to compensate for his lack of real blackness, he'd cultivated the bushiest Fro in the company and had more shikis than ten dudes put together. But Woodcock knew his shit, Harrison reflected, watching his busy hands. The Syrette came first and the Captain relaxed, closed his eyes. The bandages came next, big, soft white ones, stemming the blood. Why the fuck does he keep shakin his head like that, Harrison wondered, watching Woodcock trying to bandage the chest wound.

"Chopper comin?"

"Shoulda been here by now," Harrison grumbled. "Hey, Griot,

83

get Belmont to check that chopper, willya?" Sadly, he watched the bandages lose their whiteness and become a slow, thick crimson.

In the ambulance wagon Blackman came awake as blood dripped into his face from the wounded man above him; he could taste it in his mouth. The wagon jolted on; he didn't know how long they'd been in it, only that it was going to Nurse Helen Gibson's Colored Hospital. He'd heard someone giving directions: Nurse Helen Gibson's Hospital at City Point. Would Walt Whitman be there?

Weeks later, when he was able, he sat in the small hospital yard near the main road, watching the traffic come and go, the soldiers, caissons, wagons; the civilians coming in for their food. At first, visitors from the regiment were many; then the regiment moved on; he would have to catch up with it when he was able. One day he saw a fine pair of mares drawing a wagonette. It was driven by an old black man, his face curled in a perennial grin. In the back sat a young white woman, unbent by the fortunes of war, although her man was nearly in rags and her own clothing desperately but neatly arranged. Most of the people who came in for rations played the humble game and so passed practically unnoticed by the Union soldiers who saturated the streets. The young woman looked neither left nor right. From that first day forward, Blackman watched them pass, as regularly as a mechanized timepiece, on certain days of the week. He'd almost stopped noticing, when they passed one day, a Union officer in the back seat with the woman. Beneath his cap, the officer's hair shone like new brass and there seemed to be something so familiar about the angles of his face that Blackman came to his feet, and he walked more that day than he had in all his weeks at the hospital. Twice more he watched them, and when next they came, Blackman limped quickly to the disbursing place where the civilians picked up their rations.

While the officer and the woman were inside, the officer's presence making it possible for her to get more than her proper share, Blackman was sure, he approached the old man.

"What's your name, old man?"

His face was wrinkled, his eyes yellow and tired. His frame seemed to have been rammed down into his body. For a moment, perceiving his life as completely as he knew his own, Blackman wavered, but by now the old man, having studied the stripes on Blackman's tunic, whipped off his hat.

"Nigger," Blackman said angrily, "put on your goddamn hat. Don't play that nigger game with me."

Without a wasted motion, without a change of expression, the man replaced the hat. "Yes, sir, Mister So'jer."

"Your name?"

"Flood, sir. Those the people I work for, so dat's my name. We used t grow t'baccy. Tom Flood."

"Where your people live, Flood?"

"Green Pines Plantation, we used t call it."

"What do you call it now?"

"Green Pines Plantation."

"Old man—" Blackman began, then stopped and started again. "Where is it?"

The old man turned stiffly and pointed. "Two mile direckly up dis here road, n a mile n a half from the lef turn on dis here road."

Blackman pointed, too. "Two miles up this road and then a left turn. Is that right?"

The old man nodded vigorously. "Dat's right Mister So'jer. Whooee. You sho some smart." He chuckled and closed his eyes, as if he would go to sleep.

"How many people on the plantation, Mr. Flood?"

His eyes flickered open.

"Mr. Flood? How many people?"

"Ah, well now, jus me n Missy Flood. N her fren, the Yankee.

85

Most de niggers done run to freedom. Her moma's dead, n her daddy and brudders is wid de Se'cesh in Richmond. She ain got nobody but me."

"How about you, Mr. Flood, you got a family?"

"Naw, not now. But I had me a fam'ly. Long time ago dere at Green Pines and I guess—doan member to clearly now—ol Master Flood hit a hard spell back in thirty er thirty-five—I disremembers—young man den, too. Enyway, he sold em down Sippi way to the cotton people. Took em down dere hisself—coffle o people—jus a-walkin. Never saw em again." Nearly every black man in Virginia told the same story: land burned out by tobacco and the slaves sold downriver except for the ones kept for breeding.

Blackman watched the old man gaze out at the past, then said, "You know you're free now, Mr. Flood. Why do you stay?"

The old man pushed back his hat and played with the reins. Blackman saw a genuine smile break across his face. "A ol nigger like me, I got t scheme. Doan want t be no deadweight, Mister So'jer. Gonna make me my break soon."

"You promise, Mr. Flood?"

"I promise, son."

"You know something else, Mr. Flood?"

"What's dat, son?"

"You ain't no nigger, Mr. Flood." Blackman turned and as he did, Mr. Flood said, "See you, son."

He saw Blackman that very night.

Blackman left the hospital under the cover of dusk and limped briskly down the road, leaving whenever he thought there might be a patrol, and returning to it when it seemed safe. He reached the turnoff without incident, darkness having come. He listened to the peepers as he walked, and the other night sounds, and a ghostly mist began to rise, covering the ground like a blanket.

The trees began falling away before the unplanted tobacco fields; then came the shacks, the row of barns for storage and tools. The mansion, like so many Blackman'd seen, rose up in the clearing, struggled to dominate it, but the weeds and wild berry bushes were straggling back. Another few years, Blackman thought, and the house would be strangled by nature, crumble away back to the earth; and the scars upon the land itself would fade away. Like my revenge, Blackman thought. It'd go unnoticed in the night, except by those touched by it, just another of those wounds of wartime, another gnatbite of human intercourse.

He thought of the young woman again. He would plant black seed in her so that what she hated would always be next to her, its heart beating time with hers for three quarters of a year, and if she tried to rip it out and succeeded, she would still have the memory; it would stalk her on nights like this for her entire life; she would sleep behind barred doors, flinch at the sound of every black voice and weep at the sight of every black face. She would not have her officer to console her; he would despise her (yet in some strange way, perhaps, desire her all the more, outside the bonds of marriage). More, he too would think of nights like this and grow uneasy about his women, uneasy about himself, and would nightmarishly over and over again imagine the sheer audacious horror of it, a black man barreling through centuries of monumental and ritualized taboo to revenge himself.

The officer's horse was in the stable, the mares barricaded at the other end. Blackman picked up a length of iron; he'd use it only as a last resort. He trembled now, the fury of his vengeance leaking; shut up once, now shrilling silently for outlet, the time near. No, he told himself, pausing and taking deep, calming breaths. It must be precise, as ordered as the coming of day and the passing of night.

He found the kitchen door to the mansion open; it moved before him without sound. Blackman stepped quickly inside and eased it shut behind him. A pinpoint of orange grew into a small yellow flame, suspended in the black void, but as the flame grew, so did the form it lighted. Blackman knew first that it was a man, then a black man, and then Mr. Flood. He sat eyeing Blackman with a slight smile and Blackman wondered if Mr. Flood was going to turn out to be a nigger after all.

With dramatic slowness, although Blackman received the distinct impression that he could move much faster, if necessary, Mr. Flood raised one finger to his lips. Blackman heard a slight rustling on the table, looked down, and saw that with his other hand Mr. Flood was pushing forward a revolver. Once in the light, Blackman could see it was a Colt 1850 model. He took the gun and nodded his thanks. Mr. Flood stood up, took Blackman's sleeve and led him up a curve of stairs, one step at a time. Mr. Flood might've been Charon and Blackman a lost soul in mid-passage on the Styx. They gained a carpeted hallway and glided down it until Mr. Flood stopped. He took Blackman's wrist and placed it against a door, then tapped him on the shoulder. Blackman felt him leaving. The hall smelled of old and dusty things, of decay just barely kept at bay.

Blackman pushed against the door; it moved soundlessly. He went in and closed it behind him and remained still, measuring the room by its feel. His nose told him that it was a woman's room, filled with scents and powders. Now, on the other side of the room he saw the bed, outlined by its canopy. The snores of the exhausted reached him, his and hers, and Blackman eased across the floor under the cover of them. Close to the bed the odors of sex hung in the air; Blackman stood at its foot and saw them, turned away from each other, each returned from the coupling to his own realm. He enjoyed this moment of power over the sleeping couple; he held the gun lightly, admiring its cold strength, the destruction of which it was capable. He moved to the man's side, enjoying the prevision of shock the officer would have when he woke and found himself in the middle of the white man's nightmare.

Blackman reached down and firmly grasped the man's shoulder, felt his fingers pressing hard into the flesh and saw the man's eyes open, widen, felt him start, and Blackman brought down the butt and barrel of the revolver on his face and the officer

88

went limp under his fingers, his eyes snapping shut. Blackman pulled a chair to the side of the bed and pulled the officer up, placed him in it. He used garments to tie him in and stuffed bloomers into his mouth; the unresisting, limber body sagged quietly.

Ho turned to the girl. His fingers, a part of the night, pulled back the coverlet, and as the cool air attacked her body, he ripped at her gown. She jerked around to exclaim at the officer, saw the bed empty, perceived with fright, his sagging frame in the chair, and then, with rising horror, saw the black man before her, and fainted. Almost with the precision of cleaning a rifle Blackman finished ripping off the gown, and as he climbed into the bed, kneeled there, he heard muffled sounds from the white man. He got down and checked the knots, made sure the man's eyes were clear of the gag, and returned to the girl, entered her brutally, found her large enough, far larger than legend said she would be. The man in the chair mumbled, bumped and Blackman was sure that if he'd not been gagged, the walls of the room would've burst with his screams.

The girl came awake moving with him, her arms reaching up to encircle his back. Blackman paused to throw them down. Fully awake now, she began to scream, and Blackman hit her; she stopped at once, and sobs broke out of her mouth; yet there was something grasping, firm, even greedy down where he was, down where the officer couldn't see, and it continued until she fainted again. Sensing eyes on them—for a moment Blackman thought he, too, had fainted—Blackman pumped exaggeratedly for long moments while pulling and pushing with equal dramatics the woman's huge breasts.

After a while weary, he climbed down, and looking in the man's direction, casually wiped his penis on the bed coverings. By now the room had turned a silver-gray with the approach of dawn, the same silver-gray that had signaled the start of so many battles. The man had a haunted, hungry look on his face; even in this light, his thin blue eyes made Blackman feel that he was looking through windows out into a universe empty of life. He looked down. The man had an erection; his loins disclosed still wet, still glistening, sperm. He's already come, Blackman thought, but he still wants it. Blackman leaned over him and struck his penis with the barrel of the gun. "Now, now," he said.

Blackman was ready to leave, but he paused, thinking. Then he returned to the bed and lifted the woman from it; her body was hot, her skin dry and her odor fetid. He carried her to the man and set her facing him upon his lap, lifting her up until his eyes said Yes, and then allowing her to slide down upon him, still in her faint. As he left the room he could hear the man's chair making bumping noises against the floor.

As Blackman rejoined his regiment, the Virginia landscape was beginning to fill with Union soldiers, all black, and he marveled at this, passing through unit after unit, and saw in this gathering of black death the awesome vengeance of the North; Ethiopia finally unleashed to destroy her captor; and after battles, skirmishes, actions, expeditions; after reconnaissances, operations, affairs and demonstrations; after engagements, raids, sieges and assaults, expeditions, attacks and captures, he learned but would not believe, that the XXV Army Corps had been formed. Nearly one hundred thousand black men under arms, infantrymen by the tens of thousands, cavalrymen by the thousands, artillerymen by the hundreds, all black, all poised, echoes lingering of Poison Springs, Fort Pillow and the Crater. Wherever Blackman looked there was history, bravery and blackness, but he knew they were not all there, pawing the cold December ground of Virginia.

Another hundred thousand were rampaging with Sherman, Steedman, Morgan and Thompson; Blackman heard of them at Atlanta, Savannah, Nashville and Murfreesboro, shattering the Army of Tennessee.

He could not believe that these officers as he knew them, this nation as he knew and understood it, or the wishes of its people as he'd perceived them, would allow, would deliberately place

100,000 black men under arms, in one given area and have them as a single, murderous unit, learn what it was truly capable of.

Charleston fell in February; the XXV Army Corps remained inactive.

Petersburg and then Richmond, through which burning city marched twelve regiments of blacks, including horse, but the XXV Army Corps remained inactive until the war ended at Appomattox, and Blackman only shrugged.

*Drumtaps*

> We found our Corps broken up, our divisions taken from General Weiztel and placed under strangers; our brigades scattered, our regiments ordered into temporary service with white brigades, our fractured command placed in the rear and on the flank. It was clearly not intended that the colored troops would win any glory in the last events of the war.
>
> MAJOR GENERAL WILLIAM BIRNEY

> . . . to the six regiments of cavalry now in service, there shall be added four regiments, two of which shall be composed of colored men.
>
> Army Reorganization Bill of 1866, Section III

# TWO

He might labor for the nation's wealth, and the nation took the results without thanks, and handed him as near nothing in return as would keep him alive. He was called a coward and a fool when he protected the women and children of his master. But when he rose and fought and killed, the whole nation with one voice proclaimed him a man and brother. Nothing else made emancipation possible in the United States. Nothing else made Negro citizenship conceivable, but the record of the Negro soldier as a fighter.

W. E. B. Du Bois
BLACK RECONSTRUCTION IN AMERICA

# 7

*Cadences*

*The room seemed the same.*
*The faces seemed the same.*
*But now maps of the United States, particularly the West,*
*covered the walls. Men with pointers walked to the maps and*
*spoke of rebuilding the South, expanding into the West, of un-*
*tapped wealth in the mountains; they spoke of trade with the*
*Orient and the building of railroads. Some spoke of Indian*
*savages and Chinese and Irish laborers who would have to be*
*sacrificed so that Anglo-Saxon civilization might progress.*

*And they spoke of money, government loans and subsidies, of*
*$48,000 per mile, maximum, and they all agreed that rails were*
*what the nation now sorely needed; the money was nothing*
*beside an industrious Anglo-Saxon civilization, which would*
*shine from sea to sea.*

*Finally, one of the Army officers present gained the floor, a*
*general, and he spoke: "You've expressed some concern about*
*the Indians, but they aren't the single worry for the Army.*
*Squatters rest on lands that belong to the railroads. People*
*believe that just because they've gone great distances in covered*

*wagons, they have the right to own any land upon which they come to rest and see no tangible sign of ownership. But law and order will prevail, the Army will see to that.*

*"As to the Indians, we have a network of forts that stand in Indian Territory; not nearly as many as we need, but there you are, the fortunes of war. But we have increased the strength of the Army in the very regions where the track is going down and in neighboring areas. As a matter of fact, four new regiments— the 9th and 10th of horse and the 24th and 25th of infantry— are assigned there—"*

*The question was matter-of-fact: "Are those the niggers?"*

*The General answered smartly. "Yes, sir, those are the niggers. Gentlemen, taking the lesson from our British cousins, we're merely employing one group of natives, the niggers, to fight another group of natives, the Indians. The strategy has met with marked success in the British dominions; we would be seriously amiss if we failed to use the same method."*

Colonel Ben Grierson was tired of Fort Leavenworth, tired of the inaction, of the people. He missed the crude civility of other posts back East. At moments he even missed the war; it'd not always left time for the fermentation of the hatreds he now had to deal with daily.

If the 10th was to survive, it'd have to get out of this place. A few more cases of pneumonia and regimental strength would be severely impaired, as if the Commanding General cared. Left to the General, they could all die, Grierson included, the Colonel knew. The General himself had assigned the 10th's area, low, wet, slow-draining ground, and he'd forbidden the blacks to roam anywhere between the fort and the town on pain of courts-martial.

A gentle, patient man, a lover of music, Grierson was fast losing patience as he continued to assess the problems of getting his regiment in combat-ready order. He'd had to upbraid his recruiting officers who were sending in anything black they could

96

get their hands on instead of the best, the most fit. The officers themselves were another problem; few, blessed few, wanted to serve with the blacks, and Grierson knew that Hatch, commanding the 9th Cavalry (Colored), was having similar problems. Maybe Custer'd set the tone. He'd been offered Hatch's job but turned it down. Luckily, perhaps, he got the same job with the 7th, all white. Just as well. The 9th was better off without him; too flamboyant a man; could be to compensate for the rumors concerning the degree of his manliness. They were extremely vicious rumors, Grierson mused, but where there was smoke, wasn't there fire?

After the officers, horses. Grierson hadn't liked the animals when he went to war. It'd been an accident, his winding up in the cavalry, and on horse then, he led three regiments on a six-hundred-mile raid through Mississippi, a great help they said, when they brevetted him major general, in the Vicksburg operations. The raid taught him that horses had to be good to begin with. Such was not the case now. Private traders and Army dealers alike tried to sell the 10th horses only good for the bone factory. Great Lord! The 10th would be patrolling distances out here that made his six-hundred-mile raid look like an afternoon canter. Out here a man's horse was his life, his veritable life.

And the men knew whites didn't like them, tried to flimflam them at every opportunity. The whites were creating an explosive situation. Even black men would only take so much. Hatch'd already had his hands full with a mutiny. It happened while the regiment was moving from Louisiana through Brownsville, Texas.

Brownsville, Grierson thought. Wasn't that where the last battle of the Civil War took place? What an ugly little place it must be.

Taking out his inkpot, quill and paper, Grierson tried to compose in his mind what he would say to his wife on paper. It eased him immensely to be able to share his problems with her.

"Colored troops," he wrote in his closing, "will hold their place in the Army of the United States as long as government lasts."

He was up late making decisions and rose in the morning long before reveille was sounded, setting things in motion. He felt better then, and for the first time exulted in the belief that his regiment would not be destroyed by the bigotry of General Hoffman or anyone else, and would become, in time, one of the most famous in the Army.

Surveying the regimental square, still cloaked with mist, Grierson's eyes fell on the inseparable companions, Sergeant Major Blackman and Sergeant Harrison, the large and small of the regiment. They'd been made noncoms as soon as they walked into camp, bearing their discharge papers; there weren't too many blacks who could read and write. And Harrison had a good singing voice, Grierson recalled; he was blessed.

Out there, Grierson thought with relief, Indian Territory, he'd mold himself a crack regiment with men like those two, Leavenworth was nothing but a jail for the 10th.

Indian Territory stretched flat and painfully monotonous, an uncanny region, Blackman thought. Still it was land, the only real wealth a man could ever know. But it needed beating, murdering, sundering; it required the noise and motion of thousands of machines and hundreds of thousands of people who were willing, *eager*, to claw its wealth from between the stones that nestled on it like miniature tombstones. He knew the eastern seaboard was already cluttered with the poor, the adventurers, the bewildered, the flotsam of European upheavals, and they were still coming. Now that the war was over they were beginning to trickle across the nation like a small stream of water seeking the path of least resistance. They were straggling out to the edge of the land; there they poised, noses up, eyes wandering slowly from north to south, east to west, smelling what, seeing what? Their futures on that bleak horizon? For they had come too far to have left anything behind, these priceless but dispensable vanguards for the rich; and they had to be protected, more or less, as they

98

ventured unwashed, unschooled and uncertain to places where they could finally carve up the land and insert into it their bruised and ragged roots.

But, Blackman thought, the land was already occupied. The maps indicated that: *Indian Territory*, shared by the Indians of all nations. They knew that in the sharing of the land lay the essence of wealth. It wasn't man's anyway; he merely thought it was. But how could a man own, possess from horizon to horizon what'd been there before man came, and would remain long after man'd gone?

Still, it was a soldier's job to enforce and protect the rules of the time in which he lived—if there was nothing he could do about the rules. Perhaps in time. And the rails. They hypnotized Blackman as he rode, flung wide of his company, C, horse color, bay. They were simply two steel lines that glinted in the sun, supported by crushed stone and creosoted pilings; they came out of one horizon and vanished toward another; to Cheyenne, Wyoming, so far, the rumors said, like a Bowie knife across the throat of the Indian.

The Indians.

They were a small people, Blackman saw with some amazement; everyone talked as if they were giants, superhumans, and they weren't red, but brown, closer in color to the blacks than anything else. They knew the land as well as they knew the backs of their hands; they appeared from nowhere and vanished into nothingness, or, like gnats, hovered on the horizon awaiting the full flow of perspiration, the complete toll of exhaustion among the soldiers before striking.

Blackman came to know the pain of saddle blisters, the shuddering of the horse muscle beneath him, the flow of the wind on his face at full gallop. Months passed and Spencers burned out, horses collapsed, company after company trotted out to its baptism of fire against the Cheyenne, Kiowa and sometimes the gandy dancers. Captain Armes had become known as bad luck; his first encounter with the Indians resulted in the death of

99

Sergeant Christy; he himself was wounded. On his next outing, one man was killed and nineteen wounded. Company F, as long as Armes was with it, was an unlucky company.

On the Kansas Pacific Railroad, engines with flatcars loaded with ties, steel and men rattled westward, and the boomers followed the tracks in broken, tilting covered wagons, lean cattle strung out behind them. Bonneted women and girls looked wonderingly at the black men in blue, and their men watched the horsemen with open suspicion. This was a joke way out here, niggers on horse in Army uniforms. Cain't trust them no more than the redskins. Days, endless days of patrol passed, and the caring for horses and Colts and Spencers.

Brit Johnson broke up some of the monotony. He was a large, rough man, going to what some thought was fat. There were four or five other black men like Johnson, although Blackman had never met them; they were as legendary as some of the Indians. Johnson had carved out his own life in the West, not with groups, but alone, riding out of horizons on horses as big and evil as himself. The white traders and railmen talked about Johnson behind his back; no one spoke ill of him to his face. He was one of the rare men who, if asked properly by the Army, would go to the Comanches and retrieve whites who'd been captured by them. He'd always been successful, too, making many white men sorry they'd ventured that last expected gesture a husband makes for his wife. For once the Indians had had their women, the husbands were both laughingstock and the objects of an insincere pity. Maybe that was Johnson's way of dealing with the white man; he'd sure bring your women back for you.

And Johnson brought in liquor at a price the black soldiers could afford; the white traders charged them three times what they charged white soldiers. Washing in the horse trough, black skin rippling over solidly hewn muscles, Johnson would tell Blackman and Harrison of the black families making their way into the West, of places where they were settling and their problems of schools, food, water and plain survival. He would talk about the "Chinee" on the western end of the line digging through solid mountains or blowing up canyons and often themselves, racing with the Irish workers on the eastern end, while the bosses stood back and watched it all and made wagers on their men.

A day or two of storytelling, drinking secretly, for it was forbidden on Grierson's posts, hunting down a job or two from traders or wagon parties, and Brit Johnson would vanish to return unannounced to another of those ramshackle collection of huts and houses the Army called forts.

From Fort Riley Grierson commanded an understrength regiment of seven hundred and two men, and they were strung out from Riley, Larned, Hays and Harker, and deep into Indian Territory. Although the regiment had been involved in several skirmishes, Grierson knew there was more to come, and it would come as the rails pushed the redman further and further to the wall. Colonel Grierson fretted that so much time was spent on escorting stage coaches, protecting rail gangs, scouting and protecting trains. The regiment was shaping up as nicely as possible under adverse conditions, but trouble was brewing.

He'd been told that the meetings at Medicine Lodge had insured peace, and indeed, some of the chiefs said they'd accept a reservation plan; others had not. Winter was in the air and congressional delays had prevented the ratification of the treaties. That puzzled Grierson. He'd been led to believe that Congress was in a hurry for peace. Short of peace, he knew, his regiment would have to kill a lot of Indians. Could that be what Congress really wants, he asked himself with a slow-dawning kind of horror. He shrugged it off. Even if the Indians were raiding more, they wouldn't do anything until spring. He could gather most of the regiment back to Fort Riley. They could have band concerts and Sergeant Harrison could sing.

Abraham Blackman, once back at Riley, knew that singing and concerts could only help relieve the monotony of garrison duty so much, then no more. Detachments shuffled back and forth between Arbuckle, Gibson and Riley for more training, building, but mostly just to have something to do. There were fights, but they were to be expected. A horseman made himself a drinking ring, a horseshoe nail bent in a circle with the head up, to fight with, and until its newness was dated with a little head blood, it wasn't a real drinking ring, and you weren't really a cavalryman. There were also desertions by men who'd done well in the field, but couldn't stand garrison duty. Others did what they had to do and paid the penalties, the hard drinkers, for example, who got caught; they took their punishment inside barrels or on top of them without murmur.

It could've been different with women around. There were laundresses assigned to each detachment, usually tough old black women who smoked pipes and had muscles as large as the men. They were the widows of runaway slaves who'd come West before the war. Others had followed the recruits out. The prostitutes in the one-road towns were nearly all white. Even though the soldiers of the 10th were willing to pay double the going rate, the whores wouldn't have them; their white customers would complain, if not kill them. So there was that quietly bubbling fury of semen backed up to the gut, only to be released by masturbation, Bible-reading or rape. But Arbuckle was drawing a lot of colored people to it; there'd be some women there after a while.

Winter closed suddenly about the forts occupied by the 10th, a squadron here, one there, but most were sheltered at Riley. Powerful winds sighed and blew across the endless plains and the snow came, settled, drifted. Stark, tortured shapes lay like dead, twisted bodies; streams that rushed to join rivers froze over and were found by those occasional scouting or mail parties only by their depressions in the snowscapes.

Another spring came. Like a woods animal its color changed slowly and subtly from white to gray to brown; green teased with its appearances on tree, bush and plains grass. Brooks, streams and rivers now thawed, filled to overflowing with the melted ice and snow, rushed furiously and noisily along their prearranged channels, sometimes cutting out new ones. Within Riley the corduroy walks sank and bobbled in the spring mud. The bellies of the horses were thick with it, the faces of the troopers spotted with it.

On such a spring day Blackman was detailed to deliver the mail to Fort Gibson. He left Riley at a slow gallop, his horse striding over the soft ground with ease. Once Riley lay somewhere behind him, a sense of uneasiness overtook Blackman; he thought it was because of the hollow sound of the ground under him. He imagined deep, deep wells there, great empty mouths awaiting patiently the fitting of teeth and tongue, of throat. He wondered about that image as he rode on, letting the bay run at its own pace, for it'd not stretched itself out much during the winter. Blackman held his face directly to the warming south wind, made even milder by the heat of the sun.

He hadn't realized his eyes had been closed until he opened them with a start, a chill spreading slowly along his spine. What was that? He stared hard at the eastern horizon, stopped his horse and swung him around and around. Nothing. When the sun was directly overhead, he dismounted to eat. His horse, hobbled, nibbled at the young grass. He ate hurriedly, wanting to reach cover before the sun went down. If someone was following him; if, he would find it hard to trail him once he got into the heavy woods. In fact, Blackman thought, I might be able to surprise him.

He was mistaken. Before entering the woods, he'd doubled back several times, then guided his horse into the stream nearby. While making his way, slowly and carefully up the stream, he came upon the skeleton and mail pouch of Filmore Roberts. Roberts had been detailed to carry the mail to Gibson during the winter and failed to return to Riley. Parties that made their way from Gibson to Riley said he never arrived. Roberts had been listed as a deserter.

Lost, Blackman thought. And here we'd thought the poor bastard had gone to California. The wolves and coyotes'd got to him. Meat in the middle of winter, and the little fellas did the rest. Damn near clean as a whistle. He took the weathered, mildewed and half-eaten leather pouch and continued downstream until he found a place in the rocks just back off the stream. There he hunkered down, his rifle within easy reach, his Colt loose in its holster, his horse staked up on the grass nearby. Blackman was chewing his dried beef when the two Indians materialized before him, for a moment seeming to be a part of the shadows and of the sound of the stream. They held up their right hands in greeting and Blackman stifled a move to grab for his Spencer. He stood and raised his own hand. Each Indian stepped forward and took his hand and gave it a single shake. Comanches, Blackman thought. The taller Indian reached slowly toward Blackman's head. Blackman watched him, shifting his eyes quickly to the other Indian and then back to the slow-moving hand of the first. The fingers touched his hair beneath his hat. He took the hat off, now sensing what it was the Indian wanted. The Indians smiled and nodded. They both touched his hair.

"It is like the hair of the buffalo," the taller said wonderingly.

"Yes," said the other. "Like the buffalo."

"Sit," Blackman said, gesturing to the ground. They were mission Indians or, at least, that was where they'd learned their English. He smiled. "You've been following me?"

They glanced at each other. "You knew?"

Blackman shrugged.

The second Indian said, "We knew you knew when we saw you'd doubled back in your tracks. Mail soldier," he said, matching Blackman's shrug. "But black with buffalo hair. There's much talk of the buffalo soldiers."

There was no reason now for not having a fire, Blackman thought, and he took his Bowie knife and reached for twigs, cut them and put fire to them. He stepped near his horse, gave him a pat and brought back some branches. Squatting before the fire again, he passed his meat around.

"Buffalo soldiers good soldiers," the taller Indian said.

"Brave," the other said.

Buffalo soldiers, Blackman thought. Better than the names the whites gave them: Brunettes, Africans, Moacs and the old reliable nigger. He'd have to tell Little David and the others about the name. But, he thought, feeling a surge of panic, what were these Indians going to do? He'd invited them to his fire and fed them, as was the custom between men, weren't they going? Where'd they leave their horses? Were they going on—getting dark, fast—or staying? Why didn't he trust them? They'd made him believe, the officers, that you couldn't trust Indians. The only good Indian was a dead Indian. (And the only good nigger was a dead nigger.) He gathered more branches and sat down again. To hell with it. If they stayed, all right, if they didn't, all right.

As soon as the fire was up, casting soft shadows, the smaller Indian went for spruce branches, brought them back, lay down and went to sleep. The taller Indian, looking into the flames spoke:

"I am called Man in the Rain. He is Wolf Heart." He raised his eyes to Blackman's. "Why have you come, you black soldiers with the buffalo hair? What have we done to you? It is said among many tribes that your brothers often came and lived with us and were free men. Now you are here like the white soldiers killing us."

Blackman was surprised. Yes, there was something wrong with it; he'd always felt that, but riding at the gallop with Indians shooting rifles, spears and arrows at you, you just never got down and discussed it, and once you were safe, back in a fort somewhere, you were so glad to be there that you didn't wish to even think about what might've happened. He said heavily, "We are like braves. We do as we're told."

Man in the Rain said, "That is no excuse for a man. It is an excuse for a woman dressed like a man."

Fighting words, Blackman knew, in any other place, at any other time. He laughed scornfully. "Does a brave dare defy the chief? Does he ride off to start his own war?"

"It has happened," Man in the Rain said.

"It's happened with us, too," Blackman said, "but not all at once and not to large numbers of soldiers. And it hasn't happened to lots of braves. Time captures all of us, Man in the Rain, and we do what we must. I'm ordered to take your land; you're ordered to kill me, and that, for now, is all there is to it."

They listened to the stream as they sat unmoving and silent, each trying gently to fathom the other man. Without anger the Indian said, "I see the end of the Indian people. I see them inside reservations that're bordered with wire and rope, growing beans and melons and corn, the work of women, herded into places by soldiers, black and white, carrying their rifles that shoot many bullets without loading; I see them pushed there by missionaries who talk of the love of Christ, but do the work of the Devil. White men who say they came to help us in the Agency are another instrument of our destruction. Those long lines of covered wagons filled with weary, frightened men and juiceless women and mewling babies who believe their god better than our Manitou will fasten the gate on the reservation. Buffalo soldier—"

"My name is Abraham."

"Buffalo soldier Abraham, it's strange. Once we roamed this land from ocean to ocean, the old ones tell us. We'll be exterminated trying to hold on to a small part of it. You black people who have nothing, who let yourselves be dragged from far, far lands in chains, and who've believed, really believed that the white god was also your god, will survive us, multiply because you *do not fight*, will not fight the white man."

"Nobody multiplies faster than the white man, Man in the Rain, and his bullets multiply even faster."

"Even so, one day you will want more than to be left alone; one day you'll tire of the white man killing you one by one, like stragglers in a buffalo herd, and you'll fight. That will come long after you've helped him to kill me. But it will come."

Blackman nodded. That day would surely come, and if it did, and he was still alive and Man in the Rain was still alive, the Indian could have his land back.

Man in the Rain and Wolf Heart were gone in the morning. Morose, and without having breakfast, Blackman continued on toward Gibson. He wished now that he'd been sent to Arbuckle to see the black people there. When he got to Gibson he would be billeted overnight by himself, close to the stables. A drink from a trader or from under the sutler's counter would cost him at least twice what it cost the white soldiers. He'd eat by himself and wouldn't be able to get the rawest white private to feed his horse. Man in the Rain, you don't know the half of it.

# 8

As the rails were pushed together by the gangs of Chinese from the west and the gangs of Irish from the east, the Indians were squeezed, and like mercury ran north and south, the soldiers relentlessly chasing and killing them, or herding them onto the proliferating reservations.

By now Blackman had lost too many horses to count; the last two he remembered only because of the circumstances, the first being the forced march to rescue Lieutenant Colonel Forsythe trapped by Cheyennes on the Republican River. Blackman'd taken his squadron the last twenty miles on foot, into the center of the stench of dead horses and men. The second horse went in the actions along the North Canadian, also against the Cheyenne, in the middle of a blizzard. The 10th pinched the Indians against the Washita to await the arrival of Custer's forces which were to lead them to a reservation; instead the 7th slaughtered them, men, women and children. Those who escaped froze to death; Blackman, leading his squad and Harrison's, found many of them, old men, old women and babies, purpled and wrinkled like prunes, their eyes shut gently against death.

Then Sheridan moved the regiment from Riley to Gibson to Wichita. "Right smack in the middle of all of em," Harrison said on the marches. "Kiowa, Cheyennes, Comanches and Arapahoes."

"But we got the easy duty," Blackman said, glancing over his shoulder at the lines of troopers and wagons. "Camp Supply, where they're already quiet."

At Camp Supply, Blackman and Harrison peeled off, followed Captain Byrne into the fort. The other companies and squads would continue to pacify the Indians, drive out boomers, catch whiskey peddlers, escort stages, wagon trains, carry mail, and the most luckless of them would wind up at Medicine Bluff to build an entire regimental post from scratch. Here, Blackman thought, he'd be able to start smelling like himself instead of his horse. Out of the field. There'd be Indians here too, but. . . .

No, they wouldn't be quite like the ones who rode out of the sun shooting. Those, no matter how uneasy you felt about it, you had to kill in order to keep from getting killed. A nice arrangement for the white man, very nice. Two for nothing. You could always leave at the end of your enlistment, he told himself. To where, for what? The Rebels were taking back the South, and they didn't want you in the North. Where did that leave you? Riding a horse, killing Indians to keep from getting killed. A very good arrangement, indeed.

Colonel Grierson, on a visit to Camp Supply, watched as the Indians began to arrive in April, the result of extensive winter operations. Sheridan didn't gave a damn if it'd been winter or not; round those Indians up. It'd paid off and the Indians were coming in by the thousands. There were so many surrendering that he felt that peace was now only months away. Since Grant's election things'd changed in the Indian Agency. Men of the cloth instead of soldiers and businessmen would look after the Indians, especially men from the Society of Friends. On the other hand, the Indians who chose to stay off would be considered hostiles, fair game for the military.

The new agents were conscientious men, Grierson had found, always interceding on behalf of the Indians. And they seemed to hold a proprietary interest in his black soldiers, as if the Quakers and the Quakers alone had been responsible for freeing them from slavery. They seemed not to care that a third of a million blacks, in service and out, had done much to secure their own freedom. But almost alone of the whites, the Quakers seemed to regard the buffalo soldiers as men. Whatever their short-comings, which would be revealed in time, men like Lawrie Tatum, the local agent, would be a leavening for this godawful, raw frontier.

Grierson's mind turned back to the building of the fort at Medicine Bluff. He was extremely disgruntled at the inability or unwillingness of the Army to provide engineers to help build the new fort. Rock had to be quarried, mortar made, logs hauled, split, seasoned and put up, and his men had to do it all—and still maintain a degree of military readiness to handle the main business, the Indians. In any other regiment, Grierson knew, desertion would be the order of the day and grumbling would be heard. But his men appeared to take pride in accomplishing the impossible. What the 10th had managed with its fractured detachments made Grierson proud. Both Sheridan and Sherman expressed especial interest in the men of his regiment, as well they might.

Still, Grierson wistfully wished for better discipline, an impossible thing he knew, in the face of all that was asked of the 10th. But, once settled in the new fort—Fort Sill he'd heard it'd be called—in a true regimental home, things would be better. The black settlements at Arbuckle, growing daily, would help to improve the atmosphere, too. For just a moment Grierson wondered if that private from E Company—Kewconda —was right when, while drunk, he marched around the post claiming that he, Grierson, and the other officers were a bunch of goddamn sonsabitches. A smile almost broke over Grierson's bearded, ascetic face. Some of his officers weren't much better

110

than the men. Lieutenant Doyle had set a bad example hunting down Lieutenant Lebo and Lieutenant Badger and actually getting off a round at Captain Gray, the peacemaker in the whole drunken affair. How could you expect the men to behave when their officers were running amuck? A court-martial, suspension from rank and pay for six months, and confined to post for the same time for Doyle; he'd never make captain with his penchant for whiskey.

Outside near the stables, Abraham Blackman merely sighed when he looked at the horses that'd been sent to them from the 7th; they were half dead on their feet. Captain Carpenter had already lodged another bitter, useless complaint with Grierson who'd forwarded it on to Sheridan and Sherman. But it wouldn't do any good. Past complaints had come to nothing. The 10th still got the dregs. Even the new black recruits looked like bottom-barrel material from the small towns of America. But the looks, Blackmen knew, were deceptive. You could always whip recruits into shape or if, you, their sergeant couldn't do it, the Indians would. There wasn't anything you could do with a horse that'd galloped its last mile. A black man came in because there wasn't much else to do out there. The Army told you you got prestige and a life of order, and the black men believed most of it, Blackman observed, and went along with it. The white commands had their hands full with the troopers they'd drawn, outcasts, misfits. Or the innocent youngsters who found out all too quickly that Army life wasn't quite like the recruiting people said. Who else would be out here fighting a thousand battles over thousands of square miles but men who had nothing else to do and no place else to go?

Leaving the stables, Blackman walked out to watch the Indians streaming in, their faces downcast, and in silence. He viewed them compassionately and expansively for the moment. Just that morning he'd returned from Arbuckle with Little David. The black homesteaders were getting settled in now. Those shacks put together with buffalo chips were slowly vanishing. It was a long journey from the settlements to the nearest woods, and crop-tending and looking after scrub cattle—food—had to come first. Well, right up there with sex, for the babies were still coming, breaking into the world in the middle of the night accompanied by the screams of their mothers and the smell of insides turned out; all that life in the middle of so much blood. Many died, but many more survived. Black babies were used to surviving, and the women over there were as tough as the men, had to be. Blackman had seen some of them in the fields, harnessed to the plow, grunting, when the horses and their men were ailing. The women came as black as berries and three times sweeter. They took their sex the way they took their breakfasts when food was available; a lot of it at one sitting. Blackman knew when he left camp that he was going to get him some; couldn't nobody tell him different, and he had. She'd been a young widow, fully as tall as he, and almost as broad. She'd been ample. They'd made her mattress of dried leaves and grass and cornshucks sing and whimper, had raised that good funk up from between them. Now Blackman worried about one thing: there'd always be somebody on furlough when he wasn't, and the girl was greedy; she wore a man out. Night came early to the plains and the sweetness of the earth lingered in the air like an aphrodisiac. Naw, she wasn't likely to be sitting through all that waiting for a squadron sergeant major.

The Indians were talking hurriedly among themselves in the wake of the arrival of a detachment of troopers and a wagon. Their eyes followed the wagon. The braves looked straight ahead, as if wishing to be apart from the others. Now, their eyes were alight with something. What? Blackman hated to move from this corner that was so well shaded, yet gave him a view of the entire parade ground. He saw David Harrison hurrying toward him, and he was relieved; he didn't have to move; Harrison would tell him what was going on.

"What is it?" he asked.

"Brit Johnson. You hear about it?"

Blackman shook his head. He'd been thinking about Arbuckle, and now he thought of Harrison there with his fat little woman. "No." It could not be good news. Couldn't be, leaping like brushfire through the fort. "He dead?"

Harrison pulled on his pipe he brought out of his boot top. "Yeh. B'tween Weatherford and Griffin."

"Anybody else?"

"Three whites with im. All dead. Killed the horses to get some cover, but didn't do em much good."

"Comanches?"

"Yep."

Blackman scarcely heard the answer. This was why the Indians'd come alive. While they were in the ration line, humbly getting their supplies and therefore pledging allegiance to the white man, *some* of them were still out there fighting. Blackman took off his hat, carefully studied its broad brim and waved it back and forth across his face. "Scalped em, too?"

Little David Harrison had lit his pipe. He nibbled on the stem. "Yeh," he said, finally, looking at the Indians with scornful eyes. "Cut is prick off, too. Cut im open and stuffed that little dog of his inside him, Choko. Why they do im so bad? They knew im."

"Afraid of him. When one man does all that to another, he's afraid, that's all." He slapped his hat back on and, grabbing it by the brim, pulled it down over his eyes. Well, they'd have to bury him. He supposed that was Brit there in the back of the wagon. Read over him and bury him. He wasn't the first and he sure won't be the last. At least there were three whites dead with him, and three to one wasn't so bad. As far as the Indians were concerned, he bet, four to none was about as good odds as you could get. The line of Indians seemed to have straightened; the downcast faces had come up; there was muted fire in the eyes, and Blackman

113

understood it all. He rose and followed Harrison to the wagon and for a moment stood with his friend measuring the great pool of dry, blackened blood that had stained the canvas wrapping.

Belmont had set off the flare and now, still with his ear pressed to the receiver of the radio, he looked up at the sky with a great outpouring of relief, for he'd heard the unmistakable flutter of an oncoming chopper. He glanced down at Captain Blackman, still out from Woodcock's shot. Those bandages were sure catching blood. C'mon in here, baby, he thought, swinging his eyes up once again, up and over the tree line. Goddamn. Sure looked bad for Captain-Brother. But don't die, baby, he thought. You could make it a whole new army, a *new* one, man. Belmont fingered the clipping in the pocket of his fatigues; never went without it. Good luck, better than a rabbit's foot. Better, he guessed, than the mezewzy Doctorow carried. The helicopter came down slowly, with its familiar downdraft, and before it touched the ground two stretcher bearers hopped out and raced toward them. Once the Captain was on the stretcher, they all grabbed hold and ran for the craft. At times like these, Belmont hated his radio, but it wasn't bad enough to throw it away. He'd done that before when the shit hit the fan. Just said the radio was out and fuck it, leave it there, right on the trail or somewhere for the slopes— No. The Captain'd said that shit was out in his company. Even VC wasn't accurate, he'd said, because no one in the fuckin Army knew who was a Communist or a member of the NLF. And furthermore, he'd said, the Army didn't care. Different in his company. Don't get trapped into using all those silly titles, those racist names that came so easily, because we're in the same situation, and using them names the way the white boys did just sort of blurred the recognition of that fact. Goddamn Captain. Way out here in the Nam, puttin the shit together.

Sergeant Harrison counted the men. He knew all the faces and knew they were all there, but he counted anyway. You could want a face to be so safe, you could make it be with you, while it

114

was laying back there in a paddy half dead. When you counted you worked with numbers, not the faces. All there. He gave the pilot the okay and the craft rose, the ground fell away, and he sighed with relief. Got out again. How many times do you go in and come out in one piece? And, you know, you could *not* come back one time through no fault of the VC. Crazy fuckin brass flyin choppers shooting anything that moves on the ground; goddamn crackers on the gunships pifflin niggers, and bombers tired of carryin bombs, Zwat! right down your back. Overtaken by a furious sadness, he told himself, "One of these days you ain't comin out, that's all."

Woodcock had hooked up the plasma and it was flowing. Doctorow was holding the bottle numbly, trying not to study the Captain's face. Although he'd checked the Captain's pulse only a second ago, Woodcock found his fingers back digging into the wrist, lightening, funneling all his sense of touch into his fingers to feel. There, he had it; there was still one, going lightly, about one-thirty. C'mon, Captain.

Johnny Griot watched the green fields slide back under them. He was sitting back to back with Antoine and he wondered if Antoine was aware of the sequence of events that led to the Captain's getting hit. They were advancing on the two 47s, the Captain in front, and he'd jumped up to draw their fire to keep him, Griot, Antoine, Harrison, Doctorow and the others from walking into the interdicting fire. Weren't too many captains around doin that shit, Griot reflected, and not too many who went out with squads in their companies, one after another as a matter of habit. Aw, shit, man, you can make it. C'mon, Captain.

The warrant officer pilot had heard of the Captain. What he'd heard was that he was gitting the niggers ready for black power as soon as the plane took off from Tan Son Nhut. From what he'd heard about the situation back home, they didn't need any more niggers running around with guns, like those Panthers and things. Maybe the Captain would die. Looks like he got hit bad. That would end all the black power shit in this sector, anyway, the WO thought. Keep this sumbitch on three-quarter power and give im a chance to kick in.

"They got im and they're on the way in, Major Whittman," Faulkner, the radioman, sang out as Whittman re-entered the CP.

Whittman stopped. "Dead or alive?"

"Belmont says he's hit bad. But I guess he's alive."

"Umm," Whittman said. He went to the corner he used as an office and sat down, pulling out another Roi-Tan. He looked out over the tree line; they'd be coming from the north. Well, he thought, if he's hit bad enough, he doesn't have to be dead; he'll be out of the Army in any case. The pain in the ass, twenty years a pain, dating from Korea where they'd met, would be over. All the accumulated guilt of his rise and Blackman's marking time would be over. But would he ever get over the time Blackman told him to his face, and he, Whittman, was a captain at the time and Blackman a silver looey, that he owed his promotions to his skin, not his skill? Now that Whittman was moving on to colonel, although Blackman never mentioned it, the old truth was hanging out again; for Blackman should've held the same rank or higher. He knew it, too, damn his charcoal ass, Whittman thought, and Blackman knew Whittman knew it.

He chomped hard on his cigar and thought, Die, you black sonofabitch, this is a white man's army.

# 9

Colonel Grierson slowly, almost reverently, pulled on his dress uniform. Now returned after a two-year absence, he felt like a stranger back with the 10th, here at Fort Concho. Bitterly he reflected that Fort Sill, built by his men, must've been an almost perfect fort for, once built, the Army undoubtedly had found it too good for blacks, and so here they were, in Texas. The 10th had done well during his absence. Together with its sister regiment, the 9th, and the 6th they'd ended the Red River War.

Once again the regiment was scattered all over hell. He hoped the other forts, which he hadn't inspected yet, were at least as good as Concho, which was one of your ordinary forts. Other units of the 10th were at Davis and Stockton and Griffin and McKavett.

And during his absence, the 10th became efficient with the Gatling gun, but there was some question about the effectiveness of the weapon; in fixed situations, all right, but horse thieves, hard-riding Mexicans and quick-moving Indians didn't give you much chance to get up your Gatling. Earlier, Grierson checked the lists and was pleased to note that there remained in the regiment many men he knew and liked. He chuckled; he hadn't seen Kewconda's name. Almost lovingly he'd stroked the names of Sergeant David Harrison and Sergeant Major Abraham Blackman.

The Colonel put the finishing touches to his uniform, its blue with yellow trim, and stepped out of his room, found his staff, in white gloves, ready. They saluted snappily and he returned it. Yes, there was something about being in dress blues. Briskly now he strode toward his place on the parade grounds, knowing that each man behind him was skip-hopping into step.

It pleased him to be standing before the regiment, or what was here of it on this fine May day. The colors whipped and skipped in the hot Texas wind, and the line of troopers in full dress sat stiffly on their well-controlled, handsomely groomed horses, the detachments told their companies by the colors of their animals, bay, sorrel, black and calico.

Sweetly to Grierson came the drumtaps and bugle calls; the commands from the captains, lieutenants, sergeants; they echoed down the line of black, brown, ginger and high-yellow men. The Colonel felt then, as he always did at dress parades, when the flag whipped and the lines moved evenly, that the Army was a special thing for special men. There was honor here, he thought, and courage, and devotion to duty, and enough glory for every man in an Army uniform, regardless of his color. And Grierson was confident then, so much so that for seconds at a time his eyes grew wet, that the Army would one day soon sing of these black men and their bravery, and take them to its bosom without reservation for, even excluding the Civil War in which they'd done well, they'd been outstanding in this no man's land. He had the faith that his Army would make up for its past misdeeds.

Now Alvord with his heavy-butted walk, came over the grass to within five precise paces of Grierson, threw a salute and bellowed:

"All present or accounted for, sir."

Grierson returned the salute, wheeled, and squared and walked to the reviewing position, his aides at his heels. Once again the commands cracked out and the line wheeled into fours, reins jangling.

118

God they look good, Grierson thought, but those horses up close!

At eyes right, Blackman fastened his eyes on the Colonel; looks pretty much the same. Goin to have trouble though. His eyes went forward again. Yes, sir, trouble. The old man doesn't know too much about Apaches, Kickapoos, Lipans, Mescaleros or Texas Cheyennes. And wagon trains're backed up on the Brazos, filled with settlers waiting for the Indians to be cleared out. Colonel Shafter from Fort Duncan was going to lead an expedition out; Grierson would remain at Concho, getting used to things. At least, that's what everyone was saying.

Little David Harrison was sure the Colonel's eyes had twinkled when he rode by at the head of his squad. Good to have him back, Harrison thought. They were having enough trouble with the Indians, but the Rangers'd been bothering all the black soldiers. Easier to shoot than Indians, Harrison reasoned. Well, it was going to be a long summer on the horse, he thought. Shafter would head a big push, all black. Just before the parade, he'd seen detachments of the 24th and 25th Infantry regiments arriving outside the fort. This was going to be something.

But it was mid-July before they moved out, both Shafter and Grierson wishing to insure every possible advantage for the troops. Beyond that, Shafter looked for success that would reflect brilliantly on his own record; this expedition to the Staked Plains could give him a great boost toward general officer status.

As they left the fort with sixty-five wagons, a herd of beef, one company of the 25th, two of the 24th and six of the 10th, plus Indian scouts, Blackman growled to Harrison, "We should've left in May. This is killing weather; no water weather."

"Don't worry," Little David said. "It'll be plenty cool when this four-month campaign is over."

A trail of flying dust marked their journey across the plains until they camped at Rendlebrock Springs where Captain Nolan was relieved of command and court-martialed for not vigorously pursuing a trail left by a group of Indians. They moved on.

In August, the salt from their perspiration making white the uniforms of the troopers, they broke off four companies from the main body and with four pack mules and a medical wagon, followed Shafter westward. Shafter was determined to find and kill Indians or so dazzle them with his display of power that they would flee of their own accord to the reservations.

Even if it kills us, Blackman thought, as they pounded into Casa Amarillas, looking for Indians and water, of which they found neither. Shafter's panic was apparent to Blackman and Harrison. The column moved slower now, scouts peeling off now and again to check for water; no one spoke about Indians anymore. Whenever they found clay which did not also give up drinking water, they filled the horses' hoofs with it to ease their suffering, and every day they walked their mounts at least five miles. They knew that Colonel Shafter was hoping to rendezvous with the supply column in ten days; Blackman and Harrison agreed it would be closer to eighteen or twenty.

"If the Indians don't catch us out here," Blackman said. He found the Staked Plains eerie, absolutely desolate. Nothing could live out here for long. Even the light was strange, reaching them flatly, tinting the land in colors not seen before. And the silence.

Twelve days later, walking now more than riding, they came on the skeletons of hundreds of buffalo, shot, skinned; the meat, unwanted, was rotting in the heat. No wonder, thought Blackman, the Indians were running off the cattle herds of the whites. The white buffalo hunters had deprived them of their food; they would deprive the whites of theirs.

They moved on to White Sand Hills, found no water, force-marched into New Mexico to Dug Springs where they found not only water, but a large Indian trail as well which Shafter eagerly set out to follow with four days' ration of food.

But, in the process they were ambushed on a night when the mid-September cooling breezes swept through the tents of the exhausted soldiers. Relieved that there were no injuries, Shafter ordered Blackman to round up fifty men with the best horses possible, and they followed the trail of the raiders through the night and into daylight to an empty village. Shafter ordered it burned.

He stalked around the village chewing his bottom lip. He'd been out some forty-odd days with nothing to show for it but some notes on the terrain and the location of springs. No hostiles captured, none killed. "Sergeant major," he barked at Blackman. "Get a detail up on that hill and set up a marker. Call it Monument Spring. It'll guide the wagons to fresh water here."

Blackman turned his face to hide his smile. Soldiers had to leave their monuments; something had to remain of victory or defeat, and a cunning soldier like Shafter could turn this unfruitful expedition into victory, if not for the present, for the future.

Wearily Shafter turned back and knew the troops behind him were relieved. They'd been out ninety days. They returned to Fort Concho to discover that the Kickapoos and Lipans were raiding almost to within sight of the forts of the 10th, then dashing away to the Rio Grande and crossing it. Reluctantly, General Ord issued the order of hot pursuit:

> . . . the use of colored soldiers to cross the river after raiding Indians, is in my opinion, impolitic, not because they have shown any want of bravery, but because their employment is much more offensive to Mexican inhabitants than white soldiers.

In the brown-blue mountains of Saragossa and the Santa Rosas they caught up with the Indians and methodically destroyed them and their villages and returned to base after almost a year in the field. Colonel Grierson felt his men deserved something and he gave orders for a massive Christmas party, something to pick up the morale which was visibly sagging.

Blackman was duty sergeant that night. He saw Little David as he rode by outside, his coat buttoned up against the winter. Going to St. Angelo's, Blackman thought. Little David Harrison had been looking blue lately; maybe a night in town drinking and chasing around with one of those Mexican or German whores would make him feel better.

121

The Christmas party had made Harrison feel an inexplicable sadness, as though the Army-ordered smoothness of his life had been disturbed by some unevenness in the path of things. He wished Blackman hadn't the duty. He wanted to sit and talk with him about the Army, away from the Army, as they'd done so many times before. He'd joined it in 1863; he was thirty-six now, with eight two-year hitches behind him. Eighteen years altogether of horseshit, ass blisters, bad food; of guarding the white man's railroad, escorting his families, chasing Indians for him and sometimes killing them; of incompetent captains and lieutenants, laughter and scorn from white soldiers—except when you saved them from being castrated or scalped. And for what? David Harrison asked as he trotted through the high, freezing wind. You'd think that someone, somewhere, sometime would get up and say, loudly and clearly, Oh, look how well those fellows are doing for America. But, naw. The more you did, the less they wanted to recognize it.

These were the things he wished to talk to Blackman about, for Harrison had thought often lately about desertion. He could hear Blackman laughing: "Who, *you?*" Harrison probably wouldn't have deserted, he now agreed. The low desertion rate was another regimental badge of honor. Only eighteen men in fifteen years. The white 4th had close to two hundred in less time. Harrison wouldn't have hurt the regiment like that. A man could always get lost in the field or let it be thought that he'd been captured during a fight with the Indians.

In town now, Harrison dismounted and tied up before Nasworthy's Saloon; he could hear the piano from the street. For a moment he hesitated, listened to the wind as it sifted down the street, like a voice whispering to him. He strode up the crude wooden steps, entered and walked directly to the bar. "Whiskey," he said, and a glass was shoved at him.

Nasworthy quickly poured the drink and retreated to the end of the bar, clutching the trooper's money. Harrison stiffened then, as two men approached, one on either side of him; they leaned on their elbows and smiled down at him. Harrison glanced toward Nasworthy and read of his trouble in the saloonkeeper's eyes. Nasworthy had rushed from his corner with glasses as soon as the two men came up. He poured and retreated, without waiting to collect his money this time. He knew the signs. He'd compared notes with the Doan brothers up near Radziminski. He and they were in the path of the Chisholm Trail and the cowhands and bums who took it were the dregs of the West. To make matters worse, a lot of nigger cowboys were riding herd along that trail now and there were a lot of poor whites, themselves up to their necks in cattle dirt and cowshit, who didn't want to see anything black. It was a helluva lot easier to kill blacks than Indians, and there were a lot of cotton-green niggers traipsing around, trying to get up to Kansas. Nasworthy sighed as he knew the Doan boys sighed when black and white trouble loomed before their bar.

David Harrison's first inclination was to swallow his drink quickly and leave, avoid trouble, avoid giving the regiment a bad name. So he didn't know why he remained there, sipping, his eyes straight ahead.

"He kinda little to be a sergeant, ain't he?" That was the man on his left speaking.

"Hell, I don't mind his bein little, but he's a nigger, unless there's somethin wrong with my eyes. Is they?"

"Nope. He look like a nigger to me all right."

Harrison swished the rotgut around in his glass and looked at it. He could see pieces of something floating around in it. Now the man on the left was speaking to him directly.

"Boy, I guess you the only one can tell us for true. You is a nigger, ain't you?"

The man on his right bumped his shoulder. "Ain't you?"

Harrison took a solid swallow. He'd noticed that awkward escalation of noise behind them, as though people were determined not to believe what they were seeing. To his left he noticed the glint of a Bowie, and he glanced quickly at Nasworthy who, at that same moment, shifted his glance to another part of the bar.

He heard, most audibly, the cocking of the revolver of the man on his right. He finished his drink, carefully set the glass down and said, "Ahhh." He hitched up his pants and turned to leave and his breastbone ran into the point of the knife, he stopped.

"We gonna have them stripes, nigger." The man on his left. The man on his right forced the muzzle of his gun into Little David's side, but he made as if to continue forward; the knife point didn't give and he stopped and remained motionless, the center of attention in the bar into which came a sudden silence. Harrison twisted his body away from the knife, but felt the gun bite deeply into his ribs. He tried to slide past. As he did, the knife slid into his arm as easily as cutting through buffalo fat. The man on his right put a hammerlock around his neck and bent him backward. David Harrison heard one voice, tremulous, trying not to call too much attention to itself, but nevertheless speaking clearly with its familiar German accent, "You haff your fun, leaff him go."

Big Helga, whore of cowhands, soldiers, Mexicans, Indians— anything with pants and silver dollars.

The man on Harrison's left was cutting off his stripes, the right arm first. The man holding him in the hammerlock spun him around; the left arm.

"He jus a nigger private, now," someone keekawed.

"Then we best be gettin them stripes off his pants," the man with the hammerlock said, and his partner pried apart the thread and ripped them off, right side first, and then the left side. Then he was released, the yellow stripes lay in bands on the floor. Harrison started to walk off; he was already itching to get his hands on his rifle and revolver and return, for he knew they'd still be here, gloating and drinking. They were like that.

"Hold it, boy."

Little David stopped in the center of the saloon. The man who held the revolver said, "Avery, a little dancin music. It's Christmas an we all far from home. We need some entertainment. Now I hear tell these boys is right good dancers."

124

The pianist shrugged, sat down. The notes, light and bouncy, rolled beneath his fingers.

"Dance," said the man with the knife.

"Dance, nigger," said the other. He cocked his gun and the explosion of a .44 filled the room. Harrison looked down and saw a bullet hole in the floor near his feet. Avery glanced behind him, his face pale. He continued to play.

"Dance! Dance!" the men shouted together.

Little David Harrison walked slowly through the door. He wanted to hold his wounded arm, bend with the pain. But not in front of them. He kept walking. He might have walked through the door, got to his horse, ridden off and returned with his weapons. But he had to let them know he was going to do it. His angry tongue forced apart his pain-clenched teeth. "You cowshit, stinking, sonsabitches, I'll be back. I'll see how good *you* can dance; I'll dance you bastards into next Christ—"

At the door, they blew him through it. They emptied their guns in him and his blood spewed hot and steaming in the cold air, on the door and floor. Quickly Nasworthy said, feeling the weight of opinion now on his side, "You'd best be goin now, cause they'll be in here from the fort. Git on where you was goin before you stopped in here." He knew they were from the 4th regiment, taking their fun in regular clothes.

Something's happened to Little David, Blackman thought. It was late and no one'd seen him return. Now, in the shank of the night, quietly saddling up, Blackman was ready to find him. He tied another horse to his own, hoping he wouldn't have to use it. He prodded his horse into a trot, the better to keep it warm on the ride into St. Angelo's.

He came into the silent town and shuffled up the middle of the single street until he came to Nasworthy's. There he dismounted and tied the horses beside Little David's shivering mount. Taking the carbine from its holster, he walked up the steps and through the door. Nasworthy was sweeping up. Big Helga sat at a table drinking and crying. Little David's body lay in a corner, a piece of wrapping paper over it. Blackman pulled it back and saw the chevrons and stripes laying on the bloodied chest. Nasworthy approached. "When they came in I could see it was goin to be trouble. Wasn't nothin I could do. Sorry."

"Who did it?" Blackman said, stuffing the pieces of yellow into one of Harrison's pockets. They'd have to be sewed back on. But Nasworthy wasn't answering. "Who did it?" Blackman asked again.

The saloonkeeper shrugged. "Jus two tough-lookin cowhands, as best I could figure out."

"From where?"

"Dunno."

Now Blackman saw the holes in the floor.

"Tried to make him dance, too," Nasworthy offered.

Blackman smashed him in the head with his carbine and as he fell, Big Helga laughed. "Who?" Blackman asked again. He saw indecision in Nasworthy's eyes and hit him again.

"Troopers from the 4th. That's all I know."

"He vouldn't dance, do; dey couldn't make him dance," Big Helga said.

Blackman picked up Harrison's body. "Let's go," he said. Outside he tied it to the extra horse which he attached to Little David's horse. He let his own horse pick his pace, and the caravan went back to Fort Concho as another freezing gust of wind blew through town.

They wrenched open the earth in the regimental cemetery. They had a flag over his box, which they took away when they lowered the coffin into the ground, and as David Harrison's squad fired the traditional three-round salute, Blackman thought back to the day when Harrison had told him he was too compassionate with the white man. He hadn't known then if Little David was right; he didn't know it now. The white man had killed Harrison, coldly and brutally and senselessly, but hating blacks seemed to make sense to whites.

The dirt was going into the grave now.

Blackman thought, Without compassion, and I don't know if I have it, man. Without it, I become like *them* and to be *like* them, is to *be* them, and so help me God I don't want to be like them; I don't want to have done all they've done to people, places and concepts.

*Drumtaps*

Fort Concho, Texas, Feb. 3, 1881

We, the soldiers of the U. S. Army, do hereby warn the first and last time all citizens and cowboys, etc., of San Angelo (San Angela) and vicinity to recognize our right of way as just and peaceable men. If we do not receive justice and fair play, which we must have, someone will suffer—if not the guilty the innocent. "It has gone too far, justice or death."

U. S. SOLDIERS

# 10

The troop train crawled down out of the mountains, across the plains and deserts on the very tracks they'd helped protect for over thirty years. From time to time the Buffaloes saw neat, well-tended farmlands, children playing in the fields. In the towns they'd protected, they stared with hungry eyes at the buildings, the hotels, churches, restaurants, no longer all wood, but giving way to brick and fieldstone, they were not permitted to enter; the train only stopped on sidings outside the towns.

Behind them lay the West; the Indians, except for a brave, tough, persistent few, were safely behind the reservation fences. Just, Blackman thought, head back on his seat, as Man in the Rain predicted. The list of chiefs they'd encountered was long, many of the chiefs noble: Satank, Victorio, Geronimo, the Apache Kid, Mangus. Grierson, too, was behind them, promoted to brigadier. And they'd moved north to Fort Custer where Blackman had shown a young lieutenant named Pershing how to conduct a raid and escort on Cree Indians to the Canadian border. The first time he laid eyes on the crisp young officer, Blackman knew he wasn't going to slide into oblivion, like Grierson; Pershing was New Army.

There'd been the colored lieutenant, Flipper. He'd done real well during the Victorio campaign. First black man out of the U. S. Military Academy. We went out of our way to make him look good, to help him, Blackman thought, his mind now settling to the rhythm of the train. Proud as hell. Should've known it wouldn't last. Charged him with stealing commissary funds. Blackman snorted at the memories. Damned foolishness. We were handling everything to do with the commissary, because he hadn't learned how. They just meant to get him, once they saw him out riding with Lieutenant Nordstrom's lady friend. Once they court-martialed Flipper, there was the other fellow, Young. Better than Flipper, but they got rid of him, too. Sent him to Wilberforce as a military instructor.

Now it was 1898 and they were rolling east to war with Spain in Cuba. Remember the *Maine*. They'd all gone crazy back here, wanting to beat the hell out of Spain.

The train slowed, rolled to the outskirts of a small southern town. Blackman heaved up his window and leaned out for air. He turned at the voice: "Hey, you, nigger with all them stripes on your sleeve. Yall goin t war? Kin you niggers fight?"

Blackman was out of his seat, through the door and down the ramp to the ground in what felt like a single motion, and powered his left fist into the white man's stomach, felt the air go suddenly out of him, and then crossed the thin, pointed jaw with a right and the man was down, trying to get his breath, the enormity of what'd been done to him locked within his breathless frame. Blackman reached down and pulled him halfway up from the ground and drove forward again, hitting the man with such force that his shoulder made a popping sound. He was out. Blackman climbed back aboard the train. Can you niggers fight? How was that, Little David, compassion*less* enough for you?

As if intimidated by the South, the train rolled through it gingerly, passing through its mean little towns, the fields in which blacks stood staring after it, uncomprehending of the other blacks in it, who waved to them. On into Georgia, Chickamauga and Rossville, and Lakeland, Florida.

As they were embarking, Blackman looked at the ocean and thought, Out there, ninety miles away, and they've been wanting to get it for fifty years, and now it was time. They traveled the ninety miles segregated in the hold of their ship, and when they emerged at the port of Daiquiri, they loaded into boats, lost two men drowned; men, Blackman thought bitterly, who'd never seen so much water, were never trained what to do in it. They gained the shore where they were to fight as dismounted cavalry. Blackman wondered if the other horsemen, like himself, felt naked without horseflesh under them. From one kind of warfare they'd been thrust brutally and without training directly into another.

Daybreak comes strangely to this island, Blackman thought. In the West there'd been first the chill, going with the night, and in some places a mist that was burned off later by the sun. There, there seemed to be the proper order of things. But here you felt the heat even before the sun came up; you felt it damp and sticky, carrying with it a thousand flying bugs that snarled past, raking out a minute hunk of your hide in the process.

"We're here to protect American interests," the white soldiers said, in the cautious exchange of visits.

Which ones, Blackman wondered. Cheap labor, perhaps, that was an American interest. Slavery had been abolished here only a dozen years ago; it'd been the last country in the Americas to do so. That must be why there're so many black people here, Blackman thought. They spoke Spanish, but they were black and that's all the white man ever looked at, was skin, not languages. Once there'd been a hundred thousand slaves on this island.

Was America fighting for the blacks, the mestizos, or those "pure" Spaniards who wanted to be free of Spain so they could run the country, keep all the profits themselves? The money from sugar, tobacco and rum? What did soldiers know of all this? Next to nothing; they just ran to the fighting for the glory, the honor. Pershing had turned up here. And Young had somehow managed to get away from Wilberforce. Well, the more wars, the better; the faster you went up the ladder, if you were like Pershing, white.

130

For so much hollering, it was a small war, Blackman reflected, as he moved through it confidently, for the Buffaloes, the cavalrymen and the infantry, were about the best the regular Army could put into the field. The 1st Volunteers, the Rough Riders, attracted a lot of attention because of their colonel, and they became overbearing and arrogant without cause, even when the 10th, with heavy loss in officers—Shipp, Smith, Mills and Ord—had to rescue them with a charge to draw fire away from them on El Caney.

They'd landed on June 22 and the war in Cuba was over July 16, hardly a war either side could be proud of. Blackman couldn't believe it, therefore, when the Rough Riders, behaving for all the world as though they'd won the skirmish, came to the regimental ground to allow the Buffaloes to drink from their canteens, because they were "bully," and regular fellows, even if they were—you know.

## Drumtaps

> Negro soldiers were peculiarly dependent on their white officers . . . None of the white regulars or Rough Riders showed the slightest sign of weakening; but under the strain the colored infantrymen began to get a little uneasy and drift to the rear.
>
> PRESIDENT THEODORE ROOSEVELT

> If I am correctly informed as to the history of the Spanish-American War, it is reported that if it had not been for the gallant and courageous action of the Tenth Regiment of Cavalry at the battle of San Juan we might not have the privilege of having in the White House that brave soldier and "square deal" and patriotic President of ours. As I understand, had it not been for the gallantry of the Tenth Regiment of Cavalry, a colored regiment, at that battle there might not have been a sufficient number of Rough Riders left to tell the tale.
>
> SENATOR NATHAN B. SCOTT

Blackman reasoned that if the war in Cuba was any portent of things to come, horses were on the way out. They were all right for the wide, sweeping plains, but useless in terrain that was essentially mountainous. Without loss of rank, he transferred to the 25th Infantry Regiment (Colored) while the 10th was being dispatched to the Philippines, Montauk and Winooski. He would be the regimental machine gun specialist, since the 10th had done so much work with the weapon, from the Gatling on. He gave little thought to the quick war, and even less to the Rough Riders and Colonel Roosevelt.

President Roosevelt studied the report before him; it offended him from start to finish. He bristled at it. He knew when he heard of the Brownsville raid he would act quickly and with the full force of his office. The gall of those men! It didn't matter that he'd fought with many of them in Cuba. He gnashed his teeth, crimping the edges of his walrus mustache. You had to watch those people, they were completely unpredictable, yes, like children, with the exception of one or two, like his good friend and leader of Negroes, Booker T. Washington.

The President read: "They appear to stand together in a determination to resist the detection of the guilty; therefore they should stand together when the penalty falls."

So wrote Inspector General of the Army, Brigadier General Ernest Garlington, who was respectfully recommending the discharge without honor of the soldiers of Companies B, C and D of the 25th Infantry Regiment (Colored). One hundred and sixty-seven men. Garlington was further recommending that they forever be barred from re-enlisting in the Army or Navy and from employment in the government in any civil service capacity.

The report went on: soldiers in one or more of the three companies had shot up the town, wounding one man and killing another. All civilian and military authorities were agreed that the soldiers must have fired into the city proper from inside Fort Brown on the night of August 13, 1906, yet not one single man

132

from any of the companies had stepped forward to confess or to reveal which others had done the deed, although repeatedly ordered to do so. They claimed they hadn't done it and therefore couldn't confess to something they hadn't done.

Now, why wouldn't one of them, just one of them come forward, tho President wondered angrily. By God, they have to learn to apprehend their own criminals if they ever expect to become the equal of the white man, of that there was absolutely no doubt. He glanced out at the White House lawn. It gave him a sense of order, of things set precisely and neatly. Yesterday he'd been in Pine Knot where he'd shot his first wild turkey. He'd had that same sense of order.

With Taft, Lodge and others, he'd already gone over the possible repercussions that might stem from his signing of the order, War Department Special Orders No. 266, that would discharge without honor one hundred and sixty-seven black men on the eve of Election Day, 1906. It would be wise, was the consensus, not to make the order public until the day after Election. The Negroes, strong supporters of the Republican party, would not then have the opportunity to bolt it on the basis of the incident at Brownsville. The soldiers *were* guilty; look at all the testimony against them. But some of the soldiers were even claiming that townspeople, not themselves, had done the shooting. Preposterous!

President Roosevelt mashed his lips. Six of the soldiers were holders of the Medal of Honor; thirteen had been cited for bravery in Cuba. Even so, a leopard didn't lose its spots; it was not impossible for brave men to be brutal marauders. He glanced at the long list of names: First Sergeant Mingo Sanders, Corporal Edward L. Daniels, Privates Ernest Allison, Elmer Brown, Ernest English, Thomas Taylor, Alfred N. Williams, James Bailey, William Harder—what good did it do to read them?

He turned his attention back to Garlington's notes: The 25th had been sent to Brownsville from Fort Niobrara, Nebraska, only two weeks before the incident. After it, the regiment was sent to Reno for quarantining. There was no evidence that the citizens of Brownsville, whites and Mexicans, had mistreated the soldiers because of their race, although Colonel Hoyt was noted to have had grave reservations about the problems that might arise from having some of his regiment in Texas at all. Gunfire had been heard from shortly before midnight until a little after midnight. Four of fifty-seven men from B Company had been absent at roll call; Garlington had interviewed only seven men from B, none from C or D. That was bad business, if there was going to be a Senate investigation, and there were rumors of such action.

Finally the President drew out the papers at the bottom of the stack and signed them. He leaned back. There was a storm a-coming, but he would be away, aboard the U.S.S. *Louisiana*, perhaps reading Milton, on the way to see how his Big Ditch was coming. Taft would have to take over. It was done.

Abraham Blackman would not believe it. He'd ridden down to Brownsville on the train, talking with his friend Mingo Sanders; it'd been Sanders who, while they were in Cuba, convinced Blackman to switch to the infantry. Blackman had returned to Fort Niobrara immediately after leaving Sanders with the 1st Battalion at Brownsville.

Now, at Fort Reno, he was talking to Sanders, an eye out for the guards of the 26th Infantry Regiment (White), assigned to watch over the 25th.

"Didn't do it," Sanders said.

Blackman was furious, at the Army, at Sanders; for the First Sergeant loved the Army, didn't know what he'd do once he was let out.

"Was the crackers did the shooting. Claimed a soldier'd tried to assault her, a woman named Evans ran a boarding house there. You know in the South that's all you got to do is holler rape and they can't find trees fast enough. Anyhow, an old man, old black man used to be a horse soldier, name of Wheeler lived there.

134

Now Abe, the Evanses wasn't no high-toned people, you understand; they was livin in the tenderloin makin it the best way they could. Wheeler said Miz Evans was leanin over her fence and some man—must've known her—came by, put his hand on her head, said 'Hello, pet,' and kept on going. That was all. The way I figure it, she maybe thought one of the neighbors or someone'd seen it and didn't want it to get back to her old man, that she'd been jolly with the man, so she started up the old rape thing, and the crackers got upset. No, we didn't shoot; they did. I never thought the Army'd do this, though, man. I never thought it."

"Well, what're you going to do, Ming?"

The First Sergeant raised his chin and said, "I'll knock on every door I can find clear up to the White House to get reinstated."

"After all this?"

"Yes, sir! The Army's my life. Why, man, my company shared our hardtack with President Roosevelt's men, June twenty-fifth, 1898. Never forget that date."

"It sure isn't going to do you any good to remember it, Ming," Blackman said sadly.

The dismissal order was read the next morning, mist rising, the sun hidden. From a distance Blackman watched the three companies, ringed by the whites of the 26th, hand over their rifles. Some of the soldiers had tears in their eyes and Blackman hoped they were tears of anger.


*Drumtaps*

In the same year, in France, where the Army of the United States would find itself within a dozen short years, Captain Alfred Dreyfus was promoted to major and exonerated of charges of treason that had been brought against him in 1894. This was thirteen years after Mingo Sanders enlisted.

# THREE

Recruited as fighting men, in ridicule; trained and mustered into Federal service, in more ridicule; sent to France as a safe political solution of a volcanic political problem; loaned to the French Army as another easy way out—these men had carried on. In patience and in fortitude these men had served. Their triumphs of battle had been great; but their triumphs of...personal and civic decency had been greater.

Captain Arthur Little
369th Infantry Regiment

# 11

Even in her shower Mimosa heard the big jets coming into the airfield and taking off. She pictured herself aboard one, in a seat next to Abraham, heading for San Francisco, back home where all the action was. For him it would only be leave, of course, for he was determined to stay in the Army; they'd have to kick him out to get rid of him. Or kill him, she thought, but frowned at the idea.

But it was an idea that kept coming back; there were so many black men in the Nam, so damned many, as if it'd been planned that way. Two, three years ago, the press couldn't get enough of the Black Soldier, and the letters from home had told her you couldn't watch a newsclip without seeing several Brothers up there doing their thing. Suddenly it was over, without a whisper, without a kiss-my-ass, like another plan: don't film them niggers no more. So there was no longer any mention of the Brothers being on the evening news or featured in the newspapers. She hated it and that led to her hatred of her job; this was her last hitch in the Foreign Service. She'd been a believer, and done her stint in Lagos and Leo (now they called it Kinshasa) and Tokyo and now here. Forget it. She'd had her share of exotic lovers, but there wasn't anything like the home-grown variety.

It talked and thought the way you did, and that was important. Maybe it was that after a while you just got tired.

Out of the shower now, she made another drink, opened the box of books and went through them. These, of course, he'd just give away, since his classes were over. Why, she wondered, didn't he like the term "class?" She closed the box and made herself some cheese and crackers.

Outside it was just starting to grow dark. Was he on the way? Was his plane even now touching down over there? She willed it, and watched his every move from the plane to a taxi, through the streets now starting to fill for pleasure, to her building. A sudden sense of helplessness overcame her. There was nothing she could do but wait; she was quite simply the expression of faith. So, she waited.

Far to the north, the helicopter came down at the C Company Base on the battalion perimeter. The aid station people were alerted. When the WO brought the craft down and cut the engines, he looked behind him. "How's he?"

Woodcock, in the process of helping to lift the stretcher down, merely nodded, then they were all out, carrying the Captain into the station. Belmont and Woodcock waited with him. Harrison, Griot, Antoine and Doctorow gathered themselves to report to Lieutenant Buck Himes who stood watching.

As soon as he got the report and told Whittman about it, he'd go over to the aid station. If Blackman was going to make it, they'd fly him out as soon as they'd patched him up. Himes felt especially bad since the Captain'd got hit while out with a squad from his platoon. Blackman's going out with the squads was a break for the platoon leaders and his routine didn't subvert the respect the men had for their lieutenants. It made them know who was the boss, that was all, and the respect they had for Blackman filtered down to his lieutenants. Charley Company had a good rep in the field, a fact Himes was sure had done

140

much to prevent a lot of shit from going on when Blackman was conducting his seminars.

Take Colonel Greer, in line for his first star. Old Army in the sense that there was a way to do things, certain gloves you wore to handle messy objects. Here Buck Himes paused to admit to himself that he, too, was looking for a star; it'd be another twenty-five years, but he had himself a patron in Colonel Greer. It'd been Himes who filled in the rumors for the Colonel—Captain Blackman was conducting seminars in black military history—he'd told the Colonel that Major Whittman was upset and then ran down the rivalry between them, a tale that had the Colonel grinning, his silver fillings showing.

Buck Himes had put it to the Colonel that there was nothing wrong in Blackman's telling his troops the *truth*, and as Himes went on he knew the Colonel himself hadn't known, and from here on out would take the time to study some black military history himself. Who knows, Himes'd said in so many words, you might turn out to have the answer the Army was looking for, given these times and the makeup of the troops.

What would he, Himes, do in his place? Nothing. Let Blackman give his troops the truth; this was real Black Power, real Army Power, and this gave them more than Panthers; this gave them body that related to the Army and it looked like the Army was going to have to depend on black people for a long time. Black soldiers, Buck Himes concluded, were as traditional as the Army itself.

And the Colonel had bought it. It was a solid piece of goods, black but solid, and Colonel Greer'd bought it and in so doing became Blackman's protector, immobilizing Whittman.

Buck Himes frowned when he took Harrison's report. He rushed from the CP to the aid station; shit. He'd just have to call the Colonel from there.

Colonel Greer was at dinner, but when his aide told him it was First Lieutenant Himes calling, he left the table to answer the call. "Oh," he said when Himes told him. "Oh." To himself he thought, Whittman knew there were people out in that sector that we never completely cleaned out, knew it all the way down the line. "Keep me posted, Himes. Check it out all the way to Base Hospital." The Colonel hung up slowly. Maybe Blackman was the only man who could've kept things cool around here, he thought.

It'd been the Colonel's plan, with an eye to his star, to recommend the establishment of black military history seminars for all personnel. Required. A part of basic training. Blackman would run it for officers out here. Yes, required for black and white. Now, what? One lung collapsed, and they didn't know about the leg yet. Goddamn that Whittman; he knew something had to happen out there. Bastard. He just went and fouled up all my plans. The tow-headed shithead. Who else could do it? Himes, of course, but he was going to behave anyhow. No, you needed someone like Blackman, with his battle record, efficiency reports, the respect of the men. He signaled for another martini. He sighed. Back in the old days it was a different Army; you didn't have to worry too much about these damn things.

## Blackman's Cadence

*It was in process long, long before Archduke Franz Ferdinand was shot. The slogans obscured all that. The war to end all wars. The war to make the world safe for democracy.*

*The war was laughable in a tragic way; the Europeans were fighting for very little in Europe. If that map changed again, no matter, it'd changed before, many, many times. For one decade the French held that portion, for the next two, the Germans. Or for a quarter of a century the Italians had it, or the French or the Austrians. The Poles held this for a while, then it became a possession of Prussia. Or that was Czech and this German; that Spanish, this Dutch.*

*And what of the Goths, Visigoths, Huns, Moors, Vandals, Romans, Greeks and others of relationship? No. Those people* were brothers in blood. They enjoyed their periodic wars, diffusing their languages and offspring. Such wars might've brought them a unity beyond their wildest dreams, but something happened; the stakes became greater than ever.

The eye scans the continent of Europe, falls easily, naturally, southward to the Mediterranean, then widens on the great land mass of Africa. There was where the wealth of Europe was coming from, would continue to come from for generations unimagined. The Belgians held a land area there seventy-five times larger than their homeland; Germany would've been lost in its territories in East and West Africa; the French dominated gigantic lands that stretched from the Gulf of Aden to the Atlantic; the Italians had footholds they hoped to extend. The British held everything adjacent to everyone else. These lands then, any of them larger than the nations that "owned" them, were the cause of the war. And what could Africa's people do about it? For four hundred and fifty years they had been decimated by the slave trade that initially provided European wealth, lifted it from its dark and middle ages. The African societies of family, law and religion smashed, the land then gave up its people, then gold, palm oil, diamonds, cocoa, coffee, ostrich feathers, amber, gum, spices, ivory; bauxite had been discovered, iron, oil, uranium. Who had the gold or diamonds could buy the oil to run the machines back home; who had the oil could get the gold and diamonds; who had the coffee and the peanuts and the cocoa could get some of the gold.

Take the debris of the classes of the French, Germans, British, Belgians, Italians, Dutch out of their centuries-old, stone-built towns; ship them to Africa to pioneer, build and breed and to make way for those who'd come later, bringing "civilization" to the Dark Continent. By God, what was the Ruhr Valley, Alsace or the Tyrol or the Corridor beside such a prize that lay gleaming in beneficent weather, filled to overflowing with a people God had designated through those close to Him to be drawers of water and hewers of wood?

143

*But why laughable?*

They think of Flanders' Fields, the cold, gray, damp region between the North Sea and the Scheldt, and they think of poppies nourished by the blood of thousands upon thousands of soldiers, all white. But they came after; they were the second layer of blood and bodies that nourished the poppies. Even now their uncollated bones form a hill that blots out the sun as they await collection for the ossuaries. And there are other bones.

Hushed, hushed is the record of the Africans who came when the French begged for them, who sent Blaise Diagne to get them, and they came, almost a third of a million, with their witch doctors, and marched night and day through strange, narrow streets with slick cobblestones, and stared at the villagers who leaned out of their windows staring at them, and not really caring who saved France just as long as it was saved. So the villagers croaked "Vive la France!" and waved the tricolor, and the Africans didn't understand, but marched on, far from their hibiscus and flamboyants and their exploding sunrises and purple sunsets. They marched against unending rows of polished, well-oiled, perfectly aimed German artillery, shivering with the un-accustomed cold; then they broke into a pell-mell charge and hurled themselves at the hungry lances of flame out there on the horizon; they charged machine gun nests fearlessly, believing they couldn't die because the medicine men had told them so; not unlike white soldiers who had their own witch doctors, men who carried books with crosses stamped on them and vials of water and wore funny collars. But the Africans were pulverized, smashed, pounded, body fragment by body fragment into the earth of Flanders, before Douaumont, before Verdun. But they tripped up the German advance and before it could regain its feet the white boys mustered in their blue suits to take the field as they had fifty years before, shouting "Attack! Attack! Attack!"—with élan.

Back in Africa itself, black men fought other black men, all led by whites who spoke German, English, French, Italian and Afrikaans.

*Sing no songs then of safety and democracy and humanitarianism; tell me no crude poems of Kaiser Wilhelm, of German militarism, of Hunnish atrocities; dance no dances about Verdun; read me no dispatches of the defeat of the hellish Uhlans. I know you all.*
*Sing me instead, a paean of blackness.*

They disembarked at Des Moines in July 1917. This was to be a breakthrough; up till now you could count the number of the Army's black officers on one hand, first among them, Colonel Young. He'd been a major during the Mexican Expedition, and a hero, Abraham Blackman recalled, and should have been a general by now. They'd managed to find him physically unfit for further military service rather than give him his star. To prove himself fit, Young had ridden from Ohio to Washington on horseback, through hundreds of hamlets, towns and villages; there must've been, Blackman estimated, thousands of people who'd never seen a black soldier, let alone a black colonel.

Now Blackman formed up his detachment and marched it to quarters, thinking that he wasn't sure he was going to like this officers' training business, even though the time for it had come. Some of the men marching were from the 9th, 10th, 24th, and 25th; some were draftees, still others from the black colleges. Some would be commissioned captains, first lieutenants or second lieutenants.

Blackman felt sad when he considered that in the realignment of the Army, a new division of blacks, the 92nd, had already been given the nickname, the Buffaloes. That division, however, was still on paper, but would be accompanied by another, the 93rd.

Looking around the barracks Blackman told himself that if he couldn't stand still for the less than three months of training here, he ought to quit the Army. He had no doubt that he'd be commissioned a captain, judging from certain lacks he'd observed in the others. There were to be 1250 officers; that is, they'd been led to believe that every man now enrolled in the school was practically an officer.

The first week Blackman discovered it might not be as easy as that. A machine gun specialist, he was assigned to an artillery course. He went at once to the assignment officer, Lieutenant Gahagan, a dandy little officer who couldn't wait to get to Europe.

He studied Blackman's assignment slip and handed it back. "What's wrong with artillery?"

"Sir, you know my record. I'm in machine guns. I don't know anything about artillery. My value to the Army is in machine guns."

"Well, hell, Sergeant Major, no one else's complained about his assignment. It's rear duty, you know." He winked. "You just stand back there twirling wheels and reading numbers and throwing shells into the breech. Nothing to it."

For a moment it was clear to Blackman that none of the assignments were worth a damn; that all of them would wind up in the Services of Supply, not in combat. He said, "I wouldn't want our own men to be in front of me when I start spinning and reading, Lieutenant. I just don't have any background and I don't think two and a half months here is going to give it to me. Now the machine guns—"

Damn these sergeant majors, Gahagan thought. They think their shit don't stink. He studied Blackman. This was the first black sergeant major he'd ever seen, although he knew they existed. "C'mon, Blackman. Don't be a troublemaker. The Army's trying to do something good for you people. You've got your assignment. Carry it out."

"Sir," Blackman persisted. "It's just that I think there's been a mistake and—"

Wearily, with that patronizing patience some whites have for blacks who don't understand how it goes, Gahagan said, "Sergeant Major, the Army doesn't make mistakes; it just doesn't make mistakes. Now, that's all." Mistake, huh, Gahagan thought that sonofabitch is a mistake.

Blackman agreed that the Army didn't make mistakes—unless

146

it wished to—and he arrived at this conclusion within a few days. He showed little interest in his classes, although he tried, but it was clear that the artillery instructors were not there to teach them very much. "This is our 75-millimeter cannon, this is our new 155-millimeter job. They work like this, the range is that; they fire this many rounds a minute—or should—if you don't fall asleep or run off to get laid—or stop to take a little snort. . . ."

Some of the candidates were already sporting riding crops and posing the way they'd seen the white officers do it. Blackman shook his head. Something was going to happen, had to happen. At the end of the first two weeks some of the candidates were leaving and by August, just barely a thousand men remained.

August was also the month of the Houston riot with black soldiers of the 25th Infantry Regiment killing fifteen whites and wounding twelve others. In the barracks at Des Moines there was both pride and fear. Certainly Houston was not a Brownsville; the white man really got what he asked for at Houston. But how would that affect them?

*Thirteen,* Blackman thought. He followed the news of Houston carefully. Thirteen soldiers were charged with murder, no question of self-defense? And they *would* be convicted at their trial and they *would* be hung, and we'll just go right along, pretending it has nothing to do with us, that we'll escape it because, now we're going to become officers; it'll be different for us.

And it was strange, the arguments he heard. "The boys from the 24th knew where they were, knew the rules and shouldn't have let themselves get upset about the situation. They did, now they got to pay the penalty."

Or, "Maybe they was just layin for the white man. An that's premeditated murder. Oh, I know the man ain't shit, but . . ."

"Blackman, you'd best forget Houston and stop talkin so much about it. Ain't nothin we can do about; wasn't nothin we could do before. Let sleepin dogs lie, man. You'll talk yourself into trouble."

147

And he knew it as well as he knew his name, but he couldn't stop. There was a war on, a big one. The Army owed justice at least to its men. What Army officer was unaware of the prejudice that existed and was honored above all else in the South? Putting black soldiers in places like that was like throwing kittens to sharks. Couldn't these candidates, now being out from classes like the leaves from trees in the first high wind, see that, if justice didn't prevail for the 108 men in Houston, the thirteen condemned, the others headed for life imprisonment or long sentences, they were not immune?

"It's unfortunate what happened at Houston," one of the instructors said to his class that he'd found much too quiet. His eyes came to rest on Blackman. "Some gossip undoubtedly got the whole thing started, some troublemaker. Don't listen to em. There's one in every barracks. You don't believe for a single minute, do you, that the Army would deliberately and maliciously set out to railroad 108 men; you can't believe that. The Army's not like that. It's a great organization, the finest of its kind in the world, and we'll soon prove that. What you men must remember is that colored soldiers and Army units exist because of the good will of white people. White people let you in the Army, allowed you here for officers' training, and they can break any black man or division when he or it becomes a troublemaker. You'll do well to remember that."

Blackman felt his classmates moving away from him, not physically as much as spiritually. Gold bars; they didn't want to jeopardize their own chances to get them by appearing to side with him. Now here they sat, each one hoping he'd complete the course and automatically be out of the reach of the mobs and the ropes. So, he waited for something to happen. It always did.

He knew it was happening the week his instructors began to jump on him about his work; he was shocked not so much because they were, but because they'd taken so long to get to it. His work hadn't been much, but then he also knew it didn't

148

have to be. One candidate in his heavy artillery course was passing along well, simply because he sang and danced at the officers' parties.

One day, pondering all these things, wondering where he'd be sent, he left class, unmindful of the heavy rain. He plunged into it, water clinging to his face, sliding in minute rivulets down into his mouth. He found himself mentally calling cadence as he went, and he tried to break step, slipped and crashed into a passing officer, his two hundred pounds catching little First Lieutenant John Gahagan flush in the ribs and sending him skidding along the walk on his back.

Good, thought Blackman as he scrambled to help Gahagan up. "Sorry, sir. I didn't see you."

Gahagan rejected the hand, jumped to his feet and wiped uselessly at his uniform. "You big, clumsy sonofabitch, look at this!"

Blackman, at attention, said, "Yes, sir. I'm sorry—"

"Report to my office on the double, Blackman. On the GODDAMN DOUBLE, do you hear me?"

"Yes, sir."

Beyond Gahagan, a woman stood watching, her arms wrapped around books, and Blackman wondered who she was, wanted to see her up close and talk to her. You didn't see too many black women in Des Moines, not over this way. He took a final look at her, then spun and walked rapidly toward Gahagan's office, as Gahagan, still shaking the water from his cap, followed.

In Gahagan's office, the officer said, "Blackman, you're not going to make it through this school. You deliberately knocked me down. Furthermore, you've been inciting the men over that Houston business."

Blackman stared at a point above and beyond Gahagan's right shoulder.

"We're going to arrange a transfer out of Des Moines as soon as possible. Ship you out with that Illinois or biggety New York

149

outfit. They're going over first to sweep off the docks in France so white men can fight."

Kiss my ass, Blackman thought. And then, That's that.

The rain had stopped when he got back outside; she was waiting under a tree and she smiled when he approached. "I saw it all," she said, "and if he brings charges, I'll be a witness for you. The soldiers're always complaining about how they're treated, so we've formed a kind of civilian committee to deal with the officers."

She started walking and he fell in beside her. "My name's Mimosa Rogers, and I live here and go to school here at Drake. One of the special, good darkies, you know?"

"I'm Abraham Blackman, and I'm not going to be around here much longer."

"Because you knocked that white man down by accident?"

"That and other things."

"But that's not fair!"

He said, "Maybe not, but that's the Army, and I don't really mind."

"That means you won't get your bars, doesn't it?"

"That's right, no bars."

She said, "Can't you quit when your time is up or something like that?"

"Oh, sure. But when that time comes, for some reason or other a lot of men change their minds and stay in. They start complaining a few days later all over again."

They'd walked clear across the city and were now in the black neighborhood. Great chestnut, elm and maple trees shaded the streets. Kids walked on homemade stilts, shouting with every giant step.

"Hi, Miss Rogers!" they called out and she waved and called their names.

"Well, this is where I live."

The little cottage was all white, trimmed with green. Comfortable chairs were on the porch, all facing the street and

Blackman pictured these streets at dusk, the men returning from work, clutching their battered lunch boxes; the women rocking from side to side down the last mile from their kitchens, feet aching, arms sore from washing and ironing. Dinner would be quick, perhaps leftovers, and they'd all retire to their porches to sit and rock and exchange the news of the day, pausing to hail the occasional passer-by out strolling in a clean shirt and trousers, perhaps smoking a pipe, and perhaps with some loving mongrel hound tic-clitting on the walk beside him. If not a dog, then a child or children hurrying to match the adult pace which would ultimately bring them to Doc Horton's drug store around the corner where they'd be treated to ices.

Blackman felt sharply that he wanted to be a part of it and he murmured, "It's nice, very nice." Just as softly he said, "We're having a dance Saturday night. Will you come with me?"

"That'd be fun," she said.

He wanted to hold her close for belonging to all this, this calmness, this sanity and purpose, but he just looked at her, deeply, and took her hand and held it for a moment, satisfied that her fingers closed tightly on his.

All that week the files were ransacked, Abraham Blackman's record checked and double-checked for previous trouble or hints that he would make additional trouble, with the examiners knowing full well that a single incident would be quite enough to taint his record for as long as he remained in the Army. They looked for avenues to a discharge, dishonorable, if possible, but they were denied. Typewriters clicked and clacked during the night; telephones rang, signaling the start of conversations across half the nation; telegraph wires hummed.

Blackman was praised as a man worthy enough to fit into the ranks of the 369th Infantry Regiment, the New York 15th National Guard, which the top people knew was one of the first, if not the first, unit to go overseas, but in the Services of Supply. They found the record unblemished. Then why the transfer? Doesn't want to be an officer; some enlisted men are like that, you know. Itching to get into the fight over there. He's a good man. He'll be a credit to the 369th, okay?

Okay.

Mimosa Rogers dressed slowly and carefully. She'd had her bath, a long soaking and an even more careful washing, powdering and scenting. She thought his name: Abraham. A man you trust. Kind. Like a father? No, she thought; she liked him too much for that. But he was a soldier, after all, and soldiers were here today and gone tomorrow, and now that America was in it, since April, they'd all be going over very soon, even the black ones. She paused. Maybe *especially* the colored soldiers.

She'd never been to one of the dances at the camp. She'd been asked a few times, by older soldiers, men whose mouths glittered with gold and who you knew at once to be slicker than greased watermelons. And you didn't go out with men anyway whose language was so atrocious; what would the neighbors think? Some of them. Others were eager for their daughters to meet and marry soldiers. Soldiering was one job that offered security for a black man, no matter how bad being in the Army might be. Negroes and security, the killing search. She humphed as she slid into her dress.

Mimosa knew something about soldiers and their women. There were more black soldiers than black women to go around, but there were many of those great, cow-smelling blonde farm girls who, once the barn lights were out, didn't have to think twice about being done by a black man, and their fathers, brothers and cousins couldn't do anything about, except to try to whip the soldiers when they could.

She was fully dressed and stood before her mirror, checking her appearance, but what she was really thinking was, He's going to do me. She wondered how it would be and where, for there weren't any places that she knew about. But, she'd put on a dark dress; country people didn't wear much white, perhaps because they were so close to the earth. Real close to it. She heard voices low on the front porch and then the screen door slammed. Her mother came rapidly up the stairs and knocked on her door. "Honey?"

Mimosa smiled at herself, her head bent now to slip in her second earring. "Yes, Mother?"

"You've got a caller, dear, your soldier."

Mimosa liked the formality that at times existed between them. "Come in, Mother." The door opened and Mrs. Rogers, a thin woman with sticks for legs, entered and stopped and clasped her hands together and rocked back. "My, how *nice* you look, honey."

"Do I?" Mimosa spun around looking at herself, pretending it was the first time she'd done it.

"He must be something special with all those stripes, Mimosa."

"Umm," she answered. Mother was always digging for information. "I guess I'm ready," she said, pulling on her gloves and taking her bag. He mother hovered at her shoulder as they went down the stairs.

"Mighty handsome couple," she kept repeating, and when they were down on the porch, she sidled near her husband who sat, bald and gray, in a rocker.

"This here feller look to me like he kin take care hisself with them Huns, Mamie. I done tol him I wouldn't want t be in their shoes when he git over there."

"No indeedy," Mrs. Rogers said.

"Hello," Blackman said to Mimosa. She's a knockout! he said to himself.

"Hello, Abraham."

"You look nice," he said.

"Thank you."

"Ready?"

"Yall have a good time, now, hear?" Mrs. Rogers said, as brightly as she could. She sensed something and she didn't want it to hurt her daughter or to bring shame on the family. She leaned over the railing and said to Blackman, "You take good care our daughter, Mr. Blackman, hear?"

"Yes, ma'am," he said, and smiled to Mimosa.

They walked through the tunnel of trees, the razor-sharp creases in Blackman's uniform popping as he went. Some of the men had started to use a little starch when they laundered their summer uniforms, and the white soldiers were still trying to find out how the blacks managed to keep their suits so neat, so clean, for so long. Mimosa's hand rested lightly upon his arm and he knew that in the shadows of the porches, the Negroes were watching them pass. Once when the murmur of voices in those shadows rose up when they were not quite out of earshot, Mimosa laughed and Blackman chuckled; the people were wondering where she'd got him.

They breathed deeply of the Saturday night smells: the fish caught that afternoon in the rivers, frying in spitting lard, cooking deep, soft and sweet in their coating of flour and cornmeal; the pork chops also dipped in flour, also restless in spitting hot lard; the greens simmering in fatback, the cornmeal and hoecake bread, the fried potatoes with onions. . . .

"Um," Blackman said. "Sure smells good."

She had searched him quickly and thoroughly with her eyes; there was no telltale bulge of a bottle of liquor. She wouldn't have minded drinking liquor with Abraham.

"What's a *barbacoa?*" she asked him. There would be a *barbacoa* at the dance, he'd told her.

They were almost out the neighborhood now. He said, "It's something the Mexicans did; still do, I guess. They take a cow, or pig, what's handy, split and roast it over an open fire—"

"With seasoning, I hope," she cut in.

"Oh, sure. All those cooks, each with his own secrets, and they get together and one'll try to outdo the other, and we're just watching and waiting for them to get through. Nothing like that *barbacoa.*"

They entered the white section warily. They breathed easier

154

when they were upon busier streets, and arrived finally at the drill hall.

Later, full, the barbecue over, they watched a small group of musicians tuning up on the bandstand. "We were lucky," Blackman said. He'd been bending close to her all evening, enjoying the eyes upon him that read: Damn, old Blackman been runnin around here all by hisself, ain't saying nuthin but things to git him in trouble, an all the time that's what he got stashed back somewhere. "Lucky," he said, "because they're from New Orleans, a real jass band."

A jass band! Mimosa thought. Her mother would fall out. She didn't like dancing music, hated cards, roared at the thought of anyone playing dice. The cornet player puffed his lips and played some notes. The man with the clarinet, long and thin like his instrument, grinned a golden grin. From their vantage point, Mimosa could see the women come in with their soldiers. She knew some of them, like the lead soprano in the church choir, four women said to operate out of Miss Jenkins' sporting house," and two or three of those quiet little girls, still in their teens who, she knew, talked endlessly about men and boys on their way to school and back, and who'd better be home by ten, which was a half-hour's grace period, if they could think up a lie good enough to get past their fathers.

The hall filled with music, now, the driving, relentless banjo, the cornet with its tiny, silvered notes, the clarinet with its bird-like peepings, and the restless piano. Blackman and Mimosa found themselves tapping their feet and smiling at each other, and soon, all the soldiers were dancing. Occasionally a soldier, riddled with the goodness of the sound, broke back from his partner, contrived some steps in time and broke back in, grinning. Hey! Did you see me!

Mimosa itched for Blackman to lead her to the floor; she was confident that once there, she could do something that wouldn't leave him ashamed. She'd rarely heard music that made her know she could dance to it.

Blackman didn't mind not dancing. His number twelves were rapping the floor solidly. It was enough that a real jass band was here instead of the usual Army band. They played jass that sounded like a march, whatever they did. After each number the soldiers clapped and cheered, and the musicians in their faded tuxedos grinned back.

A sudden nervousness came upon Mimosa when she noticed that all the quiet little girls had vanished; the women from Miss Jenkins' were gone, too, and four soldiers with them, she guessed. The officers and their wives were emptying the grandstand and soldiers were drifting outside. Even as she was noticing all this, the band struck up "Good Night, Ladies." The time's come, Mimosa thought.

The night air was cool. She tried not to look at Blackman as they moved, hand in hand, away from the drill hall. "Shortcut," she heard him say and heard herself say, "All right."

They stayed, however, on the camp grounds, veering this way in the shadow of buildings or that way around them. She heard keys in his hands, then they were around the corner of another building, at the door and inside.

They stood wordless for a moment and then Blackman said, "I'm a sergeant major. I get a little space all to myself a couple of days a week when I don't have to be in the barracks."

"Oh," she said, nodding, feeling a tightening in her throat. It was going to be all right then. She needn't worry about her mother snooping through her room on Monday while she was at classes to see if she could find grass stains on her clothes. A terrible way to live for someone over twenty-one.

She felt him near and raised her face. They kissed and were breathing heavily when they parted. She wanted to tell him how comfortable she felt with him, but said nothing, undressed jerkily, her back to him, and when she heard him on the cot, she turned and went to him. His huge hands went over her, like a blind man's feeling a face, for the goodness in it, and she could feel herself go wet just that quickly. She pressed her pelvis to him, tugged at his body until at last, he rose up and she slid under, feeling a hand that might have been waved in a lingering greeting, stroking not the air, but her, and she pulled him forward, felt him pause, and then it came, hard and sure and she thought, He's in me! In me! and she had her first orgasm through which she felt him stroking and kissing until she became aware of him again, sharply, and then fell into his rhythm of slow, insinuating movements, and she came again, tearing away from his lips in panic, afraid she was unable to ever again take in a breath of air, and not finishing that because his hand, holding her chin, brought her mouth back to his. She felt him now stroking deeply, striding longer and longer, curving up under things, touching places not ever touched before, and her legs began to tremble as she shoved her pelvis at him so he could stroke deeper still. He drew back with a sigh and eased forward until he could go no more. She knew he had one foot on the floor and that that leg was now beginning to tremble as he strained, slipped to the other knee for more leverage, felt his hands pulling at her buttocks for more, and then he came. She, with another high-pitched Oh! came with him and they lay panting, the sweat collecting between her breasts.

There was no moon, but the stars were out. The night filled him with apprehension. Perhaps he was thinking of Houston. His arm around Mimosa's waist, they walked back. He was glad when he deposited her safely on the porch; he would visit on Tuesday, if all went well.

It did not. On Monday his transfer came through. He was restricted to camp until Tuesday morning when he left to join the 369th Infantry Regiment in the East. When he asked if he'd be working with machine guns then, Gahagan answered: "If you can make a machine gun out of a broomstick, then, yes." Blackman posted a letter to Mimosa and took the train.

*Drumtaps*

It is perhaps not generally known that indirect Machine Gun fire originated and was developed in the Machine Gun Platoon of the Tenth Cavalry. This work of the Tenth Cav-

157

alry platoon was discussed in Europe and printed in service journals from England to Australia. . . . There are methods of fire to this day known only by a few of the old Tenth Cavalrymen. . . ."

G. J. ODEN
Captain, 10th Cavalry

# 12

"You don't live in no Des Moines," he seemed to be saying to her, although she appeared to be far away from him. "Don't nobody live in a place with a name like that. Isn't that the place the advertising guys're always talking about, 'will they like it in—'"

"That's Dubuque, Abraham, not Des Moines."

And they both laughed heartily down a long corridor, in no hurry to reach the light at the end of it.

Blackman crowded up to the bow with the others. "There it is, man, France," someone said to nobody. The wind racing from the sea stung Blackman's eyes and made them water, and he thought, Yeah, there it is. Behind him, some of the men broke out in song: "Over There." The words were caught by the wind and hurled into the sea; Blackman only caught snatches: "For the Yanks are coming, the Yanks are coming. . . ." He gazed, wet-eyed at the shore, the line of warehouses and now coming into view, roads, houses, and he turned to go back to the hold, feeling a fluttering in his stomach. There had been wars before and there would be wars again, but he'd arrived at this one where everything imaginable was being used to kill and maim. They were *not* fooling around over here; these white folks meant business.

The French officials waited inside the warm dockside offices at Brest. It was December 27, 1917, and an entire shipload of American fighting men had arrived. By spring, when the Germans would surely launch another offensive, these men would be ready. The ship was being pushed into the docks by tugboats. The officials looked appreciatively at the black faces that ringed the rails of the ship. Black, but no matter; they had used black troops quite effectively before. In fact, it was a matter of policy to use colonial troops, for attack only. They spewed out across no man's land with knives, spears and guns in hand, jabbering in their many dialects and languages to carry the attack to the Germans whose experiences with the blacks had been so limited as to be tinged with an unreasonable fear of the unknown.

A French Army band stood bravely in the stiff winds that swept off the bay, waiting for the Americans to come down the gangway. They would see, the Americans, that the French spirit was still vigorous, still fired with élan. But God, it was good to see the Americans coming. France was bleeding badly. Almost every single family had a battle casualty. Now there might be an end to it. The officials waved forward the committee with the late Christmas tidings, and, faintly, they could hear the calls aboard ship, now being moored and the gangways lowered. The black troops started down, carrying their equipment on their shoulders. The people on the dock began to clap; the band broke into another, stirring, rapid-paced tune, and the officials, smiling, stepped out of the warm offices and lined up. Even the black Americans, they thought, are big, bigger than our black troops. Look at them! What could stand against them? Their smiles broadened.

Cable P 454-S
Details Concerning Priority Schedule
Headquarters, A.E.F.
Chaumont, Haute-Marne
Jan. 6, 1918

With regard to 4 colored regiments referred to in Adjutant General's confidential letters of Nov. 28 and Nov. 30, of which one regiment at about two-thirds strength is already here, and three regiments are to be shipped as stated in your cablegram 553, these regiments will serve as infantry pioneers. . . .

PERSHING

The French generals recoiled from the cable, each searching his mind for details he might previously have overlooked, each, for the moment, giving the Americans the benefit of the doubt, but, finally, one general leaped to his feet shouting. "But what do they mean, 'pioneer!'" The other generals waited, sure that this one was voicing quite perfectly all they felt. "'Pioneer'—isn't that some word? They mean labor regiments!" he snarled. "Ah, these Americans. Don't they understand the situation here? Our backs are still wet from almost being pushed into the Marne, and we may be back there again, or even in the Atlantic. Do they have to continue playing that stupid black-and-white game? No! In times like these, let the blacks cover themselves with glory! Let them wallow in it, gorge themselves with it. Let them fight, let them fight. Damn them! Pershing must be made to understand that they must not play their silly games *here!* Not *now!*"

"Let's go to Pétain," another general suggested, "and if necessary to Foch. After all, we know what's needed, where and how soon and how much. The Fourth Army badly needs replacements and the Red Hand Division won't be functional until its losses have been replaced. I say, let's not waste time arguing with Pershing; let's go right to Pétain."

## Drumtaps

> Colored troops (four regiments): General Pétain asks for information as to their value. General Pershing replies that he is fairly sure of the value of two of the regiments (those of Illinois and New York), these regiments having served a long time on the Mexican border. However, it must be taken into account that they include a large proportion of recruits incorporated last September. The large majority of the officers are white, the non-commissioned officers are colored. He does not have exact information on the other two regiments, but will send it shortly. Incidentally, General Pershing expresses the idea of announcing in the press the entry of American troops into sector. He is also adamant that these troops not serve with the French because of the language difficulty.
>
> *Les Armées Françaises*, Tome III, Vol. 1
> Report of Conversations of Jan. 11, 1918
> between General Pétain and General Pershing

Unaware of the generals, the 369th finished a series of parades and drills to Lieutenant Jim Europe's military band, already compared to the British Grenadiers, the Garde Républicaine and the Royal Italian bands, and was assigned, as part of the Provisional 93rd Division to the 16th Division, VIII Army Corps, Fourth French Army. The French generals had won their argument.

Blackman watched the morale of his company zoom from nothing up to excellent. It was being with the French Army, he knew, and the French people. The farmers gave them wine when they had it, and food; the girls smiled at them, and the soldiers always greeted them warmly. One big, happy family now, Blackman thought. They really mean liberty, equality, fraternity. Let's see how long it lasts.

Still, he marveled at his men who all their lives had lived under the shadow of racism so blatant that none escaped. Now he found them suddenly blossoming in this French winter of 1917–18, as though it were the end of spring, summer hotly on the way. They were so grateful for the kindnesses, as little as they were, and the barest civilities, that they would charge any number of German machine guns, go on the double a thousand miles to find Big Bertha and smash her. For just the average human expenditure of kindness, the French had won themselves friends for life.

His company hurled themselves into training with a will that both pleased and disturbed Blackman. They were mortal, and there was no need of them behaving as though they couldn't be killed, just because the French liked them. He wondered if other black men in other wars had displayed as much will; he supposed so.

"God damn, les go!" screamed one company.

"Les go Goddamn!" another answered, and Blackman, caught up in the battle chant, shouted, "Again!"

He smiled. It was good being out with them. Fuck that administrative bullshit. The French didn't have time for that. Damn, they're sure looking good, he thought, goddamn good.

Some distance behind him the French officers watched. General Le Gallais nodded and smiled to the others. "They have good spirit!"

"But," whispered one of his aides, "they aren't a division. They have no artillery, engineers, trains or rolling stock. General, they have nothing but themselves!"

"Even in numbers they aren't complete, sir," another aide ventured. "Colonel Hayward is a very charming man, talented and dedicated to his men—"

"That counts for a lot," Le Gallais said, unperturbed. What

163

a huge man he is, he thought, watching the sergeant major putting several squads through drill.

"—but, sir," a third aide said. "They didn't even give them rifles! We've had to provide them. . . ."

"Thank the Almighty that we've Lebels aplenty, then," Le Gallais said, and behind his back the aides looked at each other and shrugged their shoulders.

It was a pleasure at the end of the day to get away from all that French jabbering, Blackman thought, and settle in with the guys at night. Damn! French maneuvers, French weapons and the French language. Too much. They were all right; they shared their wine and cognac and sometimes what they called food, but they didn't have the bounce, the sheer joy of life the black boys had, all in all. They always bounced back. He pulled off his tunic and flopped on his cot. The barracks were dark and the voices pitched low. He had a good company, he reflected, and a good company commander, First Lieutenant Woodcock, and good men all the way down the line. Company C, but damned if this was Charley's company. This is Blackman's company, he thought with pride. He raised up on one elbow and called out:

"Hey, Richa'd, Richa'd—"

"Sergeant Major?" the voice came back.

Richard Boston was the company's raconteur, a bright-eyed slender ex-dining car waiter. "Do *Shine* for us, man. I can't get to sleep unless you do *Shine.*"

In the darkened barracks the voices rose in unison, urging Boston to do it.

And Richard Boston, years on the New York–Chicago run, forever, or almost, taking orders from whites, his life until the Army, measured by the three-foot aisle between tables and flashes of South Bend, Englewood, Syracuse, Albany and the Hudson River, and women picked up on the train or found at overnight stops, basked in the attention of his comrades, discovered that even away from the reek of food and starched linen, he had

164

a life perhaps fuller than ever, and he said, "Okay, quiet, and keep quiet." A private, he took orders, but when it was time to do *Shine*, he gave them. He took a deep breath and began the poem:

*It was a helluva day in the merry month of May*
*When the great Titanic was sailing away.*
*The capn and his daughter were there, too,*
*And old black Shine looked like the only crew.*
*Shine was below chompin his peas*
*When the goddamn water come up to his knees.*
*He say, "Capn, O capn, I was chompin my peas*
*When the goddamn water come up to my fuckin knees."*
*He said, "Shine, Shine, get your blue-black ass down,*
*I got ninety-nine pumps to get the water back down."*
*Shine went below, but was lookin at space,*
*An that's when the water come up to his waist.*
*He said, "Capn, capn, I was lookin at space*
*When the goddamn water come up to my waist."*
*Capn said, "Shine, Shine, get your rusty ass down*
*I got a hundred pumps to get the water back down."*
*Shine went back down an ate him some bread.*
*That's when the water come over his goddamn head.*
*He said, "Capn, capn, I was chewin my bread*
*When the sonabitchin water come up over my head."*
*Capn said, "Shine, Shine, get your funky ass down,*
*Got me two hundred pumps to get the water back down."*
*But Shine hopped on the rail, all ready to dive.*
*Ol capn say, "Shine, my man, you keep me alive."*
*Say, "Shine, Shine, save poor me,*
*You'll get more money than any black man can see."*
*Shine say, "Money is good on land or on sea,*
*Take off your fuckin shirt and swim like me."*
*Ol capn's daughter rushed up on the deck,*
*Offerin pussy, her drawers round her neck.*
*Say, "Shine, Shine, baby save poor lil me,*

165

*I'll give you more pussy than a nigger can see."*
*Shine say, "Bitch, pussy ain't nothin but meat on a bone,*
*Baby, you can fuck it or suck it or leave it alone.*
*Now I like cheese, but I ain't no rat,*
*I sure likes pussy, but not like that."*
*Shine jumped in the water and met a whale,*
*And he showed that fish his swimminest tail.*
*Tired ol whale say, "Shine, Shine, you swim just fine,*
*But you miss one stroke and your black ass is mine."*
*Shine say, "You may be king of the ocean and king of the sea,*
*But you got to be a swimmin motherfucker to outswim me."*
*And Shine swam on.*
*When the news got to port, the great* Titanic *had sunk,*
*Old Shine was already back in Harlem, damned near drunk.*

Laughter rolled from one end of the barracks to the other. There were calls: "Do it again, Richa'd." "Hey, Richa'd, once more, man."

Boston lay laughing quietly to himself. "No more," he called out. "Ima start chargin for these performances."

Once in a while a laugh broke out as someone recalled Boston's inflection, or a line, and it would initiate another flurry of laughter and "Oh, gods."

Blackman's stomach muscles ached from laughing. Now the laughter was all gone and he closed his eyes. Some time tomorrow they'd be moving to Condé-en-Barrois, wherever that was, but it was all right because this was some company, man. He drifted off to a sound sleep.

Oh, this fucking Lebel, Blackman thought, and these Chauchats. This *rifle* especially! No wonder the French always talking about steel, cause the goddamn thing don't hold but so many bullets. Let's see: one in the chamber, three in the magazine? Or one in the chamber and two in the magazine? Let's see here.

But the divisional consensus was, if the French can fight with these weapons, so could they; if French wore those funny blue helmets, so could they.

This feeling for the French had come, Blackman knew, when the French scorned *Order Number 40.* The last thing the French were worried about was black men getting French pussy; if they didn't win the war, there'd be none for anybody. Maybe, he thought, this division was special. It didn't look as if it'd been torn apart at Verdun. Must be some real bad jokers in this outfit.

"Hey, Blackman, dogfight!" He scrambled up from his desk and ran outside, craning his head up toward the sky where the two planes were, looping and spinning, the French plane tailing the German. He wondered if the Frenchman was Paul Belmont; they'd heard about him, but not seen him.

Belmont took off his shoes and socks and wiggled his toes. He glanced over to where Woodcock had fallen asleep against a crate marked MEDICAL SUPPLIES. Digging into a pocket, Belmont brought out a candy bar, peeled it and chewed it reflectively. When he was finished, he lit a cigarette and reached into another pocket, extracting an envelope, and from that a yellowed clipping pasted to smudged typing paper. At the top of the clipping, he read, perhaps for the millionth time:

PAUL BELMONT, EX-PILOT, DEAD;
AMERICAN FLEW FOR FRENCH IN '18.

Belmont's own handwriting was at the bottom margin of the clipping: "N.Y. Times, Oct. 14, 1961."

The aid station's generator surrounded him with noise but he heard the muted voices of the doctors and medics inside the tent. He wondered about Captain Blackman; he wanted him to be okay. If hurt, just slightly, not killed. He saw one man, a doctor, he presumed, walking wearily from the tent, and started to call out to him, but he was suddenly afraid. He started to read the clipping:

167

Paul Pierre Belmont of 80 East 116th Street, a Negro flier who was honored by France for his service in World War I, died Thursday in Metropolitan Hospital. His age was 67.

Mr. Belmont, a Negro, . . .

They already said that, Belmont thought hotly, perhaps for the millionth time.

was born in Columbus, Ga.

He ran away from home as a boy and went to Scotland as a stowaway.

He became a welter-weight prizefighter and boxed in England, France and North Africa.

When World War I began, Mr. Belmont enlisted in the French Foreign Legion. He suffered the first of four war wounds at Verdun. While convalescing he transferred to the French Flying Corps. Piloting scout and fighter planes, he took part in many air battles.

Between wars, Mr. Belmont was a band leader at Zelli's Zig Zag Bar in Montmartre, Paris, and then operated his own night clubs, Le Grand Duc in the Rue Pigalle and L'Escadrille in the Rue Fontaine. He also ran a gymnasium for prizefighters.

In World War II Mr. Belmont was a spy in night clubs for the French underground working with the renowned Cleopatre Terrier. While serving with the French Army, he was wounded severely at Orleans. Americans helped to smuggle him out of France, when the Germans took over the country, and eventually he returned to the United States.

In 1954 Mr. Belmont was chosen to relight the flame at the Tomb of the Unknown Soldier in Paris. More recently he operated an elevator in the RCA building here.

Once again Belmont, a twenty-year-older from Springfield Boulevard, Chicago, shook his head. An elevator operator. Poor Gramps. All of it for nothing. That's what you got, man, *nothin.*

Mr. Belmont was a Chevalier of the French Legion of Honor. His decorations included the Croix de Guerre, Croix de la France Libre, Medaille Militaire, Cross of the French Flying Corps, Croix de Combat- tants, Medaille Inter-Alliée, Medaille L'Étoile Rouge and Medaille de la Victoire.

Surviving are two daughters, Mrs. Ruth Belmont and Mrs. Hilda Johnson, and two grandchildren.

168

Belmont had thought two or three times that perhaps he shouldn't let the Captain see the article. Maybe he'd react the way he believed the men in his squad might: sneer. Your Gramps sure was a silly old dude, man. Collecting five wounds and all them medals and lighting fires and shit just to wind up jetting an elevator up and down Radio City. Some cold shit, Belmont. If I was you, I'd burn that goddamn article.

So he let the clipping sit in its envelope through several of the Captain's seminars, until, one day, something in the lecture made him know that Captain Blackman wouldn't laugh at his grandfather, and he handed it to him and stood smoking, watching the Captain out of the corner of his eyes, prepared to defend his grandfather.

The Captain signaled with that hip jerk of his head when he'd finished reading.

"You're one of the grandchildren?"

"Yeah," Belmont said. The Captain didn't stand much on formality. He shook his head and scanned the clipping again. "What do you think of this?" He waved the clipping carelessly and Belmont was surprised at how yellow it was against the green of the Nam. He wasn't expecting a question like that and he thought about it.

"Well, dig, Captain, I never did understand that first war, and the second, there was Hitler, right, and all that Aryan business and what the Germans did to the Jews and gypsies? You know, I figure now they were all Chuck's thing, you know, and he just used the Brothers the way he's doin now, but right down front now. I don't know if Gramps went for the Okey-Doke; maybe. Lotsa Brothers did, lots do now." Belmont went on, searching in the Captain's eyes for some answers; there were none, and he plunged back in on his own. "So, the way I figure it, Captain-Brother, to be caught up in all that shit, whether he dug what he was doin or not, and gettin drilled five times and still comin out alive, now that's a bad dude, an can't nobody fight with that. It's a personal thing, man."

"I see," the Captain said, folding the clipping back along its creases and handing it to Belmont. "You're proud because he's a *man*, not because he was a soldier?"

"Yes, sir."

Belmont received his clipping back, heard the Captain saying, "How to go, baby. That's all it ever gets down to, who is a man and who ain't. When the flags stop flying you still got to live with that." The Captain drew back his arm, the palm of his hand down; he didn't go for that ritualized, hip, thumb, elbow shit, just skin. Fast and quick, and left you ready, if you had to be ready for anything else.

Plap! Poppin with the palms, and the Captain was gone, trying to get wings to Saigon and his babe.

The generator noise seemed louder now, and Belmont stretched, folded the clipping and put it back in his pocket.

"What's that you were readin?"

Belmont jumped; he hadn't seen Woodcock come awake.

"Nothin," he shouted back.

"Any word on the Captain?"

Belmont shook his head. Above the noise of the generator he thought he'd heard a chopper. The night flier, the one who came in for the wounded before night closed in, before the rocket attacks began. He glanced at his watch. Cool system. Bring in tomorrow's supplies, fly out the bodies and maybe those guys who would become bodies. Belmont scrambled to his feet. Woodcock got up. The chopper came in close to the station and they were forced to turn away from the flying dirt. They saw the aidmen rush out of the tent carrying a stretcher with Blackman on it; one held a bottle of plasma (still taking that shit, huh, Belmont thought). Even as the stretcher bearers approached, the crew was throwing out boxes of ammo and rations.

"He's still alive," Woodcock shouted. "They wouldn't be giving him plasma—"

Belmont nodded his head vigorously. Yeah, sure. That's the way he figured it. The Captain's stretcher vanished inside the craft, the aidmen ran back to the tent, eyes shielded, and the copter rose and head back south.

Belmont and Woodcock, almost in unison, ran toward the aidmen.

"How's Captain Blackman?" Woodcock shouted.

One of the aidmen pointed to his chest. "One lung gone."

"How about that leg?" Belmont shouted.

"Bad," came the answer, "so we got him out of here so they could handle it better if it has to come off."

"Off!" hollered Woodcock. He couldn't imagine the Captain without two legs.

"Shit," Belmont said to himself, and then straining into the sound again, "Was that all?"

"He took one through the balls," was the screamed reply, "but just the bag, didn't touch a nut. That's gonna be okay."

Belmont felt a creeping chill in his scrotum and Woodcock, for a moment, tried to imagine what it would be like to have your balls, nuts and all, shot off.

The aidmen were anxious to get away to their bunkers, and Belmont knew that they, too, should get to them because any moment now the Viets were going to open up. The aidmen pushed at each other and were off. Woodcock and Belmont now raced across the open space toward their company bunkers. Standing at the edge of them, Belmont recognized Lieutenant Buck Himes waving for them to hurry. Holding the pocket where his clipping was, Belmont pulled ahead of Woodcock, recognized Sergeant Harrison loping toward his bunker and heard the first of the incoming rounds cleaving the air toward the base. He saw Harrison get hit in midstride; a fear gripped him and he came further up on his toes and leaned forward, but a rocket round hit the ground beneath his flying feet and amid thousands of tiny, sharp pains, Belmont felt himself tumbling head first through the air. When he hit the ground a second later the pain was gone, he heard no further rounds, for he was dead.

# 13

Lieutenant Woodcock and Blackman marched together, leading their company in long, arm-swinging khaki lines, topped by their blue helmets, their blankets rolled, French style, over one shoulder. Slowly, ever so slowly, as though marching off the edge of the earth, they left the homes and small neat farms and ancient villages. Deeply rutted roads, shattered camions, the litter of useless or discarded equipment now guided their line of march. Trees, slashed and broken, showing stark white wounds, were visible everywhere. They began to pass through villages that were mounds of stones and half buildings and the walls that remained upright, were pocked with holes. From time to time, dulled by the weather, they passed piles of giant shell casings. There were almost no people visible except the military.

Imperceptibly a slight stench arose, drifted into their nostrils; it was a mixture of stale cordite, primeval earth turned up to the sun by exploding shells, rotting animals and, undoubtedly, rotting men, parts of whose bodies had not been found.

"Fatigue march, Blackman," Woodcock said, and Blackman fell back along the men giving the order.

"Damn," Blackman heard a soldier behind him whisper. He

knew the man was looking at the raw edge of war for the very first time and found it not as he'd imagined.

Up ahead Blackman saw the thin, slow-moving line of French troops. Maybe they were the ones they'd come to relieve. Beyond where the French troops were emerging from the trenches, distant, ungodly noises buffeted the eastern horizon. The French passed, going back, a few yards on their flank and greetings echoed down the line, the men from New Orleans eager to show off their French. The outgoing troops were bearded, their eyes glazed, their steps mechanical.

"You think you're going to stop them?" one French soldier asked of the line of blacks. "Phaaa! They're still too many."

"Oh, the Germans aren't so tough," another French soldier said.

"How long you been in the trenches?" Blackman struggled to ask.

"Only since April. This time," a sergeant answered, then he was past.

Some of the French hadn't seen Americans and were puzzled by their uniforms and the French Army helmets. "Who are you?" they asked.

"Americans," the blacks answered.

"Americans?" Incredulously. Americans at last.

The blacks seemed to laugh down from their uniformly large frames at the small, pinch-faced French. It's all right now, white boys. We're here, and through the French lines went the whisper, growing as it went: The Americans are here! The Americans are here!

"I thought Americans were white, like us."

"Does it matter what color they are?"

"Big. Bigger than the Senegalese."

"They look tough."

"Just wait. Next week this time they won't look so tough."

"There're white officers."

"Some black ones, too."

173

"Don't they have Chauchats?"

"Guess not. That's why we left ours."

"A regiment without its own machine guns?"

A French soldier laughed. "Maybe they're so tough they don't need them."

"No wonder they need help," one of the black soldiers said. "They sure are some puny folks."

"Looks like they caught hell in them trenches."

"Yeah, well, you got to take it as it comes, buddy. That's all you kin do. I wisht we had Springfields instead of these funny old muskets, though."

Major Little fell back beside Blackman. "Sergeant Major, did you manage to get some wire cutters?"

"One pair, sir," Blackman said.

The Major shook his head. "I just don't understand how they could send a regiment to the front without being able to supply it with wire cutters."

"No, sir," Blackman said, "but we'll keep trying."

The Major clapped Blackman's shoulder, then moved forward again.

By the time the French column had passed, Blackman had got enough wire cutters from them to serve his company; he wondered what the others would do.

Now the chatter of machine guns was quite distinct somewhere out there where not a tree remained standing, and the earth appeared scarred and scorched. The columns started down a long, curving road that took them beneath the earth's surface. They were moving more quickly as the last of the French troops straggled out. Their own French and American officers had moved up ahead to the trench entrances to guide them into position. The blacks trotted along the narrow passageways, sometimes on rotted planks, sometimes in mud and water.

When they were settled, Blackman checked his maps. They were at a place called Les Senades, somewhere in the Argonne. From their trenches they could see the balloons floating like

174

sausages in the sky. Somewhere out there, not too far away, just over the top of the trench they were never to look out over, were the Germans, doing the same thing they were. Waiting for orders.

Blackman paced his company sector; spirits were high and the men were as proficient with the Lebels and Chauchats as they'd ever be. The card and crap games went on nonstop, when the men weren't busy lengthening and strengthening and improving the trenches. Senegalese troops were on their flanks and some of the men bought machetes from them.

"What're the men going to do with the machetes, Blackman?" Lieutenant Woodcock asked one day. Blackman glanced at him. He knew very well why they were buying the knives.

"The French officers, Lieutenant, remember? They claim the Germans don't like steel."

"Oh, right," Woodcock said. "That bullshit." He mimicked one of their French officers. "'The Germans will fight you bullet for bullet, but will break and run before the steel.' Shit. That's not only Germans, Sergeant Major."

Blackman laughed. He liked Woodcock. A Howard University man. Light, bright boy. Wavy hair, but a black man, no doubt about that. He had a friend named Tanner, a black man and a painter who lived here in France, and Woodcock'd already said he planned to stay after the war. He was tired of that shit back home. If the war was doing anything for him, it was opening his eyes to the fact that there was some other place to live beside the United States.

But Woodcock was a realist, too. "Now I don't want the men to get foolish with those knives, man. The French don't mind a whole lot of black people getting killed, you know. Those machetes're to be used only as a last resort. Hell, the bayonet on these Lebels is the longest one in the world, certainly longer than the machetes."

"Yes, sir, I'll tell em."

"Tell em soon because we're taking over two new posts,

175

28 and 29, tonight and you'll be sergeant of the guard on 29; Lieutenant Platt'll have charge of 28."

"It'll be quiet," the briefing French officer told them. "The Germans didn't like our blacks and left them alone. They'll do the same with you. They're afraid of black people."

Blackman grunted. He was always very cautious with a man filled with fear.

Privates Johnson and Roberts crawled out to their listening post. Blackman, in his position, drew a blanket around him and wondered there alone, in the darkness.

The silence formed around Johnson and Roberts. They were fast friends and liked being together on and off duty. They liked Blackman because he understood this and if he could, always placed them on assignment together. The two stood in their hole looking out, moving their heads slightly and rolling their eyes as they'd been taught, seeking out any changes in the patterns of things they'd seen only a second ago.

"Shh!" Roberts said urgently, although neither had spoken a word since coming up. He leaned to Johnson's ear. "Listen."

Chin—klink!

Chin—klink!

"Wire cutters?" Johnson whispered. He wondered if the Germans were trying for a *coup de main*, as the French called it, when they raided for prisoners to find out who was fighting in front of them.

"Les go," Roberts said.

Johnson clutched both his rifle and machete. Roberts didn't have a machete. "Oh, man," he'd said. "These crackers like to see you running around with a knife in your hand. That makes you a real nigger, and I'm tired of that crap."

They crouched and crawled to where they thought they'd heard the sound, confirmed it and started back to alert Blackman and Platt. They were caught, frozen in the light of flares that suddenly blazed through the night sky. The two men gazed deeply at one another, and as the German grenades started to come, they flung themselves apart to the ground, both taking grenade fragments that all but immobilized them.

Roberts, bawling out in a voice Johnson couldn't recognize, "Sergeant o the guard! Sergeant o the guard!" aimed from a sitting position and emptied his chamber; he struggled to fit in another clip, felt it snap in and fired again at a German who, looming suddenly into the light, tumbled forward, dead. No more bullets. Johnson fired, then threw away his rifle and reached for his machete; it was three pounds heavy, eighteen inches long. In the fading flarelight another German ran up and Johnson, grinding his teeth, clubbed him into the ground with the knife.

Blackman had leaped to his feet with the first light of the flares and the first sound of exploding grenades and was now pounding through the bright light of still another flare, heading for post 29; all along the trench men flung themselves to the parapets, waiting.

Out near 29 Johnson suddenly missed Roberts, turned and saw him being carried off by two more Germans. Johnson somehow hobbled toward them and raising his machete, brought it down through the rear soldier's head. Roberts fell to the ground, drenched in the blood and brains of the German. The German in front ran as still another from behind charged Johnson, firing a pistol. Johnson grunted as each bullet struck home, but turned to meet the charge of the German. On his knees now, Johnson brought his machete up between the German's legs, disemboweling him; it was this that Blackman slipped in when he ran up followed by the watch squad, to find Johnson and Roberts, arm in arm, unconcious, but still alive.

*Drumtaps*

## Pétain to Pershing

June 6, 1918

General Rageneau has transmitted to me your desire to see the American 26th, 42nd and 32nd divisions used

177

as soon as possible on the battlefront. The American troops *already* engaged in battle provoke the unanimous admiration of the whole French Army.

Headquarters 157th Division
July 4, 1918

General Goybet, commanding the 157th Division of Infantry, takes special notice of the fact that this is the first 4th of July to be celebrated by his Franco-American division. It is a striking demonstration of the long standing and blood-cemented friendship which binds together our two great nations. The sons of the soldiers of Lafayette greet the sons of the soldiers of Washington who have come over to fight, as in 1776, in a new and greater way of independence. The same success which followed the glorious fight for the cause of liberty is sure to crown our common effort now and bring about the final victory of right and justice over barbarity and oppression.

GENERAL GOYBET, Commanding,
157th Division.

"You see how different they are."

Blackman turned at the sound of Lieutenant Woodcock's voice, a voice sweetened with cognac.

"They remember everything, the French. But they're full of shit, too. C'mon, Sergeant Major, I know you keep cognac in your quarters. I need some of it."

It was peaceful back here, Blackman reflected as they walked to his quarters, the upstairs of a respectable barn. They'd come out of the trenches a week ago and Blackman knew it wouldn't be long before they went back to them. Early that morning an American plane had flown over and dropped a bouquet of flowers with red, white and blue bands. "A happy fourth of July to the Americans in this sector," the accompanying note said, and Blackman was sure the pilot was unaware that the American troops were black.

At his side, a melancholy Lieutenant Woodcock was reciting:

"'Fellow-citizens, above your national, tumultuous joy, I hear the mournful wail of millions; whose chains, heavy and grievous yesterday, are, today, rendered more intolerable by the jubilee shouts that reach them.'"

"Frederick Douglass," Blackman said, and Woodcock winked approvingly. He was, Blackman knew, depressed by the recent flurry of courts-martial meted out to the black officers of their sister division, the 92nd, over at Bourbonne-les-Bains; Woodcock had gone to Howard with many of them.

In the barn, holding the bottle Blackman had given him, Woodcock stared through the window and said, "Cocksuckers," then drank heavily. The lieutenant now had himself a French girl and was in constant touch with Tanner who'd opened a YMCA. "The French, you see," Woodcock said, "are different. They use *savoir-faire* while they're cutting your throat, let you get a little snatch from their sisters to keep you happy."

"Hey, Luther," Blackman said. "Take a snooze. Lay down on my cot, man, and get yourself together. If you know they court-martial Negro officers for almost anything you shouldn't be running around camp drunk. Now, I think you ought to sleep some."

Woodcock sat down on the cot heavily and gazed thoughtfully at Blackman. "You're right, Abraham. Besides, you're bigger than me. C'mon, have one drink." He passed the bottle to Blackman who took a healthy swallow and slowly and deliberately corked it. Woodcock took off his shoes and lay down, his hands folded under his head.

"I don't want to die for these fuckers, Abraham. Sometimes I get scared that I will, just for nothing, man, *nothing*, and there's not one goddamn thing I can do."

"There're a couple of things you can do, Lute."

"Oh shit, I mean, you know, you got to do the right things;

179

you got a good company, you got to look out for the men, don't want to set too bad an example. . . ." He grinned. His head flopped to one side and the grin faded; he was asleep.

Nine days later the division took its first all-out barrage; it rolled in from the northeast, whistling, rattling, swooshing, to explode on or near their positions, and the Germans, endless waves of them, ran up behind it.

Blackman crouched with the machine gunners, passing belts; he felt the heavy bullets slipping through his fingers, watched the waves of soldiers come toward them, falter, break, disintegrate, being cut down like wheat in a field until those remaining turned and ran back.

The whistles blew for a counterattack. Blackman left the machine guns and bounded out into the plain with his company.

"Goddamn, les go!"

"Murderlize those white sonofabitches!"

"Kill them German crackers; make believe they're homefolks, white!"

The ground flew under Blackman's feet; he hurled a bramble of barbed wire and slipped, went down, grateful to be somewhat out of the reach of things snapping, crackling and whistling in the air, two or three feet above him. Like a boxer, he rose on one knee, then sprang to both feet and was off again, flying. Black boys he knew, but couldn't somehow recognize now, rushed past him, screaming, firing, their bayonets, long, slender knives of dull gray metal pointed at the Germans. Fearfully, Blackman ran to catch up. Up ahead, the grenades were going off; German machine guns were opening up now and German riflemen were scrambling up out of their trenches. The machine guns were ineffective; the blacks already too close, and one by one they stopped. Blackman felt as if he were breathing inside a furnace; his chest burned with each breath, and he was wheezing, his voice breaking. Even as he ran, he jumped over bodies, avoided outstretched hands that begged for help, black and white. The trench loomed up ahead and as though he were striding toward a jumping pit, his pace grew long and measured and, finally, he gathered himself, leaped up, up and out, flinching from the bullets he imagined that even now were seeking out his body; his legs stretched for the trench and then the horizon of running Germans and sparse grass and shattered trees and pulverized brown earth vanished. He crashed into the dugout and rolled to its floor, frantically looking around for Germans who might have remained. He saw none. The Buffaloes leaped, hurdled, dove and fell into the trench, and he heard Woodcock's voice urging them to fire, to take positions, to set up the machine guns now being brought up in case of a German counter-attack.

For long moments only the sound of orders, the loading of weapons and the tired breathing could be heard and then they knew the danger of a counterattack was over. Blackman placed his hot, sweating forehead to the earth, and closed his eyes. He'd be all right in a minute. He heard the others talking:

"Whoooee, that was some flyin, and I tell you, I'da run too. Buncha a screamin niggers come runnin at me like we did—"

Blackman started laughing and it overrode his fear. He saw them as the Germans must've seen them, khaki uniforms, blue helmets, French rifles and bayonets, shouting Harlemese. Soon, laughter filled the trench and for a moment Lieutenant Woodcock wondered if they shouldn't try to take the next trench since everyone was feeling so good.

Blackman hadn't moved; his legs felt unsteady and he knew if he took one step they'd turn to rubber. As soon as he got himself together, he'd ask after Richa'd Boston; he thought he saw him go down.

Later that night, when Boston's death had been confirmed, it began to rain; the trench floors, where there were no planks, turned to mud; the cooties and the rats came out in force and still Blackman traced his every step earlier that day; saw himself with the machine gunners, then with the company moving out over no man's land, himself leaping over the bramble of barbed wire and how good it felt to be down on the ground and alive. There were moments when he shook as he remembered, and he looked at Woodcock with new eyes. Now he understood how empty, how meaningless, his death, if it came, would be, and like Woodcock, he didn't want to die either. Not for nothing.

By morning the rain ended, and through the mist came rolling the yperite gas; it sank and writhed along the ground, egged on by a slow, wet wind. The gas alarm sounded and they clapped on their masks, some in time, others not, and waited for the Germans, but they didn't come that morning.

# 14

## Cadences

There was no doubt about it as the generals gathered at Chaumont, Haute-Marne; the German spring offensive had been broken. Now it was all up to the Allies to run the Germans back home and bottle up the war. Even now General Pershing was out on a tour of training camps to see if the A.E.F. was ready for the big push.

His generals found him too cautious, not a fighter, but a pacifist, a marrier of politician's daughters. Pershing wanted a million men before commencing the A.E.F.'s push; there were now a million and a quarter in France, and obviously, the tide had turned in the Allies' favor; peace rumors filled the streets every day; young boys were being captured in German trenches. Still, Pershing waited, pleading time for additional training for the Americans.

Now, in the Commander in Chief's absence, they were trying to ascertain which American units had been blooded and could spearhead the A.E.F. attack, get it going before it was all over, before the promotions ran out. Experienced troops could get going now and as each training unit completed its work, it would be poured into line.

"How about CHARLOTTE and LEONA?"

There was a momentary silence. Each general knew the speaker meant the 92nd and the 93rd divisions.

"The niggers," another general said with a sigh.

"They've done well with the French. Fairly well. Good enough for our purposes. . . ."

"Goybet loves them."

"He doesn't have much else to love, that's why."

"We ought to get them back. Use them as shock troops, the way the French do with their niggers, Algerians, Asians, Moroccans. They'd fight even better with us; they're Americans!"

"Hah!"

"Well, look, if we want to get moving before this thing ends. . . ."

"Yeah. Guess so. Let's kick it up to Black Jack. That's where he got his name, you know, he served with them—"

"Everyone here knows that—"

"Well, let's do it."


*Drumtaps*

FOCH TO PERSHING
August 26, 1918

My dear General:

The Chief of the French Military Mission with the American Army has transmitted to me the request which you addressed to him on August 16, for the purpose of securing the return of the American 369th, 370th, 371st and 372nd Infantry Regiments (Colored) which are actually on duty with the French Second and Fourth Armies, to your command. At present, such a move would have serious consequences: in fact, two of those regiments form part, as combat units, of a French division, while the other two are similarly as-

184

signed to two of our divisions. If, therefore, your suggestion was followed through, the Commanders-in-Chief of the French Armies of the North and Northeast would be obliged to immediately withdraw two of his divisions because, at the moment, he would be unable to bring them up to strength again; something that is unthinkable at this time. After thus bringing the facts to your attention, I feel sure that you will agree with me that any change made this day in the employment of the colored regiments of the American 93rd Division, which have been trained and used as combat units, would have unfortunate consequences. . . .

FOCH

Any day now, Blackman thought, this fucker is going to be over, *over!* The problem was not to get killed before it ended, and it was getting harder now, as they rolled through Hans, Séchault, Bussy Farm, Monthois, Ardeuil, Monfauxelles; through Moya Mill and Trières Farm, September hinting of winter to come. Days and nights merged into one unending lice-and-rat-and-death-smelling block of time, broken only by the barrage at Ripont.

They'd secured the town toward the end of the day. German shellfire, thought to have been silenced, opened up; the men sprinted to cover. Blackman was in a forward hole with a lead squad and he could tell by the sound of the shell coming at them that it had his name on it. He closed his eyes and trembled.

From his position, Lieutenant Woodcock heard the shell and crouched; it was going to be damned close. As he folded himself into the earth, he noted his sergeant major's position. The shell struck. Fragments hummed and whistled and snarled through the air; a wave of earth sprayed up against the purpling sky and rained back to the surface. The next shell was some distance back and Woodcock raised his head cautiously. Blackman's position was a gaping hole of fresh-black earth. There were already screams and cries emerging from it. Minutes later, when Wood-

185

cock arrived, he saw that there were only pieces of men left; it was those pieces which were screaming. Blackman was missing. Long after the shattered bodies had been carried away, squads labored in darkness to uncover what was still unfound.

First they uncovered Blackman's head, sure it was all they'd find because of the angle at which it was stuck in the ground. But the neck came after, then the shoulders, at still another angle, then the torso, arms intact, the pelvis and legs attached. He was alive and unmarked; the men who'd been on either side of him and in front and behind him had been blown to bits.

Later, in October, the 369th curved around and through the mountains at full stride, laughing with the poilu who had vowed to build a monument in their honor. A month later, the Armistice in effect, Blackman led his company from their positions; he wondered why the French soldiers were just holding ground, smiling at them as they passed. Soon they came to a river and paused. Blackman and Woodcock checked their maps.

"The Rhine," Woodcock said.

"And you are the first Americans here," a French officer said. "The very first. We are occupying Germany."

The word went back as Blackman and Woodcock smiled at each other.

"We're in Germany, man! Krautland!"

"The Rhine, buddy! Germany! We done run them bastards clear back home!"

Oh, my God, Blackman thought. It's over. We're here. Germany, the Rhine. Ordinary looking river, nothing special. Could be the Mississippi up north if it wasn't for the mountains.

The waiting was next. Blackman awoke mornings, pressed his hands to his body, touched every rib, his face; he counted his fingers and toes, shook his penis back and forth in his hand, hefted his testicles. Then he smiled and got to his feet. He wondered at the mystery of sunrise and sunset.

Every phrase from every man in the company began: "When I get back home. . . ." And Blackman thought: Now they

186

make their plans, each wanting to believe that home'll be different because they came here, because they carried arms. They plan marriages and babies and homes; they plan to have good jobs and they dream of being treated with dignity. He knew some would stay, like Woodcock, who'd stroll Paris boulevards with his women. There'd be others like him. Roberto and Johnson will ride cars in parades, when they aren't in their hospital beds. Most will go home because it is home, and around the world monuments will rise to this graveyard, this slaughterhouse. Thank God, it's over.

Evenings they gathered in the small cellar a local farmer had hastily made over into a canteen. There they drank wine, cognac —whatever was drinkable and wouldn't kill them, and they sang:

> *The cracker marines went over the top,*
> *parlay voo;*
> *the cracker marines went over the top,*
> *parlay voo;*
> *the cracker marines went over the top*
> *because at them us black boys shot,*
> *inky, dinky, parlay voo.*

> *General Ballou went over the top,*
> *parlay voo;*
> *General Ballou went over the top,*
> *parlay voo;*
> *General Ballou went over the top*
> *and fell right in a bucket of slop,*
> *inky dinky parlay voo.*

Or they sang, wallowing in sentimentality, "The Old Mill Stream," and "Madelon" or frolicked through "Won't You Please Come Home, Bill Bailey." Soldiers danced with their farm girls; old men in berets or caps sat smiling toothlessly, and Blackman, the cognac coursing warmly through his body, wanted a woman, any woman, no matter what she looked like, no matter how much like cowshit she might smell. He wanted an agreeable, warm female hole to put his penis in.

So he joined the others who were making their way from the cellar across fields to a barn where they found a line of soldiers. Blackman got on line, conscious of the silence of the men standing there; it was like the silence of the vast, communal shithouses you had to get used to in the Army.

"What's the holdup, is somebody taking two turns?"

"C'mon, c'mon, what say in there? Leave some, man."

They were edging forward, feet kicking rocks and clots of cowshit. One by one they came out, buttoning their pants and answered the question:

"How is it?"

"Good, buddy. She got herself a good one."

Now they were inside the barn, straining to listen to the unashamed voices rising from behind stacked bales of hay. Groans, gasps.

"That bitch really puts on a show," the man in front of Blackman said. "She got to bring down that come quick, man, otherwise she'd be back there till next Monday. I bet she's lickin necks, and chewin ears and givin one good twist and a guy's off, he ain't had no pussy in seven months. . . ."

When it was Blackman's turn, he saw that she was young and hard; there was an angular look about her. She didn't look like a farm girl, but like someone from Montmartre. Her hair was bobbed and she wore a sweater without brassiere under it, and a skirt without slip or underpants.

"*Allons, mon cher,*" she whispered, tucking the money from her last customer into her purse. "*Vite,*" she said, kissing him, thrusting her tongue without ceremony into his mouth. She moved her breasts mechanically against his uniform, then expertly unbuttoned his pants. His penis sprung out into her hand; she glanced down at it, grimaced, squeezed it, as if measuring. Her skirt went up with a smooth motion at the same time she eased back onto the hay; she dipped him neatly under and

188

into her, and he plunged through all the room there was and sought for more. There was room; it was wet and wide. She raised, smashed her butt against the hay and rebounded back up his penis. She moaned in French. She pressed her legs tightly together to make it tighter and he came quickly, not wishing to linger. For a moment longer she held him, then brusquely pushed him off, wiped herself with a towel with one hand and accepted her money in the other.

Back in his quarters, Blackman washed his penis furiously and rinsed his mouth repeatedly, thinking all the while, *Vive la France, Vive la France.*

## Cadences

"*Well, it's over. We've won. We kicked the shit out of the Kaiser.*"

"*Yes, we sure did. What's the tally?*"

"*The tally? Let's see. Just the dead?*"

"*That'll do.*"

"*All right. The whites: Britain, the good old U.S.A., France—Germany, too, all right?*"

"*But of course, man. Get on with it.*"

"*I'm sorry. The Russians. Shall we count them as white?*"

"*Oh, fuck! I guess so—oh, I don't know. Yes, go ahead.*"

"*Well, then, I make it close to ten million whites dead to—*"

"*And the niggers, the niggers from all over, India, Africa, Asia, places like that.*"

"*Three million.*"

"*Is that all? Are you sure?*"

"*You've got to look at it this way: they probably lost more men in our war than they could have in two hundred years of tribal wars.*"

"*Yes, you're right there. What's the population say, of India and Africa?*"

"*Ummm, maybe five hundred million.*"

189

*"Great God Almighty! Too bad the war didn't last another five years. Nothing we can do about it now. Maybe the next one. Let's send our own black bastards home; get them the hell out of France. Jesus, they're getting so much of this French cock they'll be spoiled and won't know how to behave at home. Quick! Let's get them the fuck out of here!"*

*Drumtaps*

For these reasons, immediately after the Armistice I recommended in effect that this division be sent home first of all American troops, that they be sent home in all honor, but above all that they be sent quickly. The answer came that Marshal Foch would not, pending peace, approve the transfer of any division back to the United States. In answer I told American headquarters to say to Marshal Foch that no man could be responsible for the acts of those Negroes toward Frenchwomen, and that he had better send this division home at once.

MAJOR GENERAL ROBERT LEE BULLARD
*Reminiscences* 1927

# FOUR

From the very beginning, the Abraham Lincoln Brigade was an **integrated unit**. The concepts of **real** freedom embodied in the general antifascist philosophy of the men of the Lincoln Brigade precluded any ideas of racial superiority, or minority discrimination. Such ideas were utterly alien to the men and represented, in essence, the enemy they had come so far to fight.

Arthur H. Landis
THE ABRAHAM LINCOLN BRIGADE

# 15

Cadences

"They're burning and looting the churches."

"Raping nuns, beating up priests."

"Fuck all that. They're grabbing the land, dividing it up. They're talking about a republic where there'll be no rich and no poor. Can you imagine?"

"Bad business. What if their ideas spread? I mean, we blew it in Russia, let's not do it again."

"Don't worry. We can do something with their army. You can always do something with an army; that's what armies are for, to finagle. How about it, England? France? America? C'mon, stop rapping pencils. Look. All you have to do is stay out, okay?"

"Okay."

"Okay."

"Okay."

"Okay."

"Oh! Vatican, you're in, huh, good. Leave the kid alone, will you?"

"They're anti-Christs."

"Yeah, sure, I got the message."

"We'd like to—uh, you know, say *things* . . . *it's a—well, the three of us have this image about democracy?*"

"Got you, America. France, you too? England? I understand: you talk that talk, but don't get off the pot, right? Claro, hombres claro."

As Robert Doctorow dashed out, hopefully between the rounds of incoming rockets, he saw the helicopter turning back toward the base. Harrison'd had it, he saw instantly, and Belmont, but Woodcock was struggling along the ground, his face a hard-carved mask of fear. Doctorow grabbed an arm and pulled; he felt Woodcock coming with him. They got back to the bunker and tumbled in. There were no more rockets; the chopper landed safely.

"Let's get em to the chopper," Lieutenant Himes was shouting, and they started to run with the wounded. Three steps out of the bunker Doctorow fell, carrying Woodcock and the man on the other side with him.

"C'mon, Jewboy! Let's get the fuck up—"

"My foot, you black sonofabitch," Doctorow shouted, pointing at his left foot, gashed open, bleeding. He'd stepped on a fragment as sharp as a razor.

"Sorry, man," the soldier said. Doctorow recognized him as Antoine. "Help, help over here," Antoine shouted over the pounding rotor of the chopper.

Inside the craft, lifting off again, Woodcock opened his eyes, saw Captain Blackman's eyes fluttering. Woodcock looked down in amazement at the bandage being applied to his thigh. A flesh wound, he thought, happily.

Robert Doctorow grinned openly. His foot was cut to the bone. Penicillin, a little sewing up and he'd be just fine. Now, he too gazed at the Captain and felt a little guilty that his own wound was not serious, as far as he could tell.

Blackman gazed dully at Doctorow and Woodcock; they tried talking to him. "How's it, Captain?"

Blackman looked at them a long moment before he closed his eyes again.

Luther Woodcock was sitting in the Deux Magots, straining to see through the steam-coated windows. Like everyone else there, he was in a post-Christmas depression; it would lift in another few days when the Noel signs and prayerful angels disappeared. He'd had two coffees, light, and was on his first calvados of the day. A perfect drink for the cold. By nightfall, he'd have a merry little buzz on.

Behind him he could hear people talking in Spanish. That depressed him, too, for they obviously were refugees from Spain, where another white man's war was in progress.

Outside on the gray, windy boulevard, behind the steaming windows, two men paused, one black, the other white. They were American; that was plain from their clothing. Woodcock hoped they'd come in; they seemed to be debating the point. He liked to talk to the black Americans who'd just come over to check on things back home. He did this most frequently in Paul Belmont's clubs, where they all went sooner or later.

The black man looked familiar, maybe a type, Woodcock thought. You started to think that way when you were a painter; still, he looked very familiar.

"Doesn't look like so much," Robert Doctorow was saying.

Abraham Blackman responded, "They never do, Bob, after you've read so much about them."

"Anyway," Doctorow said glumly, "this was one of the places where they hung out, when they weren't writing. Hemingway, I hear, has gone to cover the war. Maybe we'll run into him."

"Yeah. Well, do you want to go in? C'mon, I know you do."

Doctorow said, "You wouldn't mind, would you, Abe?"

"Hell no, I can use a drink. It's cold. Seeps through everything here."

No, Woodcock told himself. He's just a kid, not more than twenty-three, twenty-four. He watched them enter and nodded as they paused uncertainly. "Sit down, fellows. Americans, aren't you?"

Blackman smiled at the man and pushed Doctorow into a chair at his table and sat himself. The man looked like a real European with his beret and capecoat. They introduced themselves around and Woodcock ordered drinks. "When you first came in," he said, "I thought you were someone I knew. Sure gave me a start."

Doctorow stared reverently around the room and Blackman explained. "Bob's a writer and all the famous writers used to hang out here."

"That's so," said Woodcock. "Writers and painters. Here and a number of other places as well. What brings you to Paris, just that?" He saw them exchange glances. "Secret?"

"We're joining a brigade of Americans in Spain," Blackman said.

"Ah, I see," Woodcock said. "I don't envy you at all. It's going to get rough down there, and I hope you'll be all right." He raised his glass in salute and turned a slightly mocking glance to Blackman. Blackman smiled; of course Negroes would wonder why a black man would want to fight in Spain. He figured it was self-evident.

The Spanish voices behind them droned on and Doctorow whirled toward them and whispered to Blackman, "They're Spanish!"

"Oh, we get a lot of them these days," Woodcock said, "and there'll be more coming." He ordered another round, settled back in his chair and said, "I'd imagine the U.S. government isn't too happy about you volunteers." And to himself, especially the black ones. He'd seen the blacks from America, the Antilles and Africa gather in Paris to plead for equality before the League of Nations; Du Bois, Trotter, Diagne and others. He'd seen William Monroe Trotter shake his finger in Woodrow Wilson's startled, ascetic face. "Well," he said. "All kinds of things're

196

breaking loose here, too. The French've discovered a sizable number of fascists in their midst. They pretend to be surprised. They've even managed to beat up the Premier, right here in the Quarter. Dragged him out of his car and really whipped him. Poor Blum."

"If they can get away with beating up a Jewish Premier here in France," Doctorow said grimly, "you can imagine what it'll be like for the average Jew in Germany."

Woodcock nodded vigorously. "And there're a lot of Jewish refugees here from Germany, too. I'm afraid we're in for another one, fellows. I admire your spirit, but in the end?" He exchanged glances with Blackman once again. Blackman finished his drink and stood. Doctorow stood, too, with a final, lingering look at the place. They thanked Woodcock, shook his hand and left. They would have one more day of travel tomorrow, all in France, before reaching the Spanish border. Tomorrow night, Blackman thought; maybe by tomorrow night. . . .

The train hustled down the Rhone Valley through Mâcon, Lyons; swung almost due south through Montpellier, Béziers, Narbonne and paused for the last breath of France in Perpignan. The next stop was Le Perthus, Spain, where they disembarked and were led to a waiting bus. Other young men sat in the bus. Hesitantly, Blackman and Doctorow gave the Popular Front salute, and felt better when it was answered with smiles and greetings in a dozen languages.

Most of the men, Blackman noted, were under thirty, in fact, not long past twenty. There were two other black Americans in the group. Filled now, the bus drove off. Blackman recognized English English, German, French, Hungarian and Canadian English. As the bus moved southward, dark clouds swept toward them, bearing rain which drummed on the rooftop. The bus fell silent, as though the rain were a bad omen. They moved gingerly along old, rutted roads, bounced over stone and asphalt highways badly in need of repair, and finally arrived at Figueras where they were billeted overnight in the fortress. The next day under a clearing sky, they boarded another train, one that hobbled through villages, stopped and started in obscure places, for no rhyme or reason, then continued on. As they came into each town they were greeted by villagers who cheered and thrust oranges through the windows.

The guitars were being played inside the train; the cards were fingered until they were slick. The placid Mediterranean appeared on their left as they descended down to sea level from the easiest route along the Costa Brava.

Where had it started, this coming to Spain, Blackman wondered. Over bag lunches in parks or while hanging around on service days in the Welfare Department, they'd talked about Spain; in Bickford's or Horn and Hardart's, each testing against the other his reasons for wanting to go; were they good enough, honest enough, important enough? Over the weeks, both young men, vulnerable investigators from whom clients could get almost anything, concluded that they must go to Spain; that there in the land of Cervantes could flourish, if not murdered, the kind of life they believed America should've been able to offer its citizens. There was where fascism, racism and economic inequality could be beaten back; there the people could beat the big money.

Step after irrevocable step they came, from making inquiries to making one appointment with the recruiter, and then another and another. They spent every moment together, as if afraid no others in New York with its seven million population, felt as they did. They reinforced one another, finally, with Blackman concluding that he could fight American lynch law by fighting Spanish fascism; Doctorow concluding that he could fight international anti-Semitism by volunteering for the Republic, one which surely would, after five hundred years, renounce its official anti-Semitism.

Until they arrived in Spain they had only each other. But now they had Italians, Czechs, Poles, Irishmen, Germans, Frenchmen,

Englishmen, Canadians, Cubans—everything, Doctorow exulted as they slid through Badalona. Barcelona would be the next stop, that city of Phoenicians, Greeks, Carthaginians, Romans, Catalans. Flashes of the ocean, seen between buildings, then huge warehouses and, rising above them, the superstructures of ships riding at anchor. The train curved slightly, then shuddered to a halt, rocking on ancient springs in a yard patterned with train tracks. Old, gray buildings were on either side of them, and rising from the sea and left of them, they could see Montjuich Park.

They left the train among gathering crowds. There were more oranges, and now peanuts and hoarse cries of *"No pasarán!"* The officers from the Republican Army, smiling and waving to the crowds, lined up the volunteers. In a variety of tongues, cadence was called as they marched to their barracks. From somewhere a band broke out into a weak, reedy martial air. Blackman and Doctorow grinned at each other, straightened their backs and stepped out smartly.

There were too few days in Barcelona exploring the chilled Ramblas. Most of their time was spent listening to lectures, drawing some equipment, socks, gloves, if they were lucky, and a blanket, and then they were sent to Valencia where it was warmer, but not much, and where they had another parade, and finally, they came to rest in Albacete. Blackman, hopping from the truck, looked around and knew, somehow, that from this point forward he and Doctorow would get just what they'd asked for by coming.

But there was still time enough to explore the quiet, nearby villages, to marvel at the mountains, the wine, the people; and as they prowled through the doors closed off only by beads that rattled and swayed in the wind, Blackman was reflecting that from here, Albacete, the thousands of good guys began their Spanish sojourn to the mountains of the west, to Madrid, a salient in the ever encroaching fascist tide. From here went the Thaelmanns, the Garibaldis, the Dimitrovs, the Dumonts, the Mackenzie-Papineaus and perhaps, soon, another American brigade, the Washingtons. He felt, crouching in the cafes with Doctorow, a personal power he'd not been aware of before in all his twenty-odd years; he felt it when the locals, their coal-black eyes filled with wonder, looked at him. And he knew they were calculating their own goodnesses, their own aspirations, the sacredness of them, through the miracle of his black presence there. From what place has this huge black man, this *moro*, this *negro*, come to aid us?

This observation served him well as training progressed with Chauchats, Hotchkisses; with Rosses and Steyers, Lebels and Remingtons, many without rifling. The Steyers, someone told him, were Springfields produced by Americans for Russian use during the Revolution of 1917. Blackman hoisted one and wondered at its strange history, tried to imagine, but could not, where it would go when this war was over. The training wore on, rifle drills, parades, lectures; afternoons sometimes spent in dim bodegas wine-tasting. The end of it was at once desirable, yet vaguely unwished for, and when it came, finally, in the bull ring of Albacete, with the distribution of cartridge belts and rifles, amid the pungent odor of Cosmoline, Blackman found himself quite ready.

Trucks groaned into the ring raising dust tinged with the scent of the shit of the brave bulls; the last act of their lives. Sitting beside a well-browned Doctorow, Blackman heard the commissions being passed out as casually as the ammo, one hundred and fifty rounds per man. Askance they watched the ambulances pull into the circle, the doctors, nurses and medics gathering. Through the cacophony of running motors, the dull clack of bolts being tested home, shouts, the slam of crates upon truck beds, their destination materialized. There was a fascist breakthrough on the Jarama. This, the Abraham Lincoln Battalion, together with the rest of the International Brigade, was expected to stop it, to plug it up, to win. There was nothing more; no ringing speeches, no flags, no bands. They simply climbed into the trucks as dusk heaved down over the mountains and drove out of the bull ring to the war.

On the morning of February 27, 1937, Abraham Blackman awoke and looked for the sun; there was nothing but gray sky. Although he lay close to Doctorow for warmth, Blackman shivered, waking him. Doctorow moved quickly, shoving his rifle up in front of him. It hadn't taken long for him to get used to war, Blackman thought. "It's just me," he said.

"Oh shit," Doctorow said, getting to his feet and stamping. "My feet are so fucking cold," he said. "This place is as bad as Riverside Drive in winter. I thought Spain was supposed to be sunny and warm all the time."

"C'mon," Blackman said, getting up himself. "Let's see if we can find some warm coffee and bread."

Down the line men were beginning to stir, to move stiffly and gray to the chow wagon, where they found a batch of new men.

"Seventy-three guys," someone said to Blackman. "Just in from Albacete."

Blackman calculated quickly. With the forty that came in the other day, they were almost back up to effective strength. But he knew that no matter how many men they had, they'd fight, three or three hundred.

Oliver Law, his face sagging, drew up beside Blackman. He'd been in the group he and Doctorow met at Le Perthus, one of the blacks. The other, Alonzo Watson, had been killed in their first battle, the first Negro to die in the Spanish Civil War. Blackman hadn't got to know Watson very well, just enough to say "Hello, man," in passing. He would not be the last black American to die in these mountains.

Now Law was speaking. "How'd you like it?"

"Rough," Blackman said. They had been blooded on the San Martín de la Vega road. The Cubans and the Irish lost heavily in a raking fascist gunfire, and the Lincolns lost forty-two, twenty

201

killed. "Seems like all the machine guns are on the other side. How're you doing with yours?"

Law was a commander of one of the machine gun companies. "We got a few more guns, we'll be in good shape," he said.

Blackman smiled. More guns that'd have to be captured from the fascists.

"We'll see if we can't get you some more today," Doctorow said.

Holding their cups of hot, weak coffee and their *panecillos*, the men gathered around the newcomers. In Albacete and Morata they pulled guard duty with empty Lebels; there was no ammo for them.

"Look at that guy," Doctorow said, nudging Blackman. "Can't be more than fifteen."

"How old are you, kid?"

The kid tossed his hair and said, "Seventeen." Blackman and Doctorow looked away; if he admitted to seventeen, he was probably fifteen.

The men looked at the kid over the tops of their canteen cups.

Jesus, Blackman thought. What was he thinking, how awful that the kid was here? Still thinking of noble, right-aged soldiers who never got killed messily? Still thinking of right making might? Since when did old men fight wars? And hadn't it happened before, at Marathon, in Zululand? Wherever men fought, there you found the boys also. War was the big game humans played, and when one was over, the corpses buried, the hardware of murder sold to lesser countries for lesser wars, they began still another game. Klonsky was the kid's name. Fifteen years old, he was a player like the rest.

"I'm going to find Walt Garland," Blackman said. Doctorow nodded. He wondered sometimes how his friend felt about being black and in this war, although there wasn't a white in the Lincolns who had a prejudiced bone in his body, not even the Southerners. This war and the men who fought it were above that disease, related as it was to all others. There were many

202

Jews with whom Doctorow exchanged comments; he knew Blackman would want to do the same with other blacks.

Garland would go with him, Blackman thought, if he could find him. They'd walk quickly through the olive groves to that isolated bodega that the owner insisted on remaining in, selling his wine to any who came, confident that he would survive the war no matter who won, Republicans or Rebels. He found Garland talking to Captain Springhall, the Britisher. Springhall was just mounting a truck bed to speak to the new men. "Let's get some wine," Blackman said, and without a word Garland fell in beside him. Both knew that Springhall would give his usual brief talk, that the new men would get Remingtons, bayonets and cartridge belts, and each would fire five rounds into a nearby hillside. That would be the extent of their rifle lessons.

Without speaking, Garland and Blackman hustled to the bodega. There, they ordered *vino de La Mancha*. White wine, cool and dry. They said if you took the wine away from La Mancha, it would spoil. Okay, Blackman thought, the wine's a long way from La Mancha, and it still tastes okay. They poured most of the wine into their canteens and drank the rest from the bottle.

"One of these days," Garland said as they started back, "I want to really get around La Mancha and the windmills." They could hear the shots being fired by the new men. "There's so much I want to see and do. So much."

Garland was from a little town in Ohio. They all seemed to come from places Blackman'd not heard of before. How had they been driven to come here, these black boys who did not live in New York or Los Angeles or Chicago or San Francisco or Boston? How had the word slipped unchecked into those small towns, into Garland's home, or Law's or Watson's or the others? And how had they managed to set aside the burning considerations of their time and places? It was easy enough to do if you lived in the large cities, but the towns, the villages?

They heard whistles and shouts and started back on the run

and joined the battalion already trotting to prepared positions. To the north, Blackman heard light firing, and then recognized Oliver Law's guns answering in short bursts. He'd just tumbled into position beside Doctorow when the word to commence firing began.

Like harmless Christmas tree lights, blue flashes winked from among the olive groves; these Blackman and the others fired at. When he stopped to reload, he could hear the British and the Dimitrovs firing at them, for they were the flashes from Rebel fire which now came ripping with sharp, sibilant sounds into their sandbagged positions.

Beside him, Robert Doctorow kept looking at the sky between shots.

"Where are our planes?" he mumbled.

As if in answer, there came a call down the line for volunteers to go out and lay down the aviation signal. Doctorow seemed to shrink into his hole. Blackman casually passed the message down, as though it had nothing whatsoever to do with him. Damned if he was volunteering; that goddamned signal should've been placed last night or early in the morning, before daylight. Now, in full view of the Rebels, someone had to go out. There had to be an end to blind faith.

"Bob Pick and Joe Streisand," Doctorow said glumly. "They're going to do it." Streisand was from New York and they'd had many conversations.

Blackman leaned against his sandbags and watched the men pick up the signal. It was a T-shaped piece of cloth, and when it was down, the T had to point toward the Rebels so the planes would know where to drop their bombs.

As though in slow motion, the two ran across the road, the signal flapping between them. Even as he was fixing his end in its final position, Pick clutched his stomach, then his chest and fell, the blue flashes winking steadily. Streisand dropped his end and ran to help him, but he too went down, and for a full five minutes, they were the targets of concentrated rifle and machine

gun fire, the sounds of which seemed to have no relationship to
the flashes. They were skinned by the bullets, flayed, disem-
boweled; almost no part of their bodies remained untouched; it
was as though two huge piles of ground meat had been thrown
down upon the road.

Done with Streisand and Pick, the Rebel guns swept fiercely
back against the battalion positions at almost the same moment
runners came with the message that they were to move out; the
Spanish Republicans had already done so. Blackman and Doctorow thought of the lines he would write one day about his
experiences in the war; his notebook was already half filled. But
now he'd just finished vomiting quietly and the war seemed too
real, no longer a thing to be described and shared, but something with dangerous meaning for him.

As for Blackman, this was the moment of truth, and he knew
it was so for every man who crouched in a hole or behind the
cover of sandbags. To thrust yourself into the open, to place,
knowingly place, your body where it could be, on whim, on
bad fortune, ripped apart, taxed his will completely. He trembled
in preparation.

Rebel machine gun fire chewed back and forth in increased
intensity against their positions, snapping into the bags.

"Man," Blackman breathed. "We'd better wait."

"Crazy to go now," Doctorow said.

They didn't hear anyone else scrambling out and Blackman
couldn't see how the Spaniards were able to advance in the
face of such fire.

Neither could Bob Merriman, who knew the Spanish hadn't
advanced, but were pinned down within feet of their bunkers.
But Copic insisted on the attack, and he was the brigade commander. To make sure the attack went off, Copic sent Springhall to make the Lincolns pull out; Springhall saw the situation,
but he had his orders, which Merriman accepted reluctantly.

So Blackman was surprised when Merriman and Springhall,

racing up and down the parapet, urged them out and forward, and doing so themselves, Springhall's face was cracked before he could touch the ground and Merriman's shoulder shattered.

But Blackman was up and out, conscious of holding his arms high, possibly to ward off any bullets that sought his head. He broke over the stubbled ground, aware that he was not, at that moment, concerned with Robert Doctorow. Everyone seemed to be falling. Seacord and the two men with him, Bill Henry and Eamon McGrotty. Blackman automatically counted his crashing footsteps: One. Two. Three. Four. Five. Six. Down, down in one piece, and firing. They told you seven seconds, or was it eleven. No, seven. A joker could pick you up in his sights and blow you out of the world in seven seconds. For himself, Blackman counted six as seven. He was bigger than most men, made an easier target; and he was slower because of his size.

As he lay, fearful that he was all alone, he heard supporting fire from behind him. Glancing over his shoulder, he saw the thin lines of the British battalion coming up and being blown apart. The Dimitrovs were supposed to come up; where were they? Robbie, Doctorow, where in the hell—oh, shit, Blackman thought. But it was time to move; he'd already been down too long. He charged up, elbows covering his face. He was conscious that he was doing it, but couldn't stop.

Hey, he thought, There's that kid. Klonsky, straight hair streaming back, was flying parallel to Blackman; they saw each other at the same time. When Blackman next dove for cover, Klonsky followed. There were no tears, Blackman saw, and the kid was fighting his confusion, his terror. Surveying the boy as he panted, Blackman felt fresh sweat break out over his face, he concluded that no war, no matter how honorable or how desperate, should be fought with boys, and he felt a great rush of pity and sympathy, for he knew that could not be. He prepared to get up again. "Stay here," he said. "Rest a bit and come along later, if you want."

"No," the kid said, shaking his head so vigorously that Blackman knew he entertained the idea, but finding it unmanly in this, his first action, could not. "I'll come along with you."

"Then do just what I do, nothing else. When I go down, you go down; when I run, you run. Got it?"

"Got it."

They were up and off again, under a sky that had darkened without their being aware of it. The Rebel fire hadn't slackened at all, and Blackman was now sure they were way out front. What good would it do, he thought helplessly, if five men, or even ten, made it to the fascists' positions? Somebody messed up, he thought, as sheets of rain came driving down, underlining his helplessness; putting a period to his thoughts, as it were; making him reflect more keenly on his next move, to keep going or draw back. Up ahead, just barely visible through the rain he saw the Rebel barbed wire, curling back upon itself, curling down a line that went up and down hills and depressions. He heard someone running wildly through the mud; he turned just as Miltie Rappaport, mouth wide, eyes twin globes of whiteness, flashed past, no rifle, but one arm thrust in front, the other behind, a discus thrower frozen in motion at the moment of sighting, and Blackman thought: a grenade, and the next moment the heroic tableau was shattered as Rappaport, hit three times—Blackman could hear the rounds thudding into him— crashed and slid awkwardly along the ground.

"Up!" he screamed suddenly and frighteningly, aware of the grenade still in Rappaport's hand. At the same time he grabbed the kid's elbow, he became aware of impending darkness, and it was this, perhaps, that sent him sprinting back to the battalion position.

It seemed that he returned days quicker.

"Hold it," he heard the voice, and he couldn't understand why whoever was speaking wasn't helping them up to safety behind the bags and dugouts. Then he recognized Sam Stember, the battalion political commissar. Stember was pointing a hand-gun at them and swinging it around to others who were returning. "Back," Stember said. "Carry out your orders; no retreat was called."

Blackman found himself screaming in his rage and fear. "Sam, put that fucking gun down. *Down*, you sonofabitch! You cocksuckers carry this communist bullshit too far!"

"Fuck you, Sam, we're coming up." Another voice in the darkness.

"Yeah, Sam, where were you? Back here safe all the time? You goddamn creep! You want an attack, you attack." Still another voice.

Stember faded into the rain, into the night and those who'd returned, clambered up the bags, tumbled over behind them and lay still. They came back one by one, the fear in their eyes deeper than the night, their clothing soaked and dirty; their voices shaking.

The volunteers, Blackman among them because Doctorow hadn't returned, slithered back out after bread, sausage and cognac. Blackman strained to see the bodies; they would be in the postures of the Hollywood dead. He saw no bodies nor heard the whispers of the wounded, and yet, until now, he could've sworn that he couldn't have walked a foot over that field without finding one of the men who'd fallen that morning.

But now he had one, an unmoving piece of clay, already stiff. He forced himself to look closely at its face in the dark, to see if it were Doctorow; he couldn't tell. He grabbed it under its arms and slid it back to the position. It wasn't Doctorow. He went out again, but returned without a casualty or a body, the last man in.

"You all right, Abe?"

The hands pulled at him, almost lovingly he thought, maybe because he wanted them to feel that way.

"Bob Doctorow?"

"Wounded. In the foot. A bad one, but at least he's alive."

Blackman started to where the ambulances waited.

"They've gone back already, Abe. He'll be all right, you'll see."

He was relieved. Somehow Doctorow's life was tied to his and now that his friend lived, Blackman knew that he would, too. If, on the other hand Doctorow had been killed, Blackman would've resigned himself to his own death, the next attack, the next day. Whenever.

"Oliver Law," he said.

"Man," he heard Law say. "I didn't know you cared."

"Well," Blackman started, but Law, his eyes twinkling knowingly, interrupted. "And Walt Garland's all of a piece, too."

"Abe, you're a black chauvinist," someone said, laughing. But Blackman knew it was indulgent laughter, and it sounded good.

# 16

On the march, the truck ride, before an attack or pausing in retreat over mountain, through valley, Blackman pondered about this country, this Spain that saluted Africa from across Gibraltar. Never mind the British on the Rock. How dark the Spaniards were! Brothers? Why not? They said from Algeciras you could see Africa, and in Málaga on a hot day with the wind blowing right, you could smell Africa.

The Moors, of course, but then everyone had come to Spain at one time or another. It looked old and worn, dry and brown, and the people seemed molded right from the soil. But if these wrecked clots of earth could bring forth a democracy, a republic that worked well for all, couldn't others equally beaten, equally desperate for a change of pace in their history bring about like transformations?

But this one wasn't working so well, he thought as the Lincoln-Washingtons wound back to the east, chewing at Brihuega, Masegasa, Cogollor, Vitande and Hita. The flush was over for Blackman. The Italian-American, Greek-American, Japanese-American, pure Anglo, Irish-American names no longer set him to thinking of the purest of brotherhoods. Nor did ex-soldiers, West Pointers, organizers, ex-sailors, merchant seamen, professors and students start him to thinking of the perfect society. That Oliver Law, boss of the Lincolns coming up to Guadalajara had white boys snapping and cracking under his command, filled him with no pride; and at Guadalajara, they overwhelmed the fascists, sent the Italians who'd walked through Ethiopia in 1935 fleeing through machine gun raked Spanish arroyos.

And at Brunete, another Brother, Jimmy Rucker. "What say, man?"

"Everything's cool, jack."

"Well, all right now."

They were still marching, still riding, and he was thinking of Salaria Kee, the only Sister nurse in Spain, and trying to figure out how to cut into her when he got a chance. He'd spoken to her at the hospital while visiting Doctorow, almost ready to be invalided back home. Walt Garland took his second hit at Brunete, and Jack Shirai, the Nisei, too happy being away from the commissary, got his, with a smile on his face, ambling between the lines to get food for his men.

And Oliver Law at Brunete? At the foot of Mosquito Crest, he led the second company upward, Blackman at his side, until heavy fire forced them to the ground. Blackman lay still; Oliver Law moved forward, crawling, and then he stood, waving his pistol, screaming above the racket, "Okay fellows, let's go, let's go! Keep it up! We can chase them off that hill! We can take that hill! Come on!"

Blackman closed his eyes. He didn't want to see him get it. He opened them; Law was staring at him. Blackman hunched to get up. Oh shit, he thought. This is gonna be it. God, don't let it hurt. He glanced around. Not another man had moved. Law screamed at them again, hardly noticing Blackman, now on his feet, scurrying toward him.

Under the sound of gunfire, Blackman heard his shoes pounding on the centuries-old packed dirt and rock. Now, it's coming, he told himself, but still he hurled himself forward, his elbows held high in that angle; he no longer worried about it.

211

"Fuck em man, let's go!" he shouted, but he'd shouted into a Rebel fusillade which cut Law down, the rounds making brief, dull sounds as they tore into his body. The commander down, Blackman went down, stayed there beside the still-conscious Law until the firing died and the stretchers came.

"No use lugging me, boys. I'm finished. Put me down."

They started to lower the stretcher, but Blackman gave one of the stretcher bearers a nudge. They carried Oliver Law to safety, where he died. As the others dug his grave, Blackman made the marker:

Oliver Law 34 years old
Commander, Lincoln Battalion,
The First Known Negro Commander of
Any Integrated American Military Unit
July 8, 1937

The voice came after Blackman affixed the marker; it was a tired, gentle voice that seemed to be resigned. "Abe, Morris Wickman, too." Wickman, from Philly, a Brother and commander of the third company of the Washingtons. The gentle voice, then, was announcing that they'd lost; it was going to be black man grieving for black man, Southerner for Southerner, Jew for Jew, Chicano for Chicano. The Brotherhood was being decimated in the hills of Brunete. The "Internationale," already sung weakly, was going to be weaker.

No respite, they moved on to Villanueva del Pardilla, marching through the night, trying to reach positions near the Republicans. Some slept as they walked; some tried to hum or sing, but, finally, they shuffled along in silence, buffeting wearily against the night, and fearful that dawn would find them still on the road, exposed to Rebel guns.

They hadn't reached their positions, but they had to stop; many couldn't move another step, but lay in the road where they fell, resigned to dying with the first daylight. So, they stopped, and while half tried to eat what was available, the other half weakly dug into the earth for cover.

Too late! Blackman thought with the first sound of the Rebel planes. Too late! Canteen cups of barley water and hard rolls were spilled or forgotten as the Lincolns scurried for cover. The planes came over in groups of threes. They dove low, pulled up, circled and returned with machine guns clattering; they came back from a different direction and chewed up the roadway. Then they returned with their bombs. From his cluster of rocks and his shallow hole, Blackman looked at them as they vanished and knew even as the silence of the mountains closed in after their passing that worse was to come and it was not long in coming.

Artillery, shells rushing out of the silence from positions undetected. The rounds exploded and echoed through the mountains, like giants rushing over the earth; sometimes they came so fast that it seemed that one echo waited for another, and they all rushed together through the passes.

The planes returned over their positions and rained down bombs, large and small, incendiary and high explosive, and the dry fields nearby first began to smoke in protest, and then burst with a loud pop into roaring flame.

To Blackman at first it felt like riding a small vessel in a rough sea; the earth heaved and bucked; fragments whistled and whizzed snappingly through the air. He shouted at the top of his voice, "You can't kill me!" Then he cursed. "Motherfuckers. Cocksuckers, you can't kill Abraham Blackman! You can't kill ME!" His throat hurt and he knew he was screaming. He began whimpering next, his palms pressed tightly to his ears. No one can live through this, he told himself, no one.

From afar their positions seemed to have been obliterated, inundated by fire, smoke and more bombs. The smell of sulphur and cordite and hot metal drifted through the hills to Republican positions a mile and a half away. This was where the Lincolns were marching to when they got caught in the open. The Spaniards watched the holocaust, shuddering and muttering prayers for the Americans. From here they could see the shells

213

and bombs dropping into a grid on the earth, an area filled with the Americans who soon would be completely wiped out.

At the moment Blackman felt his bladder go, a lizard, driven mad by the barrage, sprang from its hiding place among the rocks, and its suctioned feet gripped the skin on his face for a second before Blackman, mad himself, shrieked with fear, felt his bladder go, his sphincter suddenly relax.

He alternated between a wild obsession that he would outlive this hell, now moving into afternoon, and a desire for a shell or bomb to find him with a direct hit and blow him out of his terror. The smell of his urine, his feces and his sweat merged into one ugly miasma. Blackman cried, sobbed and felt the heat fastening more fiercely upon the land than the nearby fires still blazing.

The Republicans could no nothing. Each man—there were only two hundred left of six hundred—knew that to them would fall the task of gathering the bodies and pieces of the bodies of the Americans and burying them. That they had to do; it was, after all, the least thing to do for people who'd died for their cause. The Spanish soldiers looked at each other and shook their heads. They turned back to the American positions. Were the big guns falling off? Were the planes going? Ah, yes. Hastily, the Spaniards checked their guns. The Rebel attack would come now, and without the Americans on their flank—? Now they took a final look at the ripped and savaged earth where the Rebels, now with a preponderance of mighty weapons, had all but pulverized the very rocks. Emerging from the pall of smoke, they saw a big man, as black as the smoke itself, the front of his pants wet, and running wide-legged as though he'd dropped a load in his pants, making his way toward them. Behind him came other Americans, and the Spanish thought, aha, a few did come through, but they kept on coming through the smoke, running staggering, some being helped. Squads, platoons, companies. They'd survived! The Spaniards rose from their holes, shouted, screamed and cheered: "*Viva! Viva! Viva!*"

214

All for what, Blackman thought sullenly, for they were still moving backwards, to the east, the newsmen with them. Matthews, Hemingway, Gellhorn, Taggard. But there were leaves in Barcelona, drinks passed out by Hemingway in the Majestic Hotel on Paseo de Gracia; long, sad strolls on the Ramblas, for it was ending, this dream. And there were meetings with La Pasionaria, Paul Robeson, Langston Hughes, and pussy and red wine on the run, then back to the pounding, refreshed, thinking, we're not going to give it away; they'll have to take every bit of it.

The Rebels were willing to at Belchite, Quinto, Fuentes del Ebro, Azail; and they took the life of Brother Milton Herndon. Now Blackman moved, fought and thought automatically, his main preoccupation on survival. He could shoot up a church to get a sniper. His mood was the judge of giving a prisoner his life or taking it, and with the Lincolns he plodded into Teruel where they took the town, but lost it back to the Rebels; and lost, too, El Muleton, Calades and Gandesa, were beaten down to invalids who dragged themselves from the hospitals to take up positions, and black Aaron Johnson died in one of those ugly, brown towns, not from bullets, but from the rampant fluids of pleurisy. Blackman remembered meeting him one night in Barcelona, in an upstairs restaurant, eating paella by candlelight, a young Spanish woman with him, that look of love bright in his eyes.

The bitter winter passed slowly and summer came to Aragon. Along the Ebro the heat was intense; the sluggish brown water was turning into a stream of mud. The rocky hillsides were turning bone white. Among the Internationals the knowledge of defeat was a foregone conclusion. But the attacks and counterattacks would go on.

In the hot night Blackman knew it was getting near time to cross the river. There was something fatal about the way night had come and settled, like someone pulling a blanket up over your dead face. What could you do about it? Once again Blackman thought of all the people he'd ever known, the girls with whom he'd made love. That night, more than any other night he could remember, he wished to both embrace and salute what was his; his memories, the sum total of accidents and designated acts that'd made his life.

At first he thought it was a wind, creeping softly through the night, but he didn't feel the breeze he was anticipating. It was coming from across the river, where the Garibaldis were; they were singing "Il Piave Mormorava," about the great battles in northern Italy in World War I and the deaths of dedicated men. They sang with great tenderness, and as their voices curled back through the hills, the "Internationale" surged forth with a muffled might, and "La Marseillaise"; other songs, in English, German, Catalan, Spanish, Polish, were lofted into the air, and Blackman wondered at these paeans and wished his eyes could water at them; for he knew that here, at least this night, this moment, it was all right again, whatever happened tomorrow. Men hoped and were ready to die for other men as Shango had risked the anger of the gods to bring fire from the heavens to men; such men must be punished. But the gods also knew and still did, that there were men who would accept the punishment without a murmur. Like these men singing into the night, their songs dying like sighs as the Internationals moved toward the Ebro, the oars of their boats already muffled. They would cross, try to drive toward Ascó, Fatarella and Corbera. They were *not* to recross the river, Commander Wolff told them. In other words, *when they died, they'd die moving forward.*

The Spanish morning came, smelling faintly of cork and olive, of vineyards and bread imagined hot out of the ovens of unseen *panaderías*. They rushed on in battered trucks and on foot without air or artillery support and for the first time faced the gun they'd heard about, the German 88.

Blackman found himself leading the "Moorish Phalanx" of the Lincolns: himself, Joe Taylor, Tom Page, Luchell McDaniels, whom the Spanish called "El Fantastico." Hipsters and squares;

216

cats from The Apple, cats from Blip, a small black blot among all the International Brigades gathered on the Ebro. Behind them lay Valencia, toward which the Rebels were driving with all their men, armor, planes and artillery. The war was all but over if they cut the Republicans' lines.

For a scorching July week Blackman led his squad forward or held position. They encountered numerous Moors on the Rebel side, withstood a new German bomber, the Stuka, saw the tough Franco-Belgian Brigade, all but wiped out, recross the Ebro only twenty-four hours after they'd started the attack.

Never had Blackman been aware of so much fascist might; wherever he led his men machine guns opened up or infantry fire; the big guns from the rear roared out with interminable patience; if they didn't get you with this round, perhaps the next. And the planes. If they weren't advancing, Blackman thought, of the Republicans, we aren't letting the Rebels through. How many were in those hills waiting to rush over their bodies? A hundred thousand, two, three hundred thousand. A mighty, fascist wave.

July turned to August, and in the Sierra Pandols, the Spanish Verdun commenced. Here, Blackman thought, is a place I won't leave. It seemed to him to be a natural graveyard, capable of holding millions, and already, with the skirmishes that had taken place on these hills of widows, orphans and sweethearts, the valleys no longer smelled of sun-scorched earth, olives or grapes, but of bodies rotting in the summer heat; the stench was so thick he could almost see it.

As the Lincolns cowered on Hill 666, preparing to withdraw from the pounding of Rebel Fiats, Heinkels, Messerschmitts, deals were being made.

Hitler roared.

The British lion cowered.

El Fantistico brought it up; with so many rumors it was inevitable. "Are they really going to pull out the Internationals?"

"That's what Negrin says—according to reports," Blackman said.

The Internationals were one of the cards being dealt in Paris, Washington and London. As beaten as they were, they were still taking a heavy toll of Rebels; without them, Franco's people could walk into Valencia—which they were doing anyway, Blackman reflected. They, the Internationals, would be pushed back on Barcelona. But with the real consideration that they might be pulled out, a certain caution would now set in. Home, vistas of a new life back there most certainly had displaced the dream of a Spanish republic. Who now would wish to be killed with the Republic all but shot away and the politicians wishing them gone anyway?

"I want to live now," El Fantastico said. Blackman wondered if he did, would he ever tell his children about this and how he came by the name. Would they ever, in a time when his bitterness wore off, visit Spain, slip away to the old battle sites and try to explain to the youngsters just what it was all about?

"We all want to live," Blackman said. "Let's see to it that we do; let's keep the contact better, so we'll know what every man's up to, if he's in trouble or not."

Somehow midnight, September 24, 1938, did arrive and League Commission representatives, already in the camp of the International Brigades, observed as the terms of the deal were carried out. The El Campesino Division slipped into the lines as the Internationals climbed wearily out. Their war was over.

Blackman listened to the feet shuffling as they marched out; there were not as many as before. Of 3200 men, fifteen hundred were still alive of the Lincolns. Five days later Chamberlain gave Hitler Czechoslovakia.

Of all the parades the largest was in Barcelona, down the Diagonal, ankle-deep in flowers. The cries of "Viva!" blasted at their ears all the way down to the docks. People cried and threw more flowers. "Viva!" El Fantastico threw up his arm and fist in the Popular Front salute and the crowds shouted

"*Viva!*" Girls rushed forward to kiss them all, to hell with Spanish custom, and all cried "*Viva!*" And they marched down centuries-old streets which resounded to their steady tread that gently vibrated the Roman aqueducts near the sea, and the crowd, soon to be enveloped by the fascists, screamed "*Viva! Viva! Viva!*"

"Yeah," El Fantastico said. "They know. They know what we're all about."

"Yeah. Right now they know. Today they know. Just today, man. Tomorrow is something else." Blackman shook his head at the water in El Fantastico's eyes.

Robert Doctorow, clumsy in his wheelchair, nevertheless rolled himself fearlessly through the halls, seeking out the officer's wing of the hospital. He had to see about the Captain while he could to settle the phrases and ideas flitting through his head. Now he'd have time, lots of it, to think about the book he was going to write about this lousy war and what happened to the men in it.

As Doctorow was rolling up this hall and down that one, Abraham Blackman peered up into the black face of a man he knew to be a doctor by the insignia on his collar. A major. The doctor smiled. "So you're Captain Blackman. You're going to be all right, Captain. Just fine. Some damage here and there. We're going to have to take your right leg, Captain, your right leg. Do you understand?"

Blackman shifted his eyes from those of the doctor to the man's hairline.

"And I'm afraid you've lost one lung."

Blackman said, "What's the pain around my balls?"

"You took a slug through the bag. Not a testicle, through the bag. That's the least of your worries. That's already fixed up."

"Umm," Blackman said. How did you screw with one leg? He turned now, to study his room for the first time, or to give the

219

doctor that impression. He heard the doctor say something about prosthetic devices, and he thought, fuck prosthetic devices. He thought about Mims. Get word to her? What for? Forget it, man. You're going to wind up like some of those black amputees you've seen skidding along the subway platforms, intimidating people into giving you handouts. The only pussy you'll get will be from broads who get kicks out of balling one-legged dudes. You can take your wooden leg and shove it up. How about that?

"When?" he finally asked.

"Tomorrow. Have to do it by tomorrow, Captain."

"Yeah, I suppose so. Do you know anything about my men?"

"Sorry, I don't know. On the basis that you're getting a medal, I'd suppose they were all all right." The major waited for a response. He leaned close to Blackman again and said, "A medal. You're a hero. I think it's the Medal—"

"Hey, man, can you give me something to put me back out? I don't want to have to lay here all night hurting and thinking about the leg. Okay?"

"Certainly, Captain. We were going to give you something to make you sleep anyway. By the way, you're not on anything? I mean, there's so much of—"

"No. I'm clean. Shoot me up." Blackman didn't feel like talking anymore. He wanted to be out of it. Forget the whole mess. It's over. Just get me on out of it, man. Zap me. He closed his eyes.

# FIVE

I'm sure the Pentagon itself would be of no help—they'd cover like hell. But I do know something wild, and very bad, happened in those swamps. God knows it needs to come to life.

Anonymous

# 17

## Cadences

*The windows were open, there were no fans. After all, the boys were out there in the far-flung jungles of the world without relief from the heat, why couldn't they suffer a little?*

*The uniformed men sat somewhat stiffly in the heavy chairs that had been placed around the great table. A slender, youngish four-star general entered and everyone stood; he waved them back to their seats and ran a thin hand through a shock of flaxen hair.*

*"Gentlemen," he said. "We have got ourselves some problems. Real problems." He patted his papers into a neat pile. "First off, these people want to fly."*

*"What!"*

*"Incredible!"*

*"Fly? Why they can't even walk. All they do is dance."*

*The young General raised his hand. "The politicians say they will fly."*

*A groan went up.*

*"Next, they're complaining about not having their own chaplains. To tell you the truth, I don't see too much wrong with letting them have a few chaplains. They're a church-going people,*

when they're not knifing each other to death. I mean, chaplains have a place in war."

"All right, all right. A few."

"A few, you mean. We aren't going to have that many combat troops that're colored. We don't have them in brigade strength in any single town in the country, except at Huachuca, a division, but they're sixty miles from nowhere. Let's be big and say five, General."

The General said, "Looks like we've got to have a dozen."

"Is that what the politicians say?"

"They say at least a dozen."

Several new cigarettes were lit during the silence that followed. There was no real need to argue points here; they were all after the same thing. And they were really one big family, white, Protestant, Scotch-Irish, German-Irish. Many had relatives who fought during the Revolution, Eighteen-twelve, the Civil War, the Spanish-American War. A number of the men in this room had themselves fought in World War I. One or two had designed his own uniform. Most were from the southern or border states.

"General Whittman, sir?"

"Yes, Smitty."

"The er—uh—morale, is it as bad as we've heard?"

"Worse, Smitty. That's our major problem." He shifted his feet to a wide stance. "Now, we've had riots at Murfreesboro, Gurdon—"

"Fort Dix," someone said.

"Huachuca," said another.

"Tuskegee, Polk, Livingston—"

"—Beauregard, Claiborne, Alexandria, Pollock, Esler, Bragg—"

"—Van Horn, Stewart, Lake Charles, March Field, Luis Obispo, Bliss, Phillips, Breckinridge, Shenango—"

An admiral spoke up. "We've had them at Sampson, Great Lakes, Shoemaker, Treasure Island, Norfolk, San Diego, Pendleton, Gulfport, St. Albans, Brooklyn, Hueneme, Pearl Harbor, Boston—"

224

*A voice heavily accented with the South blustered, "Now, goddammit, you just cain't take northern nigras and station em in the South—"*

*"But we did because you wanted the bases there to give your economy a boost. Government installations and all that—"*

*The four-star General raised both hands. "All right. We've got a long agenda. The rest of that problem is overseas deployment. Where do we send them? Had that little ruckus in Australia and the Aussies are nervous. Queried MacArthur and he says he can handle the black troops there now and those being sent, so that situation seems stable."*

*"But Gruening in Alaska doesn't think the Negroes ought to be sent up there to mix with the Indians and Eskimos. Undesirable, I think he said. What's he think they're going to do, overthrow the government?*

*"Panama wants us to remove a company of Negroes—"*

*"Isn't that something! That damned canal was built by niggers!"*

*The General went on. "—Chile and Venezuela will not, repeat, will not, accept Negro coast artillery units, and Colonel McBride tells me that colored troops will not be satisfactory in Liberia. South Africa, no; New Zealand looks okay; some political reservations in China. The Belgian Congo and French West Africa look sticky; the Belgians even in exile insist on no Negro troops in the Congo. . . ."*

Abraham Blackman heard a noise, a noise with a pattern and he thought it was someone snoring. But it was a voice, droning in prayer:

"—and Lord God Almighty, some of us may never see home again, or our loved ones, having this week entered the training of the soldier. Dear God, we implore you to watch over us, guide us safely through the hail of bullets, bombs and hand grenades to come, and return us home safely, whole in our devotion to you. We ask it in the name of Him who taught us to say when we pray:

"Our Father—"

Blackman trailed the voice to its source. The man they called Big Tim was leading the prayer. He was from Texas, a nice-looking cat, some white in him, a little Mexican, but mostly spade. Big Tim was on his knees; five older men who'd come in a couple of days ago were also on their knees, looking very pious, like the trustees or elders of the church Blackman was raised in when they were about to take up a special collection.

Now, someone at the far end of the barracks spoke sleepily, "What the fuck is you niggers doin? You ain't hardly got here, talkin about some goddamn bombs and bullets. They gonna send you old cats back home anyhow. Ain't that a bitch, layin around here prayin an hour before time to get up. Boy, I tell you, a nigger ain't shit."

"—as we forgive those who trespass against us, for Thine is the kingdom and the power and the glory. Amen."

Big Tim sprang clumsily to his feet and lunged down to the end of the barracks.

"You sacrilegious, no-count, zoot-suit-wearin motherfucker, how the hell you gonna innerup a *prayer* service, man? Didn't your momma teach you nuthin?"

Now Blackman recognized the complainant's voice. A guy they called Flash, from Philly. "Okay, okay, man. I'm sorry. You just broke in on my sleep. You right, man, that sure wasn't cool. Okay, Big Tim? You a man of God, I know you're gonna forgive me."

Big Tim bellowed, "You right about that. I'ma let you slide this time, Flash, but the next time I'ma be on your ass like stink on shit."

Blackman heard Big Tim striding away, grumbling. Then Flash's voice came again. "Hey, Big Tim."

"Now whatchew want, Flash?"

"Fuck you, Big Tim."

There came the sound of running feet and Flash's laughter riding hard in the corridor. Big Tim came back in, breathing hard. "I'ma break that nigguh's neck yet, you watch I don't."

For the next half hour Blackman lay in his cot, thinking. He'd been here two days now and seen almost every kind of black male come in, youths wearing sweaters with high school block letters on them; farmering young men up from the Deep South, still reeking of animal dung and their own sweat that'd crawled into the very fabric of their faded blue coveralls; hipsters in their zoot suits and hippie-dips trying to be as sharp as the hipsters, but failing; there were one or two college freshmen and several about whom he could discover nothing.

Later dressed and back from mess, he felt a tap on his shoulder and turned. It was the man they called Benjy, outa Chicago. Zoot-suit type, but unlike the other hipsters, he was a funny cat. "Where you from, man, standin around pickin up on these clowns comin in here like you was a camera or somethin?"

The observer observed, Blackman thought. He'd always thought of himself as the guy who watched the guy watching the broad with the fine legs. Now he was caught. He laughed down at Benjy and wondered what he'd look like after the Army got rid of his conk.

"The Apple, man." He could see Benjy thinking, Maybe this is another type cat, slicker n slick in them ol square clothes. Benjy pressed.

"Where at in the Apple?"

"Eighth Avenue and a Hunnert n Forty-fifth. What you know about it?"

Benjy grinned, yellow teeth bucking. "Jim, you'd be surprised at what I know."

"You know so fuckin much, how come you're in the Army?"

"I had to cut out. Some people fuckin over me. So I cut out from the turf. Give time for things to cool off, y dig?"

All the hipsters had some answer for being in. Babes givin em trouble, The Man lookin for em. A choice between jail and heavyfootin it—Blackman was sure that most of them just weren't as slick or cunning as they pretended to be. "Yeah," he said to Benjy. "If that's what you say."

"Well, damn, Big Man, why I got to lie about saving my neck?"

Blackman shrugged. He wasn't going to get dragged into any prolonged argument or discussion about something that didn't matter to him. He laughed at Benjy because he desperately wanted him to believe his story.

They both turned to watch Felson pass; he was one of the college freshmen. He was a short, fat, light-skinned youth, and he spoke in a soft voice. His long eyelashes were startling in his altogether ugly face. Parts of Felson jiggled when he walked. Benjy cut his eyes back to Blackman's. "Sho hope times don't git hard," he said.

At the end of that week, although everyone said they despised the Army, Blackman noticed that they were glad, even eager enough to get their uniforms, and as if that were not enough when they began company drill, they strutted, Blackman with them, as if every simple drill on the stubbled field was being attended by a thousand girls, parents and guys who were too sick, from one thing or another, to have been drafted. Like the man before him on the pivot, Blackman camel-walked, shot forward like a flash. He pitied the old guys who couldn't do the push-ups, and scrambled through the obstacle course like a young god, hardly breathing at the end of it, laughing at the men like Big Tim who almost always quit midway through or got hung up on the ropes or barriers.

As the weeks shot by, the company dissolved after training hours into groups; the last names became as familiar as the first names they'd been known by before the Army. Now came the teasing of Felson with his jello-ish buttocks; Benjy's head was lumpy with the conk gone; Flash had teamed with another youth named Tisdale and became known (among the more bold) as the Gold Dust Twins; Big Dick was from Bamberg, South

228

Carolina, and he had one, and would throw it upon one of the tables on the slightest provocation; he claimed he couldn't shoot straight on the firing range because it got in his way.

By now, when the groups gathered in the rec hall or in a corner of the barracks, the talk was of the Army General Classification Test. This was going to separate the men from the boys, the geniuses from the dummies, the slicksters from the squares.

Benjy announced, "I don't much care if I wind up in a service outfit. I don't wanna be shot at. All you cats talkin about how cool you was on the infiltration course with live ammo, you all can have it."

Blackman listened to it. He hoped he did well on the tests; he was ready to meet whatever came head on. No stuff about being slick and staying alive; hell, he was going to do that anyway, but he was going to do it as a full-fledged man. Being slick was the easy way out; you didn't even have to challenge yourself. Maybe he'd even wind up in Officers' Candidate School and get himself some bars. Wouldn't that look great on Eighth Avenue and Hundred Forty-fifth! He saw himself in summer lightweight tans striding through Harlem, his name and picture in the *Amsterdam News* and the *Afro-American*; the chicks would sure dig that. Be into that stuff *every* night, jack! Maybe he could even transfer into the Air Force then; they'd told him that the quota was full. Quota, he wondered. Why would they have a quota on the number of guys who wanted to fly planes and blow the Nazis and the Japs outa the sky? Thought they needed every flier they could get their hands on.

It didn't bother him that his was an all-black company. Like the others, he accepted it as the way things were, without question, because that was the way he'd lived for all of his young life, and living that way, he couldn't see any value in certain aspects of living or soldiering with whites.

Whites. They were, if not a favorite, a constant topic of the talk, and each man was grateful they were not training in a southern camp from which, nearly every day, news of riots reached them. This was good news, for the Negroes were fighting back. More often and with far more frequency they heard of lynchings, shootings and beatings, all apparently condoned by the Army, which did nothing about them.

"Sometimes," Benjy said, "I'm not even sure I'm in the same Army with them bastards. It sure don't seem like it."

It all seemed far away to Blackman. Fort Sheridan, hard by Lake Michigan, was miles away from the shootings, the humiliations suffered by other, less fortunate black soldiers. So far away that he could not conceive of these things happening to him. Emboldened, he said,

"That crap couldn't happen here. The guys from the North wouldn't take it."

Big Dick, stroking his penis, still inside his pants, looked up and said, "You Harlem and Chicago niggers really think you're somethin special, doncha? It's all you cats what's gittin blowed away Down Home. Y'git sent there and right away you gonna change things cause they ain't like they was at home. Been livin in Harlem all your life, or Southside Chicago or some other nigger neighborhood, without makin a peep. All of a sudden they can't do it to you down South. You niggers make me sick."

"Man, how you sound?"

"Goddamn burrhead. This's the first time in your life that cracker down there ever let you get away, Big Dick."

But the responses were not answers, Blackman noticed. Perhaps there were none.

Blackman scored in Grade I in the AGCT. So did Benjy who tried to conceal his elation by declaring that he hadn't tried, that he guessed at the answers, not knowing them, of course, and that there'd been some mistake. Felson had made Grade III.

I beat that college boy, Blackman kept thinking. How often had he walked through the Convent Avenue gate of City College, waiting for the day when he could leave off helping to support the family and enroll there. When he enlisted, he was driving a freight elevator in a factory in Queens. Still, he smiled to himself, I ain't so dumb. I wasted that college boy. Me and Benjy both. Shi-it.

Still elated, he went on furlough; he'd return to Sheridan for training in the Medical Corps, to which he and Benjy had been assigned on the basis of their grades. There would be WACs, too, when school began. He was anxious to go home and get back, for he knew that officers were selected from Grade I of the AGCT.

# 18

They left the barracks with a drummer and marched through the camp roads that led to the hospital compound. The drummer got cute when they came down the main hospital road, and the contingent, Blackman in the front rank, put em down and picked em up. Blackman almost laughed; if black folks couldn't do anything else, they could sure march; he hadn't seen any white boys who could match the worst Negro training company in drill. The more the white soldiers and WACs paused to watch them, the more they swaggered, until, at last, they stopped before their new barracks.

There was a roll call and a formal welcome by the Exec of the hospital and the Commander of the Medical Corps Training School. As they spoke, Blackman was noticing that the barracks was at the end of the street, hard against the eight-foot barbed-wire fence behind which an armed guard was visible. The mess hall was directly across the street, seeing it, the smells seemed to grow more intense to Blackman. Cooking, waste, garbage cans; they'd smell this for six weeks. And then they were inside, choosing the best located bunks, for others were due in for that particular class.

Later that evening, a corporal named Gummidge, who'd

232

been placed in charge of the contingent, called an impromptu meeting. Blackman looked at Gummidge and wondered why he was in the Army at all. He was a fat man who spoke with a soft voice; and his eyes were soft.

Blackman knew none of the others except Benjy; they'd all come from other camps in other parts of the country. They focused their attention on Gummidge, a man, Blackman guessed, over thirty. This, Gummidge said, moving his hands languidly on air, was the first class of Army medical corpsmen in this war. The Chicago *Defender* has already broken the news to colored people. They expected the class to do well. Hanging on our every endeavor, Gummidge said, were thirteen million Negroes. Ours, therefore was a grave and great responsibility, but he knew every man would succeed. He had felt so much pride watching the march into the hospital. Gummidge paused and his gentle, compassionate eyes wandered over the group. "That's all I wanted to say," he said. "Except, when we're finished here, we just don't know where we'll be headed. Some to service outfits"—and here Blackman saw Benjy smile—"and some to the combat outfits. There's just no telling."

The meeting broke up quietly. Blackman went outside and sat on the steps. The guard outside the fence passed slowly, like a shred of dirty brown fog, and moved out of sight. Down the street the barracks lights were all on, and Blackman could hear radios and phonographs playing. How long, he wondered, would it take him to make T-5; how long to get to OCS? There were lots of Negro outfits in training; they'd need officers. He had to do well here, maybe move up quickly, into another branch, even, where the promos came quicker. He heard footsteps on the porch behind him, but didn't turn.

"You sure lookin evil," the voice said, and then Blackman recognized Linkey, who'd just come in that afternoon.

"Am I?"

"Real evil. You Blackman, aincha?"

"Yeah."

Still behind him, Linkey said, "This looks like a solid, good deal, don't it?"

"This school?"

"Yeah, man," he said suddenly sounding impatient. "Well, it's cool for me, cause I just married the most gorgeous, well-put-together chick in the *world!*" Blackman turned just as Linkey stomped a foot and clapped his hands. "And this gives me another six weeks to be close to that fine, brown frame, jack, another month and a half!"

Momentarily Blackman envied him. "Enjoy it while you can," he said, and felt the air become suddenly charged.

Linkey bent down over him. "What do you mean by that, man? You signifyin or somethin?"

"No. Forget it, man," and Blackman shut up and turned his back to Linkey, busied himself staring at the barracks lights. Linkey moved away slowly. His movements seemed to say, You may be evil, but you fuck with me and I'll kick your ass. I'm just lightenin up on you cause you're in your mood.

Blackman heard him open the door and said, "Hey, man. I know she's fine as wine. Good luck. Don't pay me no mind."

Linkey chuckled. "Yeah, champ. Everything's solid."

The days began to unwind, to slip by in a mélange of classes, meals, conversations, leaves into Waukegan where the boogey-bears hung out, women who snapped off dicks as fast as they could come from behind buttons; or into Chicago, haunting Parkway Ballroom, the Pershing, the Black Cat, the Rhumboogie, the DuSable. Blackman caught the trains into Waukegan or Chicago; he caught the last cars back to the hospital, just in time for reveille, and walked about all day, his penis half hard from thinking how he got it in the back seat of a jitney while the driver prowled up and down South Parkway, sighing in the front seat and peeking at his rear-view mirror; or how he got some under the stone steps of the Black Cat, pants down around his ankles, his hands protecting the girl's bottom from

234

the Chicago night while the El passed overhead, casting a long sliver of nervous light; he didn't hear the lectures on materia medica or physiology or anatomy and the rest; his ears still rang with the sound of Johnny Hodges or the Duke; Lucky Millinder, Fatha Hines, Billy Eckstine singing "Stormy Monday Blues."

Basie's "One O'clock Jump" throbbed in his head; Al Hibbler's hip voice echoed over talk of rib cages, GSWs and morphine Syrettes. Erskine Hawkins and Dash and Bascomb. Blackman thought he smelled perfume at various times of the day, and at evening colors, when he stood looking toward the flag, he thought of their faces and bodies. There was so much of it out there, and from time to time, with the WACs, in here.

Just past the midway point, Benjy and Blackman, on leave together, drifted into a USO dance in Waukegan, having failed everywhere else. The record playing was a Lucky Millinder side, Sister Rosetta Tharpe singing. He saw her from across the room and he began circling, sidling, getting close. Blackman looked over his shoulder; Benjy was watching: Go on, man. Work out. If you can.

Blackman was close to her when "Sophisticated Lady" started and he held out his hand; she took it. He didn't release her when the record was over, and they moved to "The Skater's Waltz." She flowed out from him and returned, like a wave, gently, splashing over him; she had a way of caressing his neck before she slid her arm down to his waist. Blackman didn't want to stop dancing with her, and whenever he saw someone ready to cut in, he moved her across the floor.

"I could dance with you all night," he said, and immediately felt foolish.

"All right, let's."

Later, when he knew her name was Osa and she knew his, they walked around watching the other dancers; the long lean cats from Down Home who had more steps, more grace and moves than should've been allowed, and the city cats with their studied nonchalance, that Savoy-Regal cool. Downstairs at the Coke machine, the room empty, they listened to the old building creaking to the dance steps, heard two hundred feet slipping along the waxed floor in unison, *shoom, shoom, shoom-shoom-shoom; shoom, shoom, shoom-shoom-shoom.* Goddamn, Blackman thought, listen to them niggers go! Osa tilted her head backwards as if she'd read his thoughts. "I like to come down here and listen to them," she said. "I didn't think anyone else in the world could be moved by the sound. My husband wasn't."

"Married?" Blackman tried to sound casual, but he felt strangely and suddenly deprived, and inexplicably jealous. Why, he wondered. All he wanted was some pussy.

She laughed and now he could see that she was perhaps twenty-five or close to it. A grown woman. "Sure. Isn't nearly everybody?" She became coy. "Thought you had a chippie, did you, Abraham?"

"Well, I—uh—ah—," pointing to her finger as she placed her hand in his and looked, too.

"Don't wear one, baby."

"Where's he?"

"North Africa. Ninety-ninth."

A pilot, Blackman thought. "Well, since I can't take you home—"

That smile again. Warm. Teasing. Interested. "Why can't you? I live in Evanston."

"Evanston!" Blackman blurted. That meant going back past the fort, almost into Chicago, and then returning. For a moment Osa didn't look worth all the trouble, but in the next, she did; worth it and more.

They sat together on a seat facing Benjy who slept all the way to the fort. He got off shaking his head at them, but Osa smiled warmly and moved closer to Blackman when the train continued. They talked in whispers, close to each other's ears. She was from Evanston, born and raised; had gone to Drake, in Iowa. Married a year. Not sure about it.

236

When they'd given each other their pasts briefly, he said, "Osa," then whispered it. "Osa."

"You say it pretty, baby." She stroked his cheek and studied him.

"It's a pretty name."

"Say it again?"

"Osa."

"Ummm." She moved closer to him and said, "Strange, strange."

It's gonna be cool, Blackman thought. This trim is gonna be mine. He wondered what time it was; he didn't want to get caught sneaking a look at his watch. And then he thought, Hey, I could really go for this chick. Older, but—I'm gonna be detailed out before long, to somewhere, and I'd better cut on into this good thing while I got the chance. But, lord, why does she have to live in Evanston?

At last the train slowed and stopped. Blackman hesitated on the platform. "Listen," he said. "It's late and I'd better catch the next train back. I'll call you," he said with a rush, "I'll really call you, I want to call—" He stopped and listened to his voice burbling around the deserted platform, the rushing train now a low rumble in the distance. Another train, the express, blasted out of the north and roared after the local. During the moments they couldn't speak, they looked at each other. Then she took his hand and led him down the stairs inside the station. "We'll call a cab here," she said. "And go home. I'll drive you back to the fort."

She answered the question in his eyes. "Doesn't look so good at a USO thing. I've even managed to do with Coke at those dances."

They sat back in the cab and held hands. The streets were empty, quiet. Suddenly they both spoke at the same time:

| "Do you ever have the feeling that you're the only person alive in the world when it's early like this?" | "Do you ever have the feeling that you're the only person alive in the world when it's early like this?" |
|---|---|

"Jesus Christ," she whispered, and turned to look out the window.

Then they were inside her flat, the morning struggling hard to come up, and later, roaring up to Fort Sheridan in her car, sharing a quart of bitterly cold milk and a pack of cigarettes, he thought of what she had on under her coat. Nothing. He wanted her to stop, but said nothing; he placed his hand in her crotch and slid his finger in. She drove back and forth across the road, her mouth wide, her legs opening and closing, the long, brown thighs he'd mounted in so much haste earlier, trembling. She gasped, pulled over and lay her head on the wheel when she stopped. "You drive."

Before he started, she loosened his belt, and he himself slid down his pants and drawers. As he drove back onto the road, he felt her grasping it; it was already hard and steaming. She was on the floor now, her breasts quivering on the seat, and then she was making love to it. With clenched teeth, Blackman was driving straight enough, but every time he glanced at the speedometer he was doing eighty.

He called her that night and the night after, suddenly conscious of time left, the talk of places where they might be sent, filling every spare moment. He found that Benjy was forever tapping him out of daydream, and he had no energy; he just wanted to think of Osa. Blackman sought out Linkey and they talked of good women, of beautiful women and women who were good in bed, and he knew he was thinking of Osa, while Linkey was thinking of his wife.

Suddenly all leaves were canceled and Blackman panicked. The course had been shortened; assignments would be drawn within the next three or four days. Osa, he thought. I've got to see Osa! Desperate, he called and told her to park on the road outside the hospital, that he'd find her. Benjy, against his wishes, distracted the guard for him and Blackman went over the fence. She was there, waiting, and to save time they drove at top speed into Waukegan and rented a room above a bar.

They made love on the sagging, spring-sprung bed; on the gritty linoleum floor, in a creaking wicker chair, and then they drove back to the fort, Osa crying all the way and Blackman promising he'd do his best to see her again before he left.

He came back through the tall grass, crouching, hearing Benjy's voice, for Blackman's return time had been set. Benjy was already at work, distracting the guard again. "Hey, you crazy motherfucker. How's your momma today? You got a momma, white boy? I bet that's the only pussy you *ever* got next to. Does your momma wear drawers, boy? She do?"

Red in the face, the guard was walking slowly but steadily away from Benjy's voice. "Say, boy, you passed here and I didn't see nothin hangin heavy in your pants. What you got down there, a pussy? You gon go far in the Army if that's what you got man. I like a little round eye myself once in a while, specially on tender, lil ol white boys."

Benjy was signaling Blackman and Blackman was up and over the fence and onto the ground. He was so tired he just lay there. Benjy grasped for his arm. "Get up, man. I got that boy so mad he's liable to start shootin any minute. Abe, you better get the hell up from there."

Blackman got up, staggered into the barracks and got a Coke. Benjy came in and looked at him. "This nigger's in love," he said. "You a little tender for that babe, man. She got five years on you—"

Blackman glared at him. He knew all that. How many times had he gone over it in his own mind, trying to see Osa the way his father would see her, or his mother; what would it be like, being married to her?

Blackman finished at the top of the class and made some discreet inquiries about applying to OCS and, failing that, where he was going to be sent. The officers he asked smiled, admitted he'd done well, but he'd have to wait and see what happened because no orders had come in yet. When the orders did come in, they were all assigned to Services of Supply; some were

239

going east and some west. Benjy was happy, Blackman and Linkey glum. They were going to Fort Ord; the next stop would be the Pacific. Europe seemed the more civilized place; there were famous towns and cities, and everyone knew, from the last war, that European women were especially grateful to American rescuers. They were envious of Benjy.

The railroad station was a big, noisy catacomb. Linkey and Blackman had two hours between trains. Now Linkey was somewhere in the station with his wife, and Blackman and Osa were drinking coffee and sitting in long silences. When they were tired of that, they walked around the station. "I'm coming to California," Osa said. "I'm going to try. If you want me to. Maybe you're glad you're going away from an old woman like me."

"No. You know I'm not. But I don't know how long I'll be at Ord."

"I'll come for as long as you're there."

He didn't ask about her husband; had never asked about him except for the first time.

The panic came when his train was announced; then he wondered why they hadn't found a room. Had they enjoyed being sad, holding hands and showing their sadness to the world, the way the soldier and the girl did in the movies?

"Call as soon as you get settled," she said, stretching up to him, clutching the sleeve of his coat.

"Yes, I will. I will."

She stayed on the platform beneath his window, alternately crying and smiling. Linkey's wife, next to her, smiled little smiles to Linkey who leaned over Blackman to press his lips to the window. The train jerked and Blackman saw Osa's mouth fall open; bumping into Linkey's wife, she took a few tentative steps in the direction the train was moving, then stopped, giving up; her head seemed to sink beneath her shoulders. She raised

240

her gloved hand once and bent the fingers down to the palm, and the train rushed forward.

## Cadences

"If we can get it into a bomb that a plane can carry, who'll we drop it on, the Germans or the Japs?"

"We got the plane coming. They call it the Superfort."

"Good, but where do we dump the goddamn thing?"

"Doctor, do you have relatives in Japan?"

"Of course, not, Doctor. Do I look like it?"

"Were the Japs on the Mayflower? Did they settle St. Augustine? Did they carve out the West?"

"Doctor, if you'll excuse me, those are silly fucking questions."

"Think of all the words in our vocabulary that're Japanese. Know any?"

"None, Doctor, as you well know, except for menus—"

"Ever heard of anyone going to the Japanese Riviera?"

"No."

"Are the Louvre, Prado, Rijksmuseum, British Museum in Japan?"

"Goddamn it, no."

"Where did this business start, anyway?"

"Why, in Germany and then there's—"

"You bet your sweet ass, Doctor. You've answered your own question. Now let's get back to work. This fission is a pain in the ass. Fusion, that's the answer, more power, less space. Boom! You hear me, Doctor, BA—roOM!"

At their aid station at Ord they passed the days playing touch football, cards or shooting craps. They didn't have to fight the mess lines; they simply ordered enough food for the patients in the station and themselves and drew lots to see who would go get the mess cart and return it. Blackman spent some of his nights waiting on line at the communications center to call Osa,

241

others in the movies or talking about getting to San Francisco. There were no furloughs; they were all on standby.

Gnawing at Blackman was his assignment to a Services of Supply unit. Why, with his grades? He was officer material! Right now someone somewhere should be processing his papers and discovering him. Then all would be put right. But Christ, let him get detailed out to one of those miserable islands, they'd never find him, never. Linkey was his only consolation, he being even more glum than Blackman. When Blackman greeted him during the day, Linkey would invariably answer: "Man, I just ain't doin no good." Each night he wrote to his wife while on duty in the ward, and when he came out, the calls would begin for him to do *The Signifying Monkey*.

"Hey, Linkey. Do *The Signifyin Monkey*."

"No, man, do *Shine*."

"You jokers're a pain in the ass," he'd say, taking his time getting undressed, not saying yes or no. Once in bed, he cleared his throat loudly and the barracks fell silent, waiting. Linkey had a big, basso profundo voice, and he could recite with all the nuances; it was easy to laugh night after night.

But this night Linkey prefaced his recital. "I might as well go on and do it, cause I ain't gonna be with you motherfuckers much longer. I'm cuttin out to the Windy City. Big Chi. And I'm gonna think about you. For about five minutes."

A chorus of voices rose in derision.

"Nigger, shut up and recite."

"That cat supposed to be slick."

"Joadie Grinder," Linkey shouted. "And I'ma be sharp, too. Touch me and bleed to death, square cocksuckers." He laughed.

The pfc called Scovall, out of Baltimore, called out: "Stop the shit, Linkey. You gonna be just like the rest of us, over there on them goddamn beaches beggin the Japs not to shoot you in the mouth and pleadin for the infantry not to shoot you in the ass. Who you jivin?"

"Money!" Linkey shouted.

242

"Twenty dollars," Scovall shouted back.

"Fool, that ain't no money," Linkey retorted. "*Fifty* dollars!"

"I'ma call your bluff, nigger!" Scovall was out of his bunk, sliding down the barrack floor, his finger jabbing the air toward Linkey.

"Hey, Abe," Linkey said. "Collect the gelt in the morning, okay?"

Blackman said, "All right, man, now will you do *The Signifyin Monkey?*"

"In a minute. I wanna tell you." Linkey's voice sounded joyful. "First thing, I'ma get outa this nasty ass khaki. Get me three or four reee-al sharp fronts, and some of them loafers that's the style now. Then me and my old lady gonna hit South Parkway, jim; we gonna cool it from Sixty-third Street down to Forty-seventh, just tippin, jim. Naturally, we gonna fall by a few joints; take some top-shelf to the Rhumboogie, take in a show at the Regal, taste us some ribs. Then we gonna cool it back home and come outa them vines. . . ."

Goddamn him, Blackman thought. Linkey's voice was so filled with confidence, and they were all listening to him, *seeing* him do what he said he was going to do. Hey, Blackman thought. Maybe the cat does have something up his sleeve.

Scovall's voice came out of the darkness, a little shakily, Blackman thought. "Yeah, and I'ma walk on the Pacific Ocean tomorrow."

Linkey's voice, still confident and happy; "Okay, sucker. You gonna make me fifty dollars richer. You niggers ready?"

"Oh, go on, man."

"Wait. This poem is dedicated to Scovall." Linkey laughed.

*Said the monkey to the lion, one bright sunny day,*
*There's a big burly mothafucka down the jungle way,*
*an the way he's talkin bout you, he can't be your friend,*
*an when you two lock asses, one of you's bound to been;*
*he say, you king of the beasts with your shaggy ass mane?*

he gon stomp your ass till you feels no pain;
say you growlin and roarin, keepin up fuss?
Well, he gon kick your ass, jack, till you shittin pus;
he say you got a momma what's a two-bit whore,
what don't do nothin but suck, shit and snore.
Now, up jumped ol lion in a holluva rage,
his tail a-twitchin like he'd blown him some gage.
Say, which way's that mothafucka, I'll stop his shit,
and he shot through the jungle hot as a bitch.
Ol elephant was munchin some tall collard greens,
when the king of the jungle stomped out mean.
Say now, jack, gonna beat yo ass to death;
gon stomp you till you ain't got no breath left.
Soundin on me, mighty king of all beasts,
I'm show your fat ass just who is the chief.
Elephant say, man, what the hell's wrong with you?
Better find you some broad you can lay down and screw;
I don know what you talkin about,
So don start no shit's gonna git you punched out.
Ol lion jumped back and threw up his paws,
just as elephant went BAM! upside his jaw;
then grabbed lion's tail, turned im ever' way but loose;
stomped him, beat him, pure mashed him to juice.
Lion saw stars and the sun and the moon,
lay on his ass thinkin shit, I have been ruined.
From up high in a tree the monkey looked down,
say to the lion, man what you doin on the ground?
You s'posed to be king of the jungle, just look at your ass;
elephant done fucked over you from friss to frass.
Monkey waxed bold and he jumped up and down,
say to the lion, you ol jive-ass clown,
If I wasn't cool, I'd beat your ass, too—
turkey mothafucka, you jive through and through.
Monkey was cited, jumpin all around,
then his big foot slipped and his ass hit the ground.

244

*Like a flash of lightning and a bolt of white heat,*
*lion was on his ass with all four feet.*
*Say, Signifyin Monkey, your goddamn time has come,*
*that big mouth of yours no more will run.*
*Monkey say, now look, mighty king,*
*I didn't mean nothing, you the best of everything.*
*No, monkey, no, said the lion drawing back,*
*your nasty assed mouth done got you in a crack.*
*Please mighty lion, have pity on me—*
*Stomp! Stomp! say lion, fuckin wid me.*
*Now, needless to say, the monkey's no more,*
*and the jungle's quiet cause the lion don't roar.*

# 19

Morning spilled over the mountains, pitted with fast-moving gray clouds and specks of sun trying to break through. Blackman couldn't concentrate on anything as he lay in his bunk. He had the duty; he'd have to get the mess cart. Why hadn't he heard from Osa, after all those calls? What did Linkey have in mind? He swung his legs to the floor and looked at his shoes.

"Everybody in there's running a temperature," he heard one of the duty medics saying to somebody.

Tough, Blackman thought. Now he glanced around at the others starting to come awake. He didn't feel like talking to anybody this morning. Dress and get the fuck outa here, he thought, and then he paused. What's wrong with today? Why does it feel, already, so sharp, so dangerous? Ah, Osa, he thought, don't do it. Please, don't do it, baby. I love you.

But Linkey was already up and waiting for him in the latrine.

"Gotta talk to you, Abe."

Grunting, sprinkling drops of urine all over the wall and floor.

"I got the duty this morning, man."

"Okay. I'll go with you."

Shit, Blackman thought.

Within minutes they were taking long strides along dirt paths and roads toward the main mess hall, where the lines were already impossibly long, but moving at a brisk clip past the armed guards. Armed guards because of mess hall trouble; riots; wholesale battles between black and white. Armed guards kept the peace, more or less.

"How's Osa?"

"Okay." Now he'd have to ask after Linkey's wife. "How's your wife?"

"Okay. But that's what I wanted to talk to you about, Abe. I need your help."

They cut through one of the lines.

"I need your help," Linkey said again.

"For what?"

"I'ma get outa this motherfucker."

"You said that last night."

"And I meant it. Now here's what—"

The sounds around them had been growing louder; now they positively exploded. Out of the corner of his searching eye, Blackman saw a sudden, violent movement, and told himself he hadn't seen it. But he had, blurs. Three white soldiers in fatigues pummeling to the ground a black soldier who, even now was struggling to get up from the ground, his face in an appeal, mixed with anger. Now, bouncing off Blackman and Linkey, came a swarm of black soldiers. Another movement in the lines and a cluster of whites broke through, then more and more until Blackman, separated from Linkey, was engulfed; he was involved, yet apart; it was like watching an amoeba gone wild, stretching to break itself and form anew. Blackman started throwing punches, at first, measured and with snap, at every white face he saw cresting the billowing bodies. Then, in self-defense, he threw faster and faster, ducked, spun and began to feel a growing fear as he felt the weight of all those bodies writhing and pummeling. The mass opened suddenly and Blackman found himself in its center, blows raining on his face, body and legs. He went low, but stayed on his feet. Don't go down, he told himself. He grabbed a waist above which pink and white skin was visible, and came up with his knee.

"Jesus, Jesus," the man said, and melted out of his grip.

Still in his crouch, Blackman turned and eagerly sought another. This was a race riot! The middle of it! No guns. Flesh on flesh.

"Motherfuckers!" he heard Linkey bellowing. "Here's some more!" Linkey bellowed not in pain, but in some primitive triumph. Above the grunts, groans, yells, shrieks and the sounds of blows being landed, voices snarled, "Niggercrackercocksucker-blacksonofabitchfaggotpeckerwoodstinkinniggerdicklickinpaddies - kickyoassripthatbigprickoffyoukillkillkill."

Before Blackman could complete his turn, something hit his back and his arms and legs flew out and a group already on the ground jerked up and pounded him in the face and neck; one bit him. Flashes of silver and gold raced past Blackman's eyes; then they stopped, leaving in their places a sharp pain growing sharper. He covered his head with his arms and worked himself to his knees. Bam! Another sharp pain, this one in the face. Blackman slipped to one side and went down again. His fear was now turgid; he wanted to be angry. Anger. The fear was implacable and it was coming on. He felt it and suddenly began to flail out, and the more he did, the less he felt the fear. He was coming erect, growling; the more he moved and flailed, the louder he growled, then started to bellow. (Holler when you throw that bayonet in, HOLLER!) All over the plain before the mess hall, men were down, about to go down or knocking each other down.

Unmistakably a BAR, Blackman thought when he heard it banging nearby. Then there were whistles and shouts of authority. "You men! You people! Break it up! Attention! On your feet, you hear me, on your feet! Get your hands up. Up, I said, UP." More gunfire. The movement slowed, like a sea settling before a dying wind. Hands went up, as in a mass prayer. Blackman saw the trucks with machine guns mounted on the roofs of the cabins, foot soldiers with M-1s held at the ready. These last

248

began to move into the mass, herding the whites into one group, the blacks into another. A soldier next to Blackman, his face split and bleeding, shouted, "Cracker bastards tried to cut in on me on the line, three of em, like I wasn't nothin—"

"Shut up in there!" a lieutenant shouted.

From nearby Blackman—he thought it was Linkey: "Fuck you, peckerwood!"

"How's that?" Moving in threateningly, but not too far. "How's that again?"

Prodded with rifle barrels they started to climb into the two-and-a-half-ton trucks, now rolling up in a cloud of dust, the blacks into one group, the whites into another. Now ambulances came careening up, and medics spilled out to look after the wounded. The trucks drove through the fort on the way to the stockade. Black soldiers were trotting in small groups toward the mess hall. "What happened, man?" one said, addressing Blackman.

"Paddy boys jumped us on the mess line."

"Oh oh. Some more of that lame shit, huh? Anybody hurt?"

"Don't know, but there're lotsa cats layin back there."

Linkey wasn't in Blackman's truck; he hoped he wasn't back there on the ground.

The stockade was far too small to hold all the men charged with grievous assault. Lists of names were compiled; these men would go up for courts-martial. Blackman was released for evening mess.

There was an uneasy silence in the station when he arrived. It was on a street where the black and white sections merged. Scovall met him at the door, baseball bat in hand. He grinned. "Now we're all present and accounted for."

Looking around, Blackman saw Linkey sprawled on his bunk. "You okay, Abe? What took you so long, man? What they gonna do with you? You get assault, too?"

For the first time Blackman realized that this would go in his record; he'd never make OCS now. While he compared notes with Linkey, the four men who'd gone for the mess cart returned. Safely. After the meal (the cart wasn't being returned until morning) the lights were turned off and a chair propped against the door. Scovall said hoarsely, "I think it's goin to be cool tonight."

"I don't give a damn if it *ain't* cool; I got my shit." Linkey.

Blackman heard a tiny, rushing sound which terminated in a loud, metallic clack. Switchblade. No one asked if he'd used it earlier at the mess hall. Two white soldiers had been badly cut.

"You're going to ruin the spring," Blackman said.

"Oh, yeah, Abe. There's some mail for you."

Blackman's heart tumbled. "Yeah, where?"

"Nigger sounds like he don't want it," someone snickered.

Reluctantly, while sitting in the latrine in a corner, Blackman ripped open the letter. He read it once and trembled with rage. He took a deep breath and reread it, looking for clues that would make it all right again. There were none. It was over. This time, "a wonderful sailor from Great Lakes." Slowly, he ripped up the letter and stuck the pieces under him into the bowl.

He didn't sleep well that night. He thought of the sailor riding his woman, of the smiles she was turning on him, of his eyes wide at the sight of those breasts that fitted his hands so nicely.

The next morning, Linkey and Blackman stood outside the station.

"We didn't have a chance to talk yesterday. We were, what you might call, rudely interrupted." Linkey chuckled.

"Yeah. What were you going to talk about?"

"I want you to puncture my eardrum."

A wind swept through the street, scattering surface dust and candy wrappers. Blackman turned from Linkey. "Shit."

"C'mon, man."

"Do it yourself."

"Can't. Tried."

250

"Get Scovall to do it. He'll bust your head while he's at it, too."

"No. You, Abe."

"Why me?"

Linkey grinned. "Don't exactly know why. A hunch."

"What's that supposed to mean?"

"I told you. I don't know. You'll do it, won't you? Don't worry about hurting me. Got to hurt a little, but so what?"

Today Blackman wanted to hurt, and he knew it. He said, "I might hurt you bad, Linkey."

"Goddamn it, man, just do it. Don't nobody have to know about it but me and you."

Blackman stared out over the brown hills over which some infantrymen were running and said again, "I might hurt you."

"Oh, nigger, that's what it's all about? What's the matter with you?" He was getting angry now. "Let's stop the shit. You gonna do it or not?"

Blackman shrugged. "Sure. How do you want it?"

"First, let's try concussion."

Later, after the others crept out to play touch football, Linkey and Blackman went into the latrine. Linkey talked nervously. "I keep thinkin about all those guys with bad eardrums. They ain't in. Got to get back to my old lady, man. They really gonna do us in at the court-martial." He paused and looked at Blackman. "Okay, lay it on, jack."

They agreed on the left ear. "You ready?" Blackman asked.

"Go head."

Blackman's first blow was short and measuring, with the palm of his hand, but it jolted Linkey. "You okay?"

Linkey said, "Yeah."

Blackman got more leverage with the next. Between blows he asked,

"You okay?" and Linkey would answer through clenched teeth, "Shit, yeah. Git it on, man, git it on." Blackman laid it on until his hand grew sore, until his palm was as red as Linkey's ear.

"It's singin like a bitch," Linkey said. "Like a volcano going

251

off, like Niagara Falls all rolled into one. Good God Almighty. If this ain't it—"

He waited a day, then went to see a doctor. There was nothing wrong with the ear.

When they returned to the latrine, Linkey handed Blackman a 20-cc syringe with a needle attached. Blackman took it without comment, swabbed the needle with a piece of alcohol-soaked cotton. Linkey bent down so Blackman could get more light. He said, "Git it, man."

Holding the needle poised, Blackman said, "You sure you want it this way?"

Linkey exploded. "*Stick* that motherfucker, man. We ain't playin no games here."

Holding the syringe lightly, Blackman went into the ear. He felt the needle point bouncing ever so lightly against the membrane.

"Am I there, man?"

"That's it, that's it, go on, go on—" He sucked in his breath, closed his eyes and ground his teeth.

Blackman went in, pressed, felt resistance, and then he was through. Linkey gasped, shuddered and then moaned. "Goddamn it, man," Blackman hissed. "Don't jump like that! You want this fucking thing in your brain?" He withdrew the needle; there was a neat, thin stream of blood on it.

"Let's see."

Blackman handed him the works.

"That ought to get it," Linkey said with a smile. Then he leaned over a toilet and vomited.

"You okay?"

"Shit, yeah. You a crazy cat, Blackman. Thanks."

"Any time, Linkey."

Linkey didn't return to the station after he saw the doctor. He called and asked Blackman to get his clothes and bring the money, and Scovall went to the hospital with Blackman and even talked to the doctor, who said it was very likely that Private

Linkey would be discharged after treatment. Did Private Scovall know anything about the injury, which seemed to be fresh, although one couldn't always tell about eardrums?

Blackman didn't have time to miss Linkey or grieve any further over Osa. Like every other black soldier in the mess hall riot, he was going overseas on the next boat.

The engines on the ship stopped, then started up again, slowly. Blackman, who'd been laying in his bunk, twisted suddenly, and his eyes caught the startled stare of the man in the next bunk. "We stoppin," he said. Then, "Oh shit."

A stink, sharper than usual, seemed to billow up in the hold, and everyone started to move at once, climbing slowly down from their bunks, checking and rechecking packs, nervously fitting on the helmets. The men who had weapons checked them stoically; most didn't have them. What did a stevedore require a weapon for? Some of the men were evil and snarled and cursed whenever someone approached them; others were quiet, as if in reflection, or perhaps, prayer. And they were considerate; this might count toward saving their lives.

Blackman watched. There was no need to check his pack or his kit; he knew exactly what was in both. In the latter, tags, sulfa powders, morphine Syrettes, bandages. Blackman's bowels tightened. He had to fart, and tried to, turning himself up on one haunch, but he quit; he couldn't tell which would come, the gas or the feces. The PA was issuing orders, hold by hold. Lines were forming in the passageway to the latrine, each man seeming to be unaware of the many others with the same problem.

Blackman kept attuned to the noises he could hear outside the ship. Planes, he guessed from Guadalcanal, and big guns from the few ships that'd come up the channel with them. Those, he thought, must be bombs.

The slow throbbing in the belly of the ship stopped again. Blackman closed his eyes to slow his racing stomach. The engines were the technological stimuli; they ran panting to his senses, shouting to him what the absence of the sound of those engines meant.

"They're going!" came a shout.

The white soldiers of the 37th and the marines of the 1st were hitting the nets. They'd have to secure the beach and adjacent areas; Blackman's group would then go in and begin handling cargo—ammo, ammo and more ammo and then, perhaps, food. If they lost the beach?

Naw. They'd said Bougainville was easy.

Soon, too soon, Blackman found himself moving in a line, climbing the steep steps to the upper deck, where the cool sea air whipped around wisps of cordite.

As in a daze, Blackman watched the line of heaving barges dip into the sea and out of it. Some started to pull away; others were already returning from the beach. Strange, fluttering sounds rushed through the air to explode against the steep hillsides, and planes, roaring in low from the 'Canal, passed mast-high overhead, pulled up and their bombs exploded, too, as if there was no connection between the planes, already flying away, and the noise of their missiles. Pushed from behind, Blackman moved ahead to the bulkhead, found the start of the browned, wet, rope net and started to climb down. There was water in the barges.

"Shit," Blackman said.

"Get down, get down," said the young sailor at the wheel at the rear of the craft. He sounded bored.

Feeling foolish, Blackman tucked his head below the gunwales; the brave cats, he thought, can leave them up. In times past when men were so tightly packed together, the jokes came: "Man, you sure got some fine, soft buns."

"Baby, you feelin mighty good around the hindparts there."

"Turn my ass loose, motherfucker, and take hold to my dick. You know that's what you tryin to git to."

But now, nothing.

Blackman looked back at the life-jacketed coxswain. Young.

254

White. Defiant. He'd laid aside his helmet and his hair sprayed out in the wind. Somehow Blackman found that reassuring. The engine of the boat began to boil and gurgle; the craft sought a deeper seat in the water. It seemed to slide out from behind the ship, and was now unprotected from the sweep of wind. They swung wide under the bow of the ship and Blackman saw the island again. It looked different from the barge, larger, more menacing.

They headed straight in, the barge taking the waves head on, then shuddering, skidding, continued on its course through barbed wire that'd been cut. The planes kept coming, and Blackman could now see the ships firing. The barge line was crooked, Blackman saw, unable to keep below the gunwale. The explosions on the island were becoming louder. Blackman glanced behind him at the coxswain, saw that he'd put on his helmet, and grew nervous. Then he heard the first sibilant whisper of sand on the keel, just as the coxswain was reversing his engines, spinning his wheel furiously. The ramp plopped into the water without ceremony and bunched up, they ran out, crouching.

"Hit it!" someone shouted. "Spread out, spread out and dig in, what're you, 24th?"

"Yeah," a sergeant shouted back.

"Okay, dig in till I get back to you." The man ran heavily across the sand, hailing other incoming barges, a .45 held in one hand.

Downshore, a disabled barge, upended, lunged futilely at the sky. Marines fired from behind it. Three leaped from the cover of the barge, splattered through the water and gained the beach, which now seemed vast to Blackman. The marines started across to the area where the kunai grass formed the start of land, the end of beach. Two ran abreast, grenades in their hands. The third marine ran straight up, clutching a BAR. A sharp, light rattle, like seasoned bamboo sticks knocking in the wind came from the grass.

Was that a Nambu, Blackman wondered.

The two front marines, their momentum carrying them forward, pitched to their faces and lay still. The third marine stopped suddenly, as if he'd run into a chest-high wall, and fell hard on his back. He too lay still. Blackman began to sweat.

By midmorning they'd been waved off the beach and into the grass. Blackman was still sweating and wondering what he'd do if someone shouted, "Medic! I'm hit!" But the sounds of battle seemed to be bulging deeper into the island. He told himself, again, I'm gonna be cool in just another few minutes; I'm gonna be all right then. If they—the marines he now saw walking with apparent unconcern back and forth across the beach—could do it, damned it he couldn't. Even as he was watching, one marine clapped his hands to his face, blood like syrup oozing from between the fingers, and fell. Blackman wasn't sure he'd heard a shot; there were so many. But the other marines were shouting now and pointing toward a tall palm tree. Now they were firing at it, and others were calling, "Sniper! Sniper!" and they ran up to join in the firing. In the tree Blackman thought he saw an alien presence, one that did not conform to the color of the palms or the trunk. Something black fell from the tree, then a rifle, and then something familiar, splotched with red. The marines stopped firing and closed in; Blackman saw the flash of a knife and a marine swung around holding something that could've been his own penis. Another tucked the sniper's helmet under his arm, another hoisted the rifle, stock up, on his shoulder.

They were walking away laughing when the first two mortar shells hit, without warning, shattering the cluster of souvenir hunters. All save one went down, and he, the marine with the penis, started to run in the deep sand, slid, fell, crawled, got up and ran again. Blackman turned away from them; he wasn't going to hear them if they were alive; he wasn't going out into that shit, not for those guys. Medic all they wanted to, but none of this medic would they see.

Like the marines, Blackman didn't hear or see the next mortar rounds come in. In the middle of a moment of horror, when

256

the first round blew apart two men in his company lying in front of him, the second came and he felt himself flying through the air and slammed down on the sand.

The steam was all the way up and the master of the U.S.S. *President Adams* was anxious to get under way. He was under orders first to clear the beach of the wounded—an extra roster of doctors, both Army and Navy, and medics and corpsmen were aboard—and head for the port of San Francisco. On this trip the sick bay would be a virtual hospital. The seriously and critically wounded would be, the calculations said, small, and the *Adams* could handle them.

The *Adams* had left San Francisco several months ago with a division bound for Australia. From there to New Zealand, then New Caledonia and Guadalcanal, carrying troops to augment both the Army and the Navy's Fleet Marine Forces. Bougainville was the last SoPac stop this trip.

From the bridge, the master could see the first barges of the wounded making for his ship. He glanced at his watch; they'd get away in good time. Good time. He made his way down to the sick bay, to give an official presence, a kind of ranking welcome, to the wounded. The first casualty brought in was a huge black soldier, completely out, small clots of blood in his ears and nose. Nothing else as far as he could see. He patted the shoulder of a marine who held tightly to a Japanese rifle which lay beside him on his stretcher. "Don't let anybody take my souvenir, hear? It's mine, mine." The master patted him reassuringly again, then with a nod at the doctors, left and returned to the bridge; it was time to check the radio room and see if the escorts and whatever other convoy was going would be at Mutupina Point. There were times when the Slot could still be a very tough place to cross, not that he had any real fear of it any longer; hell, half the Jap Navy was at the bottom of the Slot. He began to hum "California Here I Come."

257

# 20

*Cadences*

*"Here's a boy made Grade I in AGCT."*

*"What? Let me see? Jesus, you're right. And these boogies been screaming for officers."*

*"Been overseas, too. Bogie."*

*"Yeah, a medic, though. . . ."*

*"Hell, he can be a sanitation, supply, morale or infantry officer. That little old six weeks of training."*

*"Abraham Blackman. Humm. Purple Heart for the Bogie action—"*

*"Oh, you know how that one goes. Some one or two star goes to a hospital, walks up and down the wards, handing out Purple Hearts—"*

*"I know, I know, but if this kicks back, we at least had good reasons for putting it through in the first place. Overseas. Bogie. Purple Heart and Grade I. Maybe we better go back over this stack, Ralph, and see if we can't find some more nigger second-lieutenant material; we got some quotas to fill, man."*

*"Yeah. Where we gonna send this man?"*

*"The 92nd is the only boogie outfit I know of that's gettin*

*ready for transfer overseas. We can give this man some training —he's already had combat infantry—and have him ready by the time those boys leave Huachuca.*"

"Where's the 92nd on that priority list?"

"They're number two."

"Okay. We done created ourselves a second looey named Abraham Blackman, in the image of man."

"Better not let anybody else hear you say that last thing."

"Can't you take a joke?"

"Niggers ain't no joke, Ralph."


"So you like Florence and Italy very much," he said she'd asked him.

He'd answered, "Yes."

They walked without touching, although he wanted very much to touch her, glancing across the Arno at the old section, allowing their eyes to skip quickly over the bridges that'd been blown up. He liked the way the sun touched the old houses and walls and made them look like gold.

"Up there," she said, "is the Uffizi Gallery. Of course, the paintings are not there now. The war," she finished softly.

Now he took her hand without looking at her, afraid to read a No in them. When he did look at her, saying, "This is a lovely country, and you're lovely," he was relieved to see her smile.

"The war," she said again.

"No. Not the war."

He said he'd stiffened when he saw the pair of MPs. She must've felt it, for she gripped his hand harder. Then he thought, What had they to fear? This was her country; her family, Tuscans all, had lived here for uncounted generations. When the soldiers were gone, they'd be here for perhaps another thousand generations. Still, as they drew near the staring MPs, they communicated their uneasiness to each other. He squared his shoulders and said something jolly to her as they moved out to go around the soldiers.

"Hold it, soldier," one of the MPs said.

He had stopped, and feeling the girl tremble beside him, smiled and said, "It's all right."

"Let's see your pass."

He fished it out and was relieved that they both seemed to be studying it so intensely they were not looking at the girl. One of the MPs, with a gesture meant to assure that the pass would be returned, stuck it in his pocket. The other said to the girl, "Let's see your ID."

He had felt frightened and helpless. "She has no ID," he said. IDs were carried by prostitutes, and he knew they knew it.

"Card? Card?" she said, backing up. She knew what they meant. "What is it you're doing? I'm not a prostitute?"

The MPs looked at each other and one said, "Jim, she ain't got no ID."

"Aw, she just don't want this boy to know she's a whore. No decent Eyetalian woman goes out with these boys—"

"—C'mon, you guys, you—"

"Quiet, soldier! Not talkin to you!"

He had crumbled in his silence. What could he do? One moment he owned the world and the next he was crawling over it. She didn't know them; she didn't know what they would and could do to him. How in the hell had he got in this mess, anyway? For three months they'd sat in her parent's small apartment, not touching, hardly talking, just looking at each other, while her parents smiled at them, blessed them with an unspoken benevolence. This, this, was their first time away from her parents, their first time alone.

He felt ashamed because he was afraid. Trembling himself now, he put an arm around the girl. At first she stiffened at the touch of his arm, and his fear momentarily opened on a pit of horror. He saw the flicker in the MPs' eyes. Then she relaxed against his arm.

"Look," he had said. "She's not a whore. She's a nice girl. You've got it all wrong." He probed deeply for assurance that all would be well; he walked into the pale blue eyes he looked into, seeking, and therefore never saw the club that came down on his head.

He came to in the annex of a pro station. The girl was sitting beside him. "They said we can go now," she said. She tried to smile. "They said your head would be all right."

Outside they walked quickly, but he stopped quickly when, after a long silence, she began to moan, and he turned and saw that she was crying.

"What is it?"

She did not want to be too close to him; she resisted his gentle pressure to put her head on his shoulder.

"They gave me an examination. They put me on the table where they put the whores and they—examined me." He heard her grind her teeth. She fished in her bag and took out a yellow card. She held it to him. "Then they gave me this and said I should never be without it, or I'd go to jail."

The kid—Blackman thought of him as a kid, although he was only a year, maybe less, younger than Blackman—started to cry again. Blackman didn't want to say "Tough luck, kid" or "Look, soldier, don't make a martyr out of yourself." He touched the kid on the shoulder, but he didn't want to look up with tears in his eyes again. He shook his head and Blackman understood; he'd wait. That was his job, as Morale Officer.

Blackman stared at the kid's bobbing head. Why hadn't he just gone ahead and got the pussy, like most guys, instead of parading around with that bitch holding his hand. Christ, how many complaints like this had he already fired off? Fifth Army couldn't care less about cracker MPs busting black boys seen with white babes. And even if it did, the crackers from Down Home and Up Home both would keep on doing the same thing. Pussy, who's gettin it, sure worries the white man to death, he thought.

261

Opening his desk drawers, Blackman spoke soothingly: "Okay, soldier. I'll file a complaint for you. In the meantime, I hope you and your girl can work things out. Tell her father to come see me about that card." He found the bottle of Teachers and pushed it and a canteen cup toward the kid. Then he rose and tiptoed out of the room.

Things were at the breaking point, Blackman knew, with incomplete regiments, this business with MPs, small race riots in the towns, desertions, pitched battles with white troops, and this last thing, a shoot-out and two hundred men taking off for the swamps, with arms. One of them had told Blackman: "If they come in to get us, they'll have to take us out dead, Lieutenant. We don't see the point of goin through this hell for Uncle Sammy, and we know what'll happen to us if we stand up and tell the Colonel that. We're taking our girls, food and guns."

He knew they were telling him because he got along with them, and had ever since Huachuca. Blackman's Asiatic-Pacific ribbon, with its one battle star, and his Purple Heart, had given him the edge over the other junior officers in the division. He no longer wondered what'd happened to the report he supposed was in his records from the Fort Ord riot; he was almost certain what'd happened. To save a lot of paper work, the CO at Ord had simply transferred out every black soldier involved; their records were clean, then, and so was his. In the Army the main aim was not to show up for inspection with shit on your shirttails; that was the rule from pfc up to Ike.

"This is war, goddamn it!"

The men around him in the Viareggio division headquarters had known the General would say that; he always said it, whether angry or calm, as if to remind himself of deeds to be done in this time that in others he wouldn't have thought about in the first place. But this time he was angry. He stomped about the room ranting, an imitation of Patton, except that

Patton had an Army and he only had a division and a black one at that.

The General stopped. "All right. Before we go in there and get them, why did they do it in the first place? Anybody know? Jesus, a little time in Leavenworth, maybe, and that's all, but they had to go and pull this, with the damned spotlight swinging right over our heads? I said, anybody know why they did it? No? All right, get that Morale Officer in here, that big black buck."

Hard heels cracked on the bare floor of the villa; heavy wooden doors creaked open and rattled shut.

Blackman had his feet up on the desk, his combat boots trailing dirt; he'd gone out with a patrol that morning, hiking up the side of a steep hill like a mountain goat. The patrol had been uneventful. He was tossing the clip from his carbine up and down when the phone rang. He took the message, got up and went outside and borrowed a jeep.

In his office, the General and his officers heard the footsteps coming down the hall, measured and heavy.

As he approached the office, Blackman wondered why it'd taken so long for this. Another officer could've been called, but he would have heard about it. Did being Morale Officer include answering the questions the General was surely going to put to him?"

The door opened before him and Blackman halted on the threshhold and saluted the roomful of officers. The General appraised him, his helmet, jacket, boots, .45, belt, then returned the salute. "Come in, Lieutenant." Blackman marched to the center of the room, where the General stood, and stopped. The General circled him, glancing at the papers he held in his hands.

"What happened, Lieutenant?" he asked, when he stopped and looked at Blackman.

"I don't understand, sir."

"Tombolo."

263

"Oh. Yes, sir."

"Look. What the fuck does it look like when we've already got an understaffed division"—he spat—"they call it a task force, isn't that some shit? When two hundred men take off for the swamps? You're Morale Officer, right?"

"Yessir."

"Any inkling this was coming up?"

"Yessir."

"Howzat?"

"I don't mean Tombolo, exactly, General. I mean, I knew some big trouble was coming—"

"And if you knew, why didn't you do something?"

"I did, sir. I've copies of over a hundred complaints that I've filed both with Division and Army, sir, of discrimination and segregation, of the way the men are treated by their officers—"

From behind him one of the officers said, "What do you mean by that, Blackman?"

Without turning, Blackman said, "The officers, most of them, don't even want to be with us. They don't back up the men. They spend more time complaining about them and trying to get transferred out than they do trying to build—"

"The men are cowards, by my judgment," another officer said behind the General. "All's fine if there's no opposition. But let a single German open up with a burp gun and there's panic."

"Lieutenant?" the General said.

"We think we've fought better than we had a right to under the circumstances, General."

"Listen, soldier, every man in this Army gets the same goddamn training. Are you going to stand there and tell me otherwise?"

"Yessir."

Exasperated the General spun on his heel and slammed the papers down on the desk. "You're leading to a point, Lieutenant?"

"Only that the men who deserted probably reflect the feelings

264

of most of the black soldiers around these parts." When the words were out, Blackman felt a stir behind him.

The General became ramrod stiff. "Say that again, Lieutenant Blackman."

"Most Negro soldiers around here feel the way the deserters do, but don't have the guts to do what they've done."

Another voice from behind: "Does that go for you, too, Lieutenant?"

In a low voice, the General said, "Lieutenant?"

"Yessir."

"Oh bullshit," came another voice.

"In Tombolo," Blackman said, his voice rising, "they feel they'll be fighting for themselves, not whites—"

"But the Nazis and the fascists," the General said. "Do you know what they'd do to Negroes if *they* win?"

"Pardon, sir, but the way most of us see it, is that it can't be too much worse than it is now."

"If this is the way they feel, we'd better pull this goddamn division out of here before everybody goes over and makes love with the Germans." But he knew he couldn't ask to have the division pulled. That would be the end of his career. Damn those bastards, the General thought. His old buddies. They stuck him with this boogie outfit; couldn't find anyone else who wanted to take it, and he *had* to or get bumped from the promotion lists. They'd really zeroed in on him. Churchill had visited; Clark had dragged his bony ass up here, and that Sambo-ing one-star Davis had come with a camera crew. And now this!

The General glared around the room. Who was the sonofabitch who didn't handle those complaints? Ah, shit. They'd all cover for each other, just the way I'd do. It's my ass hanging out. He glanced up at Blackman, still at attention in the center of the room. Shit. Take these people, kick them in their asses all their lives, then put them into an incomplete unit, with all kinds of shitheads for officers; court-martial a bunch of their own Negro officers and send them out to fight. What the hell for? Of course, Blackman's right. But what am I to do, let all of what's wrong come to root on *my* shoulders, ruin *my* life? Am I supposed to be the guy who says, You're right? Quit, don't fight, desert into the swamps of Tombolo and Migliarino? I can't change history. But they have deserted; the regs are clear. They won't come out with their hands up; it'll be a war between black and white, and a real one. Imagine it. In an Italian swamp.

"Goddammit!!"

Blackman caught the tones of self-pity and frustration, and he looked at the General again; gave him a closer study.

"Lieutenant," the General said. "We'll have to go in and get them. We just can't sit here."

"They'll fight, sir."

"So will we, Lieutenant. At ease for now."

The General backed up to a wall and lowered a map. He picked up a pointer. Turning to the room again, he said, "Gentlemen, we're in the middle of a war. There's no doubt that Jerry is on the run. But we're also in the middle of another, older war, and we're going to have to fight that one, too. Things've happened back home, things over which we've had no control" —he caught Blackman's eye—"or if we did, we did nothing. Those things've caught up with us, but we're constrained to behave as though those other things never happened."

The General, under Blackman's scrutiny, was white-haired and gray-skinned. Old for a two-star. Army politics, maybe. Shitty end of the stick. Must've been a redneck instead of a Bourbon. Calling to run a nigger outfit? Running head on into the past? Shit, General. The past is gonna catch up with a whole *lotta* people; you're just getting first crack. And then he wondered why he hadn't been dismissed. Blackman's eyes scanned the map.

The Gothic Line. Almost directly north of Viareggio was a German Air Force base, or used to be; they hadn't done any damage in months. South of Viareggio was Pisa and south of that, Leghorn.

"Tonight," the General was saying, "we'll take positions south of Pisa and north of Leghorn." His voice lowered as did his eyes. "G-2 tells us that elements of the German 16th SS division"—here he touched his pointer to the map; it came to rest on the fringe of Tombolo—"are infiltrating through the swamp with an eye toward cutting our line in two. That's an armored infantry division. They can hurt us if we let them dig in. This division will not take part. Repeat," he said, looking Blackman in the eye, "this division will *not* take part in the operation. We've got some IV Corps men already on the move. We'll begin the attack at oh-six-hundred. Donaldson will give you details."

Now Blackman had it, and he felt the eyes of the officers behind him burning into his back. They were asking themselves the same question he was asking: Why had the General permitted him to stay for this briefing, as undetailed as it was? The battle orders would read of an operation against the Germans, fortunately close enough to Tombolo for Tombolo to *be* the objective. No battle order would ever be discovered that would read: Commenced attack against two hundred niggers holed up in Tombolo.

The General was moving briskly out of the room, clipping off a salute. He pulled an aide into the hall with him. "Whittman, you'll take Lieutenant Blackman with you to observe—"

"But General, you shouldn't have—"

"You heard the order, Whittman. Don't give me any shit, do you understand?"

"Yessir."

"And, Whittman?"

"Yessir?"

"You bring him back with you. By the time you get back from the swamp, you'll have had someone in your office preparing a transfer for Blackman, understand? You'll transfer him over to France, somewhere away from here. Combat. Got it?"

267

"Yes, General. One question, sir?"

"All right."

"Why did you let him stay for the briefing?"

"Because, Whittman, somebody's got to know. Somebody on their side, understand, because one day the shit's really going to hit the fan, and if we don't have a point or two on our side, forget it, and we don't have any that I know of, so far. Aw, fuck it. You don't know what I'm talking about, do you?"

"No, sir."

"Just carry out my orders then."

Blackman sat in the rear seat of the recon. They moved slowly, hugging the right side of the road so the trucks could pass. The soldiers, all white, had blackened their faces. Instead of the white robes, Blackman thought. He wondered how they'd been briefed by their captains and lieutenants. How sure the General must be of himself, to send him along, Blackman now thought. Strange man. Someone to keep the record, one witness, someone who, in some way, could tell black people about Tombolo. Tombolo. He studied the dark mass that spread out on the still black horizon. Got Brothers in there and their girls, and German Army deserters. A kind of integration in that swamp that wouldn't be believed back home.

They passed the line of trucks, all empty now, and soon caught up with the infantry, just about to disperse into the edges of the swamp. A slight silverish sheen over the Apuan Alps, now hard, blue and sharp, hinted at the approach of daybreak. Already voices were coming in over the radios.

One half hour after the attack was ordered, Blackman heard the mortars and the rattle of light weapons. Groups of medics, smoking silently, paced around, staring into the woods. Blackman, Whittman at his side, walked slowly up and down the road, stopping now and again when an especially prolonged burst of gunfire caught his attention. He wondered how they were dying in there, if they were taking an equal number of whites with them, if they were proving without a doubt

268

that they'd fight their asses off if they had something to fight for, like their lives or their girls.

Whenever Whittman had to go away, he placed Blackman back in the recon under guard, and when he returned Blackman asked, "How's it going?"

"We'll get em."

"I know that. How's it going *now?*"

Whittman shrugged.

"Gettin chewed up pretty bad, huh?"

The medics started to move, to flow into the swamp and return bearing wounded and dead on their stretchers. Ambulances groaned up, took their loads and groaned away. The sun up now, Blackman drew near the line of ambulances, looking for Negroes; he saw none that first day; none the second, none the third, and there were none on the fourth day, after the infantry pulled out and the ambulances drove away for the last time.

To Whittman Blackman said, "No prisoners, wounded or otherwise, huh?"

Whittman shrugged. "General's orders."

"And me?"

Whittman ignored him. "We left them where they fell. There'll be a Graves Registration detachment sent up from our end today. They'll be buried in the military cemetery south of Florence. Killed in action. Ten thousand bucks for their wives, sisters or mothers; whoever they left. Let's go."

"I'll hitch a ride."

"No dice. The General says you stay with me."

"I'm going in. I want to see."

Whittman took his carbine and they entered the swamp. An hour's walk brought them to the first corpse, a blubbery Negro who'd died with a scowl on his face. A few hundred feet away they found two women and four black soldiers. By now the smell of death was everywhere, and tiny animals scurried away from the bodies at the sound of their footsteps. A

269

German soldier and a black American soldier; a clump of blacks, mortared into the ground. The attack had been just as devastating from the Leghorn end; Blackman'd heard it on the radio. That had taken three days.

"Jesus," Blackman whispered over and over. "Holy Jesus Christ."

Whittman's face was white and drawn. He didn't walk so close to Blackman now. Once Blackman turned quickly and Whittman jumped and raised his carbine. Then Whittman's face flushed and he lowered the gun. Blackman walked close to him and said as he jabbed Whittman with his finger, "I don't know when. I don't know how, but Whittman, I swear before God, man, before God, you motherfuckers'll pay for this."

*Drumtaps*

> *There is a place called Tombolo*
> *Where swamps are said the deepest;*
> *There is a place called Tombolo*
> *And buried there are secrets.*

# 21

Cadences

"How come you have to roust us out of bed at this hour?"

"Jerry."

"Jerry who?"

"The Germans, you ass."

"Oh. What's going on?"

"Look at that map. They're trying to bulge in through the Ardennes."

"Aw, that's stupid. You can't fight through there. We learned that in school."

"Forget school. They're doing it, and we're short riflemen all along the line. I'm checking with Ike, Bradley, Matchett and Davis on a plan to get some colored riflemen from Communications Zone. What do you think of that?"

"Is the situation that bad?"

"I can't tell you how bad it is. How'd you like to go back and start all over at Omaha Beach?"

"There goes almost two hundred years of Army policy."

"Which would you rather have go, the policy or the Army?"

"Since you put it that way, the policy, naturally."

We're crazy, every goddamn one of us, Blackman thought, as the first truckload pulled out to burrow into the winter en route to Noyon for some quick training. Eisenhower's order had been posted only last night, and look at us, volunteering. There is something innately wrong with us, with every man in this truck and in all the other trucks. We *know* the man's using us because he's in *a tight*; we *know* he don't give a shit one way or the other if we die or not. That's not right. We know he'd rather see us dead than alive, yet here we are, in December, the snow asshole deep, running out here to fight some goddamn Germans.

And he was the craziest of all.

After all this time trying to get some bars, he'd given them up in order to volunteer. Although the arrangement was tentative, pending final clarification of his reduction, Abraham Blackman was now a private first class.

The wind blew in great gusts against the canvas-covered two-ton truck. Sure was a change, Blackman thought. There'd been snow and cold in Italy, but not like this. Up here winter really meant business. Now he reflected on the speed with which his life had changed in just a few weeks. They hadn't wasted any time getting him out, bouncing him from one replacement depot to another, all the way into northern France. He wondered if the others in the truck were as anxious to kill as he was. The rules of the game being what they were, he could only, for now, kill Germans, but they were white and that was a start. They must be in a real tight to ask for niggers, he thought, slumping down into a more comfortable position so he could doze.

But even as the line of trucks wallowed through the snow and freezing cold, Blackman could not know that Eisenhower's order,

| To: | Base Commanders | Supreme Headquarters |
| To: | Section Commanders | Allied Expeditionary Forces |

Dec. 26, 1944

1. The Supreme Commander desires to destroy the enemy forces and end hostilities in this theater without delay. Every available weapon at our disposal must be brought to bear upon the enemy. To this end the Commanding General, COM Z, is happy to offer to a limited number of colored troops who have had infantry training the privilege of joining our veteran units at the front to deliver the knockout blow. The men selected are to be in the grades of Private First Class and Private. Non-commissioned officers may accept reduction in order to take advantage of this opportunity . . .

2. The Commanding General makes a special appeal to you. It is planned to assign you without regard to color or race to the units where assistance is most needed, and give you the opportunity of fighting shoulder to shoulder to bring about victory. Your relatives and friends everywhere have been urging that you be granted this privilege. The Supreme Commander, your Commanding General, and other veteran officers who have served with you are confident that many of you will take advantage of this opportunity and carry on in keeping with the glorious record of our colored troops in our former wars.

3. This letter is to be read confidentially to the troops immediately on its receipt and made available in Orderly Rooms. Every assistance must be given qualified men to volunteer for this service.

was already being scrutinized, criticized and about to be temporized. The trucks rolled on through the same storm that was covering the German advance through the Ardennes. Blackman awoke as they halted at a checkpoint. He fingered the canvas, wondering why it was taking so long for clearance. He made no sound, although the others did, when the truck backed up, turned around and went back where it came from, the other trucks following closely behind. Somebody, he thought, goofed. Now they've got to do it all over again, some other way. He closed his eyes again and succumbed to the bumping and sliding of the truck.

LT. GEN. WALTER B. SMITH to GENERAL EISENHOWER

Although I am somewhat out of touch with the War
Department's negro policy, I did, as you know, handle this
during the time I was with General Marshall. Unless there
has been a radical change, the sentence which I have marked
(without regard to color or race to the units where assistance
is most needed, and give you the opportunity of fighting
shoulder to shoulder to bring about victory) in the attached
circular letter will place the War Department in very grave
difficulties. It is inevitable that the statement will get out,
and equally inevitable that the result will be that every
negro institution, pressure group and newspaper will take
the attitude that, while the War Department segregates
colored troops into organizations of their own against their
desires and pleas of all the negro race, the Army is perfectly
willing to put them in the front lines mixed in units with
white soldiers, and have them do battle when an emergency
arises. Two years ago I would have considered the marked
statement the most dangerous thing I had ever seen in
regard to negro relations. . . .

Furthermore, I recommend most strongly that Communications Zone not be permitted to issue any general circulars
relating to negro policy until I have had a chance to see
them. This is because I know more about the War Department's and General Marshall's difficulties with the negro
question than any other man in this theater, including General
B. O. Davis with whom Lee consulted in this matter—and
I say this with all due modesty. . . .

Two days later, back at the depot, Blackman studied the new
circular. The appeal to black troops was no longer obvious. The
new "opportunity to volunteer" extended "to all soldiers with-

out regard to color or race, but preference will normally be given to individuals who have had some basic training in infantry. . . ."

The second paragraph, Blackman noted, was pure sliding on shit: "In the event that the number of suitable negro volunteers exceed the replacement needs of negro combat troops, these men will be suitably incorporated in other organizations so that their service and their fighting spirit may be effectively utilized."

Blackman turned away, replacing his bars. Angrily he turned again to the circular. Now, he thought, they know damned well that there isn't one single Negro infantry regiment in France, let alone a division. So, who'll the volunteers replace? The Negro tank groups? Negro artillerymen? Yeah? Then why're they asking for guys with some basic training in infantry?

With long, vicious strides, Blackman made for the depot's Orderly Room. He was going to request a pass; they'd give it to him. They'd be glad to be rid of a black second looey they didn't know where or how to send someplace else. Shit, I could stay on pass until the war ends, he thought, and they wouldn't miss me. Okay Paris. Okay pussy. Okay wine. Here I come. Come, come, coming.

## Cadences

*The confidential memo read:* MATTERS VITAL TO THE ARMY, TO ITS PERSONNEL, AND THE NATION. *Now they were gathered. At each place at the table a thick packet of papers lay between two sharpened pencils. A colonel with only the American Theater and the Good Conduct ribbons on his blouse addressed them:*

*"While many of you have been actually fighting, we of the Army Research Branch've been battling in our own modest way. America has come close to putting twenty million people into this war. For almost half a decade the nation has been of a single mind: win the war.*

*"We've become in that time a military society and, since that*

275

*isn't our nature, we must analyze the repercussions of such an all-out military effort, unheard of in the annals of warfare. In this study we pay especial attention to the military, which tends to coalesce the younger men, the men who one day will run the nation, so we felt it wise to see just what they're thinking right now."*

"All right, Colonel," said a general. "What're they thinking, if you please."

"Yes, sir. First and perhaps foremost, how do they view the Germans, Hitler? Fully half," he said, consulting the papers before him, "when polled, believed that, even though Hitler was wrong in starting the war, he did the Germans a lot of good."

A murmur went around the room.

"Twenty-four per cent," said the Colonel, "believe that, since Germany was the most efficient nation in Europe, they had a right to take what they required to become the controlling influence on the Continent. Almost as many thought the Germans had a good right to be 'down on the Jews.'"

The Colonel paused; he knew that, beside himself, there probably was not another Jew in the room. "Obviously, gentlemen, these polls reveal that there is no little attraction for fascism among the masses of soldiers trained to fight and die for democracy." He let the last word come out slowly, insinuatingly, and hang on the air.

"This is consistent with another poll made that asked if soldiers should take over the country. Six per cent polled were strongly in favor of it. Sixteen said they were not exactly in favor of it, but that it might be a good idea—"

"Colonel," another general called. "I can't find that poll."

"Page six, sir." The Colonel continued. "Twenty-seven per cent were not exactly against it, but thought it probably wasn't a good idea. Forty-one per cent were strongly opposed, and ten had no opinion."

"Wherever could they've got ideas like that?" one officer whispered to another.

276

"On page ten," said the Colonel, "and I won't give you the breakdown; it's there. But what the table shows is that most men polled believe that after the war they'll have the most trouble getting along with Negroes, Jews and labor unions, in that order."

Now the Colonel widened his stance, opened another paper and looked at his audience. "It looks as though we're going to have to integrate the Army." Calmly he shuffled papers until the angry voices died down. He smiled. "We base this assumption on what's going on in the Army right now. Here're the figures: In 1941 Negro troops made up zero point zero of the total U.S. forces abroad, that total being eleven point four per cent. In 1942 alone, Negro troops shot up nineteen point zero per cent, while white troops went to nineteen point six per cent. In September 1943 Negro troops and white troops deployed were equal—twenty-eight point zero per cent. From March 1944 to March of this year, Negro troops overseas have consistently remained higher than white troops, and right now, their strength is exactly ten per cent more than that of white troops overseas. Three fourths, or seventy-five per cent of all Negro strength is overseas, compared to three fifths of all white strength—and Negro strength is growing.

"The reasons are plainly the rotation system. White troops having been in combat more often, get more points, and they are coming home. The black troops, with fewer points, for less combat, are remaining—"

But the room was exploding around him.

"Integrate the Army?"

"You mean to tell me them boys are going to be left over there—"

"To get—"

"All that French—"

"All that German—"

"All that Dutch—"

"All that English—"

"*All that Belgian—*"

"*All that Italian—*"

"*All that Luxembourger—*"

"COCK!!!"

The Colonel, having heard "Italian" during the tumult, shouted at the top of his voice: "Yes! Yes! It's true! We found out that in Italy they were getting it about a third more often than white troops, and two to three times a month!"

"SEE! Oh, my God, what'll those poor European women do? My God, my God."

"Christ. The best I could do was every two months and it cost me two hundred bucks and it was my dog-assed WAC secretary on top of it, and she never even washed her snatch."

"If we don't integrate, the Europeans'll think we don't have anything but a black Army!"

"If we integrate, the white boys can keep an eye out for the black boys, you know, so they don't—"

"Hell, I'd like to serve with them boys myself—"

"General, can you get it up?"

The Colonel kept shouting, "Gentlemen, gentlemen, gentlemen! I have to tell you about the report submitted by Lieutenant General Alvan C. Gillem, Jr. Gentlemen! If approved, and circumstances seem to dictate that it has to be, we'll be taking the first steps toward an integrated Army. Gentlemen! Aren't you listening?"

# SIX

U. S. REPRESENTATIVE FREDERIC R. COUDERT, JR.: "Did I correctly understand you to say that the heart of the present policy toward China and Formosa is that there is to be kept alive a constant threat of military action vis-à-vis Red China in the hope that at some point there will be an internal breakdown?"

WALTER S. ROBERTSON, ASSISTANT SECRETARY OF STATE: "Yes, sir, that is my conception."

COUDERT: "Fundamentally, does that not mean that the United States is undertaking to maintain for an indefinite period of years American dominance in the Far East?"

ROBERTSON: "Yes. Exactly."

House Committee on Appropriations Hearings, January 26, 1954

The big question is whether the black cat can walk like a dragon here in South Vietnam and like a fairy back in the land of the Big PX.

The New York TIMES, from a series by Thomas A. Johnson,
April 29, 30; May 1, 1968

# 22

## Cadences

"I tell you," the speaker said to the small group in the dark, paneled room, "we are in crisis. The potential of that nation cannot be realized. You sit there in those expensive, leather chairs, your bottoms cushioned by foam rubber, and refuse to see the larger picture. There, right there"—he pointed to the map of Asia on the wall—"is our next enemy. Now you know how much success we had in 1917. None, and look at Russia now. How many millions, millions of people did it lose during the war, and still function? They've got people to waste. Well, we did better in 1936, in Spain, but we've been fooling around with Chiang Kai-shek for so long, and missing the boat on the commies, that we're up the creek again. Chiang is on Taiwan; Mao has the mainland. Chiang says we should go in."

From deep in the recesses of one of the chairs a voice said, "The people would never stand for that."

The speaker said, "I know that. But they will stand for us stopping a carnivorous monster like communism, eating up all the countries around it. They'll want us to go in then."

"They didn't seem to mind too much when Hungary, Czechoslovakia, Poland and East Germany got eaten up," the same voice from the chair said.

The speaker walked around the room until he stood directly in front of the chair from which the voice was coming. "There has always been a major difference, sir. We understand it, but we don't like to kick it around in public."

"The difference?"

"We consider the Russians to be white, even with its great variety of peoples. The Chinese are colored. Jack London called Japan the Yellow Peril. Loosely. He was thinking of all those millions of Asiatics, the Chinese, Indians, Thais, Vietnamese, Laotians . . . And Teddy Roosevelt agreed, and Kaiser Wilhelm, too. We really didn't have a decent Navy until the Japanese knocked off the Russians in 1905. A lot of people, sir, have advised against colored people drawing equal to whites in any shape, form or fashion."

"They might want to get even, is that it?"

"That's a real consideration, sir." Returning to his place before the map, the speaker continued. "I think we all realize that if Russia can become a nuclear power, then China will too; the white Reds'll give it to the yellow Reds; that's the way they do things. Now, I know some of you're thinking that if we can establish a wedge between them, the nuclear gift might not be made. Also, we don't know at this point if the Russians, for their own safety, would want to give the Chinese the secret.

"But even if the Chinese don't get it from Russia, we can count on their making their own. They've got to to protect themselves from Russia, and other powers that may not feel comfortable with the bomb in their possession. Including us. If we go along on the assumption that one day they will have the bombs and the systems to carry them anywhere they want to go, we have to act today, not tomorrow."

From the other side of the room came a question: "Do you suggest that we bomb them now?"

The speaker walked slowly toward the questioner. "America has said it will not ever be the first country to use the atomic bomb."

"Are you saying we won't use it, or we won't use it without provocation?"

"That would depend, wouldn't it, on the degree of provocation, and the degree of threat to any land or sea forces we might have to send into any given place?"

Another voice: "You seem to be saying, although you haven't spoken the words, that given enough provocation, China might become involved enough so that we could then drop the bomb and our people would accept our reasons. Am I correct?"

"Well—"

"For Christ's sake. We're getting so we can't even talk to each other without a lot of bullshit. Furthermore, isn't this escalating things a bit? I thought we were just going to run circles around Taiwan, keep an eye out for Matsu and Quemoy, freeze Red China out of major economic considerations and let it die on the vine."

"We're not talking about a change in any set policy. We're talking about—eventualities. Now, suppose South Korea finds it necessary to resist North Korea? Suppose the French ask us for help in Vietnam—and they're having big trouble there right now —what do we do? South Korea is a United States ward. We've always been Allies with France. Are we going to sit around and let France get her butt kicked in by some little brown communists, let a white nation take its first defeat by a colored nation, the first time it's ever happened, as far as I'm concerned, in all of history? And make no mistake about it, gentlemen. The French are concerned about this happening to them. Think, I'm telling you, not of rubber, not of the oil, not of the opium or other products of wealth that lie in these areas and must, somehow, be brought to this side of the world; think back to World War II when the Japs, little colored men, swept out of their overcrowded islands over sleeping, disorganized and corrupt China, and down the southern lands, scattering white men, Dutch, British, French,

283

*American out of their comfortable racial stereotypes. How many other little colored men, women and children, peering from behind bamboo screens and forest growths, saw for the first time that the white man was not invincible as they'd come to believe, and wondered, stunned at the new possibilities inherent in that discovery? How many white men had given over their money, lands and wives and then pleaded with the little brown men for their lives.*

*"Of course, the Japanese lost, after all. The young colored men admit this in their rooms at Oxford, Harvard, Leiden, the Sorbonne and Moscow. The Japs made a mistake. They tried to take it all, just like the white man. But we, they say, only wish the white man out of our countries, for the white man returned to our lands with startling speed at the war's end. We, say the young brown students, wish to unite the divergent sections which'd been skewered or cut at Potsdam. We do not wish for conquest or seek to exploit. We have learned this from the white beast in our midst: there are economic realities that can be gained in a sphere of like peoples. The white man does this. They ask, are there not strengths that've lain dormant among our people for centuries? The white man must go; the puppets he has placed in our midst must go."*

*Slowly the speaker let the map up. "And there're more of them than us. And if they come with the bomb and the systems for delivery, mark my words: They'll be telling us to come to Peking for tea, and do you know what? We'd better go."*

Luther Woodcock rounded the corner and came through the opened door of the room, slowing to a stop in his wheelchair. For before him, bent over the bed in which Captain Blackman lay, he saw a woman. He savored the instant in which he had the complete advantage, the view of extraordinarily good legs, a fine behind with full-curved, strong buttocks. He knew when she turned around, as she was now doing, she would be just as fine in front.

The Captain's eye were still closed, he saw, and the drainage tubes curved out of his thorax and into bottles, now filling slowly. The Captain was in a sitting position. Hastily, almost angrily, Woodcock looked for the stump on the right leg; he wanted to see it before starting a conversation with the woman. You didn't see too many black women out here. But he also wanted to assess the Captain's wounds, see if he was going to make it, shot up, stumped, but make it, anyway.

"Hello," the woman said.

"Hi."

"I'm a friend of Captain Blackman. You?"

Oh. This was the babe from down at the Embassy. "My name's Woodcock. I'm a medic in the Captain's company."

"Are you hurt bad?"

"No. I'll be outa this thing in a few days. How's the Captain?"

"He'll live."

Woodcock peered at the bed again, not able to clearly see where the leg had been amputated. "They took his leg?"

"Yes. Look, let's talk outside, all right? You wouldn't mind?"

Woodcock shook his head and she took the back of his chair, turned him around and rolled him out of the room. Did she know he'd probably wind up being a pulmonary invalid, with the pleura thickening every day? Maybe she was going to get her hat, now, anyway.

Behind him, Mimosa Rogers was studying his shaggy Afro. Certainly one of the most impressive she'd seen; it was meant to tell the world that, although almost fair enough to pass, its owner was black from his chitlins out. What wise eyes these kids had, she thought, stopping and turning him around. She took a cushioned seat before him.

Some sadness about her impelled him to gentleness. He took out his cigarettes and offered her one and lit it for her. She was in her late twenties, he guessed. Kind of Amazonian, and it was probably that that brought them together; a big man, a big woman.

285

"A buddy of mine," Woodcock began, wondering at the shyness he now felt under her cool gaze, "name of Doctorow—he's in here too—says the Captain's gonna get the Medal of Honor . . ."

"Yes. That's how I found out what'd happened. The Medal of Honor; I'm sure he's wanted that all his life." She flicked her cigarette ash viciously.

"Yeah," Woodcock said. "It's not much of an exchange."

"No." She shouldn't be giving in to her bitterness, she thought, so she asked, "Were you in his black military history seminar?"

"Yes. Really, great stuff. I mean, the Captain-Brother told us a whole lot that we didn't know, you know. A lot of the Brothers, they come over here and think they're the first Brothers to ever get into the sh—stuff."

"Into the shit. Yes, I know."

"But the Captain, like, he brought everything down front for us and—I still can't get over it. Like, you know, Chuck's been f—"

"Fucking over you—"

Woodcock smiled. "Yeah. For so long, and not letting us know, and tellin us how great it is to die for him—" Woodcock's voice trailed away when he saw a set, weary, bitter expression creep back across her face. "Well, the Captain really turned our company around, man."

She ground out her cigarette and stared at the floor. Woodcock sat silently, letting his own cigarette go dead at the filter. Once or twice he cleared his throat and thought about his thigh wound. He played with the spokes on his chair. He dropped the butt and rolled over it. "Miss," he said. She looked up, a polite smile on her face.

"I guess I'd better be getting back to the ward. Would you tell the Captain Woodcock came over to see him, please?"

"I'd be happy, too. Come back. I know he'd like to see you."

Woodcock, already rolling, nodded. "Miss, I'm sorry. We didn't want nothin to happen to the Captain, really. We all dug him and—well, we just didn't want to see nothin happen

286

to him." Woodcock gave a mighty push and rolled out of the room before the tears brimming up in the woman's eyes splashed out on her face.

She rose and walked quietly back into the room and stood staring at the drainage bottles, the shockingly empty place under the sheet, emphasized all the more by the fullness just beside it; no leg and much leg.

She'd been staring a long time and trying to analyze her feelings that lay behind the great wall of sadness, when he said, weakly:

"Hello."

How long had he been watching? What had he read in her face? She smiled. "Hello, Abraham."

A thin smile faded up and then down on his face, now stubbled with beard. Perhaps she should try to shave him.

"I've been dreaming about you."

"Don't jive me, man. You sure it wasn't about one of those rice paddy whores?"

He liked the response, she saw; his face curled for a laugh, but nothing came out. He gave a caricature of a laugh. She moved closer. "Don't talk, honey. I'll get the doctor, anyway, since you're awake."

His head moved on the pillow: No. He pointed toward his right leg. "It doesn't itch," he whispered. "I read somewhere, a guy had his leg taken off. He wakes, dig, and his toe's itching, only he doesn't have a toe, let alone a foot, ankle or leg, *to* itch." He gave his soundless laugh again, then said, in mock puzzlement, "No itch, baby."

She touched his shoulder, kissed him and went out to find Dr. Jackson, suddenly anxious to get away from the smell of the fluids in the bottles, the lingering odor of feces and urine, the mixed sweat and rubbing alcohol scents. And because she was ashamed of wanting to get away, she approached Major Jackson all the more angrily when she saw him close to, and talking softly to a chesty blonde nurse.

287

Dr. Jackson saw the anger and faced it coolly. He'd met a few of the black foreign service people in Japan and Korea; he didn't really know what to make of them. Some, he decided, were spies, had to be; others thought they had a good thing going with the travel and different experiences at far-flung posts. This one, this Miss Rogers, apparently was an old hand. Somehow, she'd gotten herself away from Saigon and even billeted with the nurses until Captain Blackman got himself together. Some pull; must've had good contacts right up to old Bunk.

He said, "He's awake, Miss Rogers?"

"Yes," she said curtly, disdaining even to look at the blonde who was smiling sympathetically at her, but she could not help but see the rather pudgy black hand clap the white-garmented shoulder of the blonde as he swept out of the office.

Back through the corridors filled with nurses, GIs, orderlies, Vietnamese help; back through the broken and punctured bodies, their smells; back through the desperately perfumed nurses, the doctors with their heavy, tired attitudes.

Dr. Jackson's eyes swept the bottles and the tubes, took in the stumped leg, gone to just above the knee. "Captain?"

Blackman worked up a weak smile, his eyes watchful, even as the doctor unpocketed his stethoscope and listened to his chest and then took his pulse. Then he said, "I'm afraid you're going to have to sit up like this for a while to help the drainage. And as soon as this"—here he touched the thigh—"toughens up, we'll start with the weights. The rest is mostly in the hands of time."

As though he hadn't been listening, Blackman said, "Where you from, Doctor?" Once Blackman knew what city a black person was from, he could almost decipher his make-up. America was peculiar that way, in the manner in which it inadvertently, or perhaps not, formulated its racial codes.

"Berkeley. You know it?"

Blackman nodded. He'd been at Ord for a short time before going to Korea. Berkeley then was the university and that ever-growing black community of former shipyard workers and Navy

288

people; of southern blacks seeking new lives on the Coast. Berkeley, Oakland and San Francisco. Wasn't there an A-train that you took from San Francisco to Oakland? He couldn't remember, but now Ellington's song, complete with the full-bodied riffles of the sax front line, jumped into his consciousness. Wrong A train. The one that hurtled Brooklynites to Harlem and Harlemites to Brooklyn for weekends of partying, that was the Duke's A-train.

"Captain. You know Berkeley?" Dr. Jackson was conscious of Miss Rogers moving closer to the bed.

"Yeah. I used to know it. Nice place."

"How about you, where you from?"

"Binghamton."

"Birmingham?"

"Binghamton. New York," Mimosa whispered.

"Oh, Binghamton. Yes. New York State. Yes. Young fellow from there, a football player, died of something like leukemia—"

"Ernie Davis, that's right."

Major Jackson slowly stuffed his stethoscope back in his pocket.

"I'd like you to get some rest now, Captain. Press your light if you want anything. I'll have to take Miss Rogers with me, but she'll be in my office or her quarters."

"Quarters?"

"I'm with the nurses for a few days, Abraham." She patted his hand and was surprised at how thin and unalive it was. "I'll be back later." She kissed him again.

"Can we talk, Miss Rogers?" Dr. Jackson asked.

"Sure."

In his office, the blonde gone, Mimosa now had only to fight down the age-old doubts of the ability a black doctor might or might not have.

For Dr. Jackson, this was old stuff; you always sensed it, even if you didn't know it. Once this doubt that managed to reveal itself, even from behind elaborate disguises, had made him doubt himself. But he had got hold of his reality. Meharry,

289

Provident and the rare black presence at Alta Bates. He knew his business, and people like Miss Rogers could be as uncertain about him as they wished.

"Miss Rogers," he began once she'd lit a cigarette, crossed her legs and settled back, waiting in that black niche where Negroes waited for the bad things to happen to them, "I have to take it that you and Captain Blackman're into a special thing. Your being here proves that, the *conditions* under which you're here. Unusual, you know?"

She waited, her eyes twin probes sinking into his face.

"He's got a bad hurt."

"I can see that, Dr. Jackson."

Okay, baby, he thought, then said, "What I wanted to know was about your future, with the Captain. I mean, there is a future?"

She caught the snideness, the suggestion that now that Abraham was broken, she'd catch the first thing smoking, and it took her by surprise. She lurched forward, uncrossing her legs, her cigarette jabbing dangerously close to his face. Boiling within her was the unjustness of it all. In Saigon she'd been waiting, ready. No Abraham. No Abraham the next morning. Worrying, but rejecting the possibility of this. Always in the back of the mind, but always rejecting it. Then, days later, Peggy, in the Ambassador's office, surprised at the quickness with which this particular award was being processed, and remembering the name, came rushing in with the news. Then pressure on Bunk to get her up here. A rough flight. Nurses not really sympathetic because she had too much pull, and finally, Abraham, broken, thin, just this side of dying. Now this jive-ass nigger doctor.

"Now, you listen to me you—"

But suddenly he changed before her eyes, became hard and in command; it had nothing to do with the Army; it went deeper and farther back than that. He said, "No, you listen, Sister. You listen!" and his finger was more formidable than her cigarette, his eyes more piercing than she could've imagined. He took her off balance and she paused, wondering. "There is a black man in there who's hurt bad. Bad. Now you come out of the Embassy to see him. I make something of that. I'm not prying, I'm concerned about Captain Abraham Blackman. Ever since you've been here, you've been carrying your ass on your shoulders with me. Well, all right. Get down. Let's talk about that man. If you're not his future, then, dammit, say so, so I can make other plans. There's nothing wrong with you. You're not my concern. He is." Suddenly and with more gentleness he said, "I know it's tough. Most women from the moment of the hurt are determined to play Hollywood, and stick to the guy through thick and thin. Right from jump. I can see, Miss Rogers, that you're thinking about whether you want to go or stay."

"Yes, you bastard," she said without anger as she started to cry. She talked through the tears. "I don't have any choice to make, Major. Yes, I'm his future, I'm his future, but I know we're both going to spend so much time thinking about the past, when he was—you know, and *he's* not going to want me now. He's too proud a black man to want to have me around doing things for him that he can no longer do for himself, and you know, these are things I have to *deal* with, *me*, and I need just a little more time, just a very little."

"Sister, I don't mean to be rough on you, but you know as well as I do that none of us have that much time, black people especially. I'm glad you came up. I hope you can arrange to stay awhile. He's through with the Army. He'll go to a hospital back home. And even when he's out, Miss Rogers, he's going to have trouble with that lung—"

"But, Doctor, he won't want to get married."

"I didn't say one thing about marriage." He looked levelly at Mimosa. "What's marriage got to do with it? You're either with him or not, and in fact, you know, that may be just the way to make it work."

"So that he doesn't feel that we got married because I felt sorry for him."

"That's right."

"And children?"

"If that happens, then I'm sure he'd want the papers and you're home without sweat."

They sat without speaking for a few moments, she wiping her eyes, grinding out her last cigarette and lighting another, until he said, "All right now?"

"As good as I'll ever be."

"Why don't you get some rest and come back later. You'll feel better. And he'll feel better, not having you there at times, wondering what you're thinking and how you feel about him now."

"Yeah," she said, standing. "He'd better get used to my being around, because I'm going to start getting ready to resign; I'm going back on the same boat or plane or helicopter that he's going back on. I mean, that's all there is to it."

Grinning, Dr. Jackson said, "Sister, that's all I was trying to find out. From what I know, you've got yourself a special kind of man."

He watched her go and wondered if perhaps he shouldn't have asked her to have a drink or dinner at what they called their club here. But she would've been too quick to sense that he was leg-hunting instead of just sharing a part of an evening with a Sister with a big problem.

The blonde swept in, her entrance making Dr. Jackson think that it'd been timed to the exit of Miss Rogers. "They want to know when they can give Captain Blackman his medal," she said.

He looked at her for a long moment, then said, "I think in a couple of weeks. I don't think he wants it."

She scoffed. "Nobody wants it, Sidney."

"I guess not." He rubbed his round, dark face and settled his chin in his hand. He gazed absently at the people passing in the corridor. "It's like everything else, I suppose, shit, and we're in it so deep, it doesn't even smell anymore. Or almost."

"But, will he take it? You know, they don't want to be embarrassed; they'd just as soon send it, with the printed notice of all that goes with it, and let it go at that. This black and white thing's got everybody jumpy."

"It's about time, Mildred. About time."

# 23

There would be no more Meursault or grass, he reflected, for a long time, if ever, Mims. Through lowered lids he studied her, having come awake ten minutes ago. Jesus H. Christ, he thought. She's gorgeous! She was sitting in a chair, her attention fixed on the newspaper she was reading. Framed in flowers (oh yes, the ceremony's soon) her strong face revealed every bone and line, every curve and angle. She looked very good indeed. Medal-dressing time. He wanted to move and look at her legs; they sure would be showing, as good legs should from under a short skirt.

He'd once read a novel where the guy was in the hospital and his girl came to see him and she ran her finger up her pussy and let him smell it, he wanted it so bad. Blackman almost burst out laughing. There were some things Mims was an absolute black puritan about. Blackman knew that was one of them. On the other hand, he couldn't see himself asking for anything like that. White folks did, or at least in that novel they did.

They're going to come marching in soon, he thought. Doctorow, who'd visited him several times in his wheelchair, and Woodcock, who'd come in his, wouldn't be marching. For Doctorow it'd be one more thing for him to note for his book. For Woodcock, what? Nothing. They'd told him of the rocket attack. Bitterly now he wondered what would've happened had he not stood up to draw fire. Here he was with one leg, one lung and one bullet hole through the sac, and Harrison and Belmont were dead anyway. Goddammit!

Buck Himes was coming and of course Ishmael Whittman, Major Whittman, and Colonel Greer. Also, he'd heard, the four-star from Saigon. Trying to make some peace with the Brothers, Blackman guessed, but it was a little late now. Even with the fast action on the medal. From Germany to Vietnam there was an uptight situation. The black kids handling the weapons, grunting in and out, being passed over for promotions, had had it with the Army's jive program of doing like it always did. From Vietnam to Germany, no officer in a racist bag was safe from a fragging, a round of 16s in the head while in the field. Maybe he was lucky to be getting out, as messed up as he was. It seemed like centuries ago, maybe longer, when he decided he'd life it through the Army.

To his secret disappointment the war ended when he was fourteen; it could've provided him an avenue of escape from the quiet little Southern Tier town on the Susquehanna River. At sixteen, he believed it when they said he could become the first heavyweight world's champion from Binghamton, and he hung out with Joe Taylor, the middleweight, and thought he was learning, tried to learn, but still hungered for the outside. Until he met one of the De John brothers—he forgot which one, there were so many—at a CYO match, one which his prospective manager attended, young Abraham Blackman believed he could go all the way. The De John boy stopped him in the second, with one of those Italianate, from-the-floor blows, designed to rip wayward vines from the earth; this was a punch much like Kid Gavilan's bolo: lucky if it connected, brilliant if it downed a man. Blackman went down and stayed; they could've counted 100 over him.

295

In shame he fled the city. His shame was compounded by the scholarships that seemed to be raining down on the black youths with whom he'd run track and played football in high school before quitting. Before he left, he'd visited his father, who, on his second marriage and second batch of children—Blackman was one of six from the first—was a janitor at IBM. He wasn't a bad father. Sometimes, with all his children, ten in number, he'd pile them in a panel truck and drive them to visit friends in Utica, Elmira or Geneva. Just one of those things, his father'd explained, about Blackman's mother and himself.

"Didn't work out." He gave Blackman twenty-five dollars, and, together with what his mother'd given him and what he'd managed to earn on part-time jobs, he left and arrived in New York with sixty-eight dollars in his pocket. His rooming house was not far from City College and, instead of taking the Broadway line down to the transfer point to Queens, he liked to walk past the campus and take the Eighth Avenue line. He wondered how the boys who'd gotten the scholarships were doing and he resolved that the first chance he got, he was going to college. The very first chance. Thoughts of college made him feel even more keenly that he'd missed out by being too young for service when the war ended. The vets were getting free educations and being paid while they studied. Maybe—

He knew very little about the Cold War; his life was centered on the people and places around 145th Street and Eighth Avenue. Occasionally he'd pack his best suit, wear his second best, and take the Greyhound home from Thirty-fourth Street, bringing gifts for the younger children in the family, and his mother, a small, frightened woman who let the world cope with her because she herself was unable to do anything with it.

Two days in town and he'd become restless, and usually left it one or two days before he planned to, hungering for New York. But once there, reading in his gray room, restlessness overtook him again. Overcome by a distressing ennui, he skipped days on his job, panicked when he came up short with the room rent.

He pleaded illness when he returned, and the factory foreman forgave him, but ran his test anyway, asking Blackman to work overtime. He knew he was caught; the white man had him at a disadvantage.

On the day he turned eighteen, he walked through Convent Avenue, took the train at 125th Street and Eighth Avenue downtown and instead of taking the transfer out to Queens, enlisted in the Army. Three squares, a profession and travel. And rapid promotion, they said. *And*, Blackman knew, the Services were now integrated, had been for a year. He left New York without looking back; the bus on the way to Fort Dix. He scored in Grade I of the AGCT, and someone said he was officer material, but at Fort Bragg, his next post, where he made corporal, no one seemed to notice. Infantry training was far behind him now, his jumps at Bragg recorded. Those had entitled him to wear the boots; he kept them sparkling, his trousers neatly bloused down over them, and when he rose, after a long sit, the Fort Bragg stomp came automatically, straightening the trousers. He was looking for European duty—France or Germany—when he was detailed to Japan for duty with the 24th Infantry Regiment. After a tour there, he was sure, he'd make it to Europe. The cats back from Germany said the duty was good, the fräuleins willing, but the Berlin Airlift had sort of tightened things up. Well, Blackman reasoned, if it was going to get *too* hot in Europe, then Japan was the place to be.

The duty was good. The only thing was, he discovered, the Japanese had a thing about color, too; they could say nigger, say it very well. Even so, like everyone else, he got himself an "Only," and functioned at half-speed while performing the garrison duties, living for the off-duty hours, the weekends, when groups of the Brothers got together with their Japanese girls and got into records, homefood or just partying; the white boys went their own ways and occasionally they met and scuffled. The Deuce-Four was as soft as any other garrison unit in Japan. It was slowly integrating, but not too fast, in spite of Executive Order

Number 9981. It was good duty for the white officers and non-coms. In fact, any duty in Japan was, with things heating up in Europe.

One afternoon in June, when he was lying around with his Mama, thinking about going back in when they finished the PX liquor he'd brought to her house, his buddies came, fatigue-sharp, and hustled him back to the base. Blackman couldn't believe it. Here he was, two weeks a buck sergeant, his Mama Only stashed away, saving his bread and taking courses by mail, and they were talking about a war. He couldn't believe it; he hadn't even washed his prick yet, and they had him on the plane, next to Buck Sergeant Whittman, whom he hated, flying over the Sea of Japan to a place called Pusan in a country called Korea, where they couldn't get it straight about who had attacked whom first.

Whittman, with his flaxen hair, had scored in Grade III, gotten his stripes earlier and assigned to Headquarters Company where he did little except to complain about serving with Negro soldiers—a fact, which gave him a lot more leisure than he could've had serving with any other regiment. And the soldiers knew he knew, and on the plane laughed at his nervousness, his clumsy attempts to quickly befriend the men with whom he'd have to fight.

Making his way through the hospital with a steady stride, Buck Himes in his wake, Major Ishmael Whittman caught the smell of a Havana and slowed. Roi-Tans were good enough for him, but just once, he thought, he'd like to try a Havana. Have to smoke it in a closet, though. Unpatriotic, what with all the business going on over Cuba. The more he thought about it, the more incensed he became. Who in the fuck would have nerve enough to smoke a Cuban cigar in a hospital in South Vietnam. Then he saw him.

A doctor he guessed, and a young one with long hair. A Jew, he suspected, who didn't want to come into the Army in the first place; probably had to drag him in to do his tour. The doctor's cigar end was heavy with gray-black ash. Whittman's mouth watered. All his life he'd hated guys who had the privileges, while he had to hump it, and in the process he'd become so used to shit that he almost didn't know anything good anymore. Havana cigars were an exception. And he knew that the further up the Army ladder he went, the more good things would come to him. But he'd never forget the old days, coming out of Elkhart, Indiana, joining the Army and getting to Europe in the Occupation forces before being sent to Japan to soldier with the Deuce-Four, an outfit few people wanted to serve with because it was mostly jigaboo; but had turned out to be good duty for him. A buck sergeant lived like a king in those days with an outfit like that, or did until Korea. Then he panicked. He'd been rough on the niggers because the officers told him that was the best way to get along with them. In Headquarters Company, all he did was sit on his ass and shuffle papers and give orders. Even the black first sergeants had to take his shit, since he was with HQ. But he couldn't read a map to save his fucking life; couldn't tell his prick from his nose, and there he was, on the way to a war. Yeah, I suckholed, he thought. Didn't want to be shot in the back; didn't want to die. It was all too quick. And he was expendable. He'd gone to the CO to plead the importance of his staying in Japan, but, the CO told him, he had no importance. He understood then that he'd been used, counted for as much as the blacks. The continuation of the shit between the privileged and those who were not; the continuation of the battle between people like those in Elkhart, who made bugles and trumpets, and those who put together the pretty girls for the magazines and movies, to whose images you threw the salute of hot sperm from a throbbing stiff cock in the quiet and loneliness of your bed. Those were girls you'd never lay a finger on, who'd never look at you, because the guys who paraded them in front of you would never have it. What you would have would be the starch-fat country girls, the whores of Times Square, Berlin, Hamburg, Tokyo, Hong Kong and Saigon. Being an officer they would be the better class of whores. He thought of Germany where the whores used the greasy rag. They took a cloth and dipped it into a jar of Vaseline, then forced it up your ass, wiggling it around as you fucked them, and when you were ready to come, they snatched the rag out, trailing shit and grease while you tumbled through ecstasy. (Well, it did feel pretty good.)

Whittman slowed again and gave a sidelong glance at the blonde nurse who was standing too close to a black major, Medical Corps. He wanted the look to convey the information that he was checking her rank and location, but she paid him no mind, intent upon what the nigger was saying, even—damn it!—touching him on the arm.

Buck Himes saw the look, saw the blonde with Major Jackson, and smiled. Ole Whittman tried to be cool, but it just wasn't in im. But he must be happy about one thing: Ole Abe's finished with the Army. He won't ever have to look at Blackman again or hear his voice or read his reports, and know that ole Abe's got his number just as sure if he had his ass under a microscope studying him, like he was some fuckin bug or other, which he is. Buck Himes saw that the nurse had a nice ass and big tits. Okay, Jackson. Better get some penicillin from him later, cause you never know out here, and a Brother believes in gettin him some leg, even if his dick falls off later, and baby, I'm a Brother.

They entered the hospital CO's office and there found Doctorow and Woodcock in their chairs, dressed with open collars. They sat down to wait for Colonel Greer and the four-star up from Saigon. Army and civilian photographers paced the hall outside, nudging each other when a nurse swished by, and Himes noted that, when the nurses saw the cameras and the civvies, man, they put something extra into the swish. Himes got to his feet. "I'm goin in to see Blackman," he said to Whittman.

For form, Whittman thought, that was something he should

do, but didn't want to do it alone. He stood quickly. "I'll go with you." Himes led the way. He'd not seen the woman before. He smiled as she turned to them as they entered the room. Ummmm mmmmm! Himes thought. He wondered what Major Whittman was thinking of her. Probably never even talked to a woman like her, black, white or yellow. Put the dude into a cold sweat, I bet, cause she'd sure let him know, one way or the other, that that jive ole white man's superiority shit wouldn't be workin with her.

But Whittman only glanced at her. He was more intent on seeing the broken man in the bed. This was white power; this is what he'd done, finally, to the nigger who'd whipped his ass in Korea. And he'd done it to the system, too, that protected Blackman from his wrath which, like Thor, he was ready to unleash when he discovered the black military history seminar. Complaining to Greer did no good; Greer was afraid of this nigger thing. Everyone was afraid of it. But I did this, Whittman thought, as he drew near the bed and met Blackman's eyes. I sent him in when Intelligence, as usual, didn't know shit from Shinola about what was out there. Now we know, with one casualty, this one. No dead. Can't count the rocket attack, that happened at the base. Now he spoke: "Hello, Abe." He watched the eyes shifting slowly, with the same old insolence, back and forth over his face.

"Hello, Ishmael."

"How goes it?"

"Well, man, I'm gonna be short in a couple of places, but not where it's gonna count."

What's he mean by that, Whittman wondered. Why do they always talk in goddamn riddles. "That's good. Well," he said more brightly, "today you're getting the big one."

"That's what they tell me. Anybody tell you they were kicking me up to major to sweeten the pot?" Blackman watched as Whittman's face revealed its surprise. "Yeah, Ishmael. Equal rank. More pension."

"That's good, Abe. I'm glad."

In the same half whisper, half-full voice, Blackman said, "No you ain't, you turkey motherfucker. You don't have to lie anymore. You can't even do that well."

Whittman took a deep breath, hoping to regain the composure Blackman was chipping away at. "Major, the past is the past—"

"—and it's catching up with you and all the others, Ish."

"Yeah, I remember. That was always your line, Abe. The past."

Mimosa Rogers looked up quickly when she heard Abraham's wheezing laugh. The lieutenant stood beside her, absently plucking flower petals and trying to smoke a cigarette, there, but not there.

"You're afraid of the past, Ish. You drop it in a hole and cover it over, like it was a stone, but it's a seed, sprouting a jungle . . ."

Ishmael Whittman shrugged his shoulders and left the room. He'd wait back in the office. He'd have to attend the ceremony, even if his attendance hadn't been ordered in that nice way. He was the nigger's boss, his immediate superior and some of whatever bullshit glory the Army was going to pass out in a few moments would reflect on him. It wouldn't hurt his promotion, if it was really in the works.

Blackman was thinking: that creep is going to make general. I know it, I just know it, and he thought back to Korea, ignoring Mims and Himes who in any case were just sitting there, as if waiting for him to get his breath back after that shit with Ishmael.

They had trained from Pusan to Osan, a couple of rifle companies, as far as Blackman could make out, and two or three other small units. He had a squad and Whittman had a squad, Whittman being in charge of both as they tried to get into position to delay the expected thrust of the North Koreans south of Seoul. But Whittman couldn't read the map, although he kept pretending he could. Every time Blackman pointed out an error, Whittman crumpled up the map. This cat don't care, Blackman thought. He's got two squads of niggers and he don't care; he won't even let me—for Christ's sake, he's so scared of losing face that he's not even worried about getting killed himself.

That was when Blackman, with that exasperated end of black patience gesture, reached for the map, which Whittman snatched away. The fight was on and Blackman remembered clubbing him into the ground with his fists and loving it, but at times recoiling from the burning hatred in the blue eyes. Each time he recoiled, he attacked even more fiercely until the eyes showed nothing, glazed over like porcelain.

Command passed over to Blackman as they retreated slowly back south, giving more time to the troops arriving at Pusan. They had one small victory at Yech'on, but it was quickly forgotten. All the white boys wanted to remember was how the 24th hit the road, running at full stride when the North Koreans came down the pike:

> *When them commie mortars begin to thud*
> *The old Deuce-Four begin to bug*
> *When they started falling round the CP tent*
> *Everybody wonder where the high brass went,*
> *They were just buggin out,*
> *Just movin on.*

It'd been easy for the singers to forget that for long days that seemed like months, there'd been only four hundred American soldiers in Korea; a pebble thrown into the charge of a dragon. Pushed back on Pusan, they broke out again when MacArthur ducked in behind the Northerners at Inch'on. The way lay north. Blackman got another stripe and heard that Whittman, now in another company, got one, too. In Blackman's squad was a tough little corporal named Handy. He hadn't thought of Handy in a long time; reminded him of Harrison. Handy'd spent some time in Germany, cooling it along "Nigger Strasse" in Berlin before coming to Japan, the Deuce-Four and Korea. Cat'd found a home in the Army, Blackman recalled. Handy made no bones about it.

On the truck ride north Handy said, "Shit, we be back in Japan in another couple of weeks, Abe." He spat tobacco at one of the paddy fields the long line of trucks was racing past. "Whew!" Handy said. "How come you never get used to the stink o shit?"

They hurtled between lines of refugees carrying their belongings on A-frames attached to their backs. "Poor fuckin gooks," one of the white soldiers said.

Handy caught Blackman's eye and winked. "Just like sayin nigger, ain't it, man?"

Blackman said, "There's a whole heap of black soldiers callin em gooks, too. Even you," Blackman finished accusingly. "Negroes here out-Whiteying Whitey. Catchin his goddamn disease just hangin out with him in these wars."

"Yeh, you right, man," Handy said. "Never thought of it that way. Thought of an awful lot of things, but not that."

But Blackman'd closed his eyes and let his body roll with the truck. They passed through Seoul at breakneck speed. The trucks shifted into high and the soldiers in them came alive, sensing that plans were changing.

In the growing darkness, Handy said, "The shit's hit the fan, Abe. Kaesong, ten to one."

"Bullshit," Blackman said. "That's only the first stop. These crackers'll have us winding up in Peking, Handy."

"Dig it," Handy said. "The Chinese say don't cross the Yalu, and Whitey says, 'Fuck you, I'm comin,' and you may be right."

*Chink-Chink Chinaman*
*Sittin on a fence,*
*Tryina make a dollar*
*Outa fifteen cents.*

The old ditty, learned in Binghamton as a child, kept coming back to Blackman in the truck as it rattled through Kaesong. Outside the city the trucks stopped long enough for gas from a dump and C-rations. Handy had fallen quiet. How did he

304

feel now, Blackman wondered. How about this Army for a home? It was one thing to be home in the Army, as Blackman was, but another to brag about how great the Army was to you, like Handy. What did Handy, ole Bubba Handy think now about those days on welfare as a kid, or of an old man who jumped from an overpass into the path of a train, just because he couldn't find a job. What, now, Bubba, of a mother left to raise twelve kids, who fucked the butcher, blew the baker and took it in the ass from the welfare inspector, so she could get more for her kids? Does all that make the Army a home, now, Bubba? Now it's pay-off time. Send your ass across the Yalu to stop 700 million Chinese who don't give a shit about you anymore than you give a shit about them, just to save the world from communism for some Whitey sonofabitch who's afraid of it because maybe it'd give other people the same things he has.

It must've been in the truck that night that Blackman decided if he got through, he was going into the reserves, try to hold onto his grade, and go to college. There was so much shit going on, he thought, I had to make some effort to try to understand it.

Back in the truck, in the darkness, Hardy said to him, "Abe?"

"Thought you was asleep, Handy."

"When the end of the world's comin, Bubba Handy don't sleep."

"Too late to sound evil, Handy. You got to pay for livin in a happy home."

"I'm thinkin when I'm evil."

"Yeah."

"The motherfuckers gonna waste us up here, Abe."

"Baby, you gettin them bulletins late."

"I thought I was slick. Whitey been fuckin over me for so long, I'm gonna make him look out for me, y'dig?"

"You better get you another slickin factory, man."

"Lemme tell you somethin: I'm still slickem him. I'ma be back

305

with a whole black skin. What's the next town, P'yongyang or Sinanju?"

"P'yongyang, but we'll have to stop before then."

When they stopped, they could feel the mountains pressing in on them. The gas cans resounded in the stillness when they were handled, opened and emptied into the trucks' tanks. Around him, Blackman saw troopers picking up pieces of paper. "Leaflets," he heard someone say. He took one and held his flashlight to it, Handy peering over his shoulder.

> Black soldiers of America. You have crossed the 38th Parallel. You are now an Aggressor against the People's Republic of North Korea. You now approach the border of the People's Republic of China. Defensive action to annihilate the Aggressor Armies will commence at once. Our battle is not against the exploited, captive Black Soldiers of America, but against the white imperialist government that threatens the peace of Asia. Lay down your arms. No harm will come to you. We welcome you as Brothers seeking freedom. Bring this with you.

The Chinese broke up the convoy an hour before dawn. The surviving trucks were turned back south, and the troops dug in. When the attack broke off, Blackman looked for Handy, and was told he was missing.

"Dead, you think?" he asked.

They didn't know.

"Captured?"

They didn't know.

A year later, after they'd been pushed back south, Blackman saw Handy's name listed as a prisoner of war, and at that moment he remembered that Handy'd taken the leaflet from him and stuffed it into his pocket that night, saying something about keeping it for a souvenir. Maybe Handy was as slick as he said he was; maybe he right now was grinning at him from some camp north of the Yalu.

Off duty Blackman haunted the Sam Gak Chi area of Seoul with the other black soldiers, picking up another stripe in the meantime. The white soldiers left that place to them and carved out others for themselves. The battle for women was far more intense and murderous than the battles against the North Koreans and the Chinese.

The UN forces took the truce; at least agreed to talk about terms, and the war, in which every nation's troops could gain a little glory, ended. Lined up at the ramps at Kimpo, Blackman remembered, black soldiers talked loudly. They were on the way home; it was over for them. They could shout from the control tower if they wanted to.

"Charlie got his ass beat for the first time. No point in makin it look like he won. He went to the Yalu and got driv back. He didn't do what he set out to do. Leave it to these cracker mothers, and right now the Yalu'd be blood red. No, this man got his ass beat, by some boney little ole colored cats. Now he kin slice it eny which way he got a mind to, but these cats done put a hurtin on Charlie."

"Abraham, are you all right?"

"Sugar, baby." He pursed his lips. After the kiss he said, "Just thinking of Whittman. He stayed in the Army after Korea and I got out and went to college. I thought that'd help to make me the first general since B. O. Davis, Jr."

"Listen, man," Buck Himes said. "We'll go on out for a few minutes so you can get yourself together before they come in here with all that shit. You want Dr. Jackson?"

"Naw. Just lemme rest a minute. Mims, you are *fine*."

When they were outside, Blackman pissed, heard his urine hissing through the tube, saw the bottle filling, frothing on the top. He still had time, he knew, because they'd certainly come in and spray the place; get that lingering bedpan smell out, among other things. They'd put up a screen so that, in the pictures, it wouldn't look like his life was tied to bottles and tubes. He thought of Whittman's face when he told him about the promotion. He started laughing and wheezing and choking. Yeah, he could laugh now, and thank Greer for getting it through, now that he was out of it, but Whittman had stars in his eyes, and the Army would give them to him; it'd given them to worse men.

Blackman rose up on one cheek and broke wind. Funny how you have to fart all the time when you're in bed. Relaxed, maybe.

Here I am worrying about Whittman and I'm all broken up. That peckerwood's got *everything* the devil gave him. Maybe I shouldn't have come back into the Army, he thought, thinking about the years after Korea, of study and jive jobs. All the time he fretted about just being one of the mob, instead of leading it; all the time trying not to lead when he found himself doing it. There were lots of cats out there who didn't want to be led anywhere, toward anything.

(I wouldn't have met Mims, if I hadn't come back in.)

Maybe the end of the marriage had something to do with his coming back. It started, just as it ended, quietly, without a ripple, conceived at a party, ending at a party, with the mutual realization that they were marking time, dancing on a dime. She didn't want children until they were set. He didn't know what she meant by set, but suspected that it meant another car and buying a home they couldn't afford in a suburb where they weren't wanted. New York is an easy place to break up in. He'd returned there to go to City College, although he knew he could have gone almost any place. In New York when you break up, you just walk out into the street with your suitcases and join all the others with suitcases or U-Haul panel trucks; or you go down into the subway or take a bus. You simply vanish among other people, battalions of police or mounds of garbage. It was 1960 and black boys who'd gone to college were starving by the legion. Martin King was marching, but the waves hadn't grown large enough to make Power realize that it could very well accommodate some black folks into its set-up. He hated the Negro insurance company where he worked in the home service department, taking care of the payments and complaints of the policyholders, and where each person sat quietly at his or her desk, faces blank, doing work for which the pay was a

308

disgrace. But the officers like to expound on black pride; working for black people, looking out for them, we must do this, we must do that, while they, in addition to their handsome salaries, drew down two big beans every time they had a board meeting and board meetings were scheduled twice a month. There were no promotions, dismissals were often summary. So the personnel sat, cowed, and Blackman with them, until one day, he picked up the phone, called his ex-wife (he'd made the trip to Juarez) and told her he was leaving; that he was going to see if he could get back into the Army, and Louise, *that* was her name, wished him good luck, but then wondered if they couldn't have a drink as soon as his plans were made.

# 24

He went home for the last time, he was sure, blazing up Route 17 through the mountains in a rented car. His mother was joining a relative in California, the biggest old folks' home in history. The kids were all gone: Chicago, San Francisco, colleges on scholarships. His father had had a stroke and didn't even know him. There was nothing anymore. Even the Susquehanna seemed shrunken with age or recoil from past events. The great chestnut trees were all cut down, victims of blight.

So he clung to the other root, already severed, but it was the last one he'd known. Louise. And about her he remembered with clarity, only the flight down to Dallas and El Paso, ringed with blue-tinted mountains. He'd checked into a hotel and the lawyer picked him up in the morning—him and five other people, and they went to the courthouse in Juarez where the photographers hung around hoping to catch a celebrity sneaking through. They were whisked from one office to another and in short time they were all clutching green-papered divorces, signed, sealed and stamped. They were back on the plane at noon, and in New York by nightfall. Louise, it was all easy come and easy go.

They gave him a commission as a second lieutenant, and with a wink promised him that he'd get up the ladder pretty fast with active and reserve duty coupled with college. No sweat. They'd bounce him down to Bragg for a little retreading and he could begin to see the world, with a tour in Germany. He'd already seen Japan and Korea, hadn't he? Again with a wink.

He kept the date with Louise the night before flying to Bragg. It was in one of those midtown bars that blacks were just beginning to feel comfortable and safe in, near the advertising agency where she worked as a researcher, a dead-end job, he suspected, but one in which she could wear a different outfit five days a week and talk somewhat knowledgeably about clients' products. Tang was a lot of crap; Micrin was colored blue water.

"Well, it's all set then?"

"Yep," he said.

"Maybe it's for the best, Abraham. I don't know."

"Yeah, maybe. Don't worry about it."

"I'm not exactly—*worried*." She laughed. "Too late for that."

"Come on over to my place."

"For what?" she asked quickly.

Just as quickly, he said, "A drink. You've never been to my place."

"Abraham—"

"We're not married. It ought to be more fun. Like it was once or twice before we got married."

"That was all, huh?"

"C'mon, Louise. You were at the party, too."

"If it was so bad, why do you want to try again?"

He looked at her a long time, then said, "It's about the only thing I know to try, Louise."

She fought hard and managed not to cry. After all, there was no point to it, now, except that she felt about as blue as she thought he did. Neither could touch the failure; it was just there. One more time then. To Billie; all her Billie records were gone. He must have them. Wish him good luck. Say sorry before he says sorry, but mostly just put it on im. Good. All night long. "Okay," she said. "Let's go."

Years later, resting back at the base at Mannheim, Blackman picked up a paper. A black face peered out at him, a tough, lumpy face ringed by a beard and a full natural. The face was familiar and Blackman looked at it a long time before reading the story and seeing the name under the photo. Bubba Handy. He remembered that he'd been charged with collaborating with the Chinese, but acquitted. Bubba Handy was now one of the leaders of the Deacons for Defense and Justice.

Blackman sat back and pondered the passing of the years. He was a silver looey now, duty in France and Germany interspersed with maneuvers, trips home, junkets to Denmark, Sweden, Spain, Italy and North Africa behind him. They'd sure kept their promise about that. But, hell, he should be a major right now, he thought, staring at Bubba's picture again. Whittman, whom he'd met in Berlin was already a captain. You'd think with so many Brothers coming into the Army now, that they'd be glad to kick some of us upstairs. No. It's the same old shit.

During his travels he'd met old vets from World War I; that old guy with the 369th living near La Rochelle. Jesus, the Army must've been a bitch for a black man then, he thought. And the guy living in Stockholm who'd fought in Spain. And in Genoa he heard about Tombolo.

With old battle maps he'd covered the west Italian coast from Milan to Leghorn to Viareggio, and then gone down to the American cemetery to find it run by a chief petty officer from the Navy. Blackman could tell nothing from the cards, except that a lot of the Buffaloes had died on the same day during the same battle. Not unusual. Track down some of white soldiers who took part in it? He almost laughed at himself. But one day, he thought, he was going to take it upon himself to tell the young legs about black soldiers, because the white man sure wasn't going to do it and do it right.

312

Martin King kept marching. John F. Kennedy was murdered. Malcolm X was murdered. Things were happening back home and the young Brothers were coming into the Army bad; not grateful anymore, if they ever were; not taking shit anymore. America was a strange place when he returned, just before his first hitch in the Nam, and he was almost glad to be out of it.

The first hitch was almost a breeze. They operated in Zone C, northwest of Saigon, close to the Cambodian border. It was before the build-up became big and steady, before troops went into Santo Domingo. And it wasn't always bad. But it seemed that the more the troops came, the badder the Viet Cong got; they were not going to be pushed out. Sometimes you thought they were, but they always came back as Intelligence screamed, "It's the people who protect them." If the Viet Cong were like the Army said, why would the people protect them? "Because they get their throats cut if they don't" was the answer. Chuck had all the answers and the shit was getting thick, and the little brown men were steady taking out big white men and the big white men became afraid.

Was that why, Blackman now wondered, nearly all the rifle companies were slowly but certainly changing colors to all black? He'd watched them come in on the big transports at Tan Son Nhut, bound down the ramps, so much bigger and badder than Negro soldiers he'd known before. Big shoulders, big arms and heavy asses; they all walked deliberately, like Jim Brown going back to a huddle. He watched them change the Army; their language seeped through everything. Officers copied their idiom so they could communicate with their men.

Blackman's own platoon was well mixed with PRs, chucks and blacks. He led it into My Suc, a ten-hut village one day midway during his hitch, and when they left it, screams dying, the huts burning, he knew he had to change the Army. *He*, not someone else, because he thought he understood it all now.

Crouched under the fringes of the rain forest waiting for the helicopters to return, Blackman avoided his men and their terrible silence. Ordinarily there would be joking, an awful sense of readiness, the rifles set to fire on automatic. Instead, this day they sat silently, smoking, but without that leisurely quality of men who know they've done a job well. They stared at their cigarettes, as if expecting them to accuse. They were all young, all indoctrinated. They'd killed people—old men, women and children —who *might've* been Viet Cong. In other words, killed them because they had the same skin color, that was what it amounted to; that's what all the training taught them without mentioning those words. There'd been other things at other villages; the legs spoke about them with the attitude: Who's Gonna Care What Happens to These Dinks Out Here? White soldiers you could understand talking like that, but black soldiers? When sometimes in Khanhoi, Lam Son Square or on Tu Do they rioted over the little brown women who Chuck felt should be for himself only.

This, Blackman thought, this My Suc was not the black and white against the brown, not really. The blacks and the whites really wanted to kill each other, not the Vietnamese, and only the fact that there *were* Vietnamese to kill prevented them, most times, from doing so to each other. Today was one of the days the Vietnamese were their each other. Today Blackman thought bitterly, catching the first throbs of the choppers, black men became like white men; they too raped, murdered and castrated; murdered in the heat of hysteria. Once, wherever the American Army had been, from Guam to Germany, its black soldiers had been its kindest; the stories of those kindnesses were legion. But today. A sickness of laughing and giggling hit everyone. The whites were relieved that blacks at last had joined them, had lost, finally that essential human quality for which they were well known. And his black soldiers had been giggling and murdering because they'd come to know what it felt like to kill without fear of punishment, in broad daylight, challenging the universe to break

314

out of position in the heavens; had come to know, like whites who'd done most of it in history, just how mothafucking easy it was to kill a colored sonofabitch. *Easy!*

No, Blackman told himself, waving his platoon into the choppers. No! We're not joining them in this shit. We ain't payin *that* price for belonging. Back at base he gave the report, leaving out, as others had and still did, the precise events that took place. He finished his first hitch, got another and arrived back in the Nam when the New Democracy was being reported all over hell, and discovered that his battalion commander was Ishmael Whittman.

Major Whittman and on his first hitch.

"Abe," he said, shaking hands slowly, "it's been a long time."

"Yeah," Blackman said. "Long enough for you to get your leaf. Can you read maps yet, man? I forgot to ask you in Berlin, you were so busy chasing that ugly, fat fräulein."

Whittman sat back. Hadn't the years and his leaf washed away this kind of business? Shit, I don't want this spade in my command. But goddamn it, they said I had to take him, that I needed another black company commander. He said, "It's been a long time and I hope, water under the bridge, Lieutenant, and what I was doing in Berlin is none of your goddamn business—"

"Listen, Ish. Don't pull that rank shit with me. I'll climb over there and beat your ass again. Now you know fucking well that the only reason you're sitting there and I'm sitting here is that you're white and I'm not. Right? So get up off it. I'm Army. I know how to take orders and I'll take Army orders, but, Major, you ain't nothin but chickenshit peckerwood to me. I thought we ought to get that straight right away. That's not water under the bridge. And another thing: in Saigon they tell me this battalion believes in using black men on point for patrol units, squads and platoons. You still don't like niggers, do you?" Blackman stood. "You still a fuckin dummy. Ain't hardly nothin *but* niggers here and you're pullin that shit."

Whittman blew out a hot gust of air. "I guess you get that one free, Abe, but there'll be no more of it. C Company's yours; take it outa here."

But Blackman'd already gone. Second Lieutenant Buck Himes, in the next thin-walled room watched him go, thinking, That niggor'o big onouch to do juot what ho oayo he'o gonno do. I ain't never heard nobody ream out ole Whittman like that. Shit! Chalk one up for Brudder Blackman.

He started the black military history seminar as soon as he figured out a program. Start with the Revolution and go on; it's all there. The Spanish Civil War. He was glad black men were there. Tombolo; the Pacific. Untapped, and these young black legs think they're doing it all for the first time, but it's been done before, over and over again. He was anxious to get started; big things were planned over here, he knew. The planes kept flying people in, the boats kept bringing them in. Every day there were new planes streaking through the sky. They were enlarging airports everywhere. Newer, bigger choppers were being used, and newspaper and television guys were saturating everything. Blackman guessed that for many of them promotion depended on a tour of the Nam. But what was all this bullshit about the Army being the most democratic institution in America? Cause guys have to get shot with each other? Shit. There ain't nothin but spooks, PRs and peckerwoods in the ranks, and the junior officers are mostly crackers—them that ain't black.

The seminar started. There were few grunts at first, all black, then more and then that white boy, Doctorow—they wanted him the hell outa there. "It's open to the company," Blackman said. "This is Charlie Company's thing and Doctorow's in the company."

He was running out of books and lists of other books, and it'd been his intention just to ask one of the Sisters at the Embassy to facilitate things for him, spring him loose from Army red tape. That simple and he'd met Mimosa Rogers. "Don't nobody live in Des Moines," he told her on their third date, and she laughed and he knew he'd found his way home after almost forty years.

She laughed now as she pulled Woodcock's Afro comb through Blackman's hair. The nurses were changing bottles, the top sheets and spraying. He could see Woodcock and Doctorow in their chairs laughing as Mimosa combed.

"Shoulda shaved you, baby. Didn't think of it, you and the major there were having such a good time."

"Never mind. I can still kick his ass with one leg."

Without missing a stroke she said close to his ear, "You can do a lot of things with one leg, Abe."

He rolled his eyes up at her, said nothing.

With almost a single motion Doctorow and Woodcock rolled their chairs apart. A flurry of khaki halted between them. Mimosa whipped the comb down and watched as Blackman watched. The four-star was talking to Woodcock and Doctorow. The photographers were taking pictures. Now the crowd came through the door. The four-star. The colonel. Whittman. Buck Himes. The four-star's people. Dr. Jackson. Doctorow and Woodstock being wheeled in by the orderlies. The shit-slinging commences, Blackman thought, studying Woodcock.

The four-star drew abreast of the bed, smiling, and at just the precise angle for the photographers to catch him, bending over the bed, the colonel pressed close behind him, Whittman pushed close to the colonel. He, Blackman, would be "lower right" in the caption.

"General," Colonel Greer said, when the photo-taking for the moment was over, "I am proud to present to you Major Abraham Blackman."

The four-star smiled sadly, reminding Blackman of those LBJ grimaces that were supposed to pass for smiles of concern. He felt the man's hand, dry and slick, slipping into his, tightening around his bigger hand a little desperately, trying to find grip, and securing some, attempting to put force into it. Blackman closed his

317

fingers over the General's hand and squeezed slightly, then a little more, and smiled up at him. The cameras were clicking. Blackman squeezed again, saw the smile lines around the General's eyes and mouth waver, his eyes question, then he released him.

"Well, Major, you've had bad luck there, and I'm sorry. I'm truly sorry. The President, Congress, the People, the Army, know this medal can't make up for what you lost. It is only a token, but it's from our hearts." He reached for the citation.

As he read it Blackman looked at Mimosa. And thought: Here I am, flat on my ass, baby, with Chuck doing his thing over me. I should've told them No. Right? That would've been more consistent with what I feel, have felt. Then a great silence would've come up over the whole thing; there'd have been nothing for black dudes hanging out in alleyways to talk about or to mimic. Now they'll talk. 'Nigger layin up there with his dick practically shot off, one leg, one lung, takin Charlie's goddamn medal. Shoulda killed the nigger.' That's how it goes, Mims. I needed a little something for myself and for my program. Yeah, baby, I got a program. Right here in bed, I've come up with a program. We gon get workin on it too, pretty soon. Mims, do you know, if a cat could control fifty cities in Africa, he could control that continent; maybe even twenty-five? I need me some land, baby, to get my thing going. Aw, Mims, these motherfuckers've put a real hurting on me. And I can't die until I hurt back. I can't. I won't. Been thinkin, Mims, been—

The powder blue ribbon was coming down over his neck. The four-star was patting down the medal and powder blue cord with white stars on his chest, just above where the tubes coming out of his thorax were concealed by the sheets.

Now the General stepped back into a space the others had created for him, and slowly, his eyes crisp, his chin steady, raised his arm in salute. Then Blackman noticed a welter of elbows, straight fingers seeking the upper edges of the right eyebrows. Colonel Greer, Whittman, expressionless, Dr. Jackson, the blonde nurse, the four-star's aides, Woodcock and Doctorow. The General cracked his salute, the other hands came down.

That's right, Blackman thought. When you get *this* mother-fucker, officers salute *you!* That makes fifty-one we got.

"Congratulations, Major!" the four-star said, shaking his hand again, this time with both hands. "Good luck." He faded out of the room, his aides with him.

Colonel Greer came forward. "Abe, what can I say?"

His eyes were cloudy, Blackman noticed. He feinted a shrug.

"Just one of those things, Colonel." The Colonel's fingers rested lightly on Blackman's good shoulder. "Could've happened to anybody."

"No, I don't think so, Abe." Colonel Greer had already sent a letter to the Defense Department's director for civil rights. He understood that the director was a civilian. Maybe he could use a combat-experienced assistant somewhere. Be easier to get through those seminars Blackman was teaching. The Colonel's fingers played lightly on Blackman's shoulder. "I'll be back to see you before you get patched up well enough to travel. In the mean-time, if you need anything, just let me know."

"Thank you, sir," Blackman said, taking the hand that'd finally left his shoulder.

Whittman was caught between coming forward and trailing Colonel Greer out. He glanced at Blackman for a clue and Black-man catching his eyes, and now sure that the Colonel was out of earshot, said,

"Good-bye, honky."

Whittman's face went red and he spun and left the room. Buck Himes moved up, flanked by Woodcock and Doctorow. "You sure are hard on that man, Brother."

"I ain't hard enough. Hey," he said to Woodcock and Doctorow. "Glad you came for the shit-slinging. How you doin?"

"Okay, Major," Woodcock said. "Congratulations."

"Yeah, Major," Doctorow said, looking at the medal. "That's impressive."

"Woodcock," Blackman said. "If you didn't have nappy hair, you could pass for white; be like Doctorow, know that?"

Woodcock and Doctorow looked at each other; Buck Himes looked at Mimosa; Blackman continued to study Woodcock, and Dr. Jackson, detecting the presence of irrationality because of tiredness, stepped forward. "I think that's about it for today. Busy afternoon." He grasped Blackman's pulse, looked down at the medal, looked at Blackman.

Doctorow and Woodcock, pushed themselves slowly out of the room, looking backward. For both, it was about the most unusual thing they'd ever heard their commander say. Buck Himes trailed them, deep in thought.

"Take this damned thing off my neck, will you, baby?" Blackman asked Mimosa. Now he could let his weariness come down. Real tired.

As she bent close, he pressed his lips to her breasts. She smiled, but worriedly watched Dr. Jackson's impassive face. She even looked at the blonde a couple of times to see if she could read something in her face.

"Let's listen to the well for a minute, Major. Then you're going to get some rest." He placed the stethoscope to Blackman's left chest and listened. Mimosa folded the medal and cord and ribbon together with the citation, and put them in the leather box they'd come in. Dr. Jackson was through.

"Major, can I stay just a couple of minutes longer?"

"No more, Miss Rogers. I want him offed into slumberland where he doesn't have to work; the body does all the work while he lays there."

"Okay."

"The usual Nembutal," Dr. Jackson said to the blonde, who whisked out of the room. "Don't look so worried, Miss Rogers," he said. "He's just tired. He's coming along fine. I suspect having to put up with all the white folks tired him out. We're kind of funny that way. All of us. See you tomorrow." He left, whistling.

"All over," Blackman said. "Took five minutes."

320

"Yes."

"Like getting a watch after fifty years with the company."

"Well—"

"Mims, can you get me a map of Africa, a good one, do you think?"

She shrugged. "I'll try, but I don't think Africa is very big on the Hit Parade out here. How about Colonel Greer?"

"Naw. No dice. If you can't get one, it'll keep, but I'd like to get doing the things I can."

"Abe, why'd you say that to that boy? You hurt him. Did you see his face?"

"Oh. Mims, I was thinking of something. Bring im over tomorrow, huh? I'll apologize—"

"But what in the hell were you thinking to say something like that?"

He studied her and knew she thought he wasn't well, that the doctor was lying. He sighed and it ached, hurt. "I was thinking of my future—"

She winced.

"—ours," he said. "Later, we're gonna have a long talk. I don't want to spend the rest of my life being bored or doing things that don't change one single thing. I wanna be an earth-*shaker*; I wanna be a prime-*mover*, and I'm forty years old and all busted up. But I'm going to try, and tomorrow, you're going to sit down, right there, and begin telling me everything you know about Africa and the people. I'm going to need you very much."

She bent to kiss him. "I'd better go now."

He waited until she was at the door then said, "And teach me how to say I love you in something African, so I can say it all the time. I don't want to use their language anymore for that."

The blonde nurse came in as Mimosa turned the corner and vanished.

# 25

## Cadences

*In civilian clothes they'd gathered from all over the world. They were pleased to see the Man from Carolina there, shaking hands, patting backs, smiling at each new arrival who had cleared the security force of at least twenty pass-checking guards.*

*Drinks were pour-your-own. No bartenders. Less risk of a security breakdown. The rooms even now were being checked again for bugs.*

*There was not a man in the room under fifty. All were uniformly erect, as if used to reviewing large units of soldiers. They all knew each other, and all were amazed—and pleased that they'd come from so far away, so many different places, to attend this meeting.*

*Without a spoken word, they moved into the briefing room. The Man from Carolina took a seat near the speaker's rostrum, and smiled out at the audience.*

*The speaker stood at the rostrum, clenching and unclenching his hands gripping its sides. "Have you had enough?" he asked softly. "Twenty-two years of integration. Twenty-two years of problems. When World War II began the list of riots was as long* as my arm. Bases around the world shuddered under the impact of those riots, so, at the end of the war, partly because we had to maintain the manpower pool, we integrated. We still have riots. They're still not satisfied. What's worse, we're attracting far too much attention in the press. We're here to discuss this problem and come up with solutions. And solutions we must have, because at the rate things are going the Armed Forces of the United States of America are being ripped apart by black racism. We just don't know if we could put a functioning service into combat against the Soviets, the Chinese or anybody else at this moment because of our racial problems." He turned to an aide whom nobody'd noticed because he'd been standing in the shadows. "Give us the basic statistics."

The aide stepped forward and raised his arm. The lights dimmed and a chart was flashed on a board behind him.

"As you know, blacks constitute officially a little over twelve per cent of the population. Unofficially, we place the count closer to fifteen per cent.

"Now, here—" a pencil of light speared from his hand and traced over a row of soldiers at ease on the chart. "—they make up just about ten per cent of all the people in the Armed Forces, over ten per cent of the enlisted men, but thirteen and a half per cent of the noncoms. They make up only two per cent of the officers, but there are three brigadiers among them. One rear admiral, too, I might add. They are ten per cent of the forces in Southeast Asia, officially, but that, too, is closer to fifteen per cent. Unofficially they are eighteen per cent of the battle deaths there, but officially thirteen."

The chart vanished from the board and the lights came up again. The aide glanced at the papers in his hand. "Every stockade in the service is fifty per cent full of blacks, at least, and they are now considered to be most fertile for breeding black discontent. We've had major riots at Mannheim, Rota and Longbinh as well as all those you're familiar with here in the States. We've had them in the streets around the world; you name the street and *we'll give you a riot date. U.S. forces are now widely known to be divided between black and white; we are, therefore, extremely vulnerable."*

The Man from Carolina made a slight gesture and the aide asked,

"Sir?"

The Man from Carolina nodded in thanks and without standing said, "I'd suggest to you all that these are the trials and tribulations of our time. But bear in mind what's been happening over the years. Our nuclear strike capabilities have increased beyond your wildest dreams. The emphasis of warfare has shifted from men to machines. So we could open the Services to these people; they could attain high percentages of everything—but in an Army, for example, that no longer really requires their services except in places like Southeast Asia or South America. These people hold nowhere near as many positions of importance in the nuclear, technological Army as they do in the traditional Army. Oh, a few guards here and there, a dial-spinner or two, a SAC pilot or navigator—offhand I'd say they add up to less than one half of one per cent of the nuclear strike force, the fist of the strike force. Do you understand?" His soft blue eyes roamed the room.

"I know you agree with me about our not wanting to call too much attention to our nuclear strike force, how large it is, where it is, how constantly on the alert. We give the public a tidbit here and there—SAC, the Mediterranean fleet, things like that—but if we told em everything, the cost of maintaining it, and I mean the real cost, we'd all be looking for Boy Scout troops to run the next day. So you fellows have to carry the brunt of public criticism, and you get some of the goodies, too. Remember all that who-struck-John about the New Democracy in Vietnam, when all the reporters and television people were out there? You remember. And you all gave noble statements.

"Well, it took the heat off. We let the right reporters go out there and you showed them what they should see. Well, the ole train slipped off the tracks, didn't it? Riots, shoot-outs, wow. But, we'll get things back on an even keel. We'll manage. Don't forget that: we've always managed. And we'll always have a great fighting force, traditional or technological—probably the latter.

"In your deliberations, therefore, it is of supreme importance that you remember that your traditional ground, sea and air units are all but extinct. That's from the horse's mouth. Now. Does that mean we don't need traditional forces? No, not at all. We can use them in South America, in Africa, if we have to, but we need those troops right here in America, and when I say those troops, I'm not talking about integrated forces. I'm talking about white forces to fight this black population out here.

"You don't think you can continue to discharge disgruntled black troopers back to the cities without something happening, do you? Those boys been machine-gunning and carrying on, learning all about weapons and tactics and strategy. Consider that." The Man from Carolina smiled expansively, stood and stretched. "I'll see you at the bar when your talks are over."

"It's all right for him to talk that bullshit," one man in the audience whispered to another. "He's far, far away from it."

"Yes, but that business about being extinct—"

"Forget it. Somebody's always got to walk in. Always."

In a corner at the rear of the room, another group of men whispered hurriedly and heatedly. "We've got the hottest potato. We got thirteen per cent of em. And a German will fuck anybody, and the fräuleins are fucking a lot of niggers. That upsets the white boys. Maybe it wouldn't be so bad if it was just the blacks, but the spics're gettin on the bandwagon, and, goddamn it, some of those smart-assed white college boys. Those conferences at Heidelberg and Kaiserslautern mean trouble, big trouble."

"If we can get back to a white Army, why not?"

"How long do you think it'll take us to get back to a white Army again?"

"Off the record?"

"If you want."

"Well, you know, you can't two-twelve the whole fuckin Army. So, seven to ten years more in Asia, maybe three to four in South America, they're goin commie, you know, fifteen years about."

"So what do we do about this volunteer Army they keep talkin about?"

"Look, we do what we've always done: put em up front. They'll get the message soon enough. Word gets around, and do you think niggers're gonna volunteer to die? As long as I'm in this Army, that's just what I've got planned for em. I shit thee not."

## Blackman's Cadence

It was a mistake. I mean to expect my enemy, which he was, always has been, to reward my service with equality. A serious misjudgment. Worse, tragic. The tactics—well, they were dangerous. I mean there were things I was catching from him, just being in his company. I could feel it deep in my soul; I could see it happening, if not to me completely, to others. Soldiering to him was just like any other gig black folks stumble into with white folks. A soldier should get the credit due him for being responsible for the most abrupt and drastic changes that can be affected on any society. Man, they sing about soldiers; give them land. Salt. Women. Money. Pensions. Medals (!). Allowances. They do the cats up in bronze. They look so noble, even the pigeon shit doesn't matter. But when they don't give you no credit, they're not obligated to honor you one bit, or to give you one mothafucking thang, baby.

Oh, maybe I wasn't too bright, like some of the legs they got running around over here now, but things came after a while. Life begins at dit-dat, yeah? A strategic withdrawal, a real one, not that line that comes out of the four-star's office every time the Viet Cong goes upside his head. (Some shit does come outa his office. Like they always findin some Viet Cong colonel's body with maps and plans on his dead ass. A massive attack

326

*planned. Yeah.) But I'm talking about a real withdrawal and a reappraisal of the best way to break Chuck's fuckin head wide open, break his will, overrun him militarily, since that's his stick, but not with that jive morality we both been dealing like a Pitty-Pat hand.*

*We insisted that we belonged, that we were Americans. Oh, yeah, we ran that down for a long time, without once realizing what the enemy always knew: the most basic instrument of warfare was possession of terrain from which to either launch an attack or to fight a defensive action. We don't have any. American terrain wasn't ours; it was in our possession only as a figment of the imagination. We didn't even share it with him. Almost four million square miles and what'd we have? Less than one-half of one per cent of it. Man, we were as free to use most of that land as animals are free to walk in a goddamn zoo.*

*What then? Guerrilla warfare; cadres would strike the cities and vanish into the black communities; acts of critical sabotage would bring Chuck to his knees. Oh, that rappin; oh, them empty phrases; oh them sacrificial lambs. Let's go to P'eng: "The people are the water and the guerrillas the fish, and without water the fish will die."*

*A great concept simply put. A concept based on like peoples. Or, like colors. A German couldn't tell a partisan from a farmer just from the color of his skin; nor could he tell a maquis from a clochard simply by looking at his skin. A black guerrilla in the United States would be just about as inconspicuous as a white guerrilla in the Nam. Inasmuch as the black communities are already captive cities, ghettos, inner cities, etc., the black guerrilla, once he steps outside those areas, is no longer a guerrilla passing unseen through the enemy territory. Now, listen to what I'm saying. He might just as well be followed by King Kong and Mighty Joe Young and the Cardiff Giant. Inconspicuous! But you know, ole P'eng's shit could work—you know where, maybe.*

*Where, where in the United States could large groups of black people assemble to learn the art of war? Where could they escape the agents and electronic devices on the ground and in the air? Which blacks among us could we truly trust? Nowhere. None.*

*Africa, yes, where sky surveillance was almost nonexistent. But Chuck saw to it that African and Afro-American relationships were chomped and stomped, but there was Africa. This wouldn't be swift, man. Everybody's in a hurry. Brother Hannibal took his time and was hurting the Romans anytime he wanted to. Like, we haven't any odds working for us. No equipment, no diplomats, only cadres of bitter civilians and Armed Forces vets. And they wouldn't be the strike force, except as individuals and under special circumstances. Our war would be quiet. And it would take time.*

*Those twenty-five cities in Africa. Not fifty. We wouldn't need fifty. Now, suppose we just moved our people over there, not as soldiers in the strict sense, and became twenty-five inter-locking colonies, learning languages and dialects and truly becoming one with the people, Brothers and Sisters without the bullshit phrases. We'd have to fend for ourselves, I guess. I don't think the Premiers or Presidents have ever wished to throw their people into direct competition with Afro-Americans. I hope that's changed a little since World War II.*

*We'd have our own communications systems; we'd have the know-how, and we'd have pilots, if we could hustle up small craft for them, to fly back and forth. Lotsa Brothers out here pushing three-million-dollar planes around. We could get things. Arms manufacturers are businessmen. We'd go through fronts, like the Israelis if we had to; we'd get the shit. And we'd get the people. America is scared. I keep hearing and reading about white folks leaving for New Zealand and Australia and Canada. Well, white folks got the bread. Black folks gonna start taking the hint; they gonna get over that African romanticism and face the fact that it's going to be hard and not always fair, and they'll go, man. Even the white man's money is fallin apart, from Wash-*

328

ington to Zurich, from Chase Manhattan to Biddly-bop Savings and Loan. Depression coming on; like the 1930s is gonna look like groovy times, compared to this one.

What else? Oh, yeah. They fuckin with the Constitution. Not that it was ever such a hot piece of paper for the Folks, but looks like right now they're ready to riddle it. We'll get the People. Hell, they might even begin a program to deport blacks to Africa. That'd be a help, but of course, you'd have more faith in the cats who'd come voluntarily.

The strike force, heh, heh. Oh, man, the strike force. In the States and in Africa we'd train these people. Tear out their minds and replace them. These could stay in America safely; they'd be invisible; they'd be as much like fish in the water as those of us in Africa would be. Work this out.

In war, like in individual combat, a cat more powerful than you can defeat himself by having too much momentum, which doesn't allow him to stop to protect himself when he chooses too. Brother Hannibal at Cannae knew this; did up the Romans real good. How do you level Troy except by deception, a device used in love and war?

In America, today, right now, there are at least thirty million Trojan Horses, or, if you will, fishes. Some know who they are; some do not. We can make it if we can win several hundred thousand to our side.

An American Trojan Horse or Pisces americanus—either one, baby; we know what we're talking about, right? Anyway, this is a person who causes absolutely no reaction when he is in places, like a governor's mansion or Burning Tree Country Club. No stillness greets him when he walks through doors of places where a person pronouncedly black would set the glasses on the bar to trembling.

People like this would be seen every day, but not perceived. How do you tear them away from the enticements of Elysium? War begins with pride in self, kind and country. The cultural revolution they talk about back home, that was going to be a big

329

*help. It could bring us a lot of fish. Oh, I know that historically mulattoes, quadroons and octaroons seem to have dealt treacherously, on the whole, with their darker Brothers, because the enemy was willing to share somewhat with them what he withheld completely from us.*

*You gotta count on some of them falling by the wayside. So be it; we'd have to help them fall a long way. How long would it take to train them? Thirty years or so. (Damn! I'll be seventy!) We would put them back in the pit out of which they climbed; make them relive the shame and bitterness of blackness, touch upon and understand why they went Down the River to Chuckville. Then we'd bring them back up, hone them, train them, pick through the past with a microscope, goad them. Step by step we'd show them the making of a military state, the interlocking connections, the cartels. We'd show the illogicality of the Soviets and Chinese wishing to conquer the U.S. What nation today could afford to take on the problems of a vassal state won by conquest, when it's so goddamn clear that no state that now exists is even close to solving its own internal problems? And we'd have to teach this: If America could make military power relevant to political bargaining with other superpowers, couldn't we, once that military power was in our hands, or short-circuited by us, bargain politically for all we never got? Wasn't America more vulnerable now than at any other time in history, man, since all aspects of its society were gathered at the toe-jam-smelling feet of its military monuments? Neutralize that power and what have you? The world's strong boy unmasked as an impotent masturbator. Most important around the world, a collective sigh that at least one superpower, the one most likely to, would no longer be able to end the world in fifteen minutes.*

*Sshhhhh. Careful. America has dependents. No talk of bringing America to its knees alone. Fish at U.S. installations in other countries would have to function in concert with those at home; neutralize the West European systems. Systems, yeah; the jugular! For in these America had concentrated its greatest*

330

strength, most of its wealth, its most cunning and clever men and machines.

Okay, say we got our force. We've penetrated the center of gravity of enemy power by the simple expedient of utilizing the enemy's weakness, his momentum, his inability to perceive anything beyond color. How large a force? Well, man, just picture any large Western city at that time of day when the offices close and everyone starts legging for home; picture all those whites crowding the buses and trams, the subways and undergrounds; picture the white floods gushing along the sidewalks of London, Paris, New York, Berlin, Amsterdam, and then tell yourself, them folks ain't white. Say it again. Again. And again, until the concept of all that means begins to take hold, maybe in the root hairs at the back of your neck. Dig their eyes, blue, green, hazel, brown, black; see the pink cheeks, the "un-Negroid" features; picture, man, picture it! White hands brushing through blond, brown, red, raven hair, and now—quickly!—superimpose upon those faces the Sphinx, Benin heads, Olmec heads, 18th Dynasty (that's all they want to give us, baby) pharaohs; see now the flash-images of movie stars, women with full pouty lips and "un-Anglo" cheekbones; see Presidents and governors and businessmen and others. See them all pass with strange little, not unpleasant smiles on their faces.

Now, fast! Transpose the faces. Set them at the controls of Advanced Massed Strategic Aircraft, in the stomachs of Polaris submarines, in subseafloor missile stations, at the controls of the Safeguard ABM systems, in the missile silos; set them there and know they are only white-looking.

Oh, yes. Take thirty years, about. Set them in NORAD, the Skylab probes, SAC, the Pentagon; to the tracking stations at Kano, Tananarive, Santa Cruz, Canton Island, Kauai, Woomera, Houston, Kennedy; to Grand Forks, Denver, Cheyenne, Omaha, to the ice stations. And sit there lookin white, but be black as a mothafucker. Get to Plattsburg, Johnston Island. Gon, Blackman! Dig it, Jesus! A fish in the crew of every

331

*AMSA—over six hundred men; at key controlling positions in eighteen hundred ICBM silos; in the crews of fifty-four Polaris oubos in the three thousand nuclear-armed tactical aircraft making it back and forth over Europe; in the crews of ground tactical nuclear weapons systems in Europe and other nations bordering Russia and China. Ah, yes. Glory, glory!*

"How's he doing?" Dr. Jackson asked without looking up from the charts; he knew the footsteps.

"He's all right," the blonde nurse answered. "Pulse fine, respiration fine. I didn't take his temperature, though. He's still sleeping. He's got the most incredible smile on his face."

Dr. Jackson looked up and smiled himself. "Maybe he thinks he's got hold of Miss Rogers. That'd make me smile, too."

## The Tattoo

How had he done it, General Whittman wondered. He felt weary striding toward the aircraft, his aides clomping behind him, wondering, he knew, what was going on. They wouldn't ask. They were good soldiers, merely following orders. The thrusters of the aircraft burned a reddish brown in the night and gave off the rushing moan of warm-up.

He hesitated with one foot on the ramp. Something made him think of Adowa, 1896. White forces living on dreams of the Romans. What a debacle that'd been. The Italians had the guns and the Ethiopians the spears, but the Ethiopians had kicked the shit out of them. Now, he accepted the hand of the pilot, Major Woodcock, which'd been extended to help him up. Inside, he went at once to his cabin, removed his jacket and cap, then squeezed through the passageway into the conference room. He wanted some minutes alone before they crowded in. He sat surveying the room, the maps, the blinking lights, the scanners. He heard the vertical thrusters being tested, then the horizontals.

Whittman's eyes came to rest on Africa. From the start he'd

332

been sure Blackman was there. There'd come ripples of things. He'd warned them and they'd let him move with the old counterinsurgency programs, but it'd been like a mosquito nudging an elephant. Africa was a big place and the Africans had changed. And somehow he'd felt that Africa was a diversion. What was there? Things seemed to go on as usual, although they had traced a number of black vets to cities there. Surveillance of Africa was started, but was never successful. Again too big, and there was always some malfunction of the equipment when passing over that continent. Maybe that was what made him most suspicious.

Then had come the phone call. The voice was the same, and Whittman immediately pictured him as he'd last seen him: in bed, in the hospital, tubes emerging from his chest, one leg missing.

"It's over, man," Blackman'd said, and Whittman believed him.

The others were now in the conference room. The thrusters roared and they were rushing straight upward. The technicians assumed their positions at the ready board. The pilot cut in to announce that they'd reached the requested altitude. Whittman glanced out. The stars were bright outside the portholes.

He said, "This is a test, worldwide systems check."

The others glanced around. This was unusual.

Whittman said, "SAC aircraft and missiles."

The technicians pressed buttons, studied their scanners.

"Nothing will work, Ishmael," Blackman had said. "It's ours. All of it. I've kicked your ass again."

"Malfunction, sir," one of the technicians said with a frown.

"Go to alternate systems."

"Nothing, sir."

"What does NORAD say?" Whittman stared at the stars while the voices, incredulous in their urgency, came and went.

"No contact with anything, sir."

"All right," Whittman said, moving toward the rows of buttons, "firing Denver."

333

"SIR!" Everyone was on his feet, hands out, imploring. "Don't launch, sir."

But his fingers were already racing over the keys. The board above him remained blank.

"They didn't go!" someone shouted, his voice joyous with relief.

Whittman regained his seat. "Have you signal from the subs?"

"Nothing, sir."

"Subsea sites?"

"Nothing, sir."

Whittman leaned back, sighed and put a cigarette into his mouth. The major general who held the light said, "Sir, we don't understand—"

Whittman signaled to the technicians and they relaxed, faces pale, swiveling their eyes from Whittman to the other brass. "It's simple, Borland," Whittman said. "We don't have any nuclear attack system, that's all. It's been captured, and for all I know completely dismantled. For the first time since 1945, we're without a nuclear deterrent—"

A change in the pitch of the thrusters made him break off. Reverse verticals. Down. One of the aides snatched the intercom, but Whittman waved him off and spoke into it himself. "This is General Whittman. We haven't reached our destination?"

"Yes, sir. We have."

"One hour's flight time, Woodie?"

"Yes, sir."

"Then it's not *our* destination, but yours. Is that right?" Whittman eyed his puzzled staff.

"I have my orders, sir." The pilot clicked off. One of the aides rushed at the door and bounced back when it failed to give. The others turned pleadingly to Whittman.

"Sir, what the fuck is going on? By rights, in eight minutes, the Soviets should have two hundred missiles in our air space, but you say the systems aren't working. That door's locked. What's Woodie up to?"

Funny, Whittman was thinking as he stood. Woodcock didn't *look* colored. "Didn't you hear me?" he said to the men in the cabin. "We're defenseless. You've been in a war for hundreds of years and you've just lost it. Don't tell me about the Soviets. You don't understand. You've just lost the war to niggers."

Over the loudspeaker they heard laughter. It was happy and mocking.

"What do you mean, 'niggers'?" one of his aides asked in a whisper, as he led the encirclement of the man they now believed insane. As they wrestled Whittman to the floor, the voice came over the loudspeaker again. "Well, sho nuff. The Gennel mean what he done said, doncha, Gennel?" More laughter. Then: "Hey, there's a message coming through from your President."

The President's face, drawn and quizzical, looked out at them from the screen. Borland flipped a switch. "Mr. President—"

"General Whittman," the President snapped.

"He's, he's—well, he just went crazy. We had to rap him one."

"Borland, is that you, General Borland?"

"Yes, sir."

"You're next in command, right?"

"That's right, sir. What the fuck is going on?" Borland screamed.

"Don't you use such language and tone to me, General."

"Sorry, sir. But, please tell us what's going on?"

Over the craft's loudspeaker they heard Woodcock: "Way down upon de Swanee Ribber. . . ."

The President said, "Listen to the silence. It's almost like a noise. It's that goddamn invisible busyness gone from all those secret things—"

"He's flipped, too," Borland said, slapping his head.

". . . dat's wheah mah heart is turning, ebber. . . ."

Whittman came to and listened to the President, to Borland,

335

to the pilot. When they landed, he knew he'd meet Blackman. All his fucking life he'd been meeting Blackman, and there was always some shit to contend with. He cocked an ear toward Borland and stared at the President. They don't believe it. They won't believe it.

"Mr. President," Borland was pleading. "We ran a world-wide systems check. They're all out. We've nothing to throw at anybody. Whittman said we'd just lost a war to the niggers. We don't understand, sir. What war, what niggers? Is this a joke, sir? Can you tell us what's going on? We just don't understand, sir—Woodie, will you shut the fuck *up*—not you, sir, someone else, a—I don't know what he is. Can you brief me quickly on what's going on, what posture we should take? We gotta have a posture. What's this business with niggers, sir? How could they do anything—"

"All de world am sad and dreary, ebrywhere I roam, oh darkies, how my heart grobes weary. . . ."